WOLFLESS

A Crystal River Pack Novel

Amy F. Worcester

TITLE: Wolfless

By: Amy Worcester

Cover Design: Publishing

Copyright 2025

Welcome
Trigger Warnings

My Darling Readers,

I love the idea of that perfect person, or a fated mate, being out there for each person. But I also wanted more than the 'save me Alpha' story line. So, I wondered what would happen if she saved herself.

During my first book, The Hunt, Celeste did just this. But now she is the Luna of the Crystal River Pack and has found herself being called upon by the Council to take in an abused wolf-less woman.

Please be aware that through this journey my characters will once again confront abuse and sexual assault. Like many of the packs, the Dark Sky pack is governed by a misogynistic Alpha who controls the she-wolves with laws and rules limiting their freedoms.

There is a little more spice in this story. But I believe it is tastefully done.

I hope you enjoy the adventure!

With much love,

Amy

Welcome

Acknowlwdgements

My Darling Readers,

I am often asked when I started writing and I typically answer somewhere around first grade. Once I discovered that you could string words together to make a story, I knew what I wanted to do when I grew up.

But of course, life and everything happened and that dream got put on hold.

After our son graduated high school, my husband encouraged me to get out and find my tribe.

The Writer's Club that meets at our local library welcomed and encouraged me through this process. They guided and helped me along the way.

My online writer's group and editor's have been a blessing. As have my readers and fans.

I also have to thank the instructors with the Citizens Police and Fire Academies with the Greenville Police and Fire Departments. They have answered many questions and helped me correct a few issues.

And a great big thank you to Demon Dave at Texas Tattoos for making my vision of the Council's crest coming to life.

But my husband and son get great big thanks for all their support. They encouraged me with my 'tippy tappy' on the keyboard and didn't object to the late nights and early mornings. They have helped me haul books across the state, been voluntold for set-up and breakdown and have done so with no complaints.

This has been an incredible journey, and I hope that you enjoy the story as much as I have had bringing the Were their world to life.

With much love,

Amy

Contents

Chapter 1

OUTCAST

Dark Sky Pack

She was mousy and plain.

Electra sighed as she looked at herself in the mirror. She looked the same. Plain brown hair, strange black eyes hidden behind brown contacts and skin that was pale from hiding in the library. She was not overly tall and was a little pudgy. Definitely not your typical beautiful werewolf.

Every year she said that she was going to start going to the gym, going to get in shape, going to....

However, she knew better.

She would go to school, the kids would be mean and cruel; especially, AJ, the Alpha's son. She would hide in the library, get lost in a book and then come back home. Mom would tell her that she's perfect. Dad would tell her that when she turned seventeen things would change.

Helena knocked on the door, "I've got to pee!"

Shaking her head, Electra pulled on her blue-green maxi dress and unlocked the door. Her fourteen-year-old sister was the epitome of young beauty. Her brown hair had blonde highlights, and her eyes were light green. And she was tall and skinny. Everyone loved Helena.

Electra left the bathroom as her sister rushed in. Their older brother, Troy, came up the stairs with their youngest sister, Athena, on his back. She was laughing loudly and urging him onward.

Just like the rest of the family, they were also beautiful. They all shared the same light brown hair and green eyes. The other kids were tanned from playing in the sun and fit from sports. And dimples. They all had adorable dimples.

Truly, Electra sometimes thought, the only thing missing was a sparkle when they smiled.

"Go finish getting ready," Troy laughed as he sat the little girl down. Athena grumbled but went into the room that the four girls shared.

"Come here," Troy said, pulling Electra into his arms. She rested her head on his chest and wrapped her arms around his waist. Kissing his sister's hair he discreetly smelled her. "I promise, it will happen when it's supposed to," he whispered.

She nodded against his muscled chest as a few tears slipped out of her eyes. She turned sixteen without a wolf. Then seventeen. And eighteen.

Every birthday it was the same. She looked no different. She felt no different. She had no wolf.

By the time Troy met his mate, all the kids except Athena, who was still too young, and Electra had a wolf. On her nineteenth birthday, there was no hug in the hallway decorated for Yule and the Winter Solstice. No reassurances as he tried to smell her without her knowing. But he and his mate stopped by for lunch.

"I think Electra should go to college," Troy announced.

"The Alpha will not allow her to attend college," their mother pointed out.

"A human college," Troy corrected. "Mom, do you know what life is like for someone who is wolf-less?"

"I know it can't be easy..."

"It can't be easy?" Electra said softly as she took off her cardigan sweater. Bruises covered her arms. "I'm a punching bag. Why do you think I always hide in the library?"

"Who's doing this to you?" their father demanded.

Looking at her younger brother and sister, she whispered, "Who's not?"

"If we don't, then they attack us too!" Jason argued.

"It doesn't matter. Once I turn twenty-one, if I don't have a wolf, I have to leave. Or become your slave," Electra said sadly, softly. She stood up and walked towards the stairs, "Happy birthday."

"Please," Claire asked her in-laws. "She's endured so much already."

"We've secured her a place in a college close to the pack lands. She can't keep living like this," Troy added. "The Alpha has taken so much from her."

It was a low blow, one that struck his parents with guilt. They all knew exactly how much had been taken from their adopted daughter. And he was right; it was only going to get worse. If she remained, she would be forced into servitude.

Eventually, their parents relented and in January, Electra moved into the dorms of the human college, part of the University of Maine system. She turned twenty. Then twenty-one. Still, she had no wolf. She had earned a scholarship and got a part-time job working in a public library.

She missed living with a pack. Even when the pack members were horrible to her, she liked knowing her family was there. That her parents loved her no matter what. She had loved the weekends when she could still go home.

Now, they could only meet off pack lands. Thankfully, her brother worked for the council and lived just outside pack lands in neutral territory.

"Are we still doing dinner at Troy's house Saturday after my graduation?" Electra asked her mom over the phone. She was twenty-three and still wolf-less. But the second Saturday in May, she would graduate with a teaching and library science degree.

"Oh, hun, we can't. The council is having a meeting, and we all have to work."

"I understand," Electra said as she ended the call.

She sat the phone down and grabbed up her old ratty teddy bear that she had had for as long as she could remember. Burying her face in its faded velvet fur, she let the tears flow.

"Teddy, the good thing about not being noticed is that you're not noticed. The bad thing about not being noticed is that you're not noticed."

As always, the old brown bear offered his comfort in silence. From the depths of her mind came the ethereal voice that she had heard all her life. The voice that her father said was her conscience, her self-guardian, if you will.

Hold fast, little one. I have great plans for you.

Electra never told her dad that there were two voices that she would hear. The ethereal one and the angry one. The angry voice would tell her that vengeance and retribution would be her gifts. The ethereal one would tell her that there was more to her life than what she was told.

She just needed to be patient. To hold fast.

As the sun dipped low outside the window where she lay curled in the fetal position, looking almost like a sleeping wolf, her dreams took her on wondrous adventures just as they always had. Tonight, when she felt low and unloved, they showed her as an army leader.

Giving the command to attack, Electra watched as the person she was dreaming of being shifted into a large angry gray wolfhound. Running towards the enemy, she bared her teeth and snapped at enemy soldiers who fell away in fear.

Reaching her nemesis, his face faded from an unknown one into the handsome and sneering face of AJ. In her dream, her large canine mouth opened and sank deadly fangs into his neck. She shook the body hard until she heard the satisfactory sound of his neck snapping.

Hold fast, little one.

The ethereal voice whispered.

We want his blood.

The angry voice demanded as the coppery taste of blood filled her mouth.

Chapter 2

BULLIES

Crystal River Pack

Summer was coming early to the Crystal River pack in central Pennsylvania. The first week of May found many families out in the main park in the heart of the city, Crystal Pass.

An open green space with the occasional tree sat at one end of the large park with the library across the street. A spacious playground and smaller green space were at the other end which was closer to the packhouse. Between the two areas was a grove of trees that covered just over two acres. A jogging path meandered around and through the three elements of the five acres that made up Franklin Park. The path was part of a larger series of paths that wound through and encircled the entire city.

Near the playground, seven-year-old Marie and five-year-old Emily were at the park with their Aunt Kiara. After spending the day with the younger sister, she had picked up the older sister from school and brought them to the park with their friends.

Emily wore a simple princess dress from her latest Disney movie craze. Her light auburn curls bounced as she played Werewolf Tag with some other kids. She was currently the werewolf and was making growling noises as she chased the other kids with pretend claws out. Her shoes had flown off at some point and Kiara had collected them.

Because she was the younger girl, more outgoing, more trusting and much more precocious, it was Emily that Kiara kept a close eye on. Every so often, she would look over at the little girl against the tree with her nose buried in a book that was years above her grade level. But if a seven-year-old wanted to read the entire Harry Potter series in a week, Kiara was not going to discourage it.

Kiara's blue eyes flicked over to where her niece leaned against the trunk of the sugar maple tree with green leaves and small greenish yellow flowers above her. She sat on grass that was already lush and green thanks to the pack Omega's and city maintenance crews. Unlike her sister's unruly curls, Marie had straight dark auburn hair that hung just past her shoulders. Her bright warm honey eyes devoured the words on the page in front of her.

In her young mind, Marie wore Hogwarts robes that were in the Ravenclaw colors. In reality, she wore knee length khaki shorts and a purple HP shirt. Her dark purple flip flops lay next to her, perfectly even with each other.

Turning back to focus her attention on her husband's younger niece, Kiara did not see the two girls approaching Marie. Or the strange events that followed.

Dee and her best friend, Taylor, both in the same grade as Marie, each grabbed a shoe and ran into the wooded area in the park. The two blonde girls laughed at the girl following them. Both girls wore name brand denim shorts and matching pink BEST FRIENDS T-shirts.

"Let's throw them in the tree!" Taylor laughed.

"Let's not," a new voice said from the shadows as a woman stepped off the running trail.

"You don't scare me! My dad is a cop! I can do whatever I want," Dee informed the voice as she prepared to throw the shoe upwards.

A woman with braided pitch-black hair and silver eyes stepped into a patch of light that filtered through the leaves above them. She wore short jogging shorts, a tank top and dirty running shoes. Tattoos covered both arms from shoulder to wrist. One leg had tattoos going just past her knee and the other stopped just above it.

"Give the shoes back," she told the girls as she leaned against a tree.

"Do you know who my father is?" Dee demanded.

"Please, do tell me," the woman smiled.

"Daniel Knight!" the little girl said as if it were impressive. To make her point, she threw the shoe, and it caught on a branch.

"And you? Are you going to also try to impress me with your parentage?"

"Stephen Chambers, you tattooed freak," Taylor said, grabbing the book and throwing it.

Celeste smirked at the two girls. Had the woman been in what she called her 'Luna Clothes' the two girls would have easily recognized her. But here, today, during her midday run, many of her tattoos were on display and her hair was pulled back in a tight braid.

She did not look like the well put together professional Luna that appeared at the school and pack events. In fact, she did not look like any other Luna and certainly did not look like an Alpha. Celeste was content with that fact.

Both girls would be too young to have a wolf or any of their senses. If they did, the wolves would be sensing two things - Alpha blood and danger. The German shepherd dog sitting beside her gave a low growl and she gave a command through their mind link sending him home. With a huff of displeasure, he followed the path behind them to the packhouse.

"Alpha," a woman said, approaching them.

"Thank you, Anna. I was hoping you heard me," she smiled, and the two girls paled as recognition hit them. "I need Daniel Knight and Stephen Chambers along with their mates in my office as soon as possible."

"Get the shoe," Celeste ordered Dee in her Alpha voice. Then turning to Taylor ordered her to "Fetch the book."

Even without their wolves, they were unable to disobey and did as their Luna ordered. Once all the items had been returned to their owner, and they half-heartedly apologized, Celeste ordered them to go with Anna to her office.

"My mom-."

"Will know that you're in trouble as soon as she sees you with my Omega," Celeste cut Dee off sharply.

Hanging their heads in shame, they walked out of the woods with Anna. Celeste offered a friendly hand to Marie and smiled at her.

"I'm Celeste, but that's a mouthful, you can call me Aunt Sles," the woman said as the little girl took her hand.

"My dad would not approve of that, Alpha... Luna," she replied as they also walked out of the woods and into the bright afternoon sun. Softly, she apologized and hung her head in submission.

Celeste laughed lightly as she hugged the young girl to her side, "I know, it's confusing. Aunt Sles is so much easier."

"That's my little sister, Emily," Marie pointed at the little princess who was running away from the new werewolf. "And my aunt Kiara," she waved at the pregnant brunette woman who was standing with a hand shading her blue eyes as she looked for Marie.

Celeste waved at her and saw Kiara visibly relax, "I always wished that they had put Peeves in the movies."

"He's one of my favorites," Marie smiled as Emily ran up to them.

"You have a lot of pictures on you," Emily said as she took the hand that Celeste offered.

"I do," she agreed. "My mate says I'm going to run out of space. Don't tell him, but he might be right."

"Luna," Kiara inclined her head.

"Kiara, you look like you're ready to pop!" Celeste said. "How much longer?"

"The doctor is saying five more weeks. The healer said seven."

"I hate to say it but go with the healer. My friend, Sammi, says that the last six weeks are the longest decade of your life."

"I agree with that statement."

"I believe that these two belong to you," Celeste kissed both girls on the head. "Why don't you go over to Mother Mae's and have some ice cream. I'll let her know you're coming."

"Are you going to join us?" Emily asked and at the gentle nudge from Kiara added; "Luna."

"Not this afternoon, I need to go take care of an issue. And I have to go to another pack tomorrow. How about I meet you for lunch on Monday?" Celeste suggested.

"Really?" Marie asked.

"Oh, yeah. My best friend has such a crush on your dad," she grinned. "Anything to make the bestie jealous."

Celeste was still thinking about how Jill was going to be jealous over her lunch with the Hot Firefighter Dad that her friend had been crushing on ever since they had met at the pack picnic two years ago. On her way to the packhouse, Celeste reached out to Mae and let her know that the two girls and their aunt would be coming over for ice cream and to put it on the Alpha's tab.

"They're in the conference room," Anna said, standing as Celeste entered the outer office and headed for her own. Celeste was not big on formalities, but knew that with people watching, Anna would have to insist on the formal interactions between Omega and Alpha.

Just like all the offices on the second floor, the furniture and built-ins were made from cherry wood. The walls in all four rooms of the Luna's office suite were pale blue. The trim and accents in Anna's office were crimson red that matched the pack colors. When Celeste had told her assistant that the office could be in her own colors, Anna explained that her wolf was a crimson red.

When Wyatt had the offices done for Celeste without her knowing about it, he had followed his mother's floor plan and made the office closest to Anna's the informal office. When she had been pregnant, the office had bothered her and she had them swapped around. Now to get to her inner sanctum, you had to go through Anna's office since the hallway doors to her office now required a key to open.

"Have them write an apology letter," she instructed as the two girls' parents arrived. "Make sure that I'm clear for the next hour or so."

"Yes, Luna," Anna smiled at her boss as she grabbed up two notepads and pencils already on her desk before she entered the conference room that was opposite Celeste's private offices.

"Please, step into my office," Celeste moved out of the doorway and motioned for the two couples to go ahead of her.

They entered and waited for their Luna to tell them to sit in front of her ornate desk. The trim and accents in her private offices were her signature sapphire blue.

Her hellhound, Teuf was currently in his German shepherd form as he entered the room and went to lay on his overstuffed bed. Before he settled, his eyes flashed red, and smoke billowed from his snout. With his warning issued, he lay down for a nap.

Celeste motioned for the four parents to sit down in her guest chairs. Once again, she was grateful to have such a thoughtful and organized Omega as her assistant. Instead of her usual two, there were four chairs. Her standard two were cherry wood and blue padding and two with padded arms that were pulled from the conference room.

The Alpha is on his way, Anna told Celeste through the mind link.

Still in her running gear, she let the two well-dressed couples sit in uncomfortable silence as she retrieved a refillable water bottle from her small refrigerator before sitting behind the large desk. The outer door opened, and Alpha Wyatt entered, eyes only for his wife as he approached and gave her a light kiss before standing behind her chair. His message was clear, he was supporting his Luna.

"I'm sure you know why I called for you to be here." Celeste said as she linked her fingers with her mates on her shoulder.

"That other girl, you know there's something wrong with her," Daniel Knight declared. "Has to be, her mother abandoned her pups. What she-wolf does that?"

"And because of something she has no control over, you think it's okay for your daughters to bully her?" Celeste continued.

"Her father is a low-level Beta, and her mother was Omega born," Stephen Chambers pointed out. "She needs to learn her place in the pack."

"I see," Celeste nodded. Wyatt squeezed her hand in support, and she could sense his predatory smile behind her as she went in for the kill. "What the fuck makes you think that you can teach your daughter to be a fucking bitch? Maybe we need to evaluate your parenting skills."

The Luna stood to her full height, just over six feet without her heels, letting her hand drop as she braced herself on her desk and leaned forward. Her eyes glowed and fangs extended slightly as her claws scratched the top of the desk.

"Angel," Wyatt said to his wife's wolf, "please don't damage the desk. That's more work for Anna."

The claws retracted but the fangs remained just as Angel remained at the front of their mind and in control of their shared body.

"Maybe you should be reminded of your place in the pack," Angel growled. "I will be reaching out to your supervisors. The actions of your children reflect back on you and on the pack. I think that a three-week suspension should remind you of your place."

She snarled as both men started to open their mouths to object. "All of you will report to Gunny Williams tomorrow morning to receive community service assignments. Your daughters will report to Anna, and they will do whatever she assigns them."

The four parents looked at the Alpha, meeting his eyes. His own wolf, Demon, pushed to the front and he snarled at them, baring his teeth. "YOU DARE TO CHALLENGE MY MATE?"

Four heads dropped in submission and offered their throats to show that they were no threat to the Alpha or his Luna.

"Get out." Wyatt growled. "Your daughters will be brought home when they have finished their apology letters."

Chapter 3

DUTIES

Crystal River Pack

Wyatt was the first to wake up to the sound of his son fussing. Aiden wasn't crying yet, but he was certainly upset. Rubbing sleep from his eyes, Wyatt sat up and quietly pulled on his black shorts. Moonlight shimmered through the open windows and French doors on either side of the large four poster bed.

Demon gave a soft growl of displeasure in their shared mind at being woken up. Since he was not sensing any danger, he returned to the recesses of Wyatt's mind. Wyatt chuckled at the beast as he walked towards the door to his son's room.

Reaching out to his nighttime patrol through the pack link, Wyatt asked for a status report. Before the Alpha had made his way around the bed and to the door to the adjoining nursery, he was assured that everything was as it should be.

Since his eyes had not fully adjusted to the darkness, the father was grateful for the nightlight that cast stars across the ceiling and walls. He walked across the pale olive-green rug on the gray tile to the round crib and immediately saw the problem. The cut out of a wolf and pup howling at the moon hung above the crib, the light glow from the back lighting shined down onto the fussy baby on the mattress.

Teuf, his wife's German shepherd hell hound, who usually slept in the oversized crib, was not there. Wyatt picked his one-year-old son up and held him against his bare chest with a strong hand against the small back while the other rested under the diapered bottom. Tiny fingers gripped chest hair as the baby went back to sleep.

Looking around he didn't see Teuf at first. Then he saw the large dog standing by the closed French doors leading out to the balcony. Walking towards the door, he saw a huge full moon that Teuf sat staring at, whimpering. A breeze blew through the open windows on either side of the doors ruffling the cream-colored curtains.

The woodsy theme with plush wolves was slowly being invaded by plush sabretooth tigers. Wyatt could only laugh at the one that was lying on the floor by the crib. His wife's hellhound and best friend had a love/hate relationship. Although Celeste assured him that they loved each other, hating each other was a lot more fun.

"She calls to you tonight, doesn't she?" Wyatt asked, placing a hand on the shepherd's head.

It is a hound's duty to answer her call!

Demon flinched at hearing the hound's thoughts in their head. After two years of marriage to his mate, neither man nor beast were used to hearing the hell hound. He did not actually physically talk, but since the mating ceremony, Wyatt had conversations with the hellhound.

The hound's thoughts would invade Demon and Wyatt's shared mind. His beast always recoiled in fear from the demonic creature. Even now, he could feel his powerful beast, an Alpha among his kind, tremble at the nearness of the hound. In his shepherd form, he was fun, loving and playful, but when the hellhound ruled, he was aggressive and protective.

Opening the door for Teuf, Wyatt softly whispered, "Go do her bidding. I've got the pup."

Giving a slight nod to the man, the dog walked through the door and out onto the balcony. As he jumped over the railing, he shifted into his full hellhound form. His shoulders were now six feet high, his fur turned pitch black as his snout, teeth and claws extended. Landing on paws the size of serving platters, he shook his body before running towards the clearing.

Under his large paws, the ground gave small tremors due to his weight and power.

Teuf hated leaving his pup alone, even though it was not actually his. Aiden was the pup of his mistress and her mate. Teuf had bound himself to her and then her mate. He would not bind himself to any of their pups. The moon goddess had promised that he would have his own mate and pups. His pups would bind themselves to the were pups.

Before he could have either, there were duties he had to perform.

She called out to him tonight. When the Moon Goddess called on a hellhound, they answered. He may have bound himself to the Alpha she-wolf, but he still did the bidding of the Moon Goddess. Just like her other chosen servants, he was there to guide and protect her children, but only as she saw fit.

It did not take long for him to reach the meadow. The three white wolves were already there. They were all pure white with bright blue eyes. The only other color on them were small patches of red just above their right paws. One in the shape of the moon, one was a star and the last was a heart.

The black hellhound laid down and watched them with his red glowing eyes. Smoke billowed out of his nostrils that the three sisters played in. Running in and out of the smoke, jumping over the large paws, rolling in the cool grass.

The moon above them shimmered as the trees bent low. The nightingale announced her arrival before they saw her. The large black hellhound flattened himself on the ground and laid his head between his paws. The three white wolves did the same across from him.

A young woman with alabaster skin and black hair stepped out of the woods. Her gown was white and airy, just like the moon beams it was made of. The many layers flowed around her gracefully. It was held in place with a chain of stars around her shoulders and another at her waist. On her crown was a crescent moon with her large sheer shawl draped over it.

The shawl was a deep blue, almost black, with silver constellations on it. As she or the stars above moved, the ones on the shawl also moved. It crested the crown and hung down, almost to her eyes. Behind her, it almost touched the ground. She had one side wrapped around her going back over her shoulder, the other draped over her arm.

"Good evening, my children," she said in a soft ethereal voice.

All four wolves whimpered in response.

"A special child of mine is coming to you. Her wolf slumbers in deep hibernation. She will be encouraged to awaken before she arrives. She is injured and lost. You may guide her, lead her but she must do this on her own."

Selene held out her hand and a necklace appeared. It was on a long pewter chain with a sleeping wolf above a crystal.

"This will help you guide her and ease the merge. Her first shift will occur under stress. Her second chance mate is here. He will sense her before he recognizes her," with a subtle movement of her hand, the necklace disappeared.

The white wolf with the star marking made a soft sound.

"Her first mate rejected her because he could not see her true self inside. His first mate abandoned him. They can have no influence from any of you."

The hellhound gave a huff.

"You must protect her. Her mate rejected her but still craves her." She sighed, "Several of my children have been hurt in many ways. But with her new mate, and the family they make together, they can all heal."

The white wolf with the moon marking whined.

"She is the Gelert. Take care of her." As she faded into mist her final words echoed through the meadow. "I have great plans for her."

Chapter 4

LUNCHEON

Dark Sky Pack

Celeste hated the women's events when the council had meetings. She typically did not go to the ladies' events; but, as it was pointed out, she was now the Luna of the Crystal River Pack, married and had a pup, so she should attend at least one. As a concession, her husband, Wyatt, agreed to take her out after the formal dinner. She had already searched the local strip clubs and had one picked out.

He agreed to take her out as she stood naked in front of him, carefully applying lotion to her many tattoos. By the time she was done, he was stroking himself and would agree to anything. If he could have exempted them from this meeting, he would have. But the Elders commanded that they would be there. Not even an Alpha as powerful as himself defied the Elders.

Despite the misgivings and reluctance of the Alphas of the Crystal River and Silver Lake Packs along with their entourages boarded the private plane and flew to Maine. The Dark Sky Pack was a very traditional pack and the pack leaders that were going to the meeting were all full blood werewolf or Lycan. Jack, a human that had served with Celeste in the Marines, remained behind as did his partner, Jill, who was a werecat.

Their arrival was marked with enough fanfare that Celeste thought that they had arrived at a movie premiere. When she expressed this to her mate through the mate link, he shook his head and gave her a small smile.

They are old school and will give the Alpha's of the stronger and wealthier packs the red-carpet welcome. Smaller packs are not invited. As my father explained it, they worry about PAPA. Prestige. Appearance. Power. Attitude.

Settling into the back of the SUV that was provided, Stephen handed Celeste a piece of paper and pointed at the itinerary for the women's events. "Luna, you'll find the address for the luncheon here."

Celeste gave the Beta a strange look because he knew that she did not like the Luna title. But then she looked at the sticky note on the top of the page.

some alphas
mated to non—
were women
not allowed
on Dark Sky Pack
lands
everything for the
women → off pack
lands

She opened her mouth to say something, and Stephen shook his head before making a motion that the Marines used to indicate that people were listening. Rolling her eyes, she sat back and pulled the sticky note off the paper.

The SUV dropped her off at the hotel where the luncheon was being held with a quiet reminder from her mate to behave. Crossing her fingers where he could see it, she promised to try. Chuckling, Wyatt kissed her temple before climbing back into the SUV and it pulled away. Looking down at her dog, she could feel his displeasure also.

"Let's get this over with," she muttered, and a growl filled her mind as Teuf hoped for raw steak.

Shortly after arriving at the luncheon, she texted her best friend, Jill. They had served together in the Marines and Celeste could not imagine her life with the large, black, male, werecat in it.

Celeste was bored out of her mind and Jill was keeping her sane by trying to get to the council meeting. So far, neither husband had conceded to that. A message popped up on Celeste's phone from Jack, Jill's human mate, listing out the reasons why his mate could not go to the Dark Sky Pack.

1. They hate werecats almost as much as humans

2. He's mated to a dreaded human

3. We're both gay

> **4. I don't want to be a widower**

As much as she hated to admit it, Jack made very valid points. She conceded this point as the women around her started the same conversation about the hot actors again. Celeste was certain that they really had no lives away from their husbands.

> **Isn't there a law about cruel and unusual punishment?**

Celeste texted and Jill replied with a cry-laughing face.

> **I'm dying here.**

> **Take Teuf for a walk.**

Jill suggested and Celeste nudged the sleeping German shepherd under her chair. He stood up and stretched and she quickly made her excuses. The luncheon was at an exclusive hotel restaurant in the nearby pila town and Celeste grabbed the leash even though her dog did not need it.

There had been two other Hunts since Wyatt had the first non-Hunt. The third one was approaching, and this would be the fourth non-Hunt. And of course, people were upset that the Midnight Sun Pack in Iceland would be holding another non-Hunt. Not the majority, but many packs still clung to the old ways.

Which led to Celeste suffering through a luncheon with Luna's that needed a good night at the strip club followed by a damned good fucking. Or maybe that's what she needed.

Once outside, Celeste let Teuf have the lead. He would sniff the air every so often and guided his mistress to the scent he was tracking. She was not paying attention and ran into a young woman. Celeste dropped the leash and grabbed the other woman's arms. Teuf sat on the sidewalk and looked up at the women.

He was quite proud of himself having found the Gelert.

"Are you okay?" Celeste asked.

"Yes, ma'am," the mousy woman said with a sniffle.

"Yeah, I'm calling bullshit." Celeste looked around and saw a café across the street. "Let me buy you lunch or at least a coffee."

The girl nodded and let herself be guided across the street. They settled in at a table and a waitress brought two glasses of water and menus with a promise to be back in a moment.

"I'm Celeste." She said, picking up the menu. "Have you eaten here before?"

"Electra and no, Alpha." She replied.

The waitress came back and brought a bowl of water for Teuf. "I'm Brandy, I'll bring you another bottle of water for your fur friend."

"You have a friend for life." Celeste smiled. "This mudslide...?" she pointed to the chocolate drink topped with ice cream and small chocolate curls.

"Absolutely delicious." Brandy smiled. "If you're planning on having dessert, I recommend the triple chocolate cake with strawberries."

"Sold. Heavy on the Kailua, please." Celeste smiled at her companion. "Electra?"

"That's fine. Can I get mine without alcohol?" she asked timidly.

"Yes, ma'am." She wrote on her little pad. "I'll have those right out."

Celeste waited until they were alone again. "Don't make me go all bitchy Alpha on you. What's bothering you?"

"I graduate from college in a few hours, Alpha." Electra sighed. "Because of this meeting, my family won't be there."

"Why the fuck not?" Celeste asked as she undid her blue jacket and took it off. She was aware of people staring at her tattoos, but she did not care. Her life story covered her body, and she was proud of every scar and drop of ink.

"They've all been told that they'll be working the dinner tonight, Alpha. My parents are lower-level betas."

"And you?"

"I'm wolf-less, Alpha." She mumbled shamefully.

Brandy returned with a tray carrying the drinks and cake slices. After serving the two women, she sat a bottle of water on the table and asked if they needed anything else. With nos from both, she walked away to take care of the other tables.

"Listen to me, Electra." Celeste said quietly with her Alpha voice forcing the younger woman to pay attention to her. The fact that the younger woman responded to the Alpha wolf's command, made Celeste wonder exactly how wolf-less she was. Humans did not respond to the commands so easily.

"Not everyone can be an Alpha. Not everyone can have a wolf. It's what we do with our lives that matter." She reached out and placed her hand over the other woman's hand. Electra tensed under her hand and nervous energy radiated from her. "It doesn't make you any less of a person."

Inside her mind, Angel sensed the energy and sat up, paying attention to the younger woman. Lifting her nose up, she sniffed the air and sensed an ancient familial line. The powerful wolf that Celeste shared a mind and body whimpered and lowered her head in respect.

A tear slipped out of Electra's eye as she nodded. "Yes, Alpha."

As the girl swiped away the tear, Angel looked through Celeste's eyes and saw the bright flash of gold. It was so quick that she questioned if she actually saw it.

"Ugh. Enough with that bullshit. Just call me Celeste. If there's others around, do all the Alpha fuckery." She took a bite of cake and made a sound of absolute pleasure. "Sweet goddess above."

Electra smiled as she also took a bite of cake.

"Now, let's talk about your graduation and party." Celeste said, taking a drink of her mudslide. "What are your parents' names?"

"Jenny and Mike Naples."

"Where were you going to celebrate your graduation?"

"Just a simple dinner at my brother's house." Electra said, not used to having someone pay so much attention to her. Attention from anyone other than her family was a rare event. Especially not with a beating involved.

"Nope. If I've got to suffer through girly bullshit, give me something awesome to look forward to." She pulled her phone out of her jacket pocket and started to search for places to host a graduation party at the last minute.

Chapter 5

INTERRUPTION

Dark Sky Pack

Alpha Anthony droned on and on and on about how the Hunt needed to return to the traditional chase and not what has been hosted for the last few years. Many packs complained about the changes that had occurred in the two years since Crystal River held their non-hunt. The main complaints came from the older generation. The younger generation and women that had suffered at previous Hunts embraced the changes.

Then you had packs like this one that wanted nothing to change. Desperately they clung to the old traditions. Refusing to change, refusing to move forward. Fighting those who tried to bring about changes and pull them into the twentieth century. Little steps, Wyatt thought, bring them into the last century and then the current one.

If there was ever a pack that was deeply ingrained in archaic tradition it was the Dark Sky pack. Other packs had enlarged the council chambers that they used to host meetings because the packs increased in number and officers. The Dark Sky pack council chambers remained the same.

Skinny tables attached to the back of the row ahead of them only allowed enough room for an Alpha and a Beta. Even that was a tight fit with the number of packs that had come. The change in the annual Hunt had become a hot button topic, and most packs did not want to change it back. Just as much as Dark Sky did not want to change their chambers.

Rock walls surrounded the multiple nine-pane windows that dated back to when the pack was founded in the early 1700s. Wyatt's pack, Crystal River, was founded earlier than that and they retained their old chambers for ceremonies and private meetings. But even they had been updated over the centuries.

Two large fireplaces at either end of this room provided warmth and light. Kerosene lanterns hung on the walls and from the ceiling casting shadows in all different directions. More than once, Wyatt saw others making subtle shadow puppets.

Most chambers now had a single platform for the Elders. The Dark Sky chambers still had a high platform in the center wall for the Senior Elder and two slightly lower platforms on either side walls for the other two Elders. This configuration created the Elder Trinity in the form of an isosceles triangle.

There was so much about this pack that Wyatt did not like. The way that they treated their Omegas was top of the list. Followed immediately by the way that they treated the females. No female was allowed in the sacred chamber. Even the Omegas that maintained the building and grounds were all male.

Also at the top of the list was this stupid meeting and Wyatt hated to admit that his wife was right about it. This whole damned meeting could have been done by email. File the complaint and let it be addressed at the next council meeting. There had to be something more to this. He looked at his brother-in-law in the chair next to him who looked just as bored as he felt. At the nod from Sirius, Wyatt rolled his eyes to show his disdain.

Sirius casually reached over and grabbed Wyatt's pen and wrote a single word on the other man's notepad.

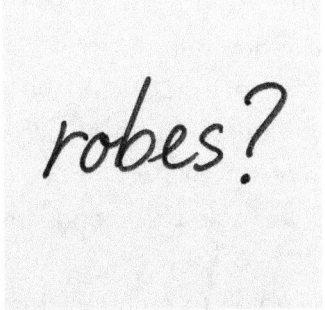

Wyatt could only smirk at yet another way that the Dark Sky Pack was still stuck in the past. And the delusion that they held any type of power or sway over the were community.

The only wolves that still wore robes were the three Elders, the Blessed Three and the High Priestess, Divine Oracle and Divine Healer, which they all reserved for ceremonies and formal events. Pack Trios, made up of a priestess, oracle and healer, would usually wear them for ceremonies such as weddings, blessings and funerals.

Not an Alpha that refused to enter the twenty-first century. Or even the nineteenth or twentieth for that matter.

Instead of looking regal and dignified as Wyatt assumed the Alpha was trying to, he looked outdated, out of touch and downright stupid. Especially with the Elders wearing casual slacks and Polo shirts and not the formal robes. This not only showed how out of touch the Alpha was, but also that the Elders held low regard for the meeting.

He had seen two of the Elder Successors earlier, both women and both barred from entering the chambers. But he knew that if they asserted their authority, even the well-trained warriors of the Dark Sky pack would concede to the will of the Elders and their Successors. And how amusing it would be to see a woman in cut off shorts and faded T-shirt for an indie rock band sitting on the high dais.

Just as he was going to mention this thought to Sirius, there was a commotion outside of the large doors. An angry feminine voice commanded that the door be opened. Reaching over, Wyatt grabbed his pen out of Sirius' hand and scribbled a message on the note pad.

I'm thinking
your sister
liven things up

Smirking, he wrote 'same' and turned the paper so that the other man could see it.

The two men grinned at each other as the double doors opened and the woman in question appeared. She shoved her way inside and her dog followed, snarling and still wearing his service dog vest.

"Come on, sweet girl." Celeste said calmly and guided a young woman inside.

Suddenly the inner sanctum reserved only for men was broken with an aggressive and domineering Alpha she-wolf and a submissive and meek human woman.

Leaning ever so slightly in his chair, Sirius whispered to his brother-in-law, "You married that."

With a proud grin, Wyatt whispered back, "Fuck yeah, I did."

"What is the meaning of this?" Alpha Anthony demanded looking at the tattooed woman. "And why did you bring that filthy whore into my house?"

As the Alpha stood, his robes billowed out around him, making him look like he was about to issue a ruling from the US Supreme Court. Or cast a spell.

"Accio brain cells," someone nearby whispered and those that heard were biting back laughter and coughing to cover it up.

Celeste let go of the girl and grabbed her dog as he lunged at the Alpha. Sirius and Wyatt moved at the same time. One placed a protective arm around the girl while the other one helped his wife hold the dog.

"What are you thinking, you stupid bitch?" The oldest son, AJ, demanded. As he stood, his robes shifted, emphasizing that they were too big for the young man.

"That stupid bitch is my wife." Wyatt hissed out. "She's also an Alpha. And a Marine. And her dog is a hell hound. But if you want," he smiled, his fangs extended as Demon pushed to the front of their mind and his voice became more of a growl, "I'll let them go."

The dog's eyes flashed red, smoke billowed out of his nose and mouth as his fangs extended partially. A low guttural growl emanated from his throat in warning as he sat at his mistress's feet. Absently, she stroked his head while he basked in the silent praise.

"You have some Betas that need the night off." Celeste said. "Mike and Jenny Naples. Their daughter is graduating college tonight."

"That wolf-less skank?" AJ sneered and Electra flinched.

"You have no right," Alpha Anthony started.

"But... I do." Elder Alpha Marcus said as he and the other two council elders spoke to each other through the mind link. With a nod from the Senior Elder Alpha, Elder Alpha Marcus continued; "We have decided that your son is not receiving the training that he needs to be a good

Alpha and leader. He will go to another pack to learn the discipline that he is lacking."

"Sirs..." AJ began.

"The decision has been made." Elder Alpha Stephen said. "Is there a pack that will volunteer?"

Celeste could only smile when Alpha James of the Marine Corps Pack stood.

"So be it." Marcus nodded. "Miss Naples, I think a change of scenery would do you some good also. And I think that Alpha Celeste would be a good teacher for you. And congratulations on earning your degree. I am excited to see you get your diploma tonight."

For the first time ever, Electra looked up at a wolf that she was not related to. When their eyes met, black eyes with a thin gold ring along the edge and similar eyes hidden behind dark brown contacts, a surge of power flooded through her. It did not last long, but the feeling that something inside her was waking up did.

A surge of power was felt throughout chambers, the flames in the lanterns and fireplaces flickered as if touched by an unfelt breeze of air in the stifling room. While the flames died down, a flash of gold filled the room from an unknown source.

The Alphas and Betas around the chamber were also looking around in confusion and Wyatt knew that he was not the only one to see and feel the power surge.

An Alpha standing close to the edge of the group quoted one of Electra's favorite lines from Macbeth. "By the pricking of my thumbs, something wicked this way comes."

She felt like there was something at the back of her mind that stretched and looked around before curling back up in the dark recess of her mind.

It's not time.

The voice was from inside her head. She had heard it before, and it was familiar and comforting. Much like hearing her mom's voice on a rough day.

Leaving the council room with the very tattooed Alpha, she found herself wondering about two things. The first was what was that sensation in her mind that she had felt earlier. And the second was why the council elders knew of her.

"Miss Naples." Senior Elder Alpha Davis said gently with a friendly smile. "We expect to see great things from you."

Yeah, sure; she thought as Celeste guided her out. *No pressure.*

Chapter 6

GRADUATION

Dark Sky Pack

The three Elders and their mates left the guest quarters that they were staying in. As they walked with their mates to the cars that the assistants stood next to, Alpha Anthony approached them. Senior Elder Alpha Davis issued a warning growl from the back of his throat and the host Alpha stopped in his tracks, bearing his neck to the three Elders.

With a soft-spoken command through the link, the Senior Elder told all the mates to go wait in the cars. They gave him slight nods as they walked past the trio escorted by their personal security details. The three assistants acknowledged their own orders and opened the doors for the women.

The elder gave a subtle glance and silent order causing the remaining security detail to spread out. This gave the Elders and Alpha privacy, but they also remained close by and ready to attack.

Every member of the all Lycan security team had been handpicked and trained by some of the most elite werewolves in the world. They came from special forces from militaries of multiple countries. The K-9s that were part of the detail were hellhounds and were bred specifically to serve the Moon Goddess and her chosen Elders.

As the guards walked them away from the Elders, the dog shifted to their hellhound forms. Each of the three dogs stood with their heads held high, even with their Lycan handlers. Their pitch-black fur stood on end making them appear even larger. The eerie and demonic red glow of their eyes refracted off the smoke that came from their large snouts and mouths that held a permanent snarl. Fangs and claws extended as foam began to form around their mouths as they drooled in anticipation of a fight.

"Tread carefully, Alpha, we have very little patience for dramatics," Elder Samuel warned with a slight growl to his voice.

"Sirs, we have prepared a feast in your honor-"

"SILENCE!" the three commanded at once. "KNEEL!"

The earth trembled under the weight of their authority. Birds in the nearby trees took flight to avoid a possible battle of wills that was looming on the horizon. The trees themselves seemed to bend in an effort to either move away from the Elders or bow in submission.

As if invisible bonds reached up from the Earth and wrapped their tentacled arms around Alpha Anthony's knees, wrists and neck, he was pulled down to cower at the feet of the men before him. Unable to fight the compulsion to follow the order, the Alpha fell to his knees and lowered his head in submission. Small indentations were formed in the hard ground where his hands and knees made impact.

Two Lycan handlers held each hellhound back as they snapped and lunged for the insolent Alpha. With a single command from the Elders, they settled down. But they remained prepared to attack and defend.

"I would think," Elder Marcus mused, "that you would want us off your lands and not digging into the secrets that your Pack keeps ever... so... carefully... guarded."

Alpha Anthony swallowed hard, and the Elders smirked at the strong scent of fear that permeated the air.

The Senior Elder stepped forward and extended a claw with which he tipped the now submissive Alpha's face to look up at him. "Know this, we answer to a Higher Authority and her patience with you is wearing very thin. I advise," he applied a little more pressure, and his claw punctured the skin, "that you look at your Pack and fix its issues. You will not like it if the council has to step in."

A look of defiance crossed his face before he controlled his expression and lowered his eyes. "Yes, Elders."

The deep warning growls from the hell hounds made the earth tremble slightly. It was as if their anger clawed its way up from hell itself.

"We are going now, and in the morning, we will leave. And Alpha," the Senior continued as moved his hand to drag his claws along the man's neck, stopping and tapping the pulse point with the bloodied claw, "Next time follow protocol. File a dispute and request a chance to speak. Don't call your own meetings."

"But the Hunt...." His voice trailed off as the rim of Senior Elder's eyes glowed a bright blue.

"The Hunt has evolved many times," the Elder Wolf growled out, his fangs extending. "It will continue to evolve as the Moon Goddess deems. It is not for us to question her motives."

The wolf receded to the back of his mind, and he retracted his claws and fangs. The three Elders moved past the Alpha that was still on his knees and towards the cars.

This is not the last we will hear of him.

Samuel warned through the Elder mind link.

No, he and his son will strike again.

Davis agreed and gave a subtle warning to the other two Elders.

Is she in danger?

Marcus asked and the other two knew who he was asking about.

"A little less than she was before," Davis assured him as they reached the cars.

They each slipped into the town cars that held their mates. Once cocooned inside their car, each of the Elders focused on their mates and the upcoming ceremony and party.

Peggy, Marcus' mate, looked at him with hope filling her eyes. "Is it really her?" she asked him, barely above a whisper.

The thin golden ring around his black eyes glowed brightly for a moment, as he smiled and nodded.

The white noise machine and scramblers were already turned on. They prevented anyone from hearing anything that they said.

"We still have to keep our distance, we cannot interfere," he reminded his lifelong mate.

"Until when?"

"The Goddess will let us know," he assured them.

She leaned into him, and he placed an arm around her shoulders.

They were both lost in their own thoughts and grief. Twenty-four years ago, their daughter had come to them and gave the exciting news that she was pregnant, and the due date was late December. With the excitement of their first grandchild, they helped their daughter, and her mate prepare to become parents.

On the night of the Winter Solstice, as they attended their host pack Yule Ball, their daughter and her family were hunted down and executed. Throats slit with silver blades dipped in wolf's bane. The baby was cut out of her mother's belly.

It was not until after the bodies were cremated and the ceremonies releasing their spirits were completed that they learned that the baby had survived. When they asked the Senior Elder if they could go get her, he simply shook his head no. He gave no further information, and Marcus was not sure if that was because he had no other information. Or simply opted to not provide what he did know.

As the car slowed, merging with traffic, they were pulled from their memories and personal thoughts. Peggy looked up at her mate of over sixty years. He smiled at her as she gently caressed his cheek.

"There's more to all of this, isn't there? More than just her being our granddaughter?"

He gave a subtle nod, "There is, but until she makes her choice, nothing can be said."

The security team split out with some remaining with the Elders and the cars while the others went ahead to the location for the graduation. It was the standard procedure for the hellhounds to return to their typical forms. Two of them resembled Rottweilers and would have guide dog vests placed on them. The third, the one that protected the Senior Elder, resembled a Cane Corso and would have a security vest and would remain with the Elders.

When they arrived at the colosseum that the graduation ceremony would be at, the guards escorted them to the seats that they had scouted out in the shadows of the last row on the upper level. The lights were off and no one else was seated up here.

Having already procured the needed security detail uniforms, the Lycan guards blended in as well as the tall warriors could. The shortest guard was a blond woman at just over six feet. The tallest was a redheaded man that stood well over seven feet.

Nodding to the nearby guards, Elder Davis indicated that they wanted some space. She acknowledged this with a nod of her own and then quietly ordered the remaining guards to begin their patrols.

Using their heightened senses, the Elders scanned the crowd beneath them. Mixed in with hundreds of humans, or Pilas, as they were commonly called, there were dozens of Alphas and Lunas. Most were the more progressive packs that agreed with the changes in the annual Hunt. Others were power hungry and trying to impress the Elders. The pack that was not there, Dark Sky, said everything about the pack and their leadership.

"They all came hoping to impress us," Samuel muttered.

"I'm not impressed," Marcus sighed. "We are going to have to address Dark Sky violating our laws. This is not something that I am looking forward to."

"We cannot, it will not be our issue to address," Davis informed the others. He smirked at the other two Elders. "Our successors will handle it. And it will be resolved before the next Hunt."

"Why is she not speaking with all of us on it?" Marcus growled.

The anger of his wolf echoed through the mind links around them. Being an Elder, he could force his way into the various mental links of the packs. With his emotions pushing to the front, all control was lost over the beast and the wolves in the crowd began to look around.

"Maybe because of that," Davis offered as they watched the crowd around them slowly find the Elders. He pushed out his authority with a warning growl forced out into the mind links throughout the building.

With more expediency than they had with finding the elders, the Alphas and their Lunas turned back to the front as the music began indicating the start of the graduation ceremony.

They watched the many pack leaders applaud and cheer as those around them did the same. Applause was given at the end of each speaker, even though it was doubtful that any of the wolves present had listened to anything being said. As the names were eventually read off and the graduates crossed the stage, the Elders spied on the Naples family.

Surrounded by the Alpha families of the Crystal River and Silver Lake packs, they were a little freer with their applause and cheering. Although the Elders did notice that they looked around frequently, as if they were afraid that the Alpha and his son would appear to punish them.

"What has the Alpha done to his pack?" Samuel asked quietly.

"He rules by fear," his mate replied.

"How many of these pack leaders are here only because we are?" Marcus asked.

"Other than Crystal River and Silver Lake?" Davis smirked. "It is doubtful that any of the others would be here if we weren't."

Samuel shook his head, "Some of their allies would have come, if for no other reason to show their alliance."

"Then let us hope that when the time comes, they support the River," Davis tipped his head towards the woman on the floor beneath them. "The trials are not over."

"How much more must be endured?" Samuel asked as the line of graduates neared the end.

"The Goddess only puts us into play," Davis said as they stood to leave. "We make our choices, and we are forced to live with the consequences."

Peggy placed a small hand on Davis's arm, even nearing a hundred, he was large and strong, looking no older than in his sixties. "Please, Elder, tell me that she will endure."

He smiled at his friend's mate as he leaned in and kissed her temple, "My dear, that is her decision."

Chapter 7
MORNING ROUTINE
Crystal River Pack

Hadrian stood in front of the stove cooking breakfast for his daughters, brother and himself. He and his girls had lived in this house for nearly two years, and he had yet to finish repainting the old avocado green kitchen. Being a firefighter, he had plenty of time off to do it since he worked a twenty-four hour shift every three days.

But one daughter wanted to paint it Ravenclaw purple. The other one thought that it should be Wednesday Addams black. He just wanted something that didn't make him think of dirty diapers.

The second issue was finding the time when his daughters weren't at each other's throats. Everyone kept telling him that the phase would pass. After all, as his father often pointed out, most of their four kids survived. Aiden had been saying that for so long that some people began to believe that he and his wife, Allison, did indeed have four children instead of three.

Currently, the peninsula is only half painted. Not a full half though as the top part of one door is different than the bottom half of another, and the door in between them, well no paint at all. Streaks of off-white paint with lines from the brushes covered six to eight inches of the cabinet itself.

He should just bite the bullet and let the construction company that redid his brother's house repaint the kitchen. He didn't know what was happening with his ex. He refused to open the large legal sized envelope that was in the mail yesterday. Now it sat on the bar as Hadrian made breakfast. Ignoring it. Just as he had the others that had come.

The front door opened and closed, and he heard his younger brother, Gerard, walking through the house. He plated the scrambled eggs and then put all four plates on the kitchen table.

"You better come eat while it's still hot!" he called out through the large open doorway into the living room.

His two daughters, Emily and Marie, both jumped up from their lime green and hot pink bean bags. They were the best presents that his sister had ever given them. If it had not been for his family, he would not have made it through the past two years.

Two years ago, the Crystal River Pack held the annual Solstice Hunt. Except when Alpha Wyatt held it, he held what he dubbed a non-hunt. All the rules were thrown out and new ones were made. There was no chase, instead the maidens had escorts, and multiple events were set up across the city.

For the first time in known history, not a single maiden was raped. Hadrian had volunteered as an escort. When he returned home that night after the Alpha and Luna were married, he found his sixteen-year-old sister asleep on the couch. After covering her up, he checked on his girls before going to bed.

Mitzi was not in bed, and he found her wedding band on the bedside table. There was also a note from her declaring that she wanted more out of life. Monday, while he was at work, he was served with divorce papers. Unsure of what else to do, he went to the oracle.

The woman smiled kindly at him and told him to be patient. Things would work out how they should. Focus on his girls and when it was time to move on, he would know. Listen to his wolf.

Every few months he got new papers. Even after they moved, they arrived at the new house. The new ones would end up with the others. In a drawer in the bedroom dresser. Ignored. Forgotten. At least until the next set showed up.

"More?" Gerard asked vaguely as he nodded his head towards the papers.

"Yup." Hadrian said, sitting down and pouring orange juice for his daughters.

"Kiara's got an appointment with the doctor tomorrow." The younger brother said. "She started nesting."

"I'll figure something out. I'm meeting with the Alpha and Luna today." The older one replied.

"Daddy, what are you going to see aunt Sles about?" Marie asked.

"Who?" both brothers asked in confusion.

"Luna told us to call her Aunt Sles. She doesn't like formerlies." Emily explained.

"Oh." The two men said in unison. The younger one added "She really doesn't" with a lopsided grin.

They continued to eat in silence. When he was through, Hadrian took his plate to the kitchen counter. He kissed both his daughters on their heads, and they hugged his neck and kissed his cheeks. Wrapping his arms around them, he lifted them as they clung to his neck and then sat them back down amid giggles and squeals.

"I love you, girls. Be good for your uncle. Rooms need to get cleaned today." He said as he grabbed his gear bag and keys by the door leading to the garage.

"Love you too, daddy." Five-year-old Emily said.

Seven-year-old Marie blew him a kiss. "I love you daddy! See you tomorrow!"

"Be safe." Gerard told his older brother. It was the closest he would come to saying that he loved his brother. It was understood without saying.

"Take care of my girls." Hadrian said just before going to the garage. Just like his brother, he did not need to say the unspoken declaration.

It was a short drive from the house to Fire Station Two on the main road through the city of Crystal Pass. They were located almost exactly in the center of the Crystal River territory. The actual center of the territory sat between them and the nearby town of Crystal Springs. Where Crystal Pass was made up mainly of werewolves, Crystal Springs was considered the human, or pila, town.

Although the wolves would often go to Springs, the pilas would rarely come to the Falls. Alpha Wyatt was working diligently to foster a better relationship with the other city. They now had a friendly rivalry that consisted of several Guns and Hoses events pitting the two cities first responders against each other. Last year, they had their first hockey game and the year before they had a seven game baseball series stretching from the Fourth of July to Labor Day.

There had been talk of a flag football league for this year. Maybe he would ask about it during his meeting today. His captain knew that he had an appointment with the Alpha and Luna in a few hours and that Station One would send another firefighter/paramedic over to cover his position while he was gone.

He parked in his regular spot between Darius and Parker. Getting out he grabbed his gear bag from the back seat of the Jeep.

"How are those girls?" Jessica Parker asked as she stood on the sidewalk.

She had three boys, Jayde, Onyx and Stone; she was certain that at least one of them would be mated to one of his daughters.

"Good. Your boys?" he stepped up next to her. He stood a good five inches above her five feet seven. She had long blonde hair pulled into a braid and bright emerald eyes, a skinny build and nice breasts for having nursed three pups. She was, like most she-wolves, beautiful.

Her husband was a deputy with the local sheriff's department. His schedule was made around hers, guaranteeing that someone was always there for the boys. An arrangement that Hadrian was very jealous of right now.

"They're good." She smiled as Darius pulled into his spot.

He jumped out, waving sonogram pictures. "Twins!" His dark face was glowing with excitement. He was about two inches taller than Hadrian. They were both muscular, but Hadrian was a little bulkier.

They both sported mustaches, one black and one red. Darius kept his head shaved while Hadrian sported his military style cut.

All three wore the standard uniform of black cargo pants, red polo shirt with the Maltese cross and their name and position. Hadrian had a single silver bugle on his collar indicating that he was now a lieutenant. Other than paperwork and reports, he really didn't see a difference between when he was a firefighter/paramedic and now that he was an officer.

They walked in and joined the rest of their twelve-member crew. Station Two had a large crew since it ran two ambulances, a truck, an engine and a rescue squad.

Around the day room and kitchen, the typical morning conversations took place. Kids. Spouses. Upcoming training. Rehashing recent calls. And there were also the new topics. Darius with his twins. The next lieutenant exam.

And the strange woman that came home with the Alpha and Luna when they attended a meeting at the Dark Sky pack late last week.

"I heard that the Dark Sky pack had kicked her out because she was wolf-less." O'Malley said.

"Yeah, well, they have a lot of old laws still in place." Parker said. She had been born and raised in the Dark Sky pack. When her mate had been in a different pack, she had been excited. When the Alpha said that she could join the fire department, she had been elated.

"Like what?" Captain McMurray asked.

"I would not be surprised if the whole reason he called that meeting was to find a mate for his daughter. If you're not mated by twenty-two, you can be forced off pack lands. She's twenty-one and still single." She explained. "Women cannot serve in a lot of positions. Police, fire, any political activity. Basically, you can be a teacher, a nurse or a housewife, all at the discretion of your husband."

"Goddess, I would have loved to see the Luna there." Thompson laughed.

"The girls told me that she told them to call her Aunt Sles." Hadrian shook his head. "I don't know what to say to that."

"She hates formalities." Gunny said from where he stood close to the door. He was a human who had served with the Luna in the Marines. Now, he worked for the pack as the security officer for humans and cooperation.

Gunny was a tall and buff Hispanic man with a flattop and clean shaved face. He took his job seriously but enjoyed kicking back and relaxing with his friends and family. "I need to talk to you about the change in the mutual aid agreement with the surrounding communities."

With that, the day officially began.

Chapter 8

OPTIONS

Crystal River Pack

The community atmosphere surrounding the pack-house was another one of Alpha Wyatt's changes from when he took over. Although the packhouse had always been open to anyone in the pack, it had not been a central hub for people to gather. He expanded the outside patio and terrace to accommodate the small hill that it sat on. Outdoor seating included small bistro tables, large picnic tables and planters with benches.

The former dining hall inside the packhouse was now run more like a restaurant. The pack members who could not pay put their meals on a tab and arrangements were made for them to pay back the Alpha. Frequently, he would find something to barter with or accept work in exchange.

He remembered so many Omegas while he was in the military that they barely scraped by with most of their checks going home to help their families. It seemed that the bigger and wealthier the pack, the harder it was on the Omegas.

At the same time, he wanted his pack members to hold their heads high and respect themselves. They would not accept charity, and he would not offer it. But he would accept artwork and interpretations of the pack crest. He often suggested volunteer hours with the pups and community services. Assisting with the farms and greenhouses was also encouraged. It was never disclosed who was 'working off a debt' and who was volunteering.

Everywhere that they went on the pack lands Crystal River, Hannah, the bubbly Omega that volunteered to be her guide, told her all about the changes. She adored the Alpha's and sang their praises.

"Even me," Hannah gushed one day when they went to Crystal Springs to the material and craft store, "they accepted me from my home pack, even with...."

A subtle movement of her hair and Electra saw the hearing aids in the other girl's ears. Unsure of what to say, she just nodded and waited for Hannah to continue. She did with a smile, not even seeming to care if others saw.

"Well, anyway, I can't hear anything in the mind link, so they made sure that I have a phone. It's connected to my hearing aids, but I still hold it to my ear because I feel weird just talking to myself."

On that trip, Electra had found some material that she liked and sketched out a dress. When Hannah had gushed over the dress, Electra offered to make one for her. The blonde had come up to Electra's rooms earlier to have her measurements taken. Once that was done, they walked down to the small café on the bottom floor of the packhouse.

Hannah joined her friends and Electra sat at the table that Celeste had told her to meet at. They had placed their orders, and the waitress brought them their drinks before disappearing into the growing crowd.

"Why teaching?" Celeste asked as people walked by, waving and saying hello to Luna as if they were friends.

"Blood makes me squeamish," Electra answered, stirring her coffee.

"Okay. So, why teaching?"

Electra looked at her confused. "I'm not understanding the question. It's not like there are a lot of options."

"Of all the things that you could have studied, why did you choose teaching?" Celeste asked.

"As a female, you can only do nursing or teaching." Electra said as if it were common knowledge.

Angel prowled and snarled in the back of Celeste's mind. The Alpha in her wanted to go rip the throats out of the pack leaders at Dark Sky. Teuf nudged her leg with his snout as the hell hound forced his way into her mind. Giving a low warning growl, he forced the Alpha she-wolf to lay down in submission before slipping out of her mind.

Celeste closed her eyes and took a cleansing breath before letting it back out and opening her eyes. Assuming that Teuf was trying to protect his new friend, she forced herself to calm down.

Smiling at the timid woman, Celeste spoke gently, keeping a tight rein on her anger and frustration. "Let me change the question, if you could study anything in the world, what would you study?"

"Anything?" Electra asked quietly.

"Anything," Celeste confirmed as a little girl ran up and crawled into her lap. The girl kissed her cheek, and the Luna hugged her before setting her on the ground and the girl ran back to her parents.

"I don't know," the woman answered softly.

"What do you like?" she asked, smiling at the little boy who brought her a flower. "Thank you, Luka. Tell your mom that I'll swing by and see her later."

"Okay," the little boy ran back to the table where his mom sat.

"I'm sorry, Luna."

"Celeste or Sles," she corrected gently as the waitress brought their lunches to the table.

"What?"

"Celeste or Sles. I hate being called Luna." Celeste smiled as Jill sat down at their table and stole a French fry. "Jill, this is Electra. Electra, this greedy thief, is my best friend. We call him Jill."

Electra looked at the large black man covered in black ink tattoos. Just like with the wolves, she could sense his beast inside him. She never understood how she could sense shifters and the different rankings. But just as it so often happened, the two voices that were always with her confirmed what she already knew.

He was from an ancient line of Siberian werecats. He was a warrior.

The large black man smiled at Electra and stole another fry. "You're gorgeous. But I'm sure you hear that a lot."

"No," Electra blushed as she looked down at her plate.

"Why the fuck not?" Celeste asked.

"I'm wolf-less." The younger woman shamefully told them.

Celeste stood up and whistled, causing the café to fall silent. "Does anyone here give a flying fu-" Jill cleared his throat reminding his friend of the children in the café, "-unny flip if someone is wolf-less?"

"I have a moody teenage wolf they can have." A woman called from the far side of the café. "No returns, exchanges or refunds."

There was a round of laughter as Celeste sat back down.

"You're in a new pack. Nobody cares if you have a wolf. Or a cat." Jill said as he pulled Celeste's plate towards him. "Or not at all."

Giving him a dirty look, Celeste took half of her sandwich. "They really don't. Why don't you take some time to figure out what you want to do."

"How did the meeting with the hot firefighter go?" Jill asked with a dreamy look.

"He's not into cats or men." Celeste laughed.

"Ha!" he said around a mouthful of sandwich. "In my fantasy, he's into both. Damn, I need Jack to hurry the hell up and get back."

"See?" Celeste said to a shocked Electra. "We have a gay werecat mated to a human and no one cares."

"They care," the waitress said bringing another sandwich and water to the table. "Because without those two, the goddess only knows what would have happened to our orphanage."

"Ahhh, thanks, Tiffy." Jill beamed as he and Celeste split the new sandwich. "I couldn't imagine my life without all my babies."

"Electra, do you like kids?" Celeste asked and the young woman nodded. "I have something for you; you'll be helping me and Hadrian-"

"Hot firefighter dad," Jill clarified as he got an eye roll from his best friend.

"-out. He has two daughters and no mate. When he's on duty at the fire station, he needs someone to watch them."

"Who watches them now?" Electra asked between bites of her own sandwich.

"His brother and sister were splitting the duties. She moved to Harbor Moon with her mate last month. And his brother is expecting their first pup in the next month or so."

"For how long?"

"As long as you want. If you don't want to, then I'll talk to Jill about having a sleep over every three nights." Celeste said with a slight shrug. "There's a couple of other ladies I'm also going to talk with."

The ethereal voice that was sometimes in Electra's mind suddenly filled it with a single word and she found herself repeating it out loud. "Yes."

Chapter 9

VISITORS

Crystal River Pack

Troy sat in the large common area of the bottom floor of the Crystal River packhouse. The center was a large round area with wings on either side. He had been told that he could go to the west wing which held the kitchens, dining rooms and entertainment. He had never been in the packhouse back home and wondered if they also had a movie theater and game room.

The other wing to the east held pack offices. The Alpha's Omega walked him down the hall and showed him the long hall of offices. Along with the Alpha's and Luna's shared office and the Beta's office, there were two conference rooms, and the door at the end of the hall that led to the large council chambers in the basement.

A human had approached them with a request to schedule an appointment. Troy was surprised that a human was there. He was even more surprised to find out that the man worked for the Alpha.

Now Troy sat and watched people go in and out of the packhouse. People of all ages and ranks came and went with ease. A group of teens were gathered across the way. Several older women sat together knitting and talking. A few old men sat out on the terrace playing chess.

There was a large restaurant and a small coffee shop café. A few kiosks were set up inside and had everything from custom pens to Crystal River memorabilia for sale. He should get his mom a magnet for her collection.

"Alpha!" one of the teens near the café called out. "Can we watch a movie?"

Troy looked over to see a very tall man wave at the teens. His extreme height and aura declared that he was more than just an Alpha. The man was Lycan dominant, and Troy felt his wolf, Jackal, tremble in submission.

"I don't care. Did you ask Terry?" Wyatt replied.

"He told us to check with you." One of the girls answered.

"If you're watching any of those Jason Momoa or Tony Stark movies, I'll chaperone!" one of the older women volunteered.

The Alpha laughed as he scooped up his squirming son from the arms of the woman. "Go on. Mom, no drooling on the electronics."

"I make no promises," she said as she followed the teens and knitting group down the hall.

"How's my little man?" Wyatt asked his one-year-old son as they approached where Troy sat just outside the large office.

"Alpha?" Troy asked, stepping towards him. He kept his eyes cast down and his arms out to side, slightly away from his body, palms out. He knew that not all packs adhered to the old ways, but he did not wish to anger a Lycan wolf.

Wyatt smiled at him. "Yes, sir?"

"I'm Troy Naples."

"Electra's brother?" he shifted the child in his arms. "I accept your submission; you may look up."

"Yes, Alpha," Troy relaxed his stance and lifted his head, but not enough to meet the other man's eyes. "I was hoping to visit her. If that is okay."

"Always," Wyatt said as his son tried to put his little fingers in his father's mouth. "I'll put you in touch with the security office, just let them know when you're coming out. Please, son, don't try to put your boogies in my mouth."

Troy couldn't help but give a small laugh, "My pup is at about the same stage."

"I'm hoping he grows out of it. Troy, this is Aiden, boogies and all."

The relaxed nature of such a powerful Alpha took him by surprise. He wasn't sure what to say. He had never been introduced to an Alpha's toddler child. And certainly not their boogies.

Aiden giggled and squealed as he bounced on his father's arm. Leaning across the large chest, the little boy stretched his arms out and opened and closed his hands.

"Oof! Oof!"

Setting his son on the ground, Wyatt scratched the big German shepherd behind his ear.

"Be nice to Oof. Teuf. Sorry, buddy."

"He'll get over it," Celeste said, wrapping her arms around his waist as Wyatt stood back up.

"Troy, this is my wife, Celeste. Troy is here to see Electra. He's her brother." Wyatt said and she held out a hand.

"We're very different from your pack." Celeste smiled. "We are a very diverse pack."

"You have no issues with her having no wolf?" Troy asked quietly.

"Why the hell are you both so hung up on that?" Celeste asked.

Troy looked at her in shock as Wyatt gave a soft chuckle.

"You'll have to forgive my mate; she's still learning the art of diplomacy."

"I know diplomacy," Celeste rolled her eyes.

"Diplomacy not at the end of a rifle barrel," Wyatt suggested with a smile.

"Whatever," she mumbled before smiling at her husband. "By the way, I am in love with her name. I'm stealing it for our daughter and Jill cannot have it."

"Where is our future daughter's namesake?" Wyatt asked, discreetly sniffing his wife.

"The library," she turned her attention back to Troy. "It's two blocks north and one block west." She explained then looked around. Celeste mind linked one of the Omega men who came over to escort Troy to the library.

"Thank you, Alpha." He said, shaking Wyatt's hand and inclining his head slightly. "Luna."

I don't like that pack. I thought that Silver Lake was bad.

Celeste said through the mind link and Wyatt replied, kissing her temple.

I know. But she is here now. I asked Mallory to give her a makeover. Hope you don't mind.

Not at all. I asked the oracle to visit her. But she said no. She said that when it was time, her mate would know.

Celeste was still confused about that and when she looked up, she saw his confusion also.

"Interesting." He murmured.

"Alpha?" They both turned to see the priestess approaching them. She wore khaki shorts and a blue T-shirt asking: I got out of bed for this?

"Love the shirt." Celeste grinned at the white-haired woman.

"Thank you. My sisters and I had lunch earlier." At their looks of concern, she waved a hand. "We do it often. I was told that there was a new wolf?"

"Yes, but she's wolf-less." Wyatt said as he picked Aiden back up and Tcuf went to the priestess

Scratching the dog behind his ear, she smiled knowingly. "I assure you, Alpha, she is not wolf-less. She has a wolf, but not a typical wolf."

"Okay. What kind of wolf?"

"Currently, she has a hibernating wolf. They are rare. They are protected and they are important." She explained with her soft smile.

"Is there anything that we need to do for her?" Celeste asked.

She is the Gelert.

The priestess answered through the mind link as she shook her head. "Will you please give her this?" She handed over a black velvet bag. Wyatt peaked inside and saw a silver necklace with a yellow crystal topped with a pewter wolf amulet. "When it occurs, it will lessen the pain of the shift."

"First shift is always uncomfortable." Celeste said, looking at the amulet in the bag.

"Nothing like this will be. They will merge and shift at the same time." The priestess gently tugged on Teuf's ear. "The moon goddess is most pleased with you, hound."

With that, she nodded at the Alphas and walked away.

What the hell is a Gelert?

Wyatt asked his wife through the link. Celeste shrugged her shoulders.

I was going to ask you.

Chapter 10

MALLORY
Crystal River Pack

After lunch with the Luna, a friendly Omega took her to the library where Electra was issued a library card and turned loose in the rows and rows of books. She had a small stack of books in her arms when her brother found her.

She checked out seven books and Troy carried them for her. They sat at a table in the nearby park and talked about the changes in her life. Including the fact that she could be in a city park without consequences or fear.

Troy had flown into Philadelphia to take care of some business with the council office. Electra knew that her brother had filed a dispute with the council, but he would not tell her about it. She did not ask. So much of what he did for the pack could not be discussed and she had quit asking years ago.

Not quite an hour later, Hannah, her Omega escort, approached with an iced coffee in one hand and her cell phone pressed against her ear with the other. With a few "Yes, Alpha" and another "Yes, Luna" she ended the call and tucked her phone away.

"Miss Electra, I am to take you to the beauty salon."

"Me?" Electra asked. She had cut her hair for so many years that she could not remember the last time a professional cut her hair. Suddenly, aware of her hair, she reached up and touched it.

"Yes, ma'am," Hannah grinned at her. "It's like what Miss Mallory says: Everyone needs a fresh start from time to time. You should always start with a new haircut."

Troy stood up and hugged her. "It's a new beginning for you, take everything that is offered."

"What about my books?" she asked as her brother walked away.

"That's not a problem, I'm headed to the packhouse after this, I'll drop them off." Hannah assured her.

The bubbly woman guided Electra over to the car and then drove to the beauty salon. Crystal Pass was a city full of trees and green spaces; parks and playgrounds abounded. And they were all open to people of all ranks and statuses.

Hannah waved and gave the latest gossip about the different pack members that they passed. She kept up a one-sided conversation, answering her own questions. Even if Electra had known any of the answers, the other woman did not slow down long enough to allow any answers.

Giving a quick wave to the woman who insisted that they do lunch, Electra nervously stepped into the beauty salon. It was sleek with glossy white floors and walls contrasted by the black lacquered shelves and reception desk. The chairs were chrome with bright lime green cushions.

The young man behind the reception desk wore a lime green t-shirt with CURL UP AND DYE on the front. He smiled broadly at her and stood up as he greeted her.

"Hi, I'm Bennett. Do you have an appointment?" he asked. He had electric blue eyes that matched the tips of his bottle blonde spiked hair. His friendly smile revealed straight white teeth and a tongue ring. He had lightly tanned skin and wore a high school class ring on his right hand.

"Electra." She mumbled.

"Oh, yeah! Alpha made the appointment." He picked up the phone and pushed a few buttons. "Hey, mom. Yeah, she's here."

A moment later, a woman with gray layered over bubblegum pink hair came out of the back. She wore a black hairdresser cape with Mallory written in lime green. Her honey-brown eyes sparkled as she looked Electra over.

"Damn. Yeah, you're beautiful."

"I'm not," Electra insisted softly.

"You are hot!" Bennett said from behind the reception desk. "But what do I know? I'm just a horny teenage boy."

"Seriously, dude?" Mallory asked her son with a small laugh. "When do you go back to school?"

"September." He said as the phone rang, and he picked up the receiver, "Mallory's Curl Up and Dye, this is Bennett, how can I help you?"

"Come on back and we'll get started on you," Mallory said, placing a friendly hand on Electra's back. "We'll have a glass of wine and talk before we start curling or dying."

"No ma'am, the salon is closed this afternoon per the Alpha's request," Bennett said into the phone as his mom guided her client to the back. "Yes, ma'am, I can get you in tomorrow..."

The teen's voice faded as they went around the wall that separated the two sections of the salon. White noise machines prevented anything said at the back of the salon from being heard by anyone at the front. Similarly, the electronic scramblers that interfered with the mind link, were anchored next to the white noise machines near the ceiling.

Reminding herself that Troy told her to start over. And that the Luna had encouraged her to open herself to new possibilities. Build a new life. One where she could do more. Whatever she wanted. The pack laws were different here, and she now had choices.

"I've never had wine before," Electra admitted as she sat in the comfortable black salon chair with lime green accents.

The same black and white theme continued in this part of the salon. Lime green lights ran along the edge of the ceiling and shined out from behind the mirrors. There were six stations with three hair washing stations. In the center of the room were eight black plush chairs with lime green piping. At the back was a hall with private rooms.

"Well, then, we should start with a blush," Mallory said, opening the wine fridge under the counter along the front wall. Grabbing two glasses, she went and sat in the chair across from her client.

"Tell me how you want me to do your hair." Mallory said, pouring wine into both glasses and then handing one to Electra.

"I don't know," she admitted softly. "The Dark Sky pack is very ummm... traditional."

"They're assholes," Mallory corrected. "I have friends from your old pack. If you'll trust me, I'll give you a kick ass haircut."

Electra replied with nervous hesitancy, "I trust you."

Clapping, Mallory popped up and covered the mirror at the station Electra sat at, "Excellent." The two walls of stations were set off center from each other and the mirrors at a slight angle preventing clients from spying while she worked. Then she turned Electra around and put a salon cape on her.

Five hours and half a bottle of wine later, Mallory pulled the cape off the mirror. "It's called mermaid ombre. Your hair was perfect for it."

Electra looked at herself in the mirror. No, not herself. The woman in the mirror was beautiful and looked confident. Her long, naturally wavy hair was now just barely past her shoulders. Her brown hair faded into pink, purple, blue and green, darkening as it went.

Reaching up and touching her hair, she watched the other woman do the same thing. It was surreal to see 'the other' her doing the same thing she was doing.

"She's beautiful," Electra said, looking at her reflection.

"Yes, she is," Mallory. "Do you know what kind of makeup you like?"

"My Alpha didn't allow it. But I like the lines at the eyes that come out."

"I love the wings." She said getting her makeup cart, "I'll show you how to do it, and I'll give you everything that we use." She was pulling out different boxes and tubes as she talked. "And we'll show off that beauty of yours."

"I'm really not beautiful. You did that. You made her beautiful." Electra motioned to the woman in the mirror.

"I only work with what the moon goddess gave you." Mallory said, opening a box and dumping out makeup brushes. "I see your beauty. Now let's see if you can see it."

She explained everything that she was using, and her pupil asked a lot of questions. Especially about the makeup tape. But with the use of the tape, Electra created perfect cat eye wings on her first try. Mallory went over the skin care routine and when they were done, she put everything that they had used, talked about or Electra had liked into a large black bag with green handles. She added the hair products and then handed the large bag over.

"I can't afford this."

"I'm your crack dealer and that is your beauty crack. First hit is free," Mallory said with a wink and small laugh. "Take the rest of the wine with you too."

"Are you sure?"

"Oh yeah. If you leave it here, I'm just going to drink it, and I already have two open here and a few at the house. Now, I can't sell you wine, I don't have a retail liquor license. But I can sell you a bottle stopper and give you a complimentary bottle of wine."

Electra laughed as Mallory waved her arms showing off her racks of bottle stoppers. "The M with the green crystals. So, I can always remember our first day together."

"That's sweet. Just for that, you get the mermaid and a second bottle. Let's do a chardonnay." Both bottles and stoppers went into a second bag that she gave to Electra.

Chapter 11

BLAZE
Crystal River Pack

Hadrian stood in his room; the walls were painted light gray to go with the dark gray and navy bedding. The furniture set was a black lacquer with chrome accents. The dresser and nightstands had three-inch long slim bar handles on the drawers.

After Mitzi left, he got rid of their bedroom set and bought this set from one of the guys in the department. He also disposed of the hideously ugly floral bedding by offering it as a prop for the next practice burn. When the fire was put out before the bedding burned, his father, the department chief, had restarted the fire.

It was the first time that Hadrian looked at the envelope of papers and considered opening it. His wolf, Blaze, was always hoping that Mitzi would return. But this morning he was in a mood and demanded that Hadrian break the bond.

We want another mate, sign the papers and break the bond.

That was the last thing that Blaze said before retreating to the back of their mind and curling up. All day, no matter what they were doing, Blaze refused to talk to him. When the girls were settled with a game in their bean bag chairs, he went upstairs and found the most recent envelope. He tore open the sealed flap and pulled out the papers.

Under the agreement, Mitzi gave up all rights to the girls. There would be no child support. No alimony. No contact. Nothing would change in their lives.

He clicked the pen and then signed the document. The pain from the severing of the bond was expected. It was not as strong as he thought it would be. The sense of relief was actually stronger.

He leaned against the dresser, head hanging as the break took place. Once it was through, a feeling of peace fell over him. Blaze let out a mournful howl in the back of his mind, and then it was done.

The papers were refolded, and he put them in the return envelope. He would drop them in the mailbox at work when he went in tomorrow. With that decision made, he tossed it into his gear bag before putting his copy in the drawer.

Downstairs the doorbell rang, and he heard his girls scrambling to answer it. Knowing that they would answer the door without him, he rushed down the stairs because they were seven and five and did not know a stranger in this town.

As suspected, the door stood wide open, and a large black man was kneeling before his daughters. ".... should never, ever, open the door without your dad saying that you can."

"Yes, sir." They both chimed but Hadrian knew that the next time the doorbell rang, they would open the door.

"Hi, I'm Jill." The large man said standing up. He must have seen the look that Hadrian made. "No, your nose is right. I'm a werecat."

"You must get that a lot." Hadrian said standing behind his daughters with a protective hand resting on their shoulders.

"I do. Followed by being called Bill. But you heard right, the name is Jill." He admitted with a small shrug.

"Why do you have a girl's name?" Emily asked bluntly.

"The name my parents gave me is Matthew. But my friends, who became like my family, gave me the nickname of Jill." He said and pulled out his phone. Showing them the picture of his little family, he pointed to each person as he named them. "That's my husband, Jack, me, and our daughter Amberley."

"I know Amberley," Marie said. "We were in Miss Wilson's class."

"Then you would be Marie, and you have a birthday coming up." Jill said looking at the older girl.

"I'll be eight!" she said excitedly.

"Just like my Amberley," ,e agreed and then looked up at the skeptical father. "Sles asked me to come talk to you. There's two options right now for while you're at work."

"Because we don't have a mom." Marie said softly.

"My Amberley doesn't have a mom either," Jill pointed out with a gentle smile, "but yes."

"Girls, go get ready for the movie," Hadrian said as he directed the girls towards the stairs. He then stepped out onto the porch and closed the door behind him.

He could feel Blaze in his head pacing anxiously. He kept putting his nose in the air sniffing. Grumbling, he huffed and returned to pacing.

"I don't like my girls thinking that they are a burden." Hadrian said gruffly. "They're not, you know."

"I know." Jill said gently. "Jack and I took over the orphanage last year. All those babies are mine. No one else may want them, but I do."

"They are my world." Hadrian sighed, "But I have obligations and responsibilities."

"I get that," Jill leaned against the porch railing. "We have two options right now. They can come hang out with us. There's nine kids in the orphanage right now. Three around their ages. We keep things fun, and they would have a room together. We have several kids that drop in for a night or two or even for a few hours."

"What's the other option?" Hadrian asked as Blaze growled.

"Calm down. We doubted that you would like that one. There are a few women that could come stay with them here. Melissa Parker, I think you work with her sister-in-law."

"She's a sweet kid, but no."

"There are two other options. Both will be at the movies tonight. Sles will introduce you."

"Okay," he said as Marie stepped out of the front door.

"Can we go ahead and put everything in the Jeep?" She asked her dad.

"I'll be right in."

"I've got to get back." Jill said, offering a hand. "The older kids were helping the younger ones to fix movie snacks. Lord only knows what that kitchen looks like now."

With a chuckle, Hadrian shook his hand and then went back inside with Marie. They loaded the camp chairs, cooler and blankets into the back of the Jeep. He sent the girls in to go to the bathroom and grab their backpacks.

What the hell is wrong with you?

Hadrian demanded of Blaze.

Something is in the air.

Good or bad?

Not sure.

Chapter 12

MOVIE NIGHT

Crystal River Pack

After Wyatt had come home from the navy and became Alpha, he made several changes. The two sister cities, Crystal Pass and Crystal Springs, interacted more. They even began a friendly rivalry with several Guns and Hoses events benefiting the Widows and Orphans programs for both cities police and fire departments.

His town, Crystal Pass, hosted an outdoor event every weekend during summer. The monthly outdoor movie held on the second Saturday was one of the most popular. People would begin gathering around six and the movie started at sundown. The movie was projected on the smooth white wall of the library that faced the city park.

Marie and Emily carried their chairs and backpacks to their usual spot next to the oak tree. Gerard and his wife Kiara were already there. The Alpha and a young woman were also there. Gerard worked for the police department and was relaxed around the Alpha.

Hadrian was not.

Although Alpha Wyatt and his unusual Luna, Celeste, always seemed approachable, they were still Alphas. And they were his Alphas.

"Alpha, this is my brother, Hadrian, and his girls, Marie and Emily," Gerard said, introducing them as they approached.

Just as he had taught them, both of his girls lowered their eyes and bared their necks. Hadrian did the same.

"Jill said that you two were pretty," Wyatt said, kneeling in front of them. "You are Marie, right?" she nodded and clasped her dad's hand. "And what are you doing for your birthday next month?"

"I don't know, sir," she mumbled.

"And you're Emily?" he asked of the younger girl who imitated her sister's actions. "Are you excited to start kindergarten?"

"Yes, sir," she answered softly.

"Your birthday is in October, and you'll be six, right?" Wyatt continued.

"I want to have a costume party for my birthday." Emily said, smiling as she looked at the Alpha.

"You know what?" he asked, smiling at the little girl. "My mate loves costume parties."

"Really?"

"Mmm-hmm." He stood up and motioned for the young woman to join them. "Donna, what do you think of costume parties?"

"I haven't been to one since I was a child." Donna admitted.

Blaze sniffed in her direction, and her wolf shook her tail at him. She was not a virgin, not mated and openly flirting. Part of him was intrigued. The other part was quite upset with both her and himself. However, if they played it right, he might just get laid soon.

But then there was another scent in the air and Blaze turned away from her. She huffed and stormed off.

What the hell, Blaze?

She's here.

Hadrian fell back into the conversation with the others about children's birthday parties. Blaze was pacing in his mind again, anxious and excited. Donna was no longer actively flirting with him. Although the blonde was pretty, she no longer held his attention. Both girls were hiding behind him and not talking to her.

"Dada! Dada!" Aiden squealed happily as his mom handed him over to Wyatt.

Her. We want her.

Hadrian looked at the wolf-less woman and felt his blood rush to his groin. Her dark eyes seemed to be solid black with a thin ring of gold next to the sclera. Her brown hair had multicolored curls hanging around her shoulders. She was pale and her makeup was light enough that he could see her blushing.

The woman wore a long empire waist purple dress and a denim jacket. He glanced down and saw that she had canvas tennis shoes and leggings. She was shy and did not know how to handle the large group of werewolves.

"I like your hair," Emily said quietly.

The woman sank to the ground and smiled at her. "Thank you. I just got it done yesterday." She said softly and held out a hand to the little girl. "I'm Electra."

Tentatively, she placed her hand in Electra's. "I'm Emily. That's my sister, Marie."

"I have three sisters; Helena, Portia, and Athena; and two brothers; Troy and Jason." She said with a smile. "My dad is a history professor and loves Greek mythology. We used to dress up as people from history and have costume competitions."

"Really?" Emily said excitedly.

"Yes, ma'am. I helped make costumes for The Wizard of Oz for the college I went to."

I like her. The girls like her. Let's keep her.

Blaze said dreamily.

It doesn't work that way.

It could.

"Can you swim?" Marie asked, stepping out and touching the multicolored curls. "Like a mermaid."

"That is something that I can do. In fact, I earned a scholarship for swim and dive at college."

"I bet your parents are proud of that." Hadrian said and saw a flash of pain in her eyes.

For just a moment, Electra remembered the shame that her family faced because of her. Wolf-less and attending a human college was bad. But then she made it worse by showing off her body in her swimsuit. It did not matter that it went from her neck to her knees and had sleeves to the elbows. It was tight and disrespectful.

"They were proud of my education." She mumbled looking at the ground.

"Do you miss your family?" Emily asked, sitting on Electra's lap.

"I do. And sometimes, it makes me sad." She admitted wrapping her arms around the little girl as if it were the most natural thing in the world. When Marie sat on the ground and leaned against Electra's side, she snuggled the little girls in close.

Acting on a long-buried instinct, the wolf-less woman inhaled both of their scents. That same strange feeling of something moving in the back of her mind twitched and stretched. The sensation was gone almost as soon as it started. But the single word that echoed in her mind from the unknown but familiar voice remained in her thoughts.

Mine.

Chapter 13

GELERT
Crystal River Pack

"I miss my mommy sometimes." Marie admitted quietly and the conversation among the adults suddenly stopped.

"That's normal, little one." Electra said gently. "There will always be a part of you that misses her. And it's okay to be angry with her. Just don't let that anger or sadness take over your life."

"Is it okay if I don't remember her? But I still miss her?" Emily asked with tears in her voice.

"Of course it is." Electra replied, squeezing the girls close to her. "We may never know exactly why she left. Even as adults, we make the wrong decisions for the right reasons."

"She left because we made her mad. We were always bad," Marie whispered as a tear fell.

Two things happened that surprised both Electra and Hadrian. She growled. Blaze whimpered and then when she growled, he yipped happily.

"No, little ones. She may have left for you, but never because of you." She kissed the top of each of their heads. "Have you ever heard the story of King Llewellyn and Gelert?"

As the two girls shook their heads no, the two Alphas had a conversation in their mind link about what the priestess had told them earlier.

"King Llewellyn had a loyal wolfhound named Gelert. Gelert was the best hunting dog he ever had. And he trusted her completely. He trusted her so much that he left her watching his infant son. The king came home one night, and the nursery was in complete disarray, and he couldn't find the prince."

"In the corner was Gelert with blood on her snout and teeth." There was a collective gasp at this, but Electra continued, "Certain that Gelert had killed the prince, King Llewellyn drew his sword and cut her head off. Just before his sword touched her, she let out a mournful howl. And then, the prince cried out for his mother."

"The queen was a werewolf and lay on the floor with her head severed from her body. The prince was hidden in the upturned crib, perfectly safe from the other wolf that had attacked to kill the poor prince."

"The king was so upset over what he did that he took the body and buried it himself. The king did it under the light of the full moon. His tears covered the ground. And when he left her there, the moon goddess came down. Every tear bloomed into a moon flower."

"The moon goddess then gave Gelert the ability to watch her son grow up, but only on nights with a moon and she could not leave that hill. King Llewellyn, struck with grief, heard her mournful howl every moonlit night until he died. The moon goddess blessed the little prince and his descendants that they would always have strong mothers who would protect their children from anything. Which is why werewolf mothers are so protective of pups."

Electra pointed to where the moon was starting to rise, "If you listen really carefully, you'll hear Gelert howl."

The whole group was quiet as the moon crested the horizon. A slight breeze rustled the leaves and there was a faint mournful howl in the distance. Both girls looked up at Electra who smiled at them. The adults all looked at each other a little surprised.

"I heard her," Emily whispered.

Electra nodded. "Now she howls for all the moms who have lost their children. Or the moms that had to leave them. And because she still mourns, I know that your mother still loves you."

"What happened to the little prince?" Marie asked.

"Gruffud ap Llewellyn ap Iowerth, now isn't that a mouthful?" She made a face, and the girls giggled. "Well, he was held prisoner by King John of England, his father and then his half-brother. But he fathered four children and among his grandchildren is Gwenllian. Do you know who she is?"

"She was the mother of Moncrief, born in secret and hidden away." Celeste said quietly, "Blessed by the moon goddess with black hair and silver eyes."

"His great grandson, also named Moncrief, is the father of the Silver Moon pack." Electra said and then noticed that everyone was looking at her. Blushing, she explained, "The downside of having no wolf in the Dark Sky pack is that you are of no use to anyone. Gives you a lot of time to read."

"Whether you have a wolf, a cat or nothing, you are always welcome and wanted here." Wyatt said softly, not wanting to wake up his son with his little head on his shoulder. "I'm glad that you are here, Electra."

"Thank you, Alpha."

We need her. And she needs us.

Blaze told Hadrian. Silently, the man nodded in agreement.

Chapter 14

BREAKFAST

Crystal River Pack

There was a light knock on the front door at six o'clock in the morning. Hadrian closed the refrigerator door and walked to the door. The multicolored cabinets no longer even caught his attention as he passed. But the small dirty finger and handprints on the glass sidelights did. Peeking through the sidelights, he was surprised to find Electra on his front porch with two grocery bags.

"I thought we said seven." Hadrian said, opening the door.

He was still in the pajama pants that the girls gave him for Christmas. They were blue with red fire trucks all over them. He was shirtless because he was certain that his girls did not understand why everyone always laughed at the matching shirt that declared firefighters like it hot.

"I'm sorry. I can wait if you want," she said looking down.

Stepping back, he opened the door wider for her to enter, "No, go ahead and come in. I was about to figure out breakfast."

"I brought stuff to make pancakes." She said walking in but not looking up. "Emily told me that pancakes with blueberries were her favorite."

Hadrian chuckled at the thought that his youngest child loved pancakes with blueberries but not blueberry pancakes. Somehow in her young mind, the pancakes were two totally different things. One delicious. The other is disgusting.

"Electra." He said, shutting the door before turning to look at her. She stopped where she was, still looking at the floor, and he moved a little closer to her. "Look at me, please."

"I'm sorry, I can't," she said in her soft voice.

"Why?"

"You're a Beta and I'm wolf-less. That's lower than an Omega."

Hadrian stepped in front of her and lifted her chin with a knuckle under her chin. He ignored Blaze and fought the sudden urge to kiss her. Where the hell did that idea come from?

"You're part of my household. You'll be treated like a Beta."

"Yes, sir," she whispered, her eyes still downcast.

"You need to act like a Beta," he told her. "The only people you submit to are Alpha and Luna. Look me in the eye."

"I can't," she murmured as a tear slipped out of her downcast eye. "You're my master now."

He cursed under his breath and then did what Blaze was screaming for him to do. Pressing his lips to hers, and keeping his eyes open and on her, he watched as her eyes widened in surprise. There was an odd golden glow that flashed from her eyes and power that emanated from her. The instant he moved away from her, it was gone. But Blaze growled a single word.

Mate.

"See?" Hadrian said softly with his face barely away from hers. "You can look at me."

"You shouldn't do things like that, sir."

"Electra let's get a few things straight. I am not your master. You are helping me with my girls; you are a member of my household. We are not like your old pack. You will be treated with respect here and not like a slave. Do you understand that?"

"No. I'm wolf-less…"

"And my mate left me. Neither of those are supposed to happen. But they did."

"I'm…"

"Beautiful. Kind. My girls already love you. And I want to kiss you again."

"Why?"

"Let's start with because my wolf wants me to. Everything else, we'll figure out when you're comfortable with the idea of me kissing you."

Unsure of what else to do or say, she simply nodded.

"I'll show you the kitchen and then I'll go get ready for work."

When he returned to the kitchen after a shower and shaving, he found his girls and Gerard at the table. Emily was in a nightgown from one of her many absolute favorite Disney princesses and Marie had unicorns on hers. They were both patiently waiting for breakfast.

Patiently because it was Electra's first morning, and they were the saints he always asked them to be. He knew it would not last.

Gerard was a younger version of himself. Even down to the similar uniform. He was a police officer, not a firefighter, and wore a blue polo instead of red.

Hadrian looked at the woman at the stove. Her mermaid hair was braided, and she wore a long peach skirt and light gray long sleeve shirt. Gray canvas shoes covered her feet and when she moved, he saw leggings under the skirt. He needed to talk to Parker; this did not seem like what you should wear in early June.

Electra turned and dropped her gaze. "It's ready when you are, sir."

"Then let's eat." Hadrian started to sit in his regular spot between his girls. But they told him to sit by his brother.

Electra placed plates in front of each of them and then went back by the stove. All four waited for her to get her plate and join them. She simply stood in the kitchen with her hands clasped together behind her back and her head tipped down.

"Electra?" Hadrian said and she lifted her head slightly and quietly gave him a soft yes. "Are you going to join us?"

She lifted her head, and both brothers saw the confusion. "Me?"

"Come sit between us." Marie smiled and patted the chair next to her. Emily did the same thing on the other side of the chair.

"Sir?" She asked, confused and surprised.

"Come join us." Hadrian smiled and she slowly made her way to the table. She sat in the empty chair without a plate. "Are you going to eat?"

"With your family, sir?"

"Yes. We eat as a family," Gerard answered as he stood up.

Electra hopped up, "What can I get for you, sir?"

"I'm just going to fix a plate for you." He answered while opening the cabinet and getting a plate. Turning around, he froze for just a moment. Then he sat the plate on the counter and pulled her into his arms for a hug. "What did they do to you?"

"You shouldn't touch me, sir." She mumbled against his chest. "I'm not worth this attention."

Gerard looked over her head at his brother. Hadrian stood up and went to her. Gently the older brother took her from the younger and held her close. Gerard went and fixed a plate and took it to the table.

"Let's eat," Hadrian whispered. "We eat as a family, and that includes you."

They sat down at the table to eat blueberry pancakes, bacon and scrambled eggs. Electra was uncomfortable since she had not eaten with werewolves other than her family since she was fifteen.

The conversation was light, and the girls were asking if they could do various things with Electra. Gerard volunteered to take them to the grocery store to get what they needed to make a cake. He preferred chocolate, if anyone was wondering.

At seven thirty, Hadrian took his plate to the kitchen counter. "Girls, make sure that you get your chores done before you make a cake. Electra, make sure that you take some time for yourself. Gerard, don't cause too much trouble."

He kissed both girls on their heads and headed for the back door.

"Daddy." Marie said and he stopped at the door. "You didn't kiss Electra."

He walked back over and kissed the top of her head before leaving for work.

Chapter 15

SLAVE
Crystal River Pack

Hadrian arrived at work a few minutes late with the rest of the crew already inside in the morning meeting. Quickly, he went and stowed his gear at his bunk and returned to the day room. The shift chief continued to go over the expected fire dangers of the day and other things they should know about. Carefully, quietly, he positioned himself close to Parker and the coffee maker as it slowed to a sputter.

Captain McMurray finished his rundown of the morning report, and the crew began to move around. Hadrian grabbed his coffee cup off his hook with one hand and the coffee pot with the other. He knew from years of experience that coffee in the fire house was in high demand. And the first cup of a fresh pot was a rare commodity.

"Parker, can I talk with you?" Hadrian asked as he poured himself a cup of coffee.

"Yeah, what's up?" she asked, sitting down at the large table in the kitchen area.

"Dark Sky pack, how do they treat those without a wolf?" he asked bluntly as he sat down across from her.

"You ever step in something gross, and you grind your boot into the grass to get it off?" She asked and he nodded, "Worse than that."

"I thought so," he said with a somber nod.

"This about that woman that came back with the Alphas?" Parker asked as other members of the crew gathered around the table.

"Yeah," he held the mug in his hands and stared at the black liquid. "She's watching the girls, they adore her.... Already... She wouldn't sit with us at breakfast. Then when she did, she wasn't going to eat with us."

Parker sighed and the weight of the sound penetrated the souls of her crewmates, "If she was lucky, the pack Alpha would have allowed her to stay with her family as a servant," she made air quotes to emphasize the fact that the other woman would not be a servant. "Since she is wolf-less, she would not be allowed to mate and may even be sterilized. She would become, ummm, an easy target for rape and abuse. She would not be allowed to work outside of her family's home. If she was lucky."

"If she was unlucky, what the hell would happen then?" Thompson asked angrily.

Parker aimed an angry look at the man, "She would become a slave for another family. Possibly a sex slave for a Beta. She could be passed around between them. She would be sterilized. What rank is her family?"

"Her father is a history professor. She didn't say what her mother was."

"That pack is not like this one. Women work outside the home at the discretion of their mates and the pack Alpha.

If she worked outside the home, it would be as a teacher or a nurse. That's it. Not even as a secretary. Certainly not as a firefighter."

"Just how badly were you treated?" Darius asked.

"My dad was a high-ranking Beta. He was a doctor, and my mom was a nurse. But both are Dark Sky for generations and are highly disappointed by me. I'm not allowed on pack lands," she looked at Hadrian. "Does she wear long sleeves and skirts?"

"That's all I've seen her in," he nodded. "And leggings."

"Shit," Parker sighed out. "She is extremely submissive, isn't she?"

"Yeah. Won't look at me, tries to do everything, and seemed lost when I asked her to join us."

"She's been raped. The leggings are an extra deterrent," she said, shaking her head. "I'm willing to bet that she thinks that you want her to perform all wifely duties without any consequences."

Blaze was just as pissed as Hadrian was. He wanted to hit something. Anything. Anyone.

The tones went off for a four-car accident and both man and beast were happy for the distraction.

Chapter 16

HOUSEWORK
Crystal River Pack

Gerard studied the young woman sitting on the floor with her back against the dark blue couch. Her brightly colored hair was the splash of color that this house and family needed. Looking at the gray walls of the living room, he again thought about how the sadness of his brother and nieces permeated the house. Various shades of gray covered the house, inside and out.

Except for the kitchen, his eyes were drawn to the avocado green cabinets at that thought. Hadrian needed to just decide what shade of gray was going in there. Then bite the bullet and buy the paint.

Suddenly, Electra gasped at a scene in the Captain Marvel movie, and he snapped a discreet picture of her. She was leaning forward, eyes wide and mouth open in surprise. It was as if she were amazed that there were female superheroes.

How was that possible? It was amazing to him that when the girls suggested a Marvel Movie, and he knew which one it would be, they had to explain what Marvel was. He decided that he would suggest a few other movies for her watch, mainly with strong female leads.

"You've never seen this?" Gerard asked.

"No, sir. This would not be allowed in my pack," she answered softly, looking at the floor.

"Your old pack, you mean," he gently corrected as he got a handful of popcorn.

"Yes, sir. I am sorry, sir," she cowered from him.

"You have nothing to fear from me, Electra," he said as the girls both stirred where they had fallen asleep in their bean bag chairs. "I am happily mated."

"I'm sorry, sir. It's a habit. I'll go finish up the cleaning now."

"It can wait. The movie is only halfway through," he said gently.

After breakfast, he sent the girls up to clean their rooms with the promise of a trip to the store and a movie after lunch. Very easily they also talked him into having lunch at a fast-food burger joint. Used to having to cook for them, take out was usually easier for lunch.

Between breakfast and when they left to go to town, Electra had cleaned the entire house from floor to ceiling. Both floors were now sparkling from her attention, and he did not think that there was a single spot that had not been cleaned.

Not only did she sweep the hardwood floors, but she also vacuumed the carpets upstairs. Even the carpet on the stairs had been vacuumed. The baseboards were also cleaned and the cobwebs in the corner that he had not noticed were now gone.

While at the store, Electra had walked quietly behind Gerard with her hands clasped behind her and head hung low. It was more than just a sign of submission. It was a silent prayer that she would not be seen. It may have worked in her old pack, but here it simply drew more attention.

Even in the drive through, she admitted that she had not eaten at a fast-food place since she was a young teen. At the age when she should have gotten her wolf but did not. Everything that he had learned about her since meeting her last night told him that her life had been hell.

Maybe his nieces were the bright spots of color that she needed in her life. And if that were true, the Crystal River Pack must be a whole damned rainbow for her.

With this thought, his eyes drooped close as she remained enthralled with the movie until the end. Gerard and his nieces slept through the rest of the movie and woke up to find Electra cleaning again. She was on her hands and knees mopping the floor with a cloth when the girls woke up Gerard.

The smell of homemade lasagna permeated the house and pulled the three of them out of their naps. Walking into the kitchen, he found the room immaculate and the only sign that she had made the lasagna herself was the running dishwasher and now empty trash can. Even the timer on the oven showed that the three of them had been out for a while as it grew closer and closer to zero.

Electra finished the floor before she stood and placed the wet rags on the back porch railing to dry. Then after she washed her hands and set the table, putting three plates out. The girls washed their hands and sat at the table, talking about the movie they had slept through. Gerard washed his hands and then fixed another plate.

"Uncle G?" Marie asked and he hummed a response. "Is Aunt Kiara coming over?"

"I don't know. I can ask her."

"Please!" Both girls chimed.

Laughing as he sat the new plate on the table before sitting at the other seat. "Electra, please join us." He said before reaching out to his mate through the mind link. "She will be here in a little bit. She's having dinner with some friends tonight."

"Are you sure, sir? There is still quite a bit for me to do."

"I'm sure," he wondered what else she could think that she needed to do in the now pristine house. "As my brother told you, we eat as a family."

"I am just a servant."

"All who eat with me, I will call him brother. All who break bread with me, I will call her sister. All who bid me join them, I will call him father and all who tend to me I shall call mother. For my pack...." Marie trailed off. "I don't remember the rest."

"You're getting there." He said encouragingly. "All who stand with me, I shall call him brother. She who breaks bread with me, I will call my sister. All who mend me shall be my mother and he who bids me join him shall I call father. For my pack is large and their needs are great. Bless me, Moon Goddess, make my plate full and my cup overflow. Give me fire in my hearth and shelter from the rain. Guide your children, be they strangers or friends, to my door to share in my blessings."

"That's beautiful." Electra said as she sat between the two girls.

"I like the short blessing better." Emily said with a grin, "Rub-a-dub-dub. Thanks for the grub!"

Gerard roared with laughter.

Chapter 17

ONE WEEK

Crystal River Pack

It was the last day of their one-week trial period. The house had never been cleaner. His girls had never been happier. And Blaze had never been grumpier.

Hadrian knew why. It was that dark eyed beauty that was already in the kitchen. Blaze was thumping his tail at the thought of her. They wanted her.

Throwing off the dark gray comforter and sheet, he went to the attached bathroom. Turning on the shower so the water could heat up, he stepped out of his black pajama pants.

Stepping under the spray, he hissed when water hit his back. Hadrian had been sent home after being burned by a falling beam during a house fire yesterday. His back was almost healed, but it was still tender.

When he arrived home unexpectedly, the girls were having lunch and Electra was on her hands and knees cleaning the trim along the floor. The first thing he saw was her round ass in the air. The image popped into his mind and Blaze yipped with excitement.

Hadrian imagined lifting her blue skirt and finding her bare for him. Wrapping his hand around his shaft, he began pumping as he thought about what she would taste like. Burying his tongue inside her cunt, he teased her nub with his thumb.

Increasing his strokes, he tightened his grip thinking that she would be tight around him as he slid into her. Resting his forearm on the shower wall, he grunted as he spilled his release onto the shower floor.

After a moment, he straightened and finished his shower. He grabbed the towel, freshly washed, folded and smelling like the woman downstairs, and buried his face in the baby blue terry cloth. Blaze growled in appreciation inside his head.

I know buddy. I want her just as bad.

Hadrian told his other half.

She's ours.

Blaze said as he soaked in her faint scent.

With the towel wrapped around his hips, Hadrian shaved and brushed his teeth. As he walked into his closet he was assaulted with her scent again. Simple, clean and his. He may deny it out loud, but he would admit to himself that Blaze was right. Hadrian felt the pull to Electra. It wasn't the same as the mate pull, it was somehow stronger yet not as intense.

His jeans and T-shirt smelled of her from her doing laundry. Having her scent on him, calmed him, soothed Blaze. Mitzi could not do that for a long time.

There were other differences between the two women. The girls were always an afterthought for their mother. Electra considered them first. She had been there for only a week, and she already knew his girls' likes and dislikes.

So far, the only thing that she had requested was to go to the fabric store over in Crystal Springs. In the past week, she had made both girls new dresses, curtains and pillows for their rooms. The material for new comforters had been ordered and he received a text notification that it had arrived.

As he stood in the hallway, he looked at Marie's room with all its bookshelves and new Harry Potter Ravenclaw curtains. Even her bed had been made, not perfectly, but more than it usually was. Her room was dark, but she had always been drawn to the darker colors and books and movies.

While he was thinking of it, he went into the room and located the flashlights that his oldest kept 'hidden' under her bed. Two of the three were dead. After checking the battery sizes, he made a mental note to get more this weekend when he went grocery shopping. With the flashlights back in their hiding place, Hadrian moved to Emily's room.

There were colors and stuffed animals everywhere. Barbie dolls and baby dolls were having a tea party at the little table and hanging out at the pool in the large plastic dollhouse. Her favorite stuffies were tucked into the bed covers that were pulled up to the pillows. Disney princesses abounded everywhere.

If he were a G.I. Joe doll, this is the room that he would want to get a twenty-four-hour pass to go to. Unlike in her sister's room, her brightly colored Disney Princess curtains were pulled wide open showing off the ruffles, lace and ribbons.

He went downstairs and found the living room empty. Even here, Electra's touch could be seen. Other than the fact that the house was now clean enough to eat off the floor, small touches of color were now in his formerly gray and navy room. Jewel toned pillows were tossed on the L-shaped couch and recliner. Small, child size blankets were neatly folded and waiting in the bean bags. One dark with book quotes and the other bright with princesses.

Typically, the girls hung out there while breakfast was being made, and he was surprised that they were not there. Following the scent of breakfast cooking and the sound of happy voices, he moved towards the large opening between the kitchen area and living room. Leaning against the doorframe leading into the kitchen, he watched Electra and his girls. With more patience than he had, she helped Marie flip a piece of toast on the skillet.

Both girls were still in their nightgowns, again one dark and one bright. Electra wore a floor length Maxi skirt and loose fitting, long sleeve sweater. When the skirt moved, he saw those damned leggings above her low-cut canvas shoes.

"I did it!" Marie squealed.

"You did," Electra encouraged. "Emily, put on the cheese and meat, please."

"Do you think daddy will like this?" Emily asked from the chair that she stood on.

"It smells wonderful," Hadrian said, smiling as his girls looked at him in surprise. "I'm sure he'll love it."

"Daddy!" Emily cried out. "We were going to surprise you."

He walked over to where they were and kissed both of his girls on their upturned cheeks. Running a hand down Electra's back, he watched her plate a slice of toast with an egg in the center. Shredded cheese and a thick slice of ham were on the underside.

"Girls," Hadrian said softly, "go wash your hands upstairs."

"But we-" Marie started.

"Go," he commanded.

They both hopped off their chairs and headed for the stairs. Hadrian took the plate and spatula and sat them on the counter. Then he gently turned Electra to face him and tipped her face up with a hand on her neck.

"Electra," he said softly, "have you ever been kissed? I mean really kissed."

"No, sir," she whispered with wide eyes that flew to his mouth before looking back down.

"I'm going to kiss you. Will you let me?" he rubbed his thumb across her lower lip.

"If you wish."

"You can tell me no."

"Sir?"

"If you don't want me to kiss you, you can say no," he lowered his head.

Feeling brave, she looked at him, "What if I say yes?"

His lips barely touched hers and he was overwhelmed with the urge to mark her. Hadrian fought against Blaze as he nipped at her bottom lip. He tilted his head with the intention of taking the kiss deeper but heard the girls coming back.

"We'll finish this later," he promised softly as he lifted his head and stepped away from her.

Chapter 18

URGES

Crystal River Pack

Hadrian sat on the back porch of his parent's house with his dad and brother. The three men looked similar with short red hair and clean faces. The father wore a black t-shirt declaring he's a grandpa- the man, the myth, the legend, and a pair of denim shorts.

Hadrian wore khaki shorts and his firefighters like it hot t-shirt. His brother wore black shorts and a gray CPPD shirt. All three were barefoot on the wooden deck.

Aiden manned the grill while his sons kept him company. He watched his oldest son sitting at the glass top table watching the woman inside with his daughters.

"What's going on with you two?" Gerard asked his brother as he leaned against the deck railing.

Looking guilty, he turned away from the window, "I don't know."

"Don't know? Or won't say?" their father pressed as he moved over and activated the outdoor white noise machine on the wall by the backdoor.

"I really can't explain it," he took a drink of his beer as looked through the door again. "It's just something that I feel like I have to do."

"Do what?" Gerard asked, feeling like he was missing part of the conversation.

"Obsidian says you need to listen to Blaze."

"Blaze says that we need to mark her," Hadrian said, shaking his head. "Keeps saying she'll wake up if we mark her."

"Your wolf has finally lost his mind," Gerard teased his brother.

"So, mark her," their father said. "She's pretty, the girls love her. What's the problem? You don't find her pretty enough?"

"I kissed her," Hadrian admitted quietly. "Last Sunday. She was helping the girls make breakfast. I sent the girls upstairs and I kissed her." He took a deep swig of his beer as he let them process that information.

"You do want her?" Aiden asked his son.

"Goddess, yes."

"What's the problem?" he asked his son. "She doesn't have the smell of a virgin."

"She's been raped," he said so quietly that even with werewolf hearing, they barely heard.

"Here?" Gerard asked angrily.

"No. Dark Sky uses it as a way of controlling women. Especially their slaves." His brother explained.

"Slavery is outlawed." Gerard pointed out. "We outlawed it before the human governments did."

"Just because the council bans something, doesn't mean it's not going to still happen." Their dad said calmly as he closed the grill and walked back to the table. "Why was she a slave?"

"It's because she's wolf-less, isn't it?" Gerard asked and Hadrian gave a soft yes and nod. "That's just stupid."

"Dark Sky is one of the worst of the Wolf Supremacist packs." Aiden said, "Humans are not allowed on pack lands. You're not allowed to 'dilute' the blood by mating with anyone other than a wolf."

The sliding glass door opened and the woman in question walked out with a tray. Her eyes were cast down as she walked with her colorful half ponytail swaying behind her. Today she wore her gray sweater and purple skirt, with the leggings that now irritated Hadrian. When he first saw them, they intrigued him. Now that he knew why she wore them, he despised them.

"Your wife asked me to bring this to you." She said softly, offering Aiden the tray.

"Thank you, dear." He smiled as he accepted the tray for the hamburgers and hot dogs on the grill. "And how are you liking your new pack?"

"I like it, sir." She said simply.

Aiden placed the tray on the table before gently cupping her chin and lifting her face towards him, "Look at me, girl."

Electra looked up at him and he saw the terror in her eyes.

"You have nothing to fear from this pack. And certainly not from anyone in this house." He told the timid girl.

"Yes, sir," she whispered as tears filled her eyes.

Aiden leaned down and kissed her temple, taking in her scent. Under the smell of soap and detergent, and the slight smell of his son and granddaughters, was a very faint scent. If you weren't looking for it, it would be missed.

Wolf.

A hibernating she-wolf, to be exact. He felt his wolf, Obsidian, push at her wolf. Letting his own wolf take the lead, he watched as she sniffed the air and then curled back up.

Both men watched as their dad's eyes darkened as he spoke with his wolf. As his eyes returned to their normal green, he stepped away from the young woman.

"Have you been to see our priestess?" Aiden asked casually.

"No, sir. I did meet with the healer the day after I arrived," she said and struggled to look up at him. "I was advised to turn away from the Dark Sky pack and practices."

"It takes time," Aiden said, picking up the tray and moving back to the grill. "My lovely mate in there, she has a very bad habit. I'm warning you in case she says that you two should go shopping."

"I fear I may have already agreed to go," Electra said. "I see what your women wear here, and I am a bit out of place."

"We are much more relaxed," he agreed as he handed her the tray of cooked meats. "Hadrian can take you to the Saturday training, if you'd like."

"Saturday training?" She asked as he opened the door for her.

"It's when the warriors gather and beat the hell out of each other, and we claim it's training," Gerard said, following her into the house. "Girls, go wash up."

"That's my line," Hadrian teased.

"I don't care who said it, girls, go wash up," Allison said as she finished in the kitchen. She wore short denim shorts and a hot pink spaghetti strap top.

"Yes, Nanna," both said as they went down the hall. They each wore simple sundresses that Electra had made.

"Why would I go to training?" Electra quietly asked Hadrian.

"To learn to fight and defend yourself," he said as he absently rubbed her back. "So, you feel more confident and comfortable."

"Women learn to fight here?" She asked in surprise.

"We do," Kiara said, placing the potato salad on the table. Rubbing her large belly, she added, "Some of us take a break."

"With each other?" Electra asked, confused.

"Yes, we have a training session and usually meet with the males at least once a month. More frequently now with the Luna. She doesn't like the segregated sessions," Allison said as the girls came back and sat down.

The rest of the family also sat down, and Electra slipped into the kitchen, with the door silently closing after she entered. Hadrian grasped the edge of the table as he forcefully stood up. The chair fell backwards with a loud thud. His mother sighed as she looked at the claw marks that he left on her table.

Closing the door quietly behind him, he approached Electra. "What's wrong?" Hadrian softly asked as Blaze whimpered in his head, pain that was not his own rippled through the wolf.

"I'm sorry," she said, wiping her eyes.

Gently, he turned her to face him and tipped her face up. As always, her hands dropped to her side. He used his thumb to wipe tears away from her eyes.

"Tell me what's wrong."

"You should go eat, sir. I do not require such attention."

"That's what's wrong, isn't it?" he said softly. "You're not used to being treated like a person."

"I am unclean," she whispered.

"In what way?"

"I am not pure. I have no wolf."

"Neither I nor my wolf give a damn," he told her as he lowered his head and brushed his lips against hers.

"Sir, you-"

"Hadrian," he corrected gently. "I am desperate to hear my name on your lips," he continued to gently kiss her.

"I... I can't," she cried softly as his hands moved to her hips and lifted her onto the counter. Shocked, her hands flew to his chest to steady herself.

"You can," he said softly against her lips.

She sighed ever so quietly and moved her hands to his shoulder. He gave a low growl as he nipped at her bottom lip. She gasped in surprise, and he dipped his tongue inside her mouth.

"Hadrian- Nope, he'll be a minute," Gerard said as he walked into and then out of the kitchen.

Laughing, Hadrian rested his forehead on hers. "Before my mother accuses me of ravishing you in her kitchen-,"

"Not in my kitchen!" Allison yelled from the dining room.

"- we should go back," he sat her back on her feet and took her hand, leading her back to the table.

"I should not join your family for your meal," Electra whispered, fear thick in her trembling voice.

"But you're part of our family," Emily said.

"I'm just a servant, Emily," Electra said gently.

"No, you're not," the little girl argued. "You're our new mom." The room fell silent with that declaration.

"Who told you this?" Allison asked.

"The sleeping dog. She said that we're hers now," Emily said confidently. "And that when she wakes up, she'll have a pup for us."

"I don't know who the sleeping dog is," Electra said, squatting between the two girls. "But it's not me. I... I can't have pups." She swallowed hard and fought back tears due to dreams taken from her years ago.

"Why not?" Kiara asked, thinking like a doctor. "There may be something that can be done."

Electra stood up shaking her head, "It's permanent."

"What do you mean?" Aiden asked as Hadrian pulled the chair out for Electra.

"Are you sure that you want me to join you?" she asked him.

"Yes," he pulled her to him with a hand on the back of her neck and kissed her lightly on the lips. "I'm sure."

Understanding that whatever happened, she did not want to talk about, Aiden did not press the subject. They enjoyed the meal with light conversation. Marie's birthday was brought up and with a little prodding, she finally admitted what she wanted to do.

"At a firehouse?" Aiden smiled. "I just happen to know the chief."

"You are the chief," his granddaughter grinned.

"Then it should be easy for him to arrange," Allison said.

"You know the police station is cool too," Gerard pouted.

"They're too young for handcuffs," Kiara said and then blushed.

Aiden rolled his eyes as his youngest son grinned and his oldest tried to keep his daughters from focusing on the comment their aunt had made.

"Electra, when is your birthday?" Allison asked, trying not to laugh at her daughter-in-law.

Softly, with her head tipped down in submission, she answered, "Winter solstice."

Chapter 19

SHOPPING SPREE

Crystal River Pack

The following weekend, Allison came and got Electra Saturday morning after Hadrian got home from his shift. They went to the mall in Crystal Springs and Electra admitted that she had not been to a mall since before she turned thirteen.

When she did not get her wolf, restrictions started. Where she could go became smaller. Who she could associate with shrank. But the worst was yet to come.

Standing in the swimsuit department of one of the stores, Electra looked for a conservative swimsuit like what she had competed in. Everything here was too skimpy and would leave her exposed. Her scars would be on display for everyone to see.

"Oh! This is adorable," Allison handed her a bikini and pushed her towards the dressing room.

"Miss Allison, I can't wear this," Electra said quietly. She looked at the red Gingham two-piece with a formed top and cheeky cut that very closely resembled a thong.

"Nonsense, you have a kick ass body."

Electra entered the small room and changed. Then she opened the door and motioned for Allison to come in.

Immediately, she saw the scars, emphasized by the cut and bright red color. She left and returned with a much more modest blue two-piece tankini with a cover up.

Feeling more comfortable, she stepped out of the room but remained in the long hallway. Allison approved and handed her a stack of jeans to try on. By the time they made it to lunch, Electra was worn out. She felt dead on her feet.

"Dad warned you." Hadrian said quietly as he wrapped his arms around her and pulled her back to his chest. Instantly, she gave into the comfort that he offered and leaned into him for emotional and physical support.

Her hair was in a French braid exposing her marking spot on her neck. The V-neck t-shirt only emphasized the spot, and he placed a kiss there. She tensed and tried to move away,

"You shouldn't do that." She warned him. "People will think-."

"Exactly what I want them to think." He whispered. Then he turned her face to him. "Do you not want to see where this goes?"

"It cannot go anywhere. I have no wolf."

"I don't care. What do I need to do to convince you of that?" he asked.

"Hadrian!" Parker called out from a table inside the restaurant.

"There's someone I want you to meet." He said, draping an arm around her shoulders. "Mom."

Allison stood up from the bench and took the girl's hands and followed her son to the table. His girls were excited to see the three boys and they ran to sit at the adjacent table. Theo Parker stood up and greeted them.

The man was dressed much like Hadrian in khaki shorts and a black T-shirt. The two men chuckled when they realized that Hadrian's shirt declared him to be a girl dad, and the other shirt declared him to be a boy dad. The woman wore short denim cut-offs and a tank top for a tea company that Electra had never heard of.

"Electra, this is Theo and Jessica Parker," Hadrian introduced with a smile and a flourish. "Those are their boys, Jayde, Onyx and Stone. I work with Jessica."

Electra looked at the other woman in surprise.

"Yes, I really am a firefighter." Parker said, answering the unasked question. "I was raised in Dark Sky. I know what you're going through."

"Your eyes are beautiful." Theo said after they sat down. He looked at her and she felt like he could see through her dark contacts. That was impossible. But the way he looked at her, she felt as though her secrets were laid bare before him.

"Thank you." She mumbled as the waitress came to get their drink orders. Everyone ordered with ease and then they waited for her. "Water, if it's not too much trouble."

"Bottled or iced?" the waitress asked with a friendly smile.

"Iced, please." Allison answered as she saw the panic start to take hold.

After the waitress walked away, the group started discussing what they were going to eat for lunch.

"Honey," Parker said gently as she pushed the menu across the table towards Electra. "They don't give a damn about rank. I mean, they do. But not like Dark Sky does."

"Have you ever met Jill?" Hadrian asked the table in general.

"You mean the big black gay werecat that's mated to a human and has taken over the orphanage?" Theo asked with a grin. "Never heard of him."

"Don't be around when that group starts drinking," Allison laughed. "Dear goddess, they get raunchy."

"You and Aiden should go to the strip bar with them," Parker smiled at her husband. He leaned over and kissed her.

"Be careful, or you'll be finding another rock name," he teased as the waitress brought the drinks and appetizers.

"I would like a little girl; Pearl or Diamond," she replied.

"Ugh, you two," Hadrian rolled his eyes.

"Seriously," Parker said to Electra, "you can start over. There's nothing..."

Parker trailed off as her eyes widened. Electra looked down at her hands in her lap.

"I'm sorry." She whispered to the other girl who nodded. "I think that you should show it to the Luna. She would know how to get rid of it."

"There's no way. It's permanent."

"I still think that you should talk to the Luna."

"She does not need to worry herself over a slave," Electra said softly.

Chapter 20

SLAVE MARK

Crystal River Pack

Celeste sat at her desk in her office listening to the man in front of her drone on. And on. And on. He had been going on for so long, she no longer even knew what the meeting was about.

She hid a giggle with a cough as a funny thought ran through her head.

This is the meeting that never ends,
it just goes on and, on my friend,
no one knows what it's about,
some shithead started talking and now I'm going to die
in the meeting that never fucking ends...

The knock on the door caused him to pause, but only for a moment. Before she had even called for Anna to enter, he was back in full swing. Please, goddess, Celeste prayed, kill me now.

"I'm sorry, Mrs. O'Donnell," Anna said, and Celeste remembered that the man was human. No wonder he couldn't get to the point.

Why could she not smell that?

"Yes, Anna?" she asked with a smile.

"I hate to intrude, but there is a detective here that needs to speak with you about an incident." Anna wore a short pink dress with cap sleeves with a black belt and peasant collar matching her black pumps. Her brown hair was pulled back in a loose braid and her eyes sparkled with amusement.

Have I told you lately how much I love you? What the hell was this waste of time about?

Even Anna's wolf laughed in the mind link. Angel growled the sentiment of *Just make it stop!*

Sharing the cost of a waterpark with Crystal Springs and Crystal Pass. Geoffrey Thompson.

You really are the best.

Celeste thanked her omega as she was standing up and offered her hand to the man, "Please leave all the information with my assistant, Mr. Thompson. It does sound like a very good investment, but as you know, I cannot make the decision on my own."

She thought again that his suit looked like it was a size too big, as if that was the best option on the rack. The olive-green suit jacket, slacks and tan shirt with a black tie made her wonder if he had served and the suit made him feel as if he were still in uniform.

Of course, she herself couldn't say much. She still wore her issued boots most of the time. But today she wore light gray slacks with a bright green satin shell under a lightweight black cardigan. And her husband's favorite pair of black stilettos.

"Of course, of course." He said, shaking her hand. "Thank you for your time and I'll leave several packets with Miss..."

"Anna." Celeste smiled.

Can you call the healer?

I'll call your mate.

Anna smiled knowingly at Celeste before ushering the human out.

A moment later, she opened the door to her sitting room and saw the two women waiting. Allison O'Reilly and Jessica Parker. Celeste smiled brightly at the two women as she walked in.

"How was your trip?" She asked, coming around the couch and hugged the older woman.

"It was wonderful," she said, embracing her Luna. She wore her police department polo shirt and cargo pants; her utility belt was still in her patrol car in the parking lot. "Every Were should go to Rome at least once in their life."

"I agree," she moved to the younger woman. "I think we need another night out."

"I think it's going to be a bit before you have one of those," Parker said, and Celeste looked at her oddly. Since it was her day off, she wore light khaki pants and a dark turquoise blouse and brown leather sandals.

"Is everything okay?" Wyatt asked as he burst into the room. He wore a starched white shirt and charcoal gray slacks. His short hair was disheveled from running his fingers through it.

"Your wife needs a hug," Anna said leaning against the wall.

"Why do I need a hug?" Celeste asked as Wyatt went to her and pulled her close.

As he always did, he closed his eyes and took in her scent. They flew open and he kissed her deeply. She was clinging to his shoulders when he lifted his head, smiling at her.

"It seems our son is going to be a brother," Wyatt said, caressing her cheek.

"Oh! Damn, is that why I can't smell anything?" she asked, leaning into him.

"Probably. I had the same thing when I was pregnant with Liam last year," Anna said smiling as she backed out, closing the door behind her.

"Alpha, do you have a moment?" Allison asked as she looked down in submission.

He connected with his Omega personal assistant, Terry, who said that he would rearrange things for as long as needed. "I'm good," he motioned for them to sit on the two gray couches. As he sat down, he pulled Celeste into his lap. The other two women sat down opposite them.

"Alphas, I was raised in the Dark Sky pack and have always heard the rumors. It was like a badly kept secret that everyone knew, and no one talked about," Parker said looking at her hands, fighting back tears.

"I do not like that pack; they are worse than the one I was raised in," Celeste said quietly. "Whatever it is that you want to tell us, just say it."

"I saw scars on Electra's arms and stomach. It looks like she was fixed. She has said a few times that she can't have kids. That it was permanent," Allison said.

Both Alphas reached out to their assistants. It did not take long for Anna to enter the room with an update. "The Beta is on his way; your parents are upstairs with Aiden. Umm, sorry," she grinned at Allison, "little Aiden."

Allison gave a small laugh, "Hopefully, my husband doesn't need a babysitter. I'll reach out to Hadrian," she said as she called her son through the mind link.

"Imogen has asked for some time with you," Anna told the Alphas. She gave a small laugh at their confused looks. "The oracle. She actually has a name."

"I never think of them having lives outside of their positions," Celeste admitted.

"It's the same for us mere mortals and you Alphas," Anna grinned. "Except for those of us who have heard you two going at it in here."

"Sorry?" Wyatt said without feeling the least bit sorry.

"I've turned on the white noise machines and set out cookies in your conference room." Anna told Celeste and moved out of her way.

"I love you!" Celeste called out from the conference room.

"Was that for you or me?" Wyatt laughed.

"It was probably for the cookies," Anna said as she returned to her desk.

"I think it is for the cookies." He said entering the conference room.

Within thirty minutes, the conference room was full and the only person not in attendance was Electra. Anna opened the door and let them know that she was on her way after making sure that the girls were settled with Jill and Amberley. A few minutes later, Electra was shown into the room.

Celeste saw the flash of anger in Hadrian's eyes when he saw her clothes. She had heard about the shopping trip with Allison even before the other women told her about it. They met for lunch at least once a week and she saw how the woman was blossoming as she lived with Hadrian and his girls.

But Electra showed up in her blue skirt, gray sweater, leggings and canvas shoes. It was as if she had pulled on armor before coming to the packhouse. It was as if she was afraid that she would be sent back to Dark Sky.

With so many Alphas and Betas in the room, Electra instinctively sank to her knees in a submissive pose. After a subtle touch from his mate, the Alpha reined in his very angry wolf as he stood up and approached the cowering woman. He offered her a hand and when she took, gently pulled her to her feet.

"Electra, there is no need for such formality." Wyatt walked her to the empty seat next to Hadrian. "Seek comfort with your mate during this trying time."

"Sir, forgive me," she said softly. "I fear you have been misled. I am merely his servant, not his mate."

The Alpha turned to his mate, and they spoke privately. She assured her mate that her hellhound stated that the young woman before the Alpha did in fact have a wolf. He then turned back to Electra and commanded her to look him in the eyes. He pushed into her mind and found the wolf curled up on herself. In the presence of the Alpha, the wolf stirred but did not get up.

Pulling out of her mind, he kissed her temple. "Sit, we have some questions, and you have the answers."

She sat in the chair and the man returned to his own chair. He spoke with the other leaders in their minds before any of them spoke again.

'Stephen, you will question her as you are the lowest ranking of the pack leadership. And the calmest.'

'Yes, Alpha.' Stephen assured his friend and Alpha.

"Electra," Beta Stephen said, "tell us what happened when you were told that you had no wolf."

She nodded as she looked at her hands in her lap. Hadrian slipped his hand between hers and gave her a light squeeze.

"When I did not have a wolf by my sixteenth birthday, I was sent to the pack priest. Dark Sky does not have an oracle or priestess. They have a priest. He..."

"Speak freely." Celeste ordered and Wyatt gave her a warning look.

Electra took a deep breath, and a tear fell onto Hadrian's hand.

"He bound me to an altar and said that he would force my wolf on me." She spoke barely above a whisper with a shaky voice filled with shame.

"How many times did he perform the ritual?" the priestess asked.

"Three times a day." She mumbled as the tears fell freely.

"For how long?" Wyatt asked.

"A week, the first time." She said as Hadrian pulled his hand away. Her shoulders slumped as she feared the good things in her life would be taken away. It was confirmed when his chair moved backwards.

Just as she resigned herself to being a slave again, large gentle hands lifted her into a lap. Strong arms engulfed her as Hadrian held her close. He was aware of the conversations going on around them, but he paid no attention to them. His focus was on the woman in his lap.

Hadrian stroked her hair as he gently cradled her against his chest. The man was outwardly calm as the beast within prowled angrily.

The door opened and the oracle entered with the healer. They both went straight to Electra. The healer touched her fingers to the young woman's forehead as the oracle placed a pink crystal in her hand.

"Stay with her." The priestess said softly as she joined her sisters for a moment. "She's going to need your strength and support."

"Emmeline." Alpha Wyatt said. "Tell us about this ritual to force her wolf onto her."

"Ritual." She snarled. "It's nothing more than torture in the name of the gods. It was never sanctioned by the Rites. It is something that some perverse old men came up with. It degrades the actual ritual."

"But there is such a ritual?" he pressed.

"There is. It is used for a wolf and a host to join in body and mind." Emmeline clarified. "The false ritual would force the wolf to the surface to protect the host."

"What happens when the wolf does not surface?" Wyatt asked.

"They may repeat the false ritual. Using the witches' power of three, they may do it three times a day, every third month for up to three years."

"What happens when this doesn't work?" he asked.

"Surgery." Electra said numbly.

"What kind of surgery?" Celeste asked, afraid she already knew.

"The kind to keep the blood pure. To not taint the blood line." She swallowed hard and closed her eyes.

Celeste stood up forcefully, her heavy wooden chair cracking the wall plaster.

"Sit down, mate." Wyatt said softly. "I know. Please quit yelling at me."

Celeste was still angry, and her eyes were glowing silver as she was pulled into her mate's lap.

Chapter 21

EVENING ALONE

Crystal River Pack

If Hadrian had known what Electra had gone through, he probably would have killed the Dark Sky pack himself. Especially the Alpha's son. From the anger that he felt emanating from the pack leadership, he would have had their support.

So much support that the Alpha had offered for him to have the next day's shift off. Hadrian declined the offer, knowing that if the schedule was off, his girls would ask questions. And he did not want to expose his young and innocent daughters to those answers.

Allison had taken the girls home and they were blissfully unaware of the hell that their beloved Electra was going through. The girls were excited to have a sleepover at Nana and Papas house tonight and with Amberley tomorrow.

When they arrived home, Electra was exhausted - emotionally, mentally and physically. Hadrian drew her a bubble bath in the large soaker tub and helped her strip out of her clothes. Reminding himself that no matter how much he wanted to destroy those leggings, he could not.

The scars on her body were atrocious. A five-inch scar across her lower abdomen where her uterus had been removed. A brand burned onto both her upper arms. One showing that she had been fixed and the other showing she was a slave.

It was done with her family knowing about it. All of it was. Because if they had prevented it, or fought it, they could have been kicked out and made rogues. Or her younger siblings could have been made slaves. Her father could have been executed and the rest of the family enslaved.

She chose to suffer so her family did not.

Through it all, she remained kind and gentle. Giving. Sweet. Everything that a man would want in a mate. Everything that Hadrian wanted in a mate.

Everything that Mitzi was not.

He noticed that the girls asked less about her. They no longer needed their absentee mother. They had Electra. Or, as Marie had taken to calling her, Momma E.

Hadrian was thinking about this as he paid and tipped the pizza delivery guy. Electra had been in their lives for almost a month, give or take, and he could not imagine life without her.

Marie had always been quiet and standoffish. Always alone, even when there were others around. He knew it couldn't be easy for her. Mitzi walked away from him and their girls, something that werewolves did not do.

And yet, a woman with no wolf, was acting more like a were mother. Drawing Marie out of her shell. Encouraging her interest in firefighting. And even suggesting that she ask about having her birthday party at the station.

The same woman who believed that her own life was limited, encouraged his daughters to aim for the sky. Emily had told her that they were told to aim for the moon. Even if they missed, they would land among the stars.

He had been surprised by her response. "The moon? We've already been there. Pick a new place to leave your own footprints."

Now, his five-year-old daughter was determined to be the first woman on Jupiter. Because everyone else wanted to leave footprints on Mars.

Leaving the pizza and sodas on the coffee table, he went back upstairs and into his room. He grabbed a T-shirt and a pair of shorts from his drawers and tossed them on the bed.

"Electra?" he said softly as he knocked on the bathroom door before opening it. "The pizza is here."

She nodded and started to stand up. Hadrian grabbed one of the baby blue towels for her. He did not avert his eyes as she stepped out of the tub. He also did not take in the lovely view in front of him, it was not the time.

Electra leaned against his chest as he held her close. "I'm sorry."

"For what, love?" he asked.

"I'm not what you want."

Letting the towel fall to the floor, he held her face between his hands and kissed her firmly on the lips. "You are exactly what I want."

"I'm not whole."

"You're perfect."

"I can't give you pups."

"I have two wonderful little girls."

"Why are you so determined to make it work?"

Sighing, he pulled her naked form against her and inhaled her sweet scent.

"When Mitzi left, I was heartbroken. I thought no one could ever make me whole again. But I had two baby girls that were depending on me. I went to the oracle, and she told me to listen to Blaze, he would know what to do and when."

"The morning that I met you, Blaze was telling me to sever the tie completely. He was anxious and, to be honest, annoying. And then you came over to us in the park and he was calm and content and happy. Something that he had not been, I have not been, in a long, long time."

"Gerard insisted on coming over and helping you with the girls. Blaze knew you were who we needed. He kept telling me that we needed you as much as you needed us. That you were what the girls needed."

Hadrian buried his face in her damp hair and inhaled deeply. For the first time, he really smelled her. There was only one word that sprang to mind – mate.

"I need to walk away from you for a few minutes." He said as man and beast fought for control. "I want to mark you and if I stay here, I will."

Surprising even herself, instead of stepping away from him, she bared her neck.

"Oh, goddess." Hadrian begged as he looked at her soft skin. "Are you sure, Electra?"

"There's something inside me telling me that you need to do it." She whispered. "It's a voice that has always been with me. It's a voice in my head, but not. I know it makes no sense."

He cupped her chin and looked at her. She had removed her dark contact lenses, and he saw thin honey-colored rings around her black eyes that flashed gold as he looked at her. "Did you start hearing her around your thirteenth birthday?"

"No. She's always been there," Electra said with a slight shrug. "Wishful thinking, maybe."

"Maybe," he whispered as he let Blaze take the lead and leaned down to kiss her. Hadrian felt his wolf slip into her mind, and he lay next to a sleeping wolf.

Pulling back, he took control and forced Blaze back into his own mind. It made no sense to him that she would have a sleeping wolf and not know. Had she never connected with her wolf? Did her wolf never reach out to her?

With even more questions than answers, Hadrian led her out to his room where he helped her into the shirt and shorts before guiding her downstairs to the living room. The pizza had cooled but was still warm enough to eat. Putting on a rom-com movie, they settled on the couch.

When the movie ended, he woke up to find her still snuggled into his chest. He looked at the nearly empty pizza box and decided that this one time, he could leave it. Picking Electra up, Hadrian carried her upstairs to his own bed. She stirred slightly as he settled them under the comforter as he spooned against her back.

Chapter 22

SLEEPING WOLF

Crystal River Pack

"You have questions." The priestess said.

Hadrian turned and saw her sitting on a bench swing placed in the garden. She wore a simple green dress with one foot tucked under her and the other gently pushing her. All around her, flowers bobbed and swayed in a breeze he did not feel.

"I do," he admitted quietly.

Looking around, he tried to remember how he got there. The last thing that he remembered was having pizza and watching a cheesy movie. They fell asleep and when he woke up, he took them to bed.

"It should be dark," Hadrian muttered.

As soon as he said this, the clouds in the clear blue sky disappeared. The sky darkened and filled with twinkling stars. For a moment he thought about saying it should be bright, just to see what happened.

Before he could, the priestess began to speak and drew his attention back to her.

"She has a wolf. One that will only emerge after she is accepted by her mate," Imogen said, standing up and walking barefoot across lush green grass towards a little gazebo. "One that will emerge once her mate fully accepts her."

"She said that she has a voice in her head. One that's always been there," Hadrian said as he stepped up into the gazebo.

The wood of the gazebo was cold against his bare feet. When he looked down, he found himself in the Star Wars pajama pants that he went to bed in. Same gray t-shirt too. Maybe this was a dream.

Discreetly he pinched himself. It hurt. So, of course, he did it again. It still hurt.

The priestess motioned for him to sit at the already set table. "Yes, she has a very strong wolf. One that can do some amazing things," she poured a cup of tea and added a slice of lemon. "Drink the tea."

He sat down and picked up the delicate cup, sipping the steaming liquid. Surprisingly, it was sweet and not as hot as he expected. Maybe he could drink tea. At least in a dream that felt real and tasted real.

"What is it that your wolf tells you?" she asked as she fixed her own cup. "Other than to mark her."

"That she needs us," he said suddenly feeling light-headed.

"The feeling will pass," she said dismissively and motioned to his head. "And you're going to forget about her wolf and this visit."

"Why?" He wondered.

Who would believe him anyway? What did I do last night? I had a tea party with the priestess in the temple garden.

Yup, he thought, go ahead and sign me up for the next psych eval.

"Let's just say that she suffered a large trauma and was severely injured. She may never bond with her wolf. Giving her false hope would only be cruel." Imogen said. "You will remember that you want her as a mate, I will not break that bond."

"Can you help her?" Hadrian asked as the world around him began to spin.

"I have done all that I can. The rest is up to her wolf," The priestess gently touched his hand. "Open your heart and let nature happen."

The gazebo and everything around him began to fade.

Taking a deep breath, Hadrian opened his eyes and looked around the dark room. Pulling Electra closer to him, he tried to remember the dream as he slipped back into a deep sleep.

Chapter 23

SATURDAY MORNING

Crystal River Pack

Saturday morning training started years ago with only warriors. It slowly opened to all pack members. Now it also encompasses the human members of the pack.

"Hadrian." A man approached them. Hadrian smiled and offered his hand.

"Gunny, this is Electra."

Electra bowed her head to him.

"I'm not Were," Gunny said bluntly. "I'm married to a were. You don't treat me any differently than anyone else. Don't ever call me sir, I work for a living."

"What should I call you?" Electra asked quietly.

"First, head up. The world is up here," Gunny said and waited for her to look up. "Much better. My name is Gunny."

Hadrian kissed her temple. "I'm going to go check in. Gunny will train you today."

She looked at him with fear. "Please..."

"You'll be fine," Hadrian assured her with a gentle caress to her cheek. He gave her a light kiss and then left her with Gunny.

"Mates can't train together," Gunny said.

"I don't have a wolf, so I can't have a mate." she said quietly.

"I don't have one either. But that doesn't stop me from having pups." Gunny said, pulling out his phone to show her a picture of his family standing on a beach. "My mate, Sammi, Marcus and Bella are our oldest, Michelle is our only single, Toby and David. Jesse and Lina were just wee little ideas in Sammi's belly."

"You have seven pups?"

"I do. Three sets of twins. And my oldest two are learning to fight," he put his phone away. "Now, let's get started on today's lesson."

They stretched out and went for a run. Then they did sit ups and pushups before using the playground equipment for pull ups. Gunny walked her through some basic self-defense moves. For someone who had never trained before, she picked it up very quickly.

"You're on a good path," Gunny said as they walked back over to the training grounds.

"Thank you," she smiled with a little more confidence than she had earlier that morning. "I was told that the girls would be here."

"They're with Sles and Sammi. I think the plan was to make cookies," he pointed to where Emily was walking around with a basket. "I asked for brownies."

"You!" a short Hawaiian woman yelled pointing at Gunny. Several men grinned at him as he continued to approach his wife. "You and your damn super sperm!"

"My sweet, lovely wife, I think you were screaming something else recently," he wrapped his arms around her and pulled her in for a kiss. "Did my damned super sperm do something?"

"From now on, when I'm in heat, you sleep on the couch," she said angrily. At the same time, she moved closer to him.

"I don't think it matters where he sleeps," Cole teased. "It's all the other activities."

"Don't listen to him," Wyatt called out from where he was helping an Omega man. "He's been moody because Wynne threatened to neuter him."

"She'll let you back in when she hits the horn dog phase," Gunny assured the younger man from his own experience.

"What's wrong?" Sammi asked as she stepped away from her mate and to Electra.

"Please don't touch me, I am unclean," Electra whispered as she moved away from the comforting hand reaching for her arm.

"Baby girl, I have seven kids under the age of ten. I can't think of the last time I was clean," Sammi grinned but let her hand fall.

"You need to get your kids," Electra whispered with her head down while watching the far tree line. She dropped to her knees and hunched her back with her hands clasped together on her legs. "I'm sorry."

There was a crashing sound at the tree line as a wolf came into view. The large black wolf went straight for Electra, shifting into a man as he leaped at her. Once the shock was over, several warriors moved to pull the man off her.

"They took me away from my pack because of you, worthless whore!" With every word, the only son of the Alpha of the Dark Sky Pack landed a punch on her body.

Gunny and Will both moved to protect Electra as Hadrian ran to her. Wyatt yanked the other Alpha back and punched him in the face.

"How dare you attack one of my pack members!" Wyatt roared. "On my land!"

"A pack member? That worthless bitch?" he yelled back. "She has no wolf!"

"She's my mate!" Hadrian screamed as he stood up.

"She can't be." AJ snarled.

Teuf sniffed at Electra to make sure that she was okay. Once he was satisfied, he turned his attention to the young Alpha. Without asking permission, he shifted into his hell hound form. Approaching the Alpha, fangs fully extended and eyes glowing bright red, anger radiated off the beast.

"Teuf," The priestess said calmly as she approached the hell hound that was now taller than her. Reaching up, she stroked the large neck and spoke silently to him.

"I can't believe that you-" The Alpha started to say, and the large black hellhound growled.

"I advise that you be quiet, or I will allow him to deliver you to the underworld before your time," the priestess warned.

Chapter 24

FIRST MATE

Crystal River Pack

The following morning, Electra was fixing breakfast when Hadrian walked into the kitchen. He had to be at work in a few hours and wanted a little bit of time alone with her. Sliding his arms around her waist, he kissed her neck.

Her bruises were already fading and that made him wonder about that. Those with wolves would heal very quickly, the higher the wolf the quicker the recovery. Gashes from the fangs and claws of the alpha wolf had already closed and were beginning to fade.

"Did you mean it? What you said?" she asked as she mixed the muffin batter. "That I am your mate?"

"Yes," he said, softly nuzzling her neck.

"We need... you should..." Electra turned off the stand mixer and braced herself against the counter. She took a deep breath and let out before continuing. "I have no wolf. My first mate rejected me because of it. I can't have pups."

He turned her to face him and made her look up at him. "Who was the idiot that rejected you?"

"The Alpha's son, A.J."

"The one who attacked you?" he asked, and she nodded. "His loss. My gain."

"Somehow, he still has control over me."

"Did you accept his rejection?"

"I have no wolf."

"Doesn't matter. Until you both break the bond it's still there."

"How do I...?"

"Break the bond?" again she nodded at his question. "You have to tell him that you accept his rejection."

"That's it?"

"That's it. Do you want to break the bond?" he asked, caressing her cheek.

"Yes," she murmured as she leaned into his hand.

"Let me find out if he's been picked up yet," Hadrian told her as he reached out to his mom. Waiting for a response from her, he leaned in and kissed her.

When his brother tapped him on the shoulder, Electra's legs were wrapped around Hadrian's waist and arms around his neck. His hands were buried deep in her hair. Breaking off the kiss, he glared at Gerard as Electra hid her face in Hadrian's chest.

"Now I know why you're not responding to mom," Gerard grinned at his scowling brother. "She said to meet her at the dungeon. She can have five minutes with him."

Electra was placed back on her feet and quickly filled the muffin pan. As she put it in the heated oven, she set the timer and gave Gerard instructions. While she did that, Hadrian got dressed and then they left to go to the police station.

Hadrian had his FD uniform polo shirt on, prepared to go in, or take the day off if needed. Electra walked down the stairs in skinny jeans that were hugging her curves in all the right places, a cropped black tank top and a shimmering sheer black loose-fitting shirt that disguised her scars.

Gerard gave a wolf whistle as he appreciated the beautiful woman in front of him. Hadrian smacked his brother on the back of his head. Looking at his older brother, he simply shrugged and admitted, "Worth it."

Unsure if his response was good or not, Electra aimed her dark eyes at Hadrian. He had seen her a few times without her contacts, and he was always drawn to the dark eyes with the thin honey-colored ring around the edge.

"Do I look okay?" she asked quietly.

"You look so fucking hot," Gerard said, and Hadrian once again smacked the back of his head. Laughing, he told his older brother, "Still totally worth it."

"Electra, you look beautiful," Hadrian assured her, and she smiled at the brothers.

That's when he understood that her old clothes had been armor against the Alphas of the Crystal River Pack. But her new clothes were a suit of armor against the next Alpha of the Dark Sky Pack. Plus, it would show that she no longer abided by their archaic laws. She was no longer a member of the Dark Sky Pack.

She was now a River.

He guided her out to the Jeep and within minutes, they were parking next to Allison's official SUV. She walked them in, and they all signed the visitor's logbook. The guard unlocked the main door, and Allison led them to the cell holding AJ.

He sat on a metal bench against the back wall. His head rested against the stone, and his hands lay in his lap. The guards had given him standard issue orange scrubs that showed just how far he had fallen.

Smelling her, AJ stood up and approached the silver bars. Sneering at her, he looked at her outfit with complete disgust, "I smell him on you, whore."

"You rejected me," she reminded him gently.

"But I've still had you," he grinned at her and then looked at Hadrian. "I took what I wanted. You can have the leftovers."

Hadrian rested his hands on her hips and kissed her hair, "You left the best part."

"Anthony Tomas Diamante Junior, I, Electra Diane Naples, accept your rejection and sever all ties and bonds between us."

She recited it just as Hadrian told her. AJ fell to the floor in pain as the bond was severed completely. Electra inhaled deeply as peace and freedom flooded through her.

As she was released from her bond, the urge for Hadrian to mark her increased. Her scent was amplified making the close proximity sheer torture for him.

Reining Blaze in, he tipped her face up to his and kissed her as AJ gasped for breath. Looking up at Hadrian, she made a single request.

"Let's go home."

Chapter 25

FREEDOM

Crystal River Pack

There was a change in Electra once she was released from her bond. She was still sweet and kind. The girls were still her world. Her complete self did not change. And yet it did.

She was no longer submissive. Her hair became shorter, and she became more comfortable wearing makeup. She wasn't quite ready for shorts or short skirts, but she did wear jeans more.

Celeste took her to the tattoo shop, and they covered her brands. On her left arm among swirls and stars was the William Shakespeare quote of *"This above all, to thine own self be true."* And on the right was the moon goddess with a hellhound.

Once her marks were covered, she became much more confident. By the time they were finishing up the plans for Marie's birthday party, she was wearing T-shirts.

Along with her newfound confidence and assertion, came a strength she did not know she had. Twice a week, the girls went to hang out with Amberley while Electra and Hadrian went to the gym. Saturday mornings she trained with Gunny.

On the morning of Marie's birthday party, she was at the training grounds with Gunny. In a pair of purple and blue knee-length tight workout shorts and a matching sports bra, her dark T-shirt discarded with Gunny's bag and bottles of water, her confidence shone through.

It was the first time that she had removed her shirt, but the late summer heat and humidity from an overnight rainstorm had the cotton sticking to her skin and irritating both her and the... other. She really was not sure how to describe the feeling that she had. Something was stirring at the back of her mind, while the growling and angry voice was present more and more.

The anger inside her that was not hers settled down when the girls and Hadrian were around. When they would go to lunch with Celeste, the temperamental hell hound would lay close to her and ignore his mistress. Often, she would hear that ethereal voice in her head while she scratched the dog's head, but the words it spoke made no sense.

I am proud of you, hound. Your reward for service is coming.

Every time that she heard this, it appeared that the dog did too and would smile at her. She did not know that dogs could smile. And she certainly did not know that hellhounds could smile. But he did. With his teeth on full display, Teuf would smile at Electra.

Currently, the dog lay on his back, sunning his stomach on a patch of lush green grass. Usually if he came with the Alpha and the Luna was not there, Teuf would stay close to where the warriors were training. But recently, he had taken to staying closer to Electra. Even now, with his eyes closed, she felt as though he was watching her.

When she and Gunny returned from their warmup run to the area that they trained at, he had her remove her shoes and they both sparred barefoot. Her strength was improving just as her skills were. Once again, she flipped him over her back with ease, and he landed with a loud oomph.

"I am too damned old for this shit," Gunny smiled as he complained.

Two years after getting out of the Marines, he still wore a modified PT uniform to spar on Saturday mornings. Frequently during the week, while working as the human liaison for the pack, he wore tactical fatigues in either camo or all black. With the heat and humidity, his PT style gray shirt with black block letters of CRYSTAL RIVER clung to him with a light sheen of sweat covering his body.

"Sorry, old man," Electra grinned standing over him.

"No, you're not. Nor would I want you to be," the human replied as he accepted her hand to help get up.

For the rest of the morning, he continued to land on his back, knees or chest each time he would attack her. Deciding that she knew his moves too well, he knew it was time to find her a new sparring partner. Taking a quick water break, he typed out a message on his phone before returning to getting his ass kicked.

And she was excelling at the challenge of kicking his ass. More than once, he had to remind her that he was merely human and would not heal as quickly as a wolf did. Behind the admonishment, was pride.

Taking the final break, he checked his phone before grabbing his water bottle, "You're going against a she-wolf next week."

"Why?" Electra asked.

"I'm not leaving you, but you need a new challenge. I've taught you all that I can by myself," he explained as he tossed her a water bottle. "And until Hadrian marks you, you're not going against any of the male warriors."

"I don't know if I want to be marked," she quietly admitted as they both took a water break.

"Which is why he hasn't marked you yet," Gunny said as he sat his own bottle on the ground and got in position to do Tai Chi as their cool down. He waited for her to join him before continuing. "His wife left him when Crystal River hosted the Summer Solstice hunt."

"Do you know why she left?"

"All I know is gossip. I would rather he be the one to tell you that. But I can tell you what I know of him as a man," Gunny said as they went through the motions of Tai Chi.

"He's never spoken ill of his ex-wife. Won't let others either. Especially, if the girls could hear or if it would get back to them."

"Is there something that they could speak ill of?" Electra asked.

"From what I have heard, yes. But that's something that should come from him," they went through the last moves and started to gather their belongings. "He puts his girls first. He loves being a firefighter. But he's started focusing more on officers and less on the fires so he's not in danger. He only goes in when he has to."

"That Saturday that he got hurt?"

"Probably the first fire he'd been involved in for months," Gunny nodded towards the man approaching them. "My kids are excited about the birthday party. We'll see you in a little bit."

"Okay." She smiled as Hadrian wrapped his arms around her and leaned in for a kiss.

"I saw you tossing him around pretty good," he said, lifting his head slightly.

"That old man?" she smiled as she toyed with the tear in the back of his shirt. "What happened to your shirt?"

"I'm fine, thanks for asking," he grinned and kissed the tip of her nose lightly. "Perseus reminded me that he was younger and stronger."

"And what did you do?"

"Reminded him that I was older and wiser."

They both looked over as a couple of passing warriors shouted that they couldn't wait for the party and then waved back.

"Who's that?" Electra asked quietly, snuggling in next to him.

"I have no idea. Apparently, the whole damned pack found out about this party. There may be more than the kids we invited."

Chapter 26

PARTY AT THE FIREHOUSE

Crystal River Pack

There were way more kids than expected.

And their parents.

And grandparents.

And aunts and uncles.

And their neighbors' second cousin's college room-mates' best friend from elementary school second grade teacher's pet goldfish former owner's ex-husbands current girlfriend.

In other words, the whole pack, and a few people from the human town, were there.

"We should have charged admission," Aiden smirked as he slapped his son on the back.

"Could have gotten a new rig," Captain McMurray agreed.

"It's a hell of a fundraising idea," Aiden agreed.

"How many people do you think are here to see how the girls act towards Electra?" Hadrian asked quietly.

"All of them," the other two men replied in unison. Hadrian groaned.

"Daddy!" Emily ran up to him holding a doll, she leapt into his arms. "Look what aunt Jill brought me!"

"You don't have an Aunt Jill," Aiden told his grand-daughter.

"Don't break his heart," a large redhead said walking up carrying an infant. "Hadrian?" he asked, and Hadrian nodded. "I'm Jack."

Shifting his daughter, Hadrian shook the human's hand, "Nice to finally meet you. Is that the Nichols pup?"

"Yeah, not sure if mom is going to make it. We took the little guy so dad can focus on his mate and daughter."

Earlier in the week, a pickup t-boned a minivan. The one-month-old had been jostled in his carrier and only sustained bruises. Mom, a human hybrid, took the full brunt of the impact and was in the pack hospital. The four-year-old daughter had to have surgery to reset her leg bone.

Hadrian and his crew were the ones to respond. He had been tasked with notifying Mark, since they had gone to school together, played football and soccer, sometimes on the same team and sometimes against. He hated that part of the job.

"I thought that all the pups at the orphanage were Jill's," Hadrian teased as the large black man wrapped his arms around Jack and gently caressed the infant.

"They are," Jill said. "Whether they are officially mine or just for a little while, they're mine."

"Oh, my goodness, Hadrian," Darius's wife, Coralie, said approaching them. "She's beautiful!"

"Thanks," he said looking for the woman with dark eyes and mermaid hair. As if she felt him looking, Electra turned towards him. He smiled at her as she stood up from helping Marie with her new custom-made bunker coat.

"Where did she get that?" the captain asked, motioning to the girl who was now spraying the hose.

"Momma E made it out of one of my dad's old coats." Emily said proudly. "She made my dress too! She said that she was not allowed to go shopping in her old pack, so she learned to sew. She's going to make my Halloween costume."

"And what are you going to be for Halloween?" Coralie asked.

"Moana."

"What happened to Merida?" her dad asked as his dad asked the same question about Elsa.

"Whichever princess she finally settles on, I'll make it," Electra said as she stepped into the group.

Hadrian placed an arm around her shoulders and pulled her close. As he kissed the top of her head, he caught the faint scent of heat. How could she be going into heat? Was this why Blaze was acting the way he was?

As if answering his question, the wolf yipped happily before rolling to his back in their shared mind.

He saw his dad and captain flare their nostrils as the scent hit them also. Blaze rolled back to his feet and growled protectively. Unmarked female in heat was a wonderful scent to any male werewolf. And even more enticing to unmated males. Glancing around, he saw the single males that were eyeing her.

"Emily, do you and Marie want to come spend the night with me and Nana?" Aiden asked with a smile and a look at his son.

Mark her.

Hadrian nodded at his father and sat his daughter down. The little girl spun around in her dress showing off the ruffles. The bodice was made from an old uniform shirt that was torn beyond repair. The skirt was from an old bunker coat and the three ruffles had CRYSTAL, PASS and FIRE DEPT on the back. The belt at her waist was made of reflective tape.

After showing off her new dress, she grabbed her grandfather's hand and pulled him over to where her sister was now climbing all over the truck.

"I think we have the next generation of O'Reilly for the fire department." Wyatt said as he joined the group. As they all lowered their heads in submission, he waved his hand. "As my colorful mate would say, none of that bullshit today. Speaking of which, she may have gone overboard on the cake."

"Please tell me that the Luna did not make the cake herself." Electra pleaded.

"Oh, no. The kitchen staff did it." The Alpha laughed and caught the scent in the air. "My dear, you smell... enticing." He gave a warning glance to Hadrian who nodded.

"Thank you, Alpha." Electra blushed.

"Ake!" Little Aiden squealed as Celeste walked over carrying him. "Ake!"

"Trust me son, I want cake too!" She handed him to his father and unwrapped the vanilla cupcake in her other hand. "What?" she asked around a mouthful of cake and gave a small piece to her son.

"You couldn't wait?" Wyatt smirked. His son shoved slobbery cake into his mouth. "The toddler slime really sets off the vanilla flavor. Thank you."

"They made cupcakes for me." Celeste grinned as she gave the last bite to Teuf. "You have to wait."

"But I'm the Alpha!" he argued with amusement.

"And I'm also an Alpha but I'm pregnant with an Alpha." She grinned and then Jack, Jill and herself all said, "You and your damned super sperm."

Laughing, Wyatt pulled her to him. "I don't think that's what you were saying about me at the time."

"If Gunny wasn't such a good friend, I'd make you fire him." She said as their son tried to push her away from Wyatt.

Wyatt kissed her lightly while little hands tried to push them apart. "No, you wouldn't. How the hell did I get you pregnant with this one around?"

"Possibly my office," Celeste grinned as she stepped back. "Yay! The cake is here. I couldn't decide what flavor I wanted." She looked sheepishly at Hadrian and Electra. "There's chocolate, vanilla, yellow and marble."

"How big is the cake?" Hadrian asked as a white delivery van backed up to the firehouse.

"Ummmm. Can I plead the fifth?" Celeste asked as the back doors were pulled open.

Kids raced over and were amazed at the large cake. Even the adults gasped as the firetruck was rolled out of the van. It was four feet long, two feet wide and three feet tall.

As Marie jumped up and down with excitement, Hadrian and Electra could only stare in amazement. Celeste walked over to Hadrian and whispered something in his ear. Then she went to the birthday girl who hugged her Luna around the neck, declaring that it was perfect.

"She has a soft spot for the ones that others ostracize." Jill said quietly as he and Jack stood next to Hadrian and Electra. "Your girls have had a hard time. But it's safe to say that those days are gone."

"It never bothered Emily. But Marie was just old enough that the other kids would hear their parents talking. She didn't even want to have a party because no one has come to them for the last two years. Then this lovely lady came into our lives."

Hadrian tipped Electra's face upwards. She lifted up on her toes and met his kiss. Dropping back to her feet, she smiled at him.

"We should go to our girls."

She said it so easily. They were hers. Hadrian was ecstatic that Electra claimed his family as her own.

Chapter 27

MITZI'S DECEPTION

Crystal River Pack

As the birthday party was winding down, the oracle approached Hadrian. Her long platinum blonde hair was pulled back in a loose braid. Just like so many others, she wore shorts and a casual T-shirt.

She gently touched his brow and then trailed her fingers down to his chest.

"You have questions that I cannot answer," she whispered to him. "There is a change happening. Blaze knows what needs to happen. She is yours. You are hers. That is all you need to know. Answer her questions honestly. Your own answers will come soon enough."

For just a moment, he felt an intense heat in his chest and then it was gone. So was the oracle.

He had experienced the same feeling before. But he could not remember when or where. The only thing he could remember was the same feeling.

He growled a warning to several single men throughout the day. They backed away but kept watching the intriguing woman. She had an unusual beauty. And she was going into heat.

The scent of virgin was not one she gave off.

Neither did she smell wanton.

She smelled of her heat and desire. But the desire was aimed at one man. One wolf. One heart.

They stopped at a little burger place for dinner and got shakes to go. When they got home, they cuddled up together on the couch.

"Hadrian, what happened with you and your ex?"

He pulled her close and kissed her hair, inhaling her scent to calm man and beast.

"We met at a Hunt, and I brought her back here. She was just seventeen and was the third child of an omega family of nine. I was twenty and just out of the academy. I knew that the first few years would be hard. She thought that because I was a Beta, life would be easier. And I'm sure to an extent, it was."

"She was pregnant with Marie before our first anniversary. Postpartum depression was hard for her. The healer recommended that she go workout, and she joined the gym over in Springs. She started feeling better, but then she had an affair with her trainer."

"I was gone, literally, a third of the time. Sometimes more. Alpha Jonathan caught her one day. I don't know if it was an accident or if he had been told. She was told to end the relationship or be sent back to her family."

"Postpartum was worse after Emily. I was afraid that I would come home and find her dead. Alpha Wyatt came home and hired her to work in the packhouse. She figured out how to block me so I could not feel when she was cheating."

"A week before the hunt that was here, I came home and could smell that she was pregnant. I knew it wasn't my baby. We hadn't been together since before Emily was born. I told her that I would take it as mine, raise it, no questions asked about the father."

"The only thing I asked of her was to be faithful. I even offered to share her with another mate if that would make her happy. We fought and argued for the whole week. She finally agreed to settle down after the hunt."

"I told my mom that we were going to work it out. I needed her help. I asked her to keep the girls so that we could go out, and work on our marriage. When Mitzi called Bridget, mom thought that Mitzi was going to surprise me. I guess she did."

"During everything that was going on that weekend, Mitzi left. The only thing that she took was what she was wearing. Left her ring and a note in the bathroom. The old house was nothing but memories. I moved us here before school started."

"That must have been so hard for Marie." Electra whispered as she wiped tears off her cheeks.

"It was. It was the main topic for quite a while. By the time she left, the whole pack knew she had cheated. And that she was pregnant. I never denied the baby. And if she were to ask, I would take the baby."

"But not her."

Hadrian smiled at her as he brushed a tear away from the corner of her eye with his thumb. "But not her. She gave me my girls, and I will always love her for that. But you, you have my heart."

"How do you know?"

"The first night I met you in the park, Blaze, my wolf, said that he wanted to keep you. Then, you told my girls exactly what they needed to hear. That it was okay to be angry with their mother. It was okay if they didn't remember her."

"It's what my dad always told me." Electra said, laying her head against his chest as she curled up against him. "I was adopted. A woman came to the door one night and handed me to my mom then walked away. The only thing that she said was Gelert. Dad would tell me the legend of Gelert, and I would listen for the howl."

"I never noticed the howl before."

"I found out later that it's usually teens out in the woods. But it still makes me feel loved."

"You are loved." Hadrian murmured against her hair. "Electra, I need to mark you."

"I know." She said and he heard fear in her voice.

"It will only hurt for a moment."

"That's not what scares me. You'll want to... to..." She sighed. "I've only ever been with ... and it always hurt."

"Look at me." She shifted and faced him at his quiet request. "I want to show you that it can be very beautiful between people who love each other. Will you trust me?"

Slowly nodding, Electra let him pull her to him for a kiss. Needing to be closer to him, she climbed into Hadrian's lap. When they broke apart, they were both panting.

"Let's go to bed." Electra suggested quietly.

Chapter 28

MARKING

Crystal River Pack

It was not the first time that they had slept together. Not even the first time that they had gone to bed together. It was, however, the first time that Hadrian would do more than just hold Electra.

He could feel her nervousness as they approached the master bedroom upstairs. Leading her to the bed, he turned the bedside lamp on. Grateful that they had both already ditched their shoes, he began to tug her t-shirt out of her jeans.

"If I need to slow down at any point, tell me." He told her as his fingers brushed against her abdomen. "I'm not sure that I can stop until you're marked, if you have any doubts..."

She pulled his face down to her and kissed him. Her hands were still on his cheeks as he pulled back a little. "I have no doubts about you," she whispered. "Just me."

"No doubts about you, either," Hadrian told her as he gathered the red cotton and lifted it over her head. She raised her arms, and he easily removed the shirt, dropping it to the floor.

Having watched her all day in his department T-shirt he had decided that was the sexiest thing she could ever wear. "You're so beautiful."

She blushed at his compliment and heated gaze. Instinctively, she moved to cover herself. Glancing at his dark hungry eyes, she reached for the front clasp of the bra instead.

A growl of appreciation rumbled in his chest as the black cotton and lace fell to join the shirt. With shaking hands, Hadrian reached out and undid her jeans. Blaze was wanting to surface and just shred the denim. The beast restrained himself as the man fought the same urge.

As he fumbled with the button and zipper, Electra untucked his shirt. With her jeans sliding to her knees, he tugged the department polo over his head. It quickly joined her own discarded clothes.

Leaning down, Hadrian kissed her, running his tongue along her lips. Sighing, she opened her mouth, and he slipped his tongue inside. She slid her hands up his chest, his hair parting for her fingers. A small moan escaped him as he guided them down onto the bed.

The comforter was cold against her bare skin. She gasped as he made his way to her breasts. He teased one nipple with his tongue, swirling circles around the little bud. As she arched her back into his caress, he lifted his head and blew cold air. Electra took a deep breath in shock of the cold and then moaned as he took her breast into his mouth.

"Hadrian..."

"Right here, baby," he said softly, moving to her other breast. "Just enjoy."

"I need..." one hand clamped onto the back of his head and the other grabbed his shoulder.

"What do you need?"

"I... I don't know," she admitted as tears filled her eyes. "I feel... empty."

He smiled as he pushed himself up and then moved over her, "I've got you, baby. You just enjoy." Kissing her until she was breathless, he left her panting as he trailed kisses down her body.

His mustache tickled and teased as he went. On his way down, he kissed the thin three-inch scar across her lower abdomen.

"Hadrian, please, don't," her voice cracked with pain.

"It's part of you," he placed one more kiss on the scar before he continued his trek.

Pausing for a moment at the junction of her legs, he inhaled the sweet scent of her arousal. Kissing his way down her leg, he pulled her jeans the rest of the way down. As he released her legs, he rested them on his shoulders.

"Electra, eyes on me, baby."

Her eyes flew to him as he ran his tongue from the bottom of her slit to the mound under pink cotton. She gasped as he pressed his tongue against her damp panties.

With a quick swipe of his claw, Hadrian tore off her panties. Pulling the material out of his way, he dipped his tongue inside her. Electra gasped and her eyes widened as she watched him feast on her juices.

"Oh, goddess!" She cried as he wrapped his lips around her nub. He gave a grunt of approval as he slid a finger inside her. She tensed, expecting the pain that she had always experienced. There was no pain and as she relaxed, pleasure began to build in her core.

Adding a second finger, he pumped them in and out as he teased her clit with his tongue. Turning his wrist, he pressed against her magic spot. As pleasure coursed through her body, her walls clamped down around his fingers. Electra tried to keep her eyes open and on him. The orgasm was more than she expected, and her eyes closed as her body arched.

Hadrian helped her ride out the orgasm. When she reached for his hand, he released her thigh and linked their fingers. Reluctantly, he pulled his fingers out and took one last lick.

Standing up he guided her legs down to the bed. Looking down at her he couldn't help but smile. She was glistening with a light perspiration and afterglow.

"Damn, you're beautiful and tasty," he leaned over her.

"I never knew it could be like that," she admitted softly with a blush. Letting go of the comforter, she ran her hand up his bicep of the arm braced by her head.

"Baby, we're just getting started."

She looked at him in wonder, "There's more?"

"There's so much more that I want to do with you," he kissed her lips lightly. "But tonight is all about you." He nuzzled her neck and kissed her marking spot. "And this."

She moaned and tightened her grip on his fingers, "I don't know..." gulping, Electra moved her head, giving him better access. "I don't know how to please you."

"Just enjoy yourself," he whispered against her neck. "I'm very well pleased right here."

"You're not going to..."

The fear was back in her voice. He needed a moment to get himself back under control. Hadrian stood up and caressed her cheek as he brought their linked fingers to his lips.

"Scoot up on the pillow, so I can join you," he smiled as he said it, his voice was calm and even.

Nothing he did showed the battle raging inside him. It was a good thing that two wolves from the Marines Pack had already taken AJ. If he was still on pack lands, Hadrian would let Blaze free and give into the bloodlust. His girls had kept it at bay after Mitzi left. He hadn't felt it at all since Electra had moved in.

When he realized that the bastard had made her fear Hadrian making love to her, an intense bloodlust coursed through Blaze.

Stronger than he had ever experienced. But as she moved, Blaze caught the scent of his mate's heat and settled down. The bloodlust left and desire quickly returned, along with the need to mark her.

Hadrian quickly stripped out of his remaining clothes. Electra looked away, a blush covering her exposed body. He lay down on the bed and covered his lower half.

"Come here," he moved his arm so she could have his shoulder. It took a moment, but she scooted closer.

When she laid her head on his chest, he pulled her to him and engulfed her in a light embrace.

"When I mark you, there will be some pain. Everything else will be pleasure."

"That is not what scares me. Whenever AJ would..." She swallowed hard.

"Rape. He would rape you," Hadrian kissed the top of her head and inhaled her scent to calm himself. "If you don't want to go any further, we'll stop. But I'm going to have to leave for a few days. And you can't leave the house."

"Why?" She sobbed.

"Have you ever had a heat?"

She shook her head no, "The healer took my womb."

"If they left your ovaries, you can still go into heat. And this is your first day of heat. And you're unmarked. You are so beautiful and with the scent of heat on you, you would be in danger. I don't know if I can stop myself."

"You would leave to protect me?" Her voice was soft and uncertain.

"I would," he nodded his head slightly and pulled her closer. It was juvenile to want his scent all over her, but he couldn't resist. "I want our first time to be nothing but pleasure for you. If that doesn't happen now, then I'll kiss you goodnight and go stay at my parents."

She lifted up on her elbow and looked down at him. "Why?"

Smiling up at her, Hadrian tucked some hair behind her ear, "Electra, the moon goddess gave me a second chance. You. She opened my heart, and you filled it. I love you, Electra."

Tears filled her eyes, and she leaned down to kiss him. The only thing between them was her wolf and crystal amulet. Had they paid any attention to it, they would have seen the yellow crystal glow bright and change to a pale green color.

But they were busy with other things. Hadrian moved her leg over his waist and began to tease her core with his fingers. Nature took over and she began to move with him.

"Electra, if you want me to stop -"

"No," she sighed out as he slipped two fingers inside her. "Just not on my stomach."

He gave a growl of understanding as he pulled his fingers out. She whimpered at the sudden loss. Grinning, he guided her to her back and then placed her hand where his had been.

"Have you ever gotten yourself off?"

"Off what?" she asked, confused.

"Oh, my sweet innocent mate," he guided her fingers in and out as she began to squirm under their shared caresses.

Once she found a rhythm, he removed his hand and watched her bring herself to an orgasm. Allowing himself a deep breath of her heated scent, he moved to get a condom from the drawer.

Without taking his eyes off her, he quickly ripped open the foil packet and rolled the condom on. Moving between her legs, he brought her hand to his mouth. As he sucked her juices off her fingers, Blaze gave a howl inside Hadrian's mind.

"Are you sure?" Hadrian asked as he kissed her palm, and she nodded.

Moving over her, he lined himself up with her and pushed in slowly. He clutched the pillow under her head in his fists in an attempt at controlling his need. Her breath caught and her eyes widened as he entered her.

"Oh, goddess..." She murmured as he began moving in her. Electra grabbed his upper arms and began moving with him. Her breathing became erratic with moans and cries.

"Wrap your legs around my waist and lock your ankles," Hadrian said as he moved to kiss her neck.

In the new position, her eyes closed tight as her orgasm built. She slid her hands up to his back and held on tightly as he increased his thrusts. Her body began to tense and arched into him.

"Electra Diane Naples, I, Hadrian Thomas O'Reilly, take you as my mate and mother of my pups."

With his declaration made, he extended his fangs and sank into her soft skin. Her orgasm ripped through her body, intensified by the marking. Claws dug into his back as she screamed her release. With a jerky last thrust, he emptied himself into the condom.

Hadrian released her neck and licked the mark sealing it. Then he kissed it and raised up looking down at her.

"It was never a thought that I would be mated," Electra said as she gently touched his cheek. "Hadrian, I don't know what to say... I don't know the vow."

"It needs to have your full name, my full name and that you take me as your mate and father of your pups."

"But I can't..."

He smiled at her as he brushed her hair away, "Marie and Emily will be yours. We can check with the priestess about binding them to you."

"Mine? They'll be my pups?"

"My love, they already are yours," he turned and kissed her hand.

"I, Electra Diane Naples, take you, Hadrian..."

"Thomas," he supplied.

"Thomas O'Reilly as my mate and father of my pups."

Once she said the words, there was a change that rippled through them. Blaze howled in the back of Hadrian's mind and his tail thumped excitedly. In the back of her mind, Electra felt something stretch and shake.

After she fell asleep, she dreamed of a large dog that lay curled up asleep. Another dog came and laid down with the sleeping wolf. Never waking up, the wolf shifted and marked the new wolf, the coppery taste of blood seeped into Electra's mouth. The angry voice seemed calm in her odd dream as she spoke to the other wolf.

I feel your frustration, mate, be patient, just a little longer.

Chapter 29

MARKED
Crystal River Pack

In the early light of dawn, Hadrian turned off his alarm and pulled Electra closer to him as he slipped back to sleep. Two hours later, he rolled over and picked up his ringing phone.

"Yeah," he said softly after clicking the green circle.

"Just wondering if you were going to join us today," Captain McMurray asked.

"Shit," he shifted the phone and focused on the little numbers up in the corner before swearing a few more times. "I'm on my way," he ended the call and kissed Electra on the cheek. "I'm late. Go back to sleep "

After he got out of bed, she snuggled down under the comforter and when he stepped out of the closet in his uniform he could hear her soft snores. Without turning on the bathroom light, he grabbed his shaving kit and headed for work.

Mom.

Hadrian called through the mind link.

Shouldn't you be at work.

I overslept.

                              Really?

He rolled his eyes at her tone.

   Yes. I need you to check on Electra. She was still in bed when I left.

                         Is she okay?

I marked her last night.

   If the girls were still sleeping, they just woke up. The neighbors also.

He laughed as he pulled into his spot.

   I'm at work and already late. Love you.

He closed the mind link hoping that his mother heard him over her celebrating.

   Hadrian walked in and the conversations stopped as they all looked at him. There was a mix of shock, respect and knowing grins looking at him.

   "Sorry, I overslept," he mumbled as he headed to put his gear away.

   "And we see why," Darius called as he went down the hall.

   Confused, Hadrian stopped and checked his fly. It was up. His shirt was on correctly. The boots were on the right feet. He touched his cheek, knowing that he needed to shave, but it wasn't that bad.

"Holy fuck, he doesn't know." Jasper said with a grin.

"Who were you with last night?" Parker asked, guiding Hadrian to the large kitchen table.

"Electra," he said slowly, not understanding what they were going on about.

"Uh-huh." Russell said.

Overhead, the speakers came to life with the tones for the engine and the truck went off. The room froze, as they all listened to the radio call for the truck, crewmembers for the engine and truck one quickly loaded up and left. Darius came back into the day room with a shaving mirror. The remaining crew members and captain stood opposite Hadrian as Darius handed him the mirror.

Confused, he took the mirror and looked at his face. Not seeing anything amiss, he looked back up at the woman and other men.

"Your neck," McMurray said.

Looking back at the mirror, he tipped it to see his neck. A large bruise with four puncture wounds was on his neck.

He was marked.

"I thought you said that she was wolf-less," Parker leaned across the table inspecting his neck.

"She is," Hadrian replied as he looked at his neck.

"It's called a hibernating wolf," the priestess said from the doorway. "They are not common. Her host suffered a great injury, and she is healing the body."

The triplets moved to him. The three looked exactly alike. Tall, slender, long platinum blonde straight hair and pale blue eyes. When they were born, they each bore birthmarks on their left wrist. A moon for the priestess, a star for the oracle and the heart for the healer.

Smiling at him, Emmeline touched his chest. "Blaze. Show him."

Hadrian's eyes glazed over as he connected with his wolf. Blaze stood next to a large wolf. He nuzzled her neck and licked at the marking wound. Laying down next to her, he licked her nose before laying his head down between his paws.

The other wolf lifted her head and sniffed. She nudged his neck and then clamped her mouth down on his neck.

I feel your frustration, mate, be patient, just a little longer.

The words that he thought he had dreamed the night before suddenly echoed in his mind. As the growling voice faced, he pushed to the front of his mind as Blaze receded to the back. Shaking his head, Hadrian's eyes cleared as the priestess removed her hand.

"She bit me last night," he told her. "She was asleep, and I thought I had dreamed it."

"They're getting stronger," Adeline, the healer, said. "When Electra broke the bond, the wolf began healing faster. She will heal even faster now."

"Watch the crystal. It will become blue," the third sister, Imogen, told him and then all three touched his neck and the mark healed instantly. The light mark of where she claimed him remained.

Emmeline gave him a blessing, and the three sisters turned to leave.

"She's in heat," Hadrian blurted.

Adeline laughed as she turned and looked at him, "You have two daughters. You know what to do."

"How?" he asked and all three cocked amused eyebrows at him. He dared not look at his crew mates, they were probably going to give him hell. "How is she in heat? They fixed her."

"Let's get one thing right." Emmeline warned. "They did not fix her. They mutilated her. Thankfully, she is of an old line. She is replacing what they took."

"Replacing..." his face went from confused to amazed. "Her womb?"

"Wait until you see what your son can do," The oracle smiled as her eyes flashed bright blue.

"Imogen!" her sisters chastised.

"She's already told Emily that they'll have a brother," she shrugged at them and left the building.

Chapter 30

BABY

Crystal River Pack

The dark bunk room was filled with a loud ringing noise, and everyone wondered whose phone was ringing. And who would be sacrificed to the moon goddess. Or the god of quiet nights on shift. With the vibrations shaking his bunk, Hadrian knew that he was the guilty party.

Since he was the only one not grumbling, out loud or through the pack mind link, the rest of the crew also knew that he was the one receiving a middle of the night phone call.

The real question was: Who the hell was calling him at two seventeen in the morning? He found his phone and tried to focus on the name on the screen. Of course, his brother would call him at two seventeen in the morning. As if he was unable to reach his older brother through the family or pack links.

He could hear the rest of the crew grumbling at the disturbance and assumed the pillow that hit him was from Parker. They had recently gotten back to bed after a false alarm. He had just got back to sleep when his phone started ringing. Accidentally hitting the speaker button, he answered the call.

"What's wrong?"

"I think Kiara is in labor," Gerard said in a panic.

"How did you think that the pup was going to get out?" Hadrian asked with a laugh as he got up. He could hear a few snickers as Parker and Darius also got up.

"I've got it," Darius said and picked up his radio, contacting dispatch.

"How's Kiara?" Hadrian asked, tossing the phone on the bed and getting his boots on.

"Threatening to rip my balls off," came the answer as Hadrian picked up the phone. He joined the rest of the crew laughing at his brother.

"Most of us don't actually do it," Parker said as she led the three down the hall. "Usually."

"I'll drive," Darius declared, opening the door out to the bay. Passing through the doorway, he pushed the button for bay two.

"We're on our way. Call mom. Have her get Electra and the girls," Hadrian told his little brother as he and Parker climbed in the back of the ambulance.

He ended the call and closed the doors. Parker knocked on the front wall letting Darius know that they were good. The engine rumbled to life, and they rolled out of the bay with lights and sirens coming on.

Hadrian called Electra who answered on the first ring. "Good morning. You're up early."

"Something woke me up," she admitted. "A weird feeling."

"Are you okay?" he asked, concerned as the ambulance turned a corner. Grabbing the bar above and planting his foot, he braced himself in place.

"I'm fine. Just a weird little feeling in the back of my head."

He smiled knowing that her wolf was stirring, "If you're sure..." she gave a soft sound of assurance. "Well, get the girls up. Mom is coming to get you. Kiara is having her pup."

"That's exciting."

He could hear her moving around, "We're pulling up at Gerard's place. I'll see you in a few. Love you."

Was it too soon to say? Possibly. But it just came out. Did it hurt that she did not say it back? A little bit. But after what he had learned about her past, he had to give her time. She would say it when she was ready. After all, they were now mated. He could feel the bond. And somewhere in the deep recesses of her mind, he could sense her wolf.

Ending the call, he glanced at Parker who was making kissy faces at him, "Shut up." He laughed and rolled his eyes at her as the ambulance came to a stop.

They grabbed the gurney and hopped out as Darius opened the door. Neighborhood lights were going on as they made their way up the walk. Gerard stood in the doorway, uncertain of what to do.

From inside the house, Kiara yelled out orders. "Go let them in. Don't leave me! Why is the door open? I'm going to kill you!"

And she's a doctor; she could do it.

Darius said through the mind link and the other two snickered.

That was the advantage of working with other Weres, you could make snide comments, and the patient and family were none the wiser. They continued to work on getting monitors hooked up and vitals taken as Kiara continued to threaten her husband's life. Gerard meekly agreed that she should kill him.

"I'm going to cook your damn balls and eat them!" Kiara threatened with a contraction as they rolled her out to the ambulance.

At least your balls will be in her mouth one last time.

Hadrian told his brother through the mind link and Gerard just glared at him.

They loaded up in the ambulance and Hadrian sat by her head. He and Parker got the gurney locked in place. Gerard sat on the side where Parker indicated. Darius closed the doors after Parker climbed up inside and took her own seat.

"If you don't mind, you can have the business end of my sister-in-law," Hadrian told Parker as he knocked on the wall.

"I don't want any man near me! Ever!" Kiara declared and then reached out for her husband. "Ger!"

"First pups are always rough," Parker soothed as they slowed down for an intersection. The horn was blown twice, and they continued on their way. "My mate still has scars from Onyx."

Kiara screamed and squeezed Gerard's hand. Parker lifted the blanket and then folded it up. She placed one of Kiara's feet on her husband's leg and the other on a hand hold.

"We're not making it to the hospital," Parker said as she worked.

Hadrian knocked on the wall as he told Darius what was happening through the mind link and the ambulance pulled over. He gently pushed Kiara into a sitting position and sat behind her giving extra support. Both he and Parker pulled on blue neoprene gloves.

"Alright, beautiful, with the next contraction, push with everything that you have in you, and we'll get this little guy out." Parker said calmly.

With Hadrian supporting her and squeezing Gerard's hand, Kiara pushed. Her breathing lessons from birthing class were forgotten as she screamed out in agony.

"I love you so much," Gerard encouraged.

"Shut up asshole! You did this!" his wife screamed.

She doesn't mean it.

Hadrian told him through the mind link as Parker told him something similar.

It's the pain talking, not her.

"That's it precious," Parker smiled at her patient. "We have a head. One more good push and we'll have you a pup."

"Fuck you, bitch," Kiara replied as the next contraction hit.

"I know, I hate her too," Hadrian agreed as he swiped away some sweat on her brow.

Kiara grunted as she pushed through the next contraction. Her claws extended and dug into Gerard's hand; he whimpered slightly.

"That's it!" Parker encouraged. "Keep pushing, don't stop! Push, push, push!"

With a final push and rush of fluids, the baby slid out of her mother and into the waiting hands of the paramedic.

"Good job, momma!" Parker smiled at the exhausted woman.

"I love you, Hadrian," Kiara said as she leaned back against him.

"You're only saying that because I control the drugs," he smiled as the pup whimpered.

Parker clamped the cord and offered the scissors to Gerard, "Daddy?"

"Daddy," he whispered as he cut where she indicated.

Parker cleaned off the baby's face and wrapped her up in a metallic warming blanket. Then she handed the bundle over to Gerard, "Why don't you introduce her to mommy?"

"Baby, we have a daughter," he said softly as he moved over to show the baby to Kiara.

"Hadrian is a good name," Hadrian suggested as he filled a syringe with a liquid.

"Jessica is better," Parker argued as she palpitated Kiara's stomach.

Kiara screamed in unexpected pain and Hadrian and Parker talked through the mind link. He quickly gave her the medicine through the IV port already placed in her arms. Then he grabbed a prefilled syringe and tore open the sealed package.

Once the second medicine was injected, Hadrian moved and laid Kiara out flat. He banged on the wall and told Darius what was going on. At the same time, both he and Parker turned off their radios.

"Sit down, Gerard," he ordered his little brother as he grabbed another saline bag.

Darius sped up and blew the horn before going through the next intersection without slowing down or stopping. A few minutes later, they pulled into the emergency room portico. The door was opened by a nurse before the box was even completely stopped.

Parker remained on the gurney with Kiara's feet resting on the mattress. Hadrian moved with the gurney as it was pulled out. He and Parker spoke with the medical staff through the mind link as they rushed down the hall.

A nurse approached Gerard. "Sir, if you'll come with me, we'll get your daughter checked over."

"Where are they taking my wife?" he asked, confused.

She just gave him a watery smile and led him to the elevator. "Let's get the baby looked after while they take care of mom."

Chapter 31

BLOOD

Crystal River Pack

Gerard sat with his parents, nieces and Electra in the waiting room just outside the nursery. Every few minutes he would get up and pace the floor before Allison would tell him to sit back down. The large room was filled with uncomfortable blue and green chairs.

There was also a long blue bench under the wall of windows that, presumably, was supposed to be a couch. Electra sat in the center of the couch with a girl on either side of her. They were asleep, or close to it, with their heads in her lap.

After about thirty minutes, Hadrian joined them in a fresh uniform. It was standard practice for them to keep at least one spare uniform in the ambulance or fire truck at all times. More than once one of the team members would need to use it due to an unexpected shift into their inner beast. Or because of gas or oil, fire, blood, other bodily fluids that you really did not want to think about.

"What the hell is going on?" Gerard asked his brother.

"The doctor and healer are coming," he answered, holding an arm out for Electra. She shifted the sleeping girls and carefully stood up. He engulfed her in a tight embrace and inhaled her scent. Instantly, Blaze calmed down now that she was close to him again.

He was only vaguely aware of the two figures that entered the room behind him.

"Gerard," Adeline, the healer, said gently. "She'll be fine."

"Kiara had a hemorrhage and lost a lot of blood," Dr. Gupta explained. "We've given her some blood to replace what she lost and have the bleeding under control. But we need specific blood to heal her."

"OK, where do we get it?" Allison asked. "Alpha? Luna?"

"Those would both be good choices," Dr. Gupta admitted. He turned and looked at the platinum blonde next to him, "Healer?"

"They are excellent choices," she smiled at the nervous father and husband. "But we would like to try something else, first," the healer said and placed a hand on Electra's back. "Electra, you come from an old line of Were. Would you give her some of your blood?"

"If you think it would help," she said and kissed Hadrian before looking over at the girls.

"We've got them, Electra," Aiden said when he saw where her eyes went.

"You won't be gone long," Adeline smiled at the maternal instinct that was driving the younger woman.

Because of her blood line and blessing from the moon goddess, Hadrian knew that Adeline could sense the wolf in the other woman. He was certain that the others could but did not know where it came from. There was an undercurrent of power that emanated from Electra as she and her wolf grew stronger.

Hadrian kissed her temple and then urged her to go with the doctor and healer. Anger and fear flowed from his brother, and he just hoped that Electra was out of earshot before Gerard said something stupid, and he knew that his brother would say something stupid. It was a given with the situation. He tried to brace himself for the impending stupidity.

"If anything happens to my mate because of that wolf-less-"

Hadrian grabbed his younger brother by the throat and lifted him off the ground. A deep protective growl rumbled in his chest as Blaze took control.

"Electra isn't wolf-less," Marie said in a sleepy voice. "Daddy put uncle G down."

"Listen to the girl," Their father warned. "Marie, why don't you and Emily go with Nana to get some coffee?"

Hadrian sat his brother on his feet, but Blaze continued to growl. The girls left with Allison and Aiden tried to get between his two sons. He tried desperately to pry his older son's hand from around his brother's neck. The more he tried, the tighter the grip became. A claw punctured the skin and blood pooled at the tip.

"She has a wolf," the priestess leaned against the doorframe, watching them with cool amusement. In her cut off shorts, tank top and sandals, she did not look much like a priestess. "Blaze, settle down. He's worried and, well, male."

Glancing at the door, Hadrian saw the priestess look behind her in the hallway before moving out of the doorway.

"Hadrian! What are you doing?" Electra demanded as she walked back in with Adeline.

She rushed over to place her hand on his and the claws immediately retracted, and his grip loosened. Letting go of his brother, he turned his attention to his mate. Cupping her cheek, he searched her face for any sign of distress.

"I told you it wouldn't be very long," the healer smirked. "We just needed a little bit of her blood. Not all of it."

"It's not there," Emmeline told Electra as she rubbed the back of her head.

"What is it?" she asked, dropping her hand.

"It's called an awakening," Emmeline said as she placed a hand on the young woman's neck. "You have what is called a hibernating wolf. She should have emerged already. But she could not."

She spoke softly in a strange language and Electra's eyes glowed gold for a moment.

"Better?" Emmeline asked as Electra's eyes returned to black.

"Yes, thanks. My head has been killing me lately," Electra said, having completely forgotten what just happened.

"Are you wearing your necklace?" Adeline asked her.

"I forgot to put it back on after my shower."

"You need to always have it." Adeline said as Emmeline suggested that she never take it off.

"Gerard," Dr. Gupta said walking back in with a smile, "your mate is asking for you."

The room watched as Gerard quickly left to go to his wife and daughter. The doctor followed him as the nurses directed him to the room. Hadrian turned his attention to the priestess who simply smiled at him.

"Soon, my child," Emmeline assured him. "Soon, she will be strong enough to join you."

Chapter 32

SCHOOL CLOTHES

Crystal River Pack

The blessing ceremony for the new pup was set for four weeks after her birth. The girls were excited about it, and both wanted a new dress. With school starting in a few weeks, Hadrian decided that it was a good time to go shopping for school clothes. But there was something else that they needed to do first.

After breakfast, he sent the girls upstairs to get ready. Marie told her little sister it was because "Daddy wants to suck on Momma E's face."

He wasn't sure which of his crew mates taught her that term, but he was probably going to kill them. Once he quit laughing.

"It's not a bad idea," he admitted. "But that would lead to other things, and I think having sex in the kitchen with the girls here is probably not a good idea."

Electra blushed as she finished loading the dishwasher, "You're horrible."

"And you usually don't complain," he replied, pulling her into his lap. "I think the girls need to go spend the night somewhere." Hadrian murmured against her neck.

Every night that he was home since he marked her, he had made love to her. She was always willing and enjoyed it. As she became more comfortable with her own body and sexuality, she became more adventurous. It had been less than a week and neither could get enough of each other.

"Hadrian...." She sighed as she cupped the back of his head.

"Woman. The girls need to go to my parents, or Amberley's or Gunny's or somewhere," he growled.

She laughed a little, "Right now?"

"Goddess, don't tempt me."

The girls were coming back down, and Marie insisted that they make a lot of noise so mommy and daddy would hear them. Both adults laughed at the innocence of children. And the guilt of being caught.

"Can you drive?" Hadrian asked Electra as he sat her on her feet.

"I can. I would use my brother's car around campus and town." She hesitated for a moment before adding, "I couldn't drive on pack lands."

"You can here," he said as the girls stomped into the kitchen. "With school starting, you're going to have to."

Electra's eyes went wide, "What am I going to do while the girls are at school?"

"What do you want to do?" he asked.

"They always need volunteers at the school," Marie suggested. "Mrs. Fox said that they can't keep anyone in the library."

"I like books," Electra admitted.

"I guess you'll have to go talk to Mrs. Fox," Hadrian grinned. "But we have other things to do today."

"What are we doing, daddy?" Emily asked as he ushered them all to the Jeep.

"We're going to go shopping," he said, and Emily squealed with excitement while Marie groaned. "Without Nana. It's not a marathon shopping trip."

He wasn't certain but was pretty sure that his oldest murmured something along the lines of 'Thank the goddess!'

Where Emily was all girl and dresses with an obsession for the Disney princesses, his oldest was a little tomboy with a penchant for the darker side. One would cheer for the princess, the other preferred the villain. One was happily ever after; the other was everything after ever after.

His youngest wanted to grow up and find her mate. She was already in love with love. The older one? Hadrian chuckled to himself as he pulled on his shoes. His dad was right when he said that Marie was the next generation of the fire department.

Following the others out to the garage, he slid into the front passenger seat as both girls climbed into their seats and fastened their seat belts. He loved how independent they were and hated how fast they were growing up. But he assumed that it was the curse of parenthood.

"I want mommy to make me a dress for the blessing ceremony!" Emily declared. "With pockets!"

"I can do that. We'll have to go to the fabric store," she said as she checked their belts. Electra opened the front passenger door and found Hadrian there.

"You're driving," he handed her the key fob.

"Okay... I don't know where we're going," she closed the door and walked around to the driver's seat and got in. Making the needed seat and mirror adjustments, she asked where they were going.

Refusing to tell her, he directed her out to the highway and then over to Crystal Springs. Once there, they took a few turns and then pulled into a car dealership.

"Are we going to see Uncle Jay?" Marie asked as they parked in front of the building.

"We are," Hadrian confirmed as he waved at an older bald man standing outside. "And he might have something for you two."

Both girls climbed out of the Jeep and ran to the man. Hadrian lifted Electra's hand to his lips and brushed a kiss over her knuckles.

"We better go before he sugars them up," he suggested, and she nodded.

There was a hint of fear in her eyes, and the tangy scent of it filled the small cab. But then, she seemed to remember that she was strong, and it faded from her. With determination, she opened the door and slid out of the car.

"You must be the young woman that I keep hearing about," the man said as they approached.

"That's our new mommy," Emily told him around the lollipop in her mouth.

"I'm Electra," she smiled and found herself being pulled into a hug.

"I'm uncle Jay," he told her. "Allison is my sister."

"Can I have a lollipop?" Electra asked when he released her. It was something that she never would have considered asking before.

"Absolutely. Let's go in and see what kind of car you want," Jay said, ushering them inside.

"Me?"

"You," Hadrian said as they sat down in his uncle's office. The girls sat at the table in the show room with coloring books and crayons. "Unless you want the Jeep, and I'll get something."

Placing a glass jar of lollipops on his desk, Jay smiled at Electra. "You. You get the sucker. You get the man. You get the adorable little girls. And you get the car."

"And what does he get?" she asked, getting a red lollipop.

"The best prize of all," Jay smiled, "he gets you."

Three test drives and half as many hours later, Electra followed Hadrian off the lot in her new Durango. After a stop at Target for a booster seat for Emily, they went to the fabric store.

Both girls had buggies full of material. Electra did too. Even Hadrian had some material picked out. As the girls were looking at the latest Disney prints, he spoke with a salesclerk about sewing machines and tables and cutting boards and patterns and thread and …. Who the hell knew that there was so much to sewing?

He had seen her using an old machine that she constantly had to adjust or fix something on. And whenever she was sewing, she had to lug the heavy avocado green machine to the kitchen table. When it was time to eat, she stashed it away.

Since the birthday party, five other firefighters had asked about either a dress or alterations. Darius and Coralie had asked if she would make blessing gowns for their twins. Not to mention that she had a mating ceremony dress to find. Or make.

Maybe he could do something in the basement, give her a place to sew. Lord knows that was a great big space just to do laundry. It should be used for something more than just a giant open space for her to clean.

Walking back over where they were discussing what dresses to make for Gerard's baby's blessing ceremony, Hadrian realized that they had never discussed a mating ceremony.

"You should probably get some material for a mating dress," he suggested as he wrapped his arms around her waist and kissed her neck. "And start thinking about what you want."

At a loss for words, she just turned and kissed him. "You and your girls to be mine. That's all I want or need."

"Well, pack law requires a little more," he smiled down at her. "My girls are wanting to be bound to you. And I want your last name to change."

"That is some really pretty material," a woman said to Emily, and both turned their attention back to the two girls.

Blaze gave a low warning growl, and the woman met his eyes. The scent was strong and unmistakable.

Rogue.

And she was openly challenging a Beta. For just a moment, Blaze pushed to the front and bared his teeth. It lasted only a mere second, but long enough to let her know to back down. She did not and instead she placed her hand on Emily's shoulder.

"My mommy is going to make me a dress. With a big skirt so I can twirl," Emily said unaware of what was happening. "And pockets."

"Girls, come here, please," Electra said as Hadrian reached out to his mom.

The rogue she-wolf tightened her grip on Emily's shoulder holding her in place. Electra's eyes glowed with gold showing through the contacts, a deep protective growl rumbled in her chest as fangs and claws extended. The she-wolf paled and released Emily as she lowered her head in submission.

"Don't touch my child," Electra growled.

"I'm sorry, Alpha," the woman said and slunk away.

Electra returned to her normal self and grabbed the back of her head, "Why did she call me Alpha?"

"You have the smell of an Alpha," Hadrian said and pulled her closer to him. He looked down and saw that the crystal on her necklace was now white. "Are you okay?"

"Yeah. What happened?" she asked quietly as Gunny approached them.

"I was a few blocks away. Is everyone okay?" Gunny said ruffling Marie's hair.

"Yeah," Hadrian replied. "I'd heard that there were some around."

"What happened?" Electra asked again.

"You started to shift," Hadrian told her as the Stevenson triplets approached them.

Robert, Roderick and Ronald were well over six feet, muscular and blonde hair with blue eyes. They were frequently referred to as the Vikings or the Swedes.

"Perseus is scouting around outside. We wanted to check in before we joined him," Roderick said to Gunny. "Are the kids okay? Ma'am?"

"We're fine," Electra assured them. She smiled at them, all the while she rubbed the back of her head and swayed slightly.

An employee came over, unaware of what happened, and stepped behind the large cutting table. "How much can I get for you?"

"I've got this, take her to the sisters," Gunny said, and Hadrian nodded, handing over his keys. Pulling out his phone and texting the Luna, Gunny turned back to the clerk. "We'll take everything that they picked out. Girls, is there anything else that you want?"

"How many yards, sir?"

"All of them."

Chapter 33

WHITE
Crystal River Pack

Emmeline opened the front door of her cottage next to the temple to find Hadrian holding a sleeping Electra. Opening the door wider, she stepped back for him to enter. He carried her to the white couch and laid her down.

The crystal chandelier in the center of the room shimmered and the crystals made soft clinking noises. The power emanating from Electra was palpable. In fact, to her, it was visible. An iridescent glow surrounded her body and seemed to brighten her alrighty bright white, ivory and gold living room.

"What happened?" Emmeline asked as she joined them after closing the door.

She moved around the square gold and glass coffee table to kneel on the white and ivory rug that covered her white marble floor. Adjusting the ivory and gold trim pillows, she placed one under Electra's head and another under her knees.

"A partial shift," Hadrian said as he brushed hair off her face. "Claws, fangs, growling."

"This is happening much faster than we expected," the priestess admitted as she ran her hands slightly above the woman's body.

"Her wolf... had the scent of an Alpha."

"That's a common mistake," she replied as she moved air away from Electra's face with her hands.

The back door to the cottage opened and one of her sisters entered. A moment later the third sister joined them. They spoke through their shared mind link, keeping Hadrian out of the conversation. It was not that they wanted to hide the well-being of his mate from him, but they could not disclose who her wolf was.

He tried to push his way into the conversation, but the three sisters locked him out. Adeline looked up at him with concern and amusement.

"I promise you," the healer assured him as she and her sisters worked, "she will be fine. She's strong, her wolf is strong. But the Awakening is difficult."

Not knowing how else to respond, he simply nodded.

Aiden and Allison both reached out to their son when they heard about the incident. Gerard showed up at the cottage and the two brothers went outside to a gazebo. Imogen knew that Hadrian would have an odd feeling that he had been there before. But she could only hope that he could not remember when she brought him there in his dream.

"That's it," Emmeline murmured as the strong wolf finally started to settle. "Sleep a little longer."

All three of them could sense the wolf curling back up to resume her deep slumber. She was not ready to open her eyes. Not ready to merge with her host. It was not yet time. Her mate was not ready. Her host was not ready.

But soon, the time would come, and they would both have to make a final decision. One that would impact not only their lives, but many around them. And eventually, all in the Were community.

Electra slowly opened her eyes and found three sets of electric blue eyes looking back at her. Blinking, she tried to orient herself. The three sisters felt the presence even if they could not see the moon goddess. They each wondered how the young woman would respond to the ethereal spirit.

> *Hold fast, my child. I have great plans for you. Be patient, my little darling, it is nearly time for you to awaken.*

Fear remained in Electra's eyes, but her body relaxed. The wolf inside her mind let out a deep breath and slipped back into her deep slumber.

"Why won't anyone tell me what happened?" Electra asked softly.

"You had a partial shift," Imogen told her. "How does your head feel?"

"Fine," she looked around the room and then at the sisters. "Where am I?"

With a nod from her sisters, Emmeline reached out to Hadrian, inviting him back into the cottage.

"You're at my cottage," Emmeline told her. "Hadrian brought you here after the rogue-."

"The girls!" Electra sat up quickly and Adeline placed a hand on her shoulder.

"They're fine," the healer assured her. "They are at Gunny's house with his wife and kids."

"Oh, goddess," Hadrian rushed over and pulled her to him. "I was so scared."

She wrapped her arms around his waist seeking his comfort. Laying her head against his chest, she sighed. His arms tightened around her shoulders as he buried his face in her hair inhaling her scent.

The three sisters knew that Electra's scent had changed slightly. The scent of wolf was now an underlying tone. Alpha wolf.

Imogen watched with amusement as Gerard sniffed the air and visibly counted everyone in the room. On his third round of counting, the oracle smiled at his confusion.

"Her wolf is waking up," The oracle clarified for him. "So, yes, you scent three wolves."

"Don't you have wolves?" Electra asked her quietly.

"We are a blessed three of witches. We have no wolves, but together, we can channel the moon goddess herself," Imogen explained. "Our mother was a witch, and our father was a Were."

"How do you...?" Electra asked and the three sisters just grinned at her. "You're revered, but you have no wolves. I don't..."

"Not all packs are like the Dark Sky pack," Adeline said gently. "We have the traits of Were, we can scent people, use the mind link and yes, we can shift, but we are limited to the goddess' nights."

"Full moons and solstices," Emmeline added. "It was ones similar to us that caused the folklore of shifting only on full moons."

"Enough about that," Imogen interrupted, giving her sisters glares. "Your wolf will merge with you in the next few weeks. When it happens, she's going to have complete control. She is aggressive and protective, more than what either of you two are used to dealing with." She looked at the two brothers.

"I saw her today," Hadrian pointed out.

"Yes, and she was still asleep," Emmeline said. "The wolf was reacting to the scent of a rogue."

"I've been around rogues before," Electra told them.

"But you did not have pups," Adeline stepped closer. "Let me see your belly."

Electra stepped away from Hadrian and lifted her shirt slightly. Adeline reached over and pushed the front of the jeans down. Carefully, she touched the small one-inch scar.

"What happened to my scar?" Electra whispered as she saw it was nearly gone.

"The line that your wolf is from is old and strong. She is healing you," Adeline let go of the cloth and pulled out the necklace. The crystal was a bright opaque white. "Soon, this will become blue and then she will awaken completely. When it does turn blue, come to us, you must speak with the moon goddess."

"Me?" Electra squeaked.

"You," Emmeline agreed. "But for now, go home, love your mate and your pups. If you need him, the hound will guide you."

Emmeline ushered them to the door, where Teuf, the Luna's hellhound, was curled up on her front porch. He stood up and stretched with a big yawn showing his sharp teeth. The large German shepherd followed them to the car and hopped in, crawling over the passenger seat and stretching out across the back seat. His head lay on the car seat, and he seemed quite content with himself.

Chapter 34

TEUF

Crystal River Pack

When Hadrian and Electra arrived at Gunny's house, no one seemed concerned that the Luna's hell hound was with Electra. Sammi made Electra stay and relax while Gunny and Hadrian went to get Gunny's car. When Gunny brought the girls home, he drove Electra's new Durango with the third row and space behind it filled with bolts of material.

Sammi motioned to the large dining room table where they could sit and talk. It was positioned in a place so that she could watch both sets of kids as she folded the laundry sitting on the large wooden table. The older kids played out in the backyard while the younger ones chilled in their play area in the living room.

Electra had learned that the swing set in the backyard was something that the pack Alpha did for all families with young children. It was one of the many ways that she found this pack different from the one she was raised in.

A happy laugh and other noises from the backyard pulled her from her dark thoughts. As if on autopilot, Electra picked up a small shirt and began to fold the laundry. Her host bustled around the lower floor between the living room and kitchen.

"It's absolute chaos," Sammi admitted as she pulled chicken out of the oven. "I would not have it any other way."

She was perfectly content with her hair in a messy bun, barefoot and wearing a pink floral sundress. Toys, doll clothes, naked dolls and the occasional shoe were scattered across the house. Even in the kitchen and dining area.

This was Sammi's kingdom, and she loved being the queen of her full and chaotic house.

Placing the chicken on a plate, she sat it inside the refrigerator. Then she popped four frozen pizzas in the double oven. Teuf sat in front of the refrigerator.

"It's cooling off. You're not going to starve," the little Hawaiian told him, and he whined as he lay down, facing the refrigerator. "He doesn't eat kibble. He prefers raw, but he's not eating raw chicken on my floor."

Electra swore she saw the dog roll his eyes.

"And he loves W-A-T-E-R. Especially in the loo. It's part of his nature. He's always hot so he likes to take dribble dribbles and splash splashes," Sammi said, trying to avoid certain words. Unfortunately, Electra was not understanding. "Well, hell. Showers and baths."

Teuf popped up on all four feet with his tail wagging excitedly.

"Bella! Turn the hose on!" Sammi called out the open back door. "Go on."

The dog ran out the open sliding door and soon they heard laughter and happy barks as the children and dog played in the water. Although he played, he kept an ear tuned in to what was going on inside. Even having fun and playing with the pups, he was on duty.

"I've probably got some clothes that the girls can wear home," Sammi said as she got a large stack of towels out of the laundry room.

Sitting at the table, she resumed folding clothes and kept up a one-sided conversation about her husband and kids. Her Alpha had made her choose between the pack or her mate. Surprising her Alpha, she chose the human and never looked back.

When the oven timer buzzed, indicating that pizzas were done, she made the kids turn off the water and took them towels. As the two women took plates of pizza outside, Hadrian and Gunny got back. Teuf finally got his chicken and lay down on the patio, watching as the four adults sat at the bar and ate pizza and salad. The men discussed the training session that was coming up. The women laughed at the antics of their respective kids.

By the time they left, the girls were dry. Well, mostly dry. Teuf was dry shortly after the water was turned off. His body heat as a hellhound took care of that. As a precaution, Sammi sent dry towels for them all to sit on. She insisted that they could return them in a few days when they arranged a play date.

The girls were excited that Teuf was going home to stay with them. Everyone knew of Teuf, and Electra could see them bragging about Teuf staying with them. The change in how the girls were treated changed drastically once the Alpha and Luna were both seen with the family.

Each night at bedtime, the two sisters would argue about who Teuf was going to sleep with. Each one wanted him to sleep with them. He always settled the issue by laying between the two doors.

He was well behaved and let them know when he needed something. He devoured the scrambled eggs that Electra made him in the morning. Gratefully accepted the meat that she gave him at lunch and dinner. When they went to the park, he ran and played like a typical German shepherd.

No matter what he was doing, he was a hellhound doing the bidding of the moon goddess. That meant that he always kept track of Electra. And her pups. Hadrian could take care of himself. Teuf knew that once her wolf woke up, Electra would be able to protect herself and her pups. But right now, she was vulnerable.

The moon goddess herself had charged him with protecting the Gelert. He would do just that.

It was the third day that he had been with them, and they all went to the park for a picnic. Teuf lay on his back, sunning his belly. Although he was asleep, he knew where his charges were. He always knew where they were.

Emily was on the swing being pushed by her dad. Electra sat on the blanket with Kiara and the baby. And Marie sat under her favorite tree with a new book.

Movement in the trees drew his attention to the girl. He had told Selene that he was worried about her being so alone. The moon goddess had scratched him behind the ear and assured him that she would come out of her shell. She had granted him a glimpse of what lay in her future.

But for now, he is still worried.

Two blonde girls sat on either of Marie. He tuned his hearing to them and linked with his mistress and her mate.

"Your mom left you," Taylor whispered. "And your stepmother is wolf-less."

"Your dad is cursed with bad mates," Dee added.

"Are you just as worthless as your mom?" Taylor taunted.

"No one around to rescue you this time," Dee grabbed some of Marie's hair and pulled it hard.

Teuf rolled to his paws and bolted towards Marie. He snapped and growled at the two bullies. Across the park, their mothers both called for them. Standing up, Dee dropped a handful of hair onto Marie's book before they ran away.

Teuf nudged the book closed and then laid his chin on her shoulder. She wrapped her arms around his neck and buried her face in his neck. Her little body was shaking as the tears fell freely.

"Come here, little one," Alpha Wyatt said as he picked up the girl and her book.

Chapter 35

ALPHA'S OFFICE
Crystal River Pack

Wyatt entered his office carrying Marie with the rest of her family following. Teuf went to his mistress who scratched him behind his ear. Wyatt sat in his chair with Marie on his lap and sat the book on his desk. He motioned for Hadrian and Electra to sit in the chairs in front of his desk.

I am not in the mood for this shit.

Celeste told her mate through their shared link. He smiled at her in understanding.

I know. We must trust your hound and the goddess.

Hadrian pulled Emily into his lap. Wyatt had reached out to his omega and Terry led in detective Marshall. He was in his mid-thirties and just under six feet with an athletic build. His olive skin was shaved clean, and he had piercing brown eyes. The rumpled gray suit was overshadowed by the high-ranking beta aura.

"Marie, you know Jack Marshall, don't you?" Wyatt asked her gently.

"Yes, Alpha," she whispered.

"Okay, I need you to tell him what happened. He's going to look at your head and then we'll get a healer for you," Wyatt said as the detective pulled a chair over.

Marie softly explained what happened by the tree. The detective prodded on a few questions here and there. When he asked if it was the first incident, she shook her head no.

For an hour she spoke of the abuse she had endured from the other kids since her mother left. The insults that the parents said were repeated by the children. How she discovered it was easier to hide in books than to face the world around her.

Electra understood completely. Her heart broke for the girl who felt abandoned. The woman cried for the little girl she once was and the child in front of her.

When she was done, Wyatt turned his attention to Emily. "Have you ever had any of these issues? Has anyone ever said anything to you about your mom leaving?"

"Yeah," she said nonchalantly. "I usually tell them to piss off." As the adults stared at her in shock, Teuf made a groaning sound as he hung his head down low. "But it's what you told me to tell them."

Seeing that she was looking at the hound, Wyatt cocked an eyebrow at him. Teuf laid down and refused to look at either his mistress or her mate.

"You hear him?" Celeste asked.

"Don't you?" the little girl asked.

"I do. But he's bound to me."

"She can commune," Adeline said from the doorway. "She will need to start training soon." She shook her head as she approached Marie. "This is not the time."

As the healer tended to Marie, Terry opened the door for the Knight and Chambers families. They had been excited when Terry reached out and told both Daniel and Stephen that the Alpha had asked them to come to the packhouse in their best attire.

Their excitement died the instant that they saw Hadrian and his family.

"I spoke to you and your daughters about their behavior," Celeste said with all friendliness gone from her voice. This was an angry Alpha that they were now dealing with. "I told you to take care of it before it escalated, and someone got hurt."

"It's no one but the mongrel," Dee said dismissively.

"Blaze," Adeline said without looking away from the girl she was tending to. "See to your mate. She is not strong enough to shift."

Hadrian pulled Electra to him and let his wolf go to hers.

"You admit to pulling Marie's hair?" Marshall asked.

"Yeah," Dee smirked as Taylor added, "She cried like a baby."

"Alpha," Stephen said. "Girls pull each other's hair all the time."

Wyatt reached over and opened the book to the page with a clump of hair and a small patch of skin still attached. "I'd cry to if I suffered that injury."

There was a rush of power and authority that filled the room. So powerful and strong that even Wyatt and Celeste were tempted to submit to it. Then the deep angry growl came.

"Go to her," Adeline told Marie as she sat the girl on her feet. "Let her see that you are okay."

Marie nodded and then rushed to Electra, "Mommy, I'm okay now."

Electra pulled the girl into her lap and buried her face in the neck of the little girl. As she inhaled the sweet scent of innocence, the growl faded and then the power subsided.

"Sleep," Adeline said, approaching Electra and her eyes that had been glowing gold, returned to black. Carefully she reached for the necklace and pulled the crystal out of Electra's shirt. It was now clear with a few veins of white running through it. "Sleep a little while longer."

Electra raised her hand to the back of her head. "What..."

Smiling, Adeline closed her hand over the amulet. When she released it, the pewter wolf was still curled up, but the head was raised as if sniffing the air. "What happened? Your wolf is trying to wake up. It will happen soon."

"I have no wolf," Electra argued softly.

"You do. A very strong wolf," Adeline corrected. "Alpha, if I may suggest something?"

"Speak your mind," Wyatt ordered the healer.

"Postpone any punishment for the parents until the pack's Labor Day picnic. And between now and then, have the two girls live with Electra."

He looked at the woman curiously and then she spoke to him through the mind link, and he smiled.

"Agreed," Wyatt said. "Electra, I know that Gunny enjoyed using my credit card the other day, but if you need more material or anything, please let us know."

"Thank you, Alpha. I don't even have a place to put everything that he bought. Some of it is still in the cars," Electra replied with a small laugh.

"Speaking of which," Celeste said, "I need to get with you about some dresses. And other things."

Wyatt pulled his wife into his lap and placed a kiss on her dragon tattoo on her collarbone. "Don't hide my friend."

"I am not going to allow my daughter to live with that... wolf-less... worthless... thing!" Andrea declared, pulling Dee towards her.

"Then your children can stay at the orphanage while you and your mate are in the dungeon," Wyatt growled with his eyes flashing. "Your choice. Obey your Alpha or suffer the consequences."

"I'm sorry, Alpha," she said, lowering her head.

Chapter 36

HOUSE GUESTS

Crystal River Pack

Electra looked from the Alphas to the healer after the other two families left, before she finally admitted, "I don't know what to do with these new little girls. How do I treat them?"

Adeline walked over and hugged her, giving her the only advice that she could, "Treat them the same as your own pups. Give them chores, punishment, love and praise." The healer looked at the four children, ignoring the other parents, "The moon goddess and the innocence of childhood will take care of the rest."

Comforted by the simple words, Electra nodded, and the healer cupped her cheek. Adeline moved in and soundlessly whispered into Electra's ear, using her witchcraft to ensure that it was only Electra that heard her words, "They have always guided you and protected you. But there are some trials that we must endure. Lessons we must learn. Hold fast, little one, she has great plans for you."

***

Shortly before Dee and Taylor arrived, Jack and Jill came by with bunk beds. Electra had one set up in each of the girls' rooms. Celeste sent over bedding for the two friends to use. At first, they were going to have Emily and Marie share one room and the other girls could have the other.

This was not what was intended for the next few weeks. They needed to be immersed in the family and treated no differently. With that decision made, Electra told the sisters to choose which of the friends would stay in their room.

When Dee and Taylor arrived that afternoon and were not happy. When they learned that they would not be sharing a room they were even more unhappy. And they let everyone know it. With the innocence of a child, Emily was oblivious to the tension.

"You're staying in my room!" Emily said excitedly as she grabbed Dee by the hand and dragged her upstairs.

Each girl was given a set of sheets, a pillow and a comforter. Neither knew how to make a bed. Hadrian stopped Electra from doing it for them. Marie showed them how on her own bed and then left them to figure it out themselves.

At dinner, Marie started washing vegetables and Emily set the table. Dee and Taylor were upset when they were told that they needed to help with chores. The two girls had never had to do so much before.

After dinner, the whole family helped to clean up. Again, the two new girls did not know what to do. Both went to bed instead of staying up with the family. A few minutes after they were in bed, Electra came in to tuck them in.

"Why are you being so nice to us?" Dee asked quietly.

"I know what it's like to be the outcast," Electra said with a sad smile. She lifted her sleeve up and pointed out the brand that was barely visible under her tattoo. "I was basically a slave. No one should be treated like that."

With that, she kissed the girl on the forehead and left the room. When Emily came to bed, Dee pretended to be asleep and listened to the girl and her stepmother whisper. They exchanged endearments and Electra kissed her temple before she left again.

In the morning, the girls all sat in the living room with books as Hadrian and Electra fixed breakfast. When it was time for him to leave, he kissed Electra and then all the girls on their heads.

After breakfast, Emily insisted on watching Cinderella, who she was going to be for Halloween. This week.

One of the firefighter's wives stopped by to see Electra about her making a dress. She brought old bunker gear and old uniform shirts. They talked for a few minutes, and Electra took measurements of the four-year-old. She was not comfortable asking for payment, but the woman gave her a hundred-dollar bill.

As they were leaving, a woman from down the street stopped by to see about Electra making her daughter a few dresses for school and the yule ball. They agreed to let the teen to come by after work at her summer job.

Once that was taken care of, she measured both Dee and Taylor. She showed them all the material that she now had. They each picked a few styles that they liked. They talked about the types of clothes that they preferred, some of which their parents would not let them wear.

Sadly, Electra understood this all too well. It had been years since she lived on the Dark Sky Pack lands, but she often found herself deferring to their modest style. With all four girls watching, she drew out a few designs on her sketch pad.

After lunch, Electra laid out material on the kitchen table and used her tailor chalk to draw out patterns. As the girls read, she cut out and sewed their dresses.

For dinner they made homemade personal pizzas. It was the first time that either Dee or Taylor had done that. They laughed and joked and began to relax. Electra even snapped a few pictures and sent them to Hadrian with all four girls slightly covered with flour.

"You're not as bad as my mom says," Taylor told Electra as they sat at the table after dinner.

"That's because we don't know each other," Electra replied. "You should always make your own decisions about people."

"After we clean the kitchen," Marie asked, "can we play a video game?"

"Why don't you girls go play Mario Kart and I'll get the kitchen tonight," Electra suggested.

That's how the two bullies made new friends. Homemade meals. Handmade clothes. Wholesome fun.

Electra and Hadrian treated them just like their own daughters. They had chores. Received praise. If they did something wrong, they were corrected. Electra never lost her temper. Hadrian kept his cool, no matter what.

And having three eight-year-old girls in the house tried a man's patience.

Chapter 37

BUT DADDY

Crystal River Pack

The sun was not quite up and the windows in the master bedroom were just barely starting to lighten. Down the hall, the girls were giggling over who knows what. There was the occasional shushing sound followed by a warning or admonishment of waking up the parents. Aiden's voice echoed in his son's head as he listened to the girls.

"Count to ten, take a deep breath and remember, neither your mother nor I killed any of you four, I mean, three kids."

Hadrian was seriously starting to wonder if his dad's joke about killing one of the kids was true. He was beginning to understand why some animals eat their young. Don't get him wrong, he loved his girls, and he found himself lumping Dee and Taylor in that category.

In the week and a half that they had been here, they really bloomed. They were no longer angry and mean. They helped around the house and were nice to the other kids in the house and neighborhood.

All the girls were looking forward to the blessing ceremony tomorrow night. He had a shift at the station today and did not envy Electra having to be with them all day. She had already mentioned a trip to the park, the library and a street hockey game that was already set for tonight.

Hadrian remembered how excited he was when both of his girls were blessed. Gerard and Kiara were just as excited as he had been. Laying there, he caught the faint scent telling him that his mate was pregnant. He could only imagine how exciting it would be to have a blessing ceremony for his child with Electra.

He snuggled in closer to Electra knowing that the alarm would go off soon. "The girls are already up."

"They think that they're being sneaky putting on their dresses before we get up," she whispered back.

"Are they okay to put them on?"

"As long as they're careful. And they don't want to get caught, so they'll be really careful."

He kissed her shoulder. "I love you."

"I love you too," Electra turned slightly and met his kiss. "I better go check on them."

"I'll go," he said softly, starting to slide towards the edge of the bed. "I need coffee." He declared going into the bathroom. After doing his business he walked back out to the sound of a small crash, "Large black coffee, hot and steaming."

"That sounds good," she rolled to her back and smiled at him. "Pancakes or muffins?"

"I'm guessing that you're not on the menu?" he grinned at her as he leaned over the bed and kissed her. "Let's do muffins. Any leftovers I'll take with me and make the guys jealous."

She was laughing as he walked down the hall to Marie's room. The door was opened, and he stood just out of view watching the four girls. A stack of Marie's books had been knocked over and he decided that it must have been the crash that he heard.

Marie had a sleeveless floor length empire waist dress in dark gray with bright purple trim and lace. He already knew that she chose that to pretend that it was her Hogwarts Ravenclaw uniform.

Dee had a knee length pale pink tea dress with a navy sash and trim. Taylor had a similar dress with tiny white flowers all over the pale blue material with white lace at the hem.

Emily had a bright teal peasant dress. She was barefoot and twirling in the middle of the room. Her curls flowed around her head making her have to swipe it out of her face as she giggled.

One of the girls loudly shushed her.

"Those are some really pretty dresses," Hadrian said, stepping into the doorway.

All four gasped as they turned to see him smiling at them. They all looked at the floor guiltily.

"Do we have to take them off?" Emily asked, twisting from one direction to the other, her skirt swishing around her.

"Yes," he leaned against the doorframe with his hands in his pajama pants pockets.

"But daddy..." Taylor said and then her eyes widened as she realized what she said. "I'm sorry, Mr. O'Reilly."

He walked over and hugged her to him and kissed her head. "It's quite alright."

"How come you give us so many hugs and kisses?" Dee asked.

"That's what daddy's do," he said, holding his arms out for the other girls who quickly snuggled into his embrace.

"Ours don't," Taylor whispered.

"You can always come get a daddy hug from me," Hadrian said around the lump in his throat.

Little did he know he would be the one that the two would come to from then on. When Dee would meet her mate in ten years, it would be Hadrian and Electra that she would call. And Taylor would seek sanctuary for her brother and herself much sooner.

Chapter 38

BLESSINGS

Crystal River Pack

The meadow was beautifully decorated with pink twinkling lights creating a small canopy above a white bassinet. Gerard stood next to Kiara with their baby in the decorated white bassinet in front of them. Pink and white satin encircled the bassinet in swags with the crest of the pack hanging on a golden chain.

With the sun going down, more people were arriving. Aiden and Allison stood with Kiara's parents. Hadrian hoped he did not have to remember their names. His was a presidential name... George Washington or James Monroe or Millard Fillmore. Rutherford. Damn, he hoped that her dad's name was Rutherford.

He found himself wondering what they had named the baby. As was tradition, her name had not yet been spoken. Not even the priestess knew what the name was.

More and more people arrived, filling the hallowed meadow on the temple grounds. The Alpha and Luna were there as was the Beta and his family. The Luna wore her trademark heels and tonight she wore a simple blue sundress recently made by Electra. She had kids of all ages vying for her attention. Giving up, she sat on the ground and was quickly swallowed up by the group of children.

With his wife distracted, Alpha Wyatt removed his tie and undid the top two buttons on his white shirt. Tucking the tie into his jacket pocket he saw Jack and Jill across the way with the kids from the orphanage. Jill grinned at him and removed his tie. Several others followed the Alphas example.

Soon the moon was high, and the priestess joined the large crowd. She and her sisters wore the robes of their calling, used only for blessing and other special ceremonies. Sapphire blue silk with white and crimson embellishments and a pale blue stole. On one end of the stole was the bright crimson triquetra and on the other was the symbol of their position. Moon, star or heart.

With a nod to the parents, the priestess took her place in front of the bassinet. Kiara handed her the baby, and she and Gerard stood on either side of the priestess. The baby fussed for a moment, and Emmeline drew a symbol on the small forehead with her finger, and the infant was calm and relaxed.

"Welcome, one and all to the blessing of this child. Would the grandparents please join your children?"

She gave a moment for the two sets of parents to join them. Hadrian watched as his parents guided Kiara's parents to the front. Wyatt helped Celeste to stand, and people rushed to collect their children from the smiling Luna.

"Very good. Kiara, have you and Gerard chosen a name?"

"We have," Kiara smiled at her husband who smiled back.

"Gerard, do you accept this pup as yours and promise to honor, protect and guide her throughout her life?"

"Yes."

"Alpha Wyatt, do you accept this pup into your pack, offering her protection and sanctuary throughout her life?"

"I offer myself and my pack for this pup," he said the well-practiced line and meant it.

"Luna Celeste, do you accept this pup into your pack, offering her guidance and love throughout her life?"

"I offer myself and my pack," she said as she shifted her son and another toddler in her arms. "Quick question... whose child do I have?"

There was a rumble of laughter as Kiara's sister claimed her daughter with a soft spoken 'sorry, Luna.'

Smiling, the priestess continued as she recited the blessing.

"Blessed be your breath; may you breathe deep as you take in power. Blessed be your eyes as they look to the future and the skies. Blessed be your ears as you listen to the world around and the moon goddess to guide you. Blessed be your tongue as you speak only truth and taste only the sweetness of life. Blessed be your hands as you grasp what the world and moon goddess provide. Blessed be your feet as they carry you through this world and the next."

Stepping back, Emmeline handed the infant to Imogen who held her close.

"Blessed be the mate that you will someday find. Blessed be the pups that you will raise. Blessed be the wolf who chooses your body as a host. Blessed be by the love of your family. Blessed be by the moon goddess above."

She stepped back and Adeline took her place with the baby.

"Blessed be this body that you have received. May it grow in strength and knowledge. Blessed be the wolf body that you will share. May you both be strong and fast. Blessed be by the earth below."

"Kiara, Gerard," Emmeline said, "speak your daughters' name."

Looking at each other and then at their daughter, they spoke in unison. "Jessica Diane O'Reilly, may the moon above remind you of the cosmic miracle that you are."

The howl started with the Alpha and Luna and then the family. The rest of the pack joined in. As it died down, a lonely howl answered them from the distance.

Electra rubbed the back of her head as that strange feeling washed over her again. Imogen noticed and focused on the amulet around Electra's neck. The white lines in the clear crystal deepened to a dark blue and the wolf shifted its shoulders and turned her head. But it did not curl back up in sleep.

The oracle forced a smile as she and her sisters heard the foot falls in the woods. Teuf tipped his nose in the air and sniffed. Just as he connected with his mistress, the warning went out through the pack.

Rogues.

Chapter 39

CRISIS

Crystal River Pack

Electra was not part of the pack and did not hear the alarm. But she sensed the change in Hadrian and the rest of the pack. He kissed her and then hugged and kissed all four girls.

Deep in the recesses of her mind, she felt the change. Whatever was in her mind was not fully awake. But it was guiding her to protect the pups. Both hers, and the others.

I smell a filthy rogue.

The angry voice was strong in her mind as it growled. There was a sharp pain in her mouth as it felt as though it tried to change shape and new teeth tried to force their way out.

A soft hand of the priestess landed on her shoulder and the pain and stirring receded.

Hadrian was looking around, gathering Electra and all four girls together. Sammi came over with her brood and smiled at him.

"I'm taking Electra and the girls to the orphanage with me," Sammi told him as she folded them in with her group.

Gerard pushed Kiara and the newborn towards Sammi, "Keep them safe."

Sammi and Celeste were both pregnant and could not shift, so they gathered the children and took them to the orphanage. Other women and children of the pack were also gathering there. Within minutes, the women were entertaining the children in the basement.

Electra stayed with Kiara and her parents, James and May Madison, as they took all the children to the basement of the orphanage.

Converted from the old high school, the ground was built up around the first floor taking it from a three-story building to two. Walls were reinforced and windows removed. Two emergency tunnel entrance/exit and a false tunnel remained.

Going to the safe house was no longer a scary event for the children of the pack. As the kids piled in, they spread out to various activities, video games, laser tag, movies. There were also bunk rooms and a nursery. A fully functioning and stocked kitchen could last for up to two weeks.

Yes, even with the shelter full of hungry teenagers.

Celeste's favorite change that Jack and Jill did was not in the basement. Although, the hidden armory that was under the back patio was a close second favorite. During the renovations, they raised the sides on the roof, giving more protection to the humans as they stood guard.

Celeste, Gunny, Jack and Jill took up posts on the roof with AR-15s and radios. The sandbags and faded lawn chairs along with other items on the roof made it feel like one that they had spent many nights on while deployed.

"It's nights like these that I miss Doc," Jill grumbled over the radio.

"Me too," Celeste agreed. "I'm hungry. Would it be wrong to ask one of the women to make me something to eat?"

"Probably," Gunny laughed.

"Glad I don't have to deal with a pregnant bitch to get my babies," Jack snickered.

"Ahhh, this feels like the good old days," Jill chimed in.

"You two going to run off to supply later?" Gunny laughed.

They stood post and remembered the good times that they had while deployed. Their nights around pretend bonfires. Sending new recruits out on a snipe hunt. Covering for Jill and Celeste as they went on runs in their Were forms.

"How many times did we have to go get Teuf from motor pool?" Gunny asked and the others half laughed, and half groaned.

"That damned asshole has a fucking tractor tire as a fucking toy!" Celeste rolled her eyes at the antics of her hell hound.

"Heads up," Jack called. "Movement on the east perimeter."

That's all it took for the four of them to return to Marine mode. They were silent until Celeste called out that the warriors were on their way back. Jack kept his eyes on the movement that he had spotted and did not relax until he saw the large hellhound emerging from the tree line.

Once out of the woods, the dog shook his large body and returned to his shepherd form. He took up a patrol around the orphanage. His eyes continued glowing red.

The pack remained on high alert throughout the rest of the night. No other incidents were reported. The following day, the surrounding Alphas were notified of the rogue activity. As were the elders.

All three elders arrived early in the morning. Elder Alpha Marcus was the only one that lived in the United States. And his pack was on the other side of the country. Wyatt and Celeste both wondered if there was more to this than what they suspected.

Chapter 40

PACK PICNIC

Crystal River Pack

There were a few things in life that were absolutely certain. Everyone had to pay taxes. Everyone will die. The Alpha was completely in love with his wife. The Luna currently has an insatiable sweet tooth.

Every family made sure to have at least one dessert for their beloved Luna. Electra had made lemon bars and golden brownies.

She still laughed when she thought about Celeste stopping by the house yesterday. Electra had been baking and told the Luna that she was worried about what the other pack members would think of her. Although the Blessed Trio had said that she did indeed have a wolf, it was hard to believe after so many years of being called a disgrace because she did not have a wolf.

Celeste had looked at her angrily and declared, "It doesn't matter what the rest of the damned pack thinks. I'm their fucking Luna and I say they're going to love you." As Electra sat the glass pan on the trivet, the Luna's face and voice softened, "Are those lemon bars?"

And after the Luna left with the entire pan of lemon bars, Electra made a double batch of single-serve apple pies.

Now that they were at the picnic, all four of the girls were running around with other kids. Marie had brought her latest book, but the other girls convinced her to go play with them.

The training grounds had been converted for the picnic with bounce houses and other activities. One of the more popular was what he described as messy twister. Watching the teens and tweens being hosed off after a round made her grateful that neither of her girls wanted to play.

Hadrian stood with his arm around Electra's shoulders as they talked with some of the other firefighters and their mates. Several of the women loved the dress that Emily was running around in today. Every so often the little girl would stop what she was doing and simply twirl.

"That's her requirement for every dress," Electra grinned as Emily stood in the middle of the playground and twirled her blue gingham checked sundress. "I have to twirl."

"And pockets," Hadrian added.

"I love dresses with pockets," Tanisha gushed.

"It's like designers think that we don't carry things also," Yolanda complained.

"You have purses," her husband countered.

"Because we don't have pockets!" all the women chimed at once. They all gave a little laugh as they bonded over the curse of women's fashion.

"And when you do have pockets," Tasha said, putting her hands in her front pockets which stopped at the end of her fingers, "they are useless."

"I'm constantly losing my phone," Parker complained. "I swear, cargo pants were created by a woman who was tired of carrying around a damned purse."

"I got Eliza some cargo pants," Yolanda laughed. "I literally watched her pants hop across the floor. She had a huge bullfrog in her pocket."

Her husband Mark laughed, "I hear her screaming and get in there and she's up on the dryer with this frog on the floor. Kudos to Eliza, I don't know how she got it in her pocket!"

"Marie brought home a snake a few months ago," Hadrian shuddered. "It took Gerard and me two hours to catch that damned thing."

"I remember that!" Parker laughed. "Emily opened the door, and it just slithered out."

"I can't say I'm upset that I missed that," Electra laughed. "Snakes creep me out."

"It looks like the Alpha is about to make announcements," Theo said, pointing at the stage where the Alpha and Luna were standing by a microphone.

"Good morning, pack!" Wyatt called out and the group responded with a loud "Good morning, Alpha!"

"Let's start off by confirming that yes, my mate is indeed pregnant with our second pup," the pack cheered for them and the couple embraced, sharing a light kiss. This caused another round of cheers. "She informs me that the baby is the cause of her sudden sweet tooth.

Gentlemen, I'm going to give you the best marital advice I was ever given."

Tipping her face up to his, Wyatt kissed Celeste. "Yes, dear."

The she-wolves cheered, and the men laughed.

"I don't care what the question is, the answer is always yes, dear. And if you think it makes you less of a man, this came from a man expecting his eighth pup. So, can my parents move in? Yes, dear. Can we repaint the house? Yes, dear."

"Can Doc move in with us?" Celeste asked.

"Yes, dear," Wyatt answered. "Along with announcing our baby, I get to announce other events."

He listed off the families that had newborn pups. Each new pup got a round of cheers.

"I also get to announce that we have a new mating, and my lovely wife is hoping for a mating ceremony soon. If you have a little girl, you know who I'm talking about. Electra Naples has mated with Hadrian O'Reilly."

The firetruck in the parking lot blew the horn and flashed the lights. Hadrian laughed as Electra wrapped her arms around his neck and pulled him down for a kiss.

Resting his forehead on hers, he held her close as their friends and his family cheered around them. "Marry me?"

Her dark eyes filled with tears as she softly whispered yes.

Chapter 41

MERGE

Crystal River Pack

E mily lay on the blanket asleep between Electra and Allison. Taylor and Dee had returned to their own families. The girls were sad to go and preferred to stay with Hadrian and his family.

Hadrian and his dad were involved in a football game with the fire department against the pack police. Gerard and Kiara had already gone home with a very cranky pup.

Marie sat with the Parker boys as they watched the flag football game. The boys watched, and she read the latest Percy Jackson book.

The pack was beginning to disperse as the afternoon began to turn into evening. School would start on Wednesday, and people were reluctant for summer to end.

Electra began rubbing the back of her head. Allison had noticed that she was doing this more and more often. Every time she asked, the younger woman brushed it off as a headache. Allison was certain it was not just a headache.

Emmeline and Imogen sat down with them as Electra began to twitch her head. Her breathing became labored and erratic.

"Is she okay?" Allison asked as she mind linked her husband and son.

"Can you feel it? There is power in the air," Imogen smiled as the air all around them seemed to crackle.

"She's fine," the priestess said calmly. "Don't fight this Electra. It's time. Trust your wolf, she knows what to do."

Electra hunched forward and gagged as if she had a large object thrust into her mouth. A little spit and blood came out of her mouth as fangs extended and then retracted.

"Baby?" Hadrian asked when he came to a stop next to her.

"He's here," Emmeline said as he placed their hands together. "Let her lead, Electra."

She shook her head as bones and joints cracked throughout her body. She would shift partially and then return to her human form. "Why... now?" She struggled to get out.

"Ask her why. She's never lied to you. Trust her," Emmeline encouraged as a small crowd gathered.

"Are you sure she's strong enough?" Adeline asked.

"She is," Imogen replied, kneeling next to Electra. "Accept your destiny. Accept your responsibilities. Tell me why you have awoken now."

All movement of Electra's body stopped. Looking up at the healer, her eyes glowed gold, barely dimmed by the contacts. She growled out the answer just before she shifted and ran for the tree line by where Marie and the boys sat.

Emmeline hummed softly as Teuf nudged her arm. She placed a hand on the dog's shoulder. The hell hound sat by the priestess and seemed to smile at her.

Chapter 42

PROTECTION

Crystal River Pack

The pain coursing through Electra's body was almost unbearable. Her limbs grew and shrank as her skull shifted and returned. Her back arched and her joints moved. Fire coursed through her veins; power flowed around her as the air pulsed in waves flowing through those surrounding her.

Following the advice that Imogen gave her, she reached out to the voice that had always been there and begged for guidance. She demanded forcefully.

Why? Why now?

A calmness and understanding flooded through her as the wolf inside awoke. Eyes inside her mind that had been long closed and dormant, snapped open and Electra saw the world in a new way. Blinking her physical eyes, the dark contacts that she had worn since she was nine were forced out. The golden glow increased as the large wolf stretched in her mind.

"My pups," Gelert growled just before she shifted the human body into her own.

There was no fumbling and falling as the human body adjusted to the new form. Gelert was old and experienced. She had lived a hundred lifetimes in different hosts. Memories of her past lives drove her forward.

Leaping over the children, the large wolf stood between them and the pack of rogues that were creeping through the woods. She let out a deep protective growl and warning bark. Her ears twitched as she heard the movement behind her and knew that Hadrian and Theo were getting the kids.

Theo ushered the four pups away as Hadrian carefully approached his mate.

The rogue scents were strong even as they hid in the shadows. Movement to her right distracted Gelert for just a moment. The leader took the opportunity to attack the large wolf.

Gelert swiped at the leader as she snarled at the other man. She wanted their blood. She needed it. The taste of it had already filled her mouth and nose before any had even been spilled.

No.

Electra told her other half. She herself had suffered at the hands of others. She would not do the same to someone else.

"You don't scare me, you hybrid bitch," the man said.

Gelert bared her teeth and prepared to strike.

"Those are my daughters," a second woman said, stepping out of her hiding place.

"You gave them up," Hadrian argued. "You left us! You broke the bond and divorced me!"

"And I want them back!" Mitzi yelled at him.

"It's too late," Hadrian told her. "You won't get them."

"I'll appeal to the council. They'll want girls to have a mother."

"Do what you think you need to do. But you will never take my girls from me," Hadrian warned.

"Get off my lands," Wyatt commanded. The other rogues flinched at the order, but Mitzi stood firm.

"It seems that I'm still a member of the pack," Mitzi sneered.

"In that case, Gunny, arrest that bitch for child abandonment," Wyatt smiled back with his canines extending and eyes glowing bright blue. "Arrest the others for trespassing."

Her smile faltered as silver cuffs were placed on her wrists. The five were led away and placed in waiting patrol cars parked where they had been playing football. As they pulled away, Adeline placed a blanket over Gelert as she shifted back into the human form.

"Sit down," the healer encouraged.

Hadrian kneeled in front of Electra. "I love you. But I need to think of my girls right now," he kissed her before he stood up and walked away.

Chapter 43

HEARTACHE

Crystal River Pack

Electra had been hurt before. She had been abused. She had been raped. She had been humiliated. She had been cast aside. She had been mutilated. She knew that she could survive this too.

Maybe.

Nothing had ever hurt as much as this excruciating pain before. Never had all her hopes and dreams been yanked away so quickly. It had been years since she had any of either. Within two months she had a lifetime of both. She was even content with not having a wolf.

And then she had a family and a pack and a wolf.

Now she had none of it. Even the powerful wolf that she had connected with so wholly for a few brief moments had receded to the back of her mind. Once again, it was unreachable. As if the wolf had never been there.

The healer gave her a tonic, and she slept most of Tuesday. Not in the bed that she shared with Hadrian. She slept in a cold, lonely, empty bed in the packhouse. The mattress was soft and the sheets soft with a high thread count and the comforter plush. But she was not comfortable, and she could no longer sleep.

Electra did not need an alarm to tell her that the girls would be getting up and getting ready for school. Today was the first day of school. Emily's first day of kindergarten.

She would not be there for her girls.

Rolling over, she hugged the cheery pink blanket to her chest and let the tears fall. She thought of the gray comforter and sheets that were practical and masculine. They were what she wanted to see surrounded by the bluish gray walls and darker gray carpet. Not the pink cheerfulness that made her think of Emily. Or the full bookshelves that reminded her of Marie.

As she lay in the borrowed bed, wearing borrowed clothes, feeling as if she were living a borrowed life, her little family felt just as broken as she did.

***

"Emily, you need to get dressed," Hadrian told her for the fifth time. "It's your first day of school. You wanted to show off one of your new dresses."

"Mommy should be here!" the five-year-old yelled at him.

At least that one talks to me. He thought as he looked at the closed door to Marie's room. Since he told the girls that they were going home without Electra, she had spoken only one word to him.

"Why?"

Hadrian found himself wondering if he had done the right thing. Even his parents looked at him disapproving. He hadn't talked to Gerard, but his sister Bridget had called to tell him that he was an idiot.

The door downstairs opened, and he smelled his brother. Giving up on coaxing his girls out of their rooms, he went downstairs. Kiara was with him, and she was carrying Jessica.

"Thanks for coming over."

"I've never missed a first day of school," Gerard pointed out. "Marie, why aren't you dressed?"

"We're not going to school," she informed her uncle. "Not until mommy comes home," her chin trembled, and her voice was shaky. "She was going to work in the library and take us to school and have lunch with us and," with angry eyes, she pointed at her father, "HE made her go away. So, we're on strike until mommy comes home and you can tell him."

"Marie, there are other things-."

"Tell my father that when mommy gets home, we'll be in my room," Marie turned and went back up the stairs.

A moment later, their backpacks filled with school supplies slid down the stairs. Marie had a sparkly camo and Emily had a glittering unicorn complete with sequenced horn and matching lunch box. Both now lay at Hadrian's feet.

"Girls," Kiara called up the stairs, "let's go get some donuts. You can go in your PJ'S."

They both rushed down the stairs and hugged Gerard before slipping on their shoes by the door. Kiara kissed

Gerard before throwing a dirty look at Hadrian and following the girls to her car outside.

Gerard shut the door before turning on his brother. "I'm going to say this once and only once before I listen to your side. You are the biggest fucking idiot on the face of this fucking planet. Now," he took a deep breath and let it out on a sigh, "tell me why you let such a great woman who your daughters adore, and your wolf and you love, walk the fuck out of your damn life."

"Mitzi," Hadrian said and walked into the kitchen. He scraped scrambled eggs out of the pan into the trash.

Gerard sat down at the table and picked up a piece of bacon, "What about her?"

"She came back and is threatening to take the girls," he sat down across from his brother and rested his forehead in his hands.

"Mom said that she's in the dungeon. She can't do anything from there."

"I have to think of the girls. How does it look if I mate with a woman I barely know?" He asked looking up with tears in his eyes. "I love her, but my girls have to come first."

"Okay, but how are you thinking about them right now?" he asked, picking up toast. "Do you know what life was like before Electra? Kids picked on the girls. Marie spent so much time in the library because she could hide there. Your third grader is reading at an eighth-grade level. Your kindergartener can read and write."

"Now, their mother left, and you left their stepmother. What's the common factor? You. If Mitzi is threatening to take the girls, she now has ammunition."

"Like what?" Hadrian demanded.

"You're unstable. Which, she can argue, is why she left."

"I've been here! I stayed! I've taken care of the girls! I dried their tears! I did everything that I could!"

"Including turning the pack against you," Gerard pointed out around his toast. "Practically everyone loves Electra. We named our daughter after her. Plus, what are you going to do with the girls while you're at work?"

"We can go back to you-."

"Nope," he interrupted. "Let me stop you right there. I have my own daughter to raise now."

"Maybe mom..."

"Good luck with that," he said, standing up and heading for the coffee pot. "I have a message from mom." Reaching over, he smacked the back of his brother's head. "Pull your head out of your ass."

"I don't know what to do!"

"Figure it out," he drank his coffee and then rinsed his cup. "Give me a ride to the packhouse."

"Fine. Finish up in here while I get my gear bag."

Chapter 44

NOT HIM

Crystal River Pack

It was the fourth call of the day. And the fourth person who refused to have Hadrian tend to them. As he pulled into the hospital emergency room portico, he knew it was best to stay where he was.

After the second call, Darius grabbed Hadrian by the arm when they got back to the station house. With his anger not even close to being hidden, he informed the other man, "I hate being in the back. You better get this sorted out."

Gerard was right. The whole pack hated him right now. Including himself. He called Kiara to check on the girls. They still refused to talk to him.

Aiden stopped by the station earlier and pulled his son into the office. Hadrian remembered when he was younger and got in trouble at school. He had sat in the same chair as his father lectured him.

"Son, I can't tell you what to do. But I can tell you that I think you're making a huge mistake. You're miserable. The girls are miserable. And I'm damned sure that she's miserable."

"Dad, Mitzi is threatening to take the girls," Hadrian had explained. "She threatened to go to the council."

"Then marry your mate and bind your girls to her."

If only it was that easy, Hadrian thought. Blaze grumbled in the back of Hadrian's mind. Even his own wolf would not talk to him.

"O'Reilly four-four-three," came over the radio and confirmed that even dispatch was upset with him. Since his dad, an uncle and a couple of cousins were in the department, he was usually just called him by his first name. Not today. Today it was his last name and helmet number. At least they weren't using his rank.

Yet.

"O'Reilly four-four-three responding," he said into his microphone.

"You have been asked to report to Mr. O'Donnell's office at your earliest convenience."

Now the Alpha wanted to talk to him. He confirmed that he was to report to the Alpha and then signed off. Hadrian was banging his forehead against the steering wheel when the door opened, and Parker climbed into the passenger seat.

"Do you need Tylenol?" she asked. "Or something stronger?"

"Stronger," he groaned. "I've been called to the Alphas office."

"We heard that," she turned in her seat and looked at him. "I know everyone is telling you what to do; and I promised Theo that I'd keep my mouth shut. You're one of my closest friends, I love you, you big idiot. I get that you're doing what you think you need to, and I respect that. If you want to talk, I'm here."

"Do you think I did the right thing? Honestly?"

"Honestly, no. I think you made a rash decision. Your heart and mind were thinking about the girls. But they were ruled by fear."

"What should I do?"

"Go talk to Electra. And before you throw your relationship away, go talk to the Alpha about your options and rights."

"I love you, too."

"Of course you do. I'm awesome."

Chapter 45

WYATT'S OFFICE

Crystal River Pack

Tuesday morning, Wyatt headed down to his office and greeted Terry with a request rather than his typical greeting, "Terry, get me the divorce papers for Hadrian O'Reilly. Please and thank you and all that other shit."

Having anticipated it, and being slightly more all-knowing than Beta Stephen, the papers were already pulled and on the Alpha's desk. Wyatt had read through the divorce papers and then called Sonya, the pack lawyer, who reviewed it. Once he was comfortable with his decision, he requested that Hadrian come to his office.

Sonya had gone down the hall to work in the conference room until he needed her. Wyatt was on a call with a neighboring Alpha concerning the rogues. He was certain that there was more than what they had arrested.

Terry sent him a message saying that Hadrian had arrived. Wyatt asked Sonya to join them and then scheduled a time to call the Little Ridge Alpha back. As he hung up the phone, he called out to Terry through the mind link.

Standing up, Wyatt walked around his desk as the door opened. "Come on in, Hadrian."

"Thank you, Alpha," he said, baring his neck as he shook the other man's hand.

"Come sit down, Sonya Johnson will be joining us also," Wyatt motioned to the conference table. "Before she gets here, there's something that I want to talk to you about."

Sitting down with the Alpha was something that Hadrian never thought that he would do. But this was his Alpha and if the Alpha wished to tell him he was an idiot, Hadrian would let him. He nodded as he looked at his hands in his lap.

"I don't know what's going on with you and Electra, that's not really my place. If it starts affecting the pack, it will become my place. I may not be the best person to speak with, but we have three Elders here," Wyatt placed a friendly hand on the man's arm. "Marcus is easy to speak with. If you can get past the creepy eyes. He has these black eyes with just a thin ring of gold."

"Sir?" Hadrian asked looking up. He was about to ask about the unusual eyes when the door opened, and Sonya walked in.

The lawyer wore a bright blue skirt suit that emphasized her deep blue eyes. She had dark brown hair with traces of silver that she called her wisdom highlights. Crow's feet and laugh lines showed that she had a fun side along with her all-business demeanor.

After introductions and pleasantries, the three of them sat down around the table. Sonya pulled out three folders from her briefcase. Handing each man a copy of the papers she pulled out her glasses.

"Effectively, your ex-wife gave up all rights to your children. However, she claims postpartum and that she made a mistake."

"Do you think she has a chance?" Hadrian asked.

"Very slim," she smiled. "You were very smart to wait on signing the agreements. The first ones had joint custody."

"I never looked at the first ones," he admitted.

"The fact that she kept modifying them should help, right?" Wyatt asked.

"Yes. Did you keep your copies?" the lawyer asked, making a note on the legal pad.

"I have all of them," he admitted.

"Good. I'll have someone collect them. We'll make copies and return the originals to you," she took her glasses off and looked at him. "Do you mind if I ask why you chose to sign them now?"

"Well, ummm..." Hadrian took a deep breath and slowly let it out. "About a week before that, my wolf started getting antsy and irritable. The oracle had told me when Mitzi left, Blaze would know when to break the bond."

"Blaze is your wolf?" She asked, scribbling on a notepad.

"Yes, ma'am. That morning, he told me that he wanted a new mate. He said it was time, and I signed it."

"And when did you meet ..." she looked at her notes, "Electra?"

"That night," Hadrian smiled, thinking back to how calm Blaze became around her. How the girls opened up to her so readily. "My girls seemed to fall in love with her at first sight. And Blaze was just as smitten. Honestly, so was I."

"I remember when I met my second mate," she smiled at him. "It wasn't all fireworks, and I need you now. It was more of a slow burn that I couldn't and didn't want to get away from."

"Just wanted to curl up and watch Hallmark movies with her for the rest of our lives," Hadrian grinned.

"Exactly. I already had the wow and now, I wanted the steady."

"I fucked up," Hadrian's shoulders slumped in defeat. "How do I get her back? The girls want their momma E back and I walked away from her."

"When Noah and I had our first big fight, like so big that I thought he was going to leave me at Ole Miss, he sent me a key with an address. He got me access to the Mississippi Hills pack law library," she smiled remembering the feeling of excitement and love that washed over her. "When I graduated, he didn't make me pick my pack or him, he asked where we were going to raise our pups. But mostly, he supported me and listened."

"Don't look at me for advice," Wyatt held his hands up in surrender. "I was crazy stalker guy for ten years. I'm still figuring this shit out."

"Listen to your girls, all of them," Sonya grasped Hadrian's hand in hers. "And listen to your wolf."

"He's not talking to me right now."

"Then take advantage of the Elders being here. They really are smart wolves," she suggested.

Chapter 46

ELDERS WISDOM

Crystal River Pack

T he three elders were sitting outside at a large round picnic table as Hadrian left the packhouse. He considered walking by without stopping. After all, they are *The Elders*. He was just some random wolf.

He paused a short distance from the table and debated with himself. That is what the position of Elder was for – guidance. But they were Alphas. How could they understand what a simple man such as himself was going through?

Did they even have mates?

They chuckled at something that was probably said in their protected mind link. One of them cut the others off with a single sentence, "Behave, you two. We have a young man who needs our knowledge."

"Yes, Senior Elder Alpha Davis," the other two Elders said with a slight bow of their heads.

"Are you going to stand there? Or are you going to ask us your question?" the darker skinned Alpha asked.

Bowing his head he approached them and bared his neck, "Forgive me, Alphas, I was advised to seek your guidance."

"Sit down," the one who made Hadrian think of an older, and smaller, version of Dwayne Johnson said. "I am Davis, these are my colleagues, Samuel and Marcus."

He sat where Davis indicated and kept his head down, "My name is Hadrian."

"Hadrian, look up," Marcus said from across the table. "I think you can tell a lot about a person by looking at their eyes."

He looked up and found himself staring into the eyes that looked just like Electra's. Air was trapped in his throat, unable to inhale it into his lungs or expel it out into the world. There had been a few times that he had seen her without her contacts. When she had finally shifted, they popped out and her eyes had that strange golden glow that he had seen before.

The old man smiled at his recognition. A simple touch on his arm and Hadrian gasped in air at the silent command.

"She is my granddaughter," Marcus said softly. "Her mother died in childbirth and her father shortly after. She was given to a family who would love her as their own. I could not take her, much as I wanted to, I cannot disobey the moon goddess."

"Why would you leave her in that horrid pack?" Hadrian asked, surprised.

Tears filled his eyes, as he softly admitted, "When I learned how she was being treated, I pleaded with Selene. She forbade me from interfering."

Davis rested his hand on Marcus' arm, "We all pleaded. But we were told that she has to face her trials alone. Until her mate accepts her."

Samuel touched his finger to the mark on Hadrian's neck. "Have you accepted her?"

"I... I... I did. And then I didn't," it was his eyes that filled with tears this time. "My ex threatened to take my daughters, and I panicked and walked away."

"Fear can cause a lot of bad decisions," Samuel told him as a shock coursed through Hadrian beginning at his mark. As it coursed through him, he felt Blaze stir and whimper for his mate. "Your wolf has distinct opinions about you right now."

"He is not happy with me," Hadrian admitted. "I feel conflicted. I want to be with Electra. But I need to put my girls first."

"Being a parent never gets any easier," Davis said, watching Samuel communicate with Blaze. "You have to find a balance. Remember, the moon goddess knows what she's doing. Trust her. If she has put a new mate in your life, it's for a reason."

Pulling his hand away from Hadrian's neck, Samuel spoke to the others through the mind link. When the others nodded in agreement, he turned his attention back to the younger wolf, "Tell us what your daughters think of Electra."

"They love her," he smiled and his whole demeanor softened as he thought of his girls with Electra. "They call her momma E and lately it's just been mommy. My oldest, Marie, hasn't spoken to me since I left Electra.

Emily, my youngest, only yells at me. They informed me this morning that they are on strike until mommy comes home."

Hadrian let out a deep sigh, "Everyone is telling me that I messed up. But I have to take care of my girls."

"What would you do if your ex had never come into the picture?" Davis asked.

"I had just asked Electra to marry me."

"There's your answer," Marcus told him. "Forget the outside forces and focus on your family."

"Everything else will work itself out," Davis added.

"A she-wolf in love will forgive quite a bit," Samuel added.

"Hadrian," Marcus said softly. "She only knows me as an elder. As much as I want her in my life, I cannot until after she meets with the moon goddess."

"I understand," Hadrian nodded. "I mean, I don't understand what is going on here. But I understand wanting to keep your secrets."

"Gentlemen," Davis said standing up. "I believe we are being summoned."

Celeste's omega, Anna, approached the table with her head lowered. The other two elders also stood and left Hadrian sitting at the table by himself. He sat there for quite a while thinking about everything that he had been told.

Reaching a decision, he stood up and walked back into the packhouse. He approached Terry who contacted Wyatt and then ushered the man into the Alpha's office.

Chapter 47

NEW BEGINNING

Crystal River Pack

Hadrian stepped back out of the packhouse and looked up at the sun. He felt good about his decision. He felt good about the plan. He felt great that the Alpha pulled some strings, and everything would be done in about twenty-four hours.

When it was all set into motion, Wyatt slapped Hadrian on his back, "This is much better than the advice that my Beta gave me. Flowers. Chocolates. Promises you don't intend to keep. According to the clock man."

He reached out to his mom, who was still not happy with him. When she didn't respond, he dialed her number on his cellphone and headed for the Jeep. He had just sat with the three Elders, demanded assistance from his Alpha and took out a loan for home improvements. And finally painting the kitchen. He could face his mother and her wrath.

Or so he hoped.

"Maybe I don't want to talk to you," Allison said as a way of a greeting.

"I'm sure that you don't. But I need for the girls to stay somewhere tonight," Hadrian said, getting in and starting the engine.

"Why?" the question was full of accusations.

"Because the house is going to be an overnight construction zone," he answered after the call was transferred to the Jeep. "Can you do it? I have to go to Springs and be back to meet the crew by five."

"What the hell are you doing?"

"What I should have done a month ago," he answered, pulling out of the parking lot. "They don't have to go to school until next week. Please mom."

"Are you going to patch things up with Electra?"

"I'm planning on it. But I need you to keep the girls tonight," he took the exit for the highway and then merged.

"You better. I like this one."

"So do I."

With that taken care of, he continued to his next stop. He found the clerk and picked out what he wanted. It took some work, and he had to lay down the back seats, but he got everything in the Jeep. Exactly how he got everything back there, he still was not certain.

Hadrian got back to the house just after he watched the first truck pull up. Opening the garage door with the remote as he pulled into the driveway next to the Durango, regret filled him again. He should get it cleaned before he takes it back to Electra. That could be dealt with at another time. Tomorrow, when there was a place for all of her material.

"Hi, Andy?" Hadrian asked, getting out and smiling at the general contractor as two more pickups pulled up.

"Yeah. Show me what we're working with. Alpha said there was an outside entrance."

"Yes," Hadrian led him around the corner of the house where there was an entrance into the basement at the front of the garage. Inside he showed the half-finished area.

"You never used the bathroom down here?" Andy asked, looking at the powder room next to the washer and dryer.

"Maybe a few times while doing laundry."

He nodded as he looked at the plumbing under the sink, "The Luna has told me that she's bringing me a Keurig in the morning. She has told me to make sure she has her coffee."

Hadrian watched as other men filed into his basement with tools, wood and drywall. Andy and another man were measuring and marking the large basement.

"Knock-knock," a woman said walking in. "Which one of you assholes is Hadrian?"

He looked at her and was certain that he was looking at Electra's sister-in-law. "Claire?"

"How dare you-?"

"Let's go upstairs so you can yell at me," Hadrian pointed to the stairs leading up into the kitchen.

"We're good down here," Andy said as he continued to work. "Just let me know when you're ready for the painters up in the kitchen."

Hadrian followed Claire upstairs and closed the door behind him.

"I doubt that Electra knows that you're here. She's too kind to send you," he said before she could say anything. "Not that I blame you for wanting to kick my ass. The whole pack, including my parents and daughters, would cheer you on."

"Good! You have a great woman!"

"I know."

"And you hurt her!"

"I know."

"You're an idiot."

"I know."

"Quit agreeing with me!"

"Sorry, but I'm an idiot trying to make up for a really stupid mistake," he sighed and ran a hand through his short hair. "And I'm hoping that she'll forgive me and take me back."

Claire stared at him for a moment. "She will," she assured him softly. "She loves you."

Chapter 48

THURSDAY

Crystal River Pack

Electra wasn't ready to face the dining hall or any of the restaurants. But she woke up hungry on Thursday morning. Quietly, she debated with herself to stay in the warm bed.

After a quick call to the packhouse kitchen, one of the Omega women said that she could bring up a tray. The Omega listed off several options and Electra made a few choices of what sounded best. It did not take long for the Omega to bring it up.

Sitting under the covers, she stared at the nearly empty wooden tray placed on the nearby table. The single crimson rose in the baby blue vase made her smile. It was the little touches that she had experienced here that made her think she could make a new life for herself.

"As much as I want to hide in bed, I shouldn't," Electra finally declared to herself as she sat at the small table with her breakfast tray. She had a new life to build. One that would not include Hadrian and his girls.

Hold fast, my child. I have great plans for you.

This time it was just the ethereal voice that spoke to her. The angry voice was nowhere to be found. It saddened her that she was not hearing the other voice that had been a constant throughout her life. Not hearing it made her reel as though part of her was missing.

After eating the fruit bowl and slice of warm banana nut bread with butter, she drew herself a warm bubble bath. Sitting in the large soakertub, she cried remembering the night that Hadrian had put her in the tub. Hehad been so sweet and kind to her. She couldn't imagine that he'd just walkaway.

But he did.

And she didn't blame him. He had to protect his pups. They were going to be her pups. She already loved them as if they were hers.

When the water cooled, she washed and then got out. No more looking back, Electra told herself as she dried off. It was time to look to the future.

She could not go home. AJ and his father would never allow it. After experiencing the freedom that she had here, she did not want to go back to slavery and solitude.

She would talk to the Luna. There was bound to be something that she could do for the pack. Plus, she still had dresses to make.

Of course, all her material and supplies along with the old 1970's Singer were all at Hadrian's house.

So were her clothes. The Luna found some clothes for her to wear. Not that she would ever wear shorts out in public. And certainly not shorts that short. Celeste had called them PT shorts and Electra had asked where the rest of them were.

Sammi came by with a few Hawaiian dresses. It really didn't matter what she wore. She wasn't going to leave her room just yet.

Electra pulled on one of sundresses that Sammi brought. Then she picked up her large coffee and book that she had found in the room.

Settling into a chair out on her balcony, she decided to read about Nancy Drew and her mystery. She was deep into River Heights and an old clock in no time. The knock on the door went unanswered as she did not hear it.

"Electra?"

Startled, Electra jumped and hit the small metal table with her coffee cup on it. The metal travel cup hit the ground and began to roll towards the edge. Coffee dribbled out of the lid as it rolled.

Both she and Celeste reached for the cup at the same time. The Luna picked up the cup and smelled the coffee.

"Goddess, I miss real coffee."

Electra smiled at her as she turned the table back up right, "It's for a good reason."

"I don't know. Aiden is teething and is cranky and I'm going to have two of these little devils."

"I would love to have that problem."

"Someday," Celeste said handing the cup over. "How are you feeling?"

"Honestly, like shit," Electra said softly. "Is it me?"

"Oh, sweet girl," The Luna opened her arms and the younger woman readily went into the embrace. "It's not you."

"He is thinking with the heart of a father, do not fault him for that," Electra pleaded softly.

"You are too kind," Celeste murmured as Electra cried on the tattooed woman's shoulder and welcomed the tenderness. Celeste held her close and rubbed her back. She had pleaded with the triplets to help Electra, to ease the pain, something.

"There are certain things that we are not allowed to interfere with," Emmeline had said sadly.

"This is one of them," Adeline added.

"The Gelert must walk alone until her mate accepts her completely," Imogen explained. "It's part and parcel of being..."

"Being what?" Celeste demanded and the three sisters looked at each other as they argued in the mind link.

"I'm sorry, Alpha," Imogen said. "We have to answer to a higher power. We must obey the moon goddess."

She had even pleaded with the elders.

"You're here because of her, aren't you?" she had accused and not one of the three denied it.

"Everything, right now, is around her," Davis had confirmed. "But we are bound by our oaths."

She had been pissed at them and left her own office. After raiding the kitchen for sweets, currently her vice, she took her decaf coffee and went to her husband's office. He was on the phone with Andy about revamping a space for Electra to have a dress shop.

"There better be a damned coffee bar in it! Hell, I'll even bring you a fucking Keurig."

And she had dropped it off at his house last night. His wife, Janie, had told her that he was working late. But would make sure that he got it. And the box of coffee pods, cups, spoons and other accessories that Celeste thought that Electra would need.

She had no intention of telling Electra about the space. Partially, because Wyatt would not give her any details. And because Celeste was not certain that she was ready for that yet.

There was a knock on the door and Celeste guided Electra back into her chair before going and opening the door.

Chapter 49

BEGGING

Crystal River Pack

I t was the Luna that opened the door to Electra's quarters. Hadrian lowered his head and bared his neck. She gave a small growl and a warning through the mind link.

I hope you're here to plead for mercy.

He nodded and admitted that he had been wrong. With a final hmmm, she walked out and left the door open for him. He took a deep breath and walked in prepared to face an angry she-wolf. The broken woman on the balcony was his undoing.

She sat with her knees to her chest. Her arms were wrapped around her legs and her chin rested on her knees. Tears streamed down her cheeks as she looked out over the grounds below. Hadrian doubted that she saw any of the people walking around looking at the changing leaves on the trees.

"I failed you," he said softly stepping out on the balcony. Electra looked up at him in surprise. "I promised you forever and I walked away at the first test."

"You had to think about your pups," she whispered.

"But I failed them too," he knelt in front of her and gently took her hands in his. "They are on strike until I bring their mommy home. Marie won't even talk to me. Emily is a complete terror. And my wolf, hell, he's pissed at me."

"I don't blame you for thinking about them first," Electra said softly as she lowered her legs.

Hadrian kissed each of her hands. "I know you don't. It's why I love you."

"I love you, too."

"I don't deserve you giving me a second chance, but I hope that you will," he stood up and pulled her to her feet. After she was standing, he sank back to his knees.

"If you give me a second chance, I promise that you will be treasured every day for the rest of your life," Tears filled his eyes, and his voice cracked as he spoke. "My life is not complete if you're not with us. My daughters need their mommy. I need my mate."

He pulled a ring out of his pocket that Claire had helped him pick. "Electra Diane Naples, will you do me the honor of becoming my wife and mate? And the mother of my pups?"

"Do you mean it?"

"Goddess, yes, I do. With every fiber of my being."

Nodding slightly, she sniffled as she said yes. Smiling at her, he slid the ring on her finger before standing up and kissing her. For the first time since he had walked away from her, Hadrian felt Blaze in his mind. He could feel his wolf prancing and pawing in excitement.

"I did a few things," he finally whispered between kisses. "I need to show you what I did to the house."

"You didn't mess up my kitchen, did you?"

"No, ma'am, but I did finally get it painted," he smiled at her. "You remember how I was talking about turning the basement into an area for the girls?"

"Did you give them the ultimate playroom?" she asked with a smile.

"Actually, no," he chuckled. "I did something completely different."

Keeping her hand in his, he guided her out of the quarters and then down to his Jeep. The three Elders sat at a table outside the packhouse and gave him a slight nod as they passed. With that small acknowledgement, he felt stronger in his decision.

Although the drive to the house was only fifteen minutes away, today it seemed to take forever. All three lights between the packhouse and their neighborhood were red and added to his anticipation. When they finally arrived, he took her to the kitchen to see the misty purple walls and dark gray cabinets.

"Oh, Hay, it's beautiful," she gushed as she ran her hand along a door on the upper cabinets. "It has Marie's purple and Emily's darkness."

"They're putting in new countertops and appliances next week," he said nervously. "We can change it, if you don't like it."

Walking over, she grabbed his face and pulled him down for a kiss. Smiling at him, she insisted, "You're not changing anything."

Smiling back at her, he turned his face and kissed one palm before turning his head the other way and kissing the other palm. He never broke their eye contact, and it made the moment a little more intimate. Taking her hand in his, he guided her over to the door room just off the kitchen.

They stood in the strange room where you could go into the basement, the kitchen, garage or backyard. He and Gerard had always called it the door room. Their mother called it a vestibule. Andy had called it an engineering nightmare. Electra called it annoying.

All four doors opened inward. But only one at a time.

"Okay," he said softly and kissed the top of her head. "Open the door and let's go down."

Nervousness flooded through them both. Electra wasn't sure what was on the other side of the door. Hadrian wasn't sure how she'd react.

She opened the door and led the way down the stairs. They turned at the landing where the inside and outside stairs met. He had always wondered why they were like that. Andy had pulled the original plans, and this had originally been a mother-in-law suite. The outside stairs ran along the backside of the garage and net with the inside stairs on a small landing about halfway between the ground floor and the basement.

Light gray tiles covered the floor with a plush tan rug. The walls were a light peach color with light tan trim. Across the floor was a three-way mirror with a dressing room on either side. In front of the mirror was a tailor's pedestal in the same light tan color.

On the rug sat a light gray couch with tan and peach pillows. To her right was a small desk with a laptop and tablet. Behind that was a wet bar with a Keurig and a tower with pods. Hanging above were coffee cups and wine glasses. There was a small refrigerator and a wine refrigerator under the counter along with a small dishwasher.

At the end of the bar was a door leading to the rest of the basement. On the wall with the stairs was a TV showing pictures of the dresses that she had made.

On the remaining wall were racks with dresses that were pending pickup. There was a high rack for the longer dresses, a mid-rack for adult dresses and two racks, one above the other, for the little girl dresses.

Electra placed a hand over her mouth as tears fell freely down her cheeks. "Hadrian," she whispered. "You did this for me?"

"I did this for us," Hadrian corrected softly. "I see how much you love making the dresses. You needed a place to do it."

He stepped off the stairs and tugged her hand until she followed him. He pushed open the swinging door and let her go in.

In the center there was a large cutting table. Along the back wall were shelves filled with material, lace, trim and spools of thread. Lining the other wall were three different dress forms. Along the opposite wall were two different types of sewing machines, a standard and one called a *serger*. He wasn't sure what that was, but the clerk had suggested it.

There was a TV that showed the outside of the house, the door to the basement and her 'showroom' on it. On the shelf below it was a radio and a printer.

"I ordered a cutting board with a grid, I hope that makes sense to you," Hadrian said as he opened the door between two of the forms to the freshly painted bathroom.

"It does," she nodded as he opened the other door to the new laundry room. "Hadrian, this is wonderful. I don't think that I can do this on my own. Not to this scale."

"Well, that brings us to the next thing that I did," he smiled sheepishly. "But we have to go somewhere else."

"Where?"

"Lunch."

Chapter 50

LUNCH

Crystal River Pack

Gerard had gotten a call from his mom saying that they had a lunch meeting with the Alpha. She told him to go by the house and get the girls some dresses. Why neither Kiara nor Allison couldn't do that was beyond him. But he went and got some dresses just as he was told. And hoped that they met his mother's standards.

After he dropped them off at his parents' house he headed back home to change into something a little more formal than his jeans and CPPD softball league T-shirt. He settled on the blue department Polo shirt with khaki pants. Kiara greeted him in a soft blue sundress with burgundy trim and sash. His young daughter was in a pink onesie with a small rainbow tutu.

Currently they were sitting in the back of the restaurant in a party room. This was not what he had expected for lunch with the Alpha. His parents were both in formal uniforms for their departments and the girls were in the dresses that Electra had made them. Emily had her hands in the skirt pockets as she spun in circles off to the side.

Marie sat in a chair reading yet another book above her grade level.

Looking from his niece and the James Patterson book to his mother, he could only chuckle as Allison simply shrugged as if she gave up.

The door opened and a family that he did not recognize entered. He had seen the younger man once at the packhouse, months ago. He had talked to the Alpha and Luna and then an omega took him somewhere.

"Hi, I'm Mike, this is my wife, Jenny. This is our son Troy and his wife Claire and their pup, Riley," The man said in general with a smile. "And our other children, Helena, Portia, Jason and Athena."

"You're mommy's family!" Emily cried out as she ran over and hugged Mike.

"Mommy?" the whole family asked, confused.

"Our Alpha told us that we were called here by your Alpha," Mike said, making a small gesture to the Alpha standing near the door with a look of disdain on his face.

"Sorry about the confusion," Wyatt said as he walked in carrying his son. The toddler squealed in delight when he saw Kiara. "Yes, there's your KK," he sat the little boy down who made his way over to her.

"Disgraceful to see an Alpha act like a nanny," Alpha Anthony scoffed as Celeste came into the room with a plate of desserts.

"Shut up," Celeste said as she dipped a cookie into her mousse. "Oh, sweet goddess."

"I know," Wyatt said as he kissed her cheek after she sat down. "I did this to you."

"You did," she smiled at him as she handed both the girls and Riley a cookie.

"Please, sit," Wyatt said as he took the chair next to his wife. Aiden was now being held by the man who shared his name. "Aiden, sorry, chief, how are things going with the department?"

Aiden sat back down as the rest of his family also took their seats and resumed the conversations.

"Well, thanks to Marie's birthday, we've had three more requests for birthday parties. And one Bachelorette party."

"Why didn't I think of that?" Celeste mused.

"Anthony, please sit down," Wyatt said as his wife slapped his hand for trying to get a piece of cake. "Where is your dog?"

"With the spooky sisters," Celeste said.

"I like that," Emmeline said entering on the arm of Elder Alpha Marcus.

"Please, don't get up," Marcus said as everyone at the table prepared to stand. "Wyatt, have you heard anything yet?"

"No, Elder," he answered as the other two elders and triplets also walked in.

"Don't even ask," Imogen said as Davis pulled a chair out for her. "I've already told you that we can't interfere. Forgive me, Alpha Anthony, the head of the table is for the highest-ranking position."

He stopped and looked at the three elders who were sitting across from Alpha Wyatt.

"She's here," Celeste said quietly. "I don't understand what Teuf is trying to tell me. She does not yet have her pup."

"Adeline?" Elder Alpha Samuel asked softly.

"I have to believe him," the healer said.

The door opened and Electra walked in. She had changed into a pair of jeans and sleeveless T-shirt showing off her tattoos. Part of her short hair was pulled up exposing her multicolored curls. She had done her makeup with the wings that she liked so much.

In short, it was clear that she no longer belonged to the Dark Sky pack.

When she saw her parents, she felt no shame in her body being on display. She was proud of her tattoos and short hair. Jenny rushed over to hug her.

"Momma, what are you doing here?"

"I'm not sure, baby. You look good. I love your hair."

"I am not staying here with that... wolf-less harlot," Alpha Anthony declared as he stood up, slapping the table.

"That door over there works both ways," Wyatt said. "But if you leave, you will have no say in the offer I am going to make."

"We can discuss it in your office later," he said storming out.

"Too bad the offer is not for you," Wyatt grinned.

Chapter 51

ALPHA VS ALPHA

Crystal River Pack

Wyatt's office door flung open and Anthony stormed in. Celeste was straddling her husband's lap with her hands held in one of his above her head. His other hand was buried in her black hair as they kissed passionately.

"I can't believe you would do that behind my back," Alpha Anthony snarled as Terry stood nervously in the doorway.

"This seems to be right on schedule," Wyatt said before nibbling on his mate's lips. "Why don't you go upstairs and start us a bath? I shouldn't be long."

"As long as you're hard, I'm good," she said as he let her wrists go.

"Always for you, mate," he replied, watching her slowly move off his lap. Her PT shorts barely covered anything, and her sports bra was pulled down exposing her breasts. She took her time putting herself back together and he enjoyed the show. Wyatt gave a warning growl, and she simply smiled at him before taking her tattooed ass out of his office and up to their apartment.

"It's okay, Terry. I was expecting him," Wyatt said to his omega that was standing in the doorway. "He won't be staying long."

Terry nodded and closed the door.

"I warned you not to leave the lunch. I offered Mike a good deal and he took it. They will not be going back with you. Some of my warriors are going to escort Jenny home to pack everything. They will be off your lands by Sunday."

"You have no right-!"

"Do not storm into my office and proceed to tell me what rights I do and do not have!" Wyatt roared back as he stood up.

They stared at each other, neither backing down. They were both strong Alphas. Anthony had age and wisdom. Wyatt had youth and worldly experience. Anthony's pack feared him, Wyatt's loved him.

"What did you offer them?"

Wyatt sat back down but did not offer the other man a seat. "Three times his current pay, a house for his family, one for Troy and his family, an apartment for Helena and college for all of his kids. And a job for his wife."

Anthony was fuming and Wyatt could tell. He smiled and warned the older Alpha, "Your ways are outdated and unpopular. Don't be surprised if more people leave your pack."

He knew for a fact that many younger wolves were moving to their new mate's packs. Speaking with another Alpha, Wyatt learned of a general feeling of discontent in the Dark Sky pack. It was being led by none other than the Alpha's oldest daughter, Danielle.

Danielle met her mate last year. A half-blooded wolf from the Dragon Moon pack in Japan. Her father had refused to allow the mating because he was not a full Werewolf. She had run away twice, and Anthony had brought her back. Now he was searching for a mate that he approved of.

And she was spearheading a quiet rebellion.

One that was picking up more support when she learned that her father planned to marry her to his nephew. Her first cousin, Henry. Among the Alphas, he was often referred to as Henry the Eighth. He had already disposed of two mates when they failed to provide him with a son.

"I don't know what you think you're doing-."

"Thinking about fucking my mate," Wyatt answered honestly. "You saw her body. She's quite delightful."

"I've heard about your trips to the clubs," Anthony sneered.

"Won't deny that. The rumors about the stripper pole in the bedroom are false. But I do like the idea," Wyatt smiled.

"You're disgusting. Carrying on like deviants."

"We are children of the moon goddess, children of the night. We *are* deviants."

"I should report you to the council," Anthony threatened.

"Okay," he mind-linked Terry who almost immediately entered the room. "When is the next council meeting? Alpha Anthony has a complaint against me."

"Crescent City pack is hosting a council meeting the first weekend of November," Terry answered. "Would you like to schedule a council complaint interview, Alpha Anthony?"

"Yes. Your Alpha is stealing my pack."

"Rebuttal and can you also do one for me?"

"Yes, Alpha. What are the charges, sir?"

"Abuse, neglect, mutilation and slavery. Against Dark Sky."

"You have no proof."

An evil smile crossed Wyatt's face and Anthony swallowed hard. Slowly the younger Alpha stood up and walked around his desk to stand in front of the older man. His smile never faltered. His movements were slow and calculated. When he stopped in front of Anthony, he was barely an inch away and Wyatt looked slightly down on him.

"I have your son's rejected mate. The one that you sterilized. The one that your son raped. The one that he attacked on my lands. The one that was beaten so often that she thought it was better to just let him. And now her family is here and no longer scared of what would happen to them."

Chapter 52

HERITAGE

Crystal River Pack

The priestess had looked to her sisters for guidance, and they all agreed that the moment of truth was upon them. The three of them went to the Alpha and gave a cryptic message, "It's time for her to learn the truth. Bring her family."

Not only had the Alpha brought Electra's family to his pack, but he also offered them a new home. One that they all eagerly accepted. Now they were preparing to reveal why the orphan had endured so much hell.

Emmeline decided that the best place for this discussion was somewhere neutral. Somewhere safe. Somewhere that nothing would be destroyed by an emotional outburst. Somewhere secluded. And somewhere that everyone would feel comfortable.

After eliminating the temple, any homes or the packhouse, she settled on the meadow garden. It was calming and secluded. Everything in it could easily be repaired or would regrow. And no one had any emotional ties to it.

Her instructions had been clear. Her parents and older brother and Helena were to come. Along with her mate, his parents, brother and his mate. The Alpha's and the Elders. Her own two sisters.

That was still a lot of people.

It couldn't be helped. She eliminated all the children. Had even made arrangements for childcare. Had second thoughts about Helena. But in the end, the nineteen-year-old was included.

The temple omegas had set up a comfortable lounging area in the center of the meadow garden near the stream. There were several outdoor couches and chairs arranged in a circle. There were also small tables, and Adeline had brewed mint and chamomile tea.

The three sisters wore the robes of their position. The Elders were also wearing their robes. The fact that all six of them wore formal robes indicated the importance of the meeting.

Emmeline always thought that the Elder robes looked like catholic priest robes. Black with a high mandarin collar, embellishments on the sleeves and stoles denoted their wolf lineage.

Just as the blessed three had markings, the Elders also had the same markings. Marcus had the moon, Davis the star and Samuel the heart. Females were always marked on the right and males on the left.

The group had settled into the garden, and the omegas had served the tea. Once it was served, they made themselves practically invisible, the few that remained melded into the background with the guards that encircled the large meadow. Teuf lay on the ground between the Alphas. He lifted his head and looked at Emmeline.

"Thank you, hound," the priestess said as she sat her tea down. "Electra, what do you know of your birth family?"

"Nothing," she admitted. When she had been told that they would be meeting with the Elders, Alphas and the triplets, she had put on a dress. It was navy blue with gold trim and a gray cardigan.

"Mike, Jenny, what do you know?" Emmeline asked.

"A woman showed up with the baby in her arms. Troy was only a few months old," Jenny said. "She said nothing to me as she handed over the baby. As she started to walk away, she said Gelert and that was it."

"Jenny walked into the bedroom and showed me the baby," Mike added. "We tried to find out who the woman was or where she came from. We were unable to find out anything. Documents were filed and she became our daughter."

Emmeline nodded. "Your mother was named Jocelyn Margareta Moncrief de Agentieu. Your father was Robert Christopher Llewellyn ap Iowern. Jocelyn was a direct descendant of Remus and Robert of Romulus. Both passed through the lineage of the Gelert. You know the legend of the Gelert, do you not?"

"Yes. She was the mother of Llewellyn's first born and beheaded because he thought she killed the baby," Electra said softly. "The moon goddess blessed her to watch him grow from her hilltop."

"There is more, but usually not discussed," Imogen added. "Gelert herself was named an Elder when her wolf chose a new host. As with the other Elders, the wolf retains memories and knowledge. Because of this, Elder Wolves do not awaken until they are twenty-one, mated and blessed by the moon goddess."

"The awakening occurs a little at a time. This allows the host to adjust to the wolf," Adeline explained. "You have experienced this. Healing. Strength. Knowledge. Compassion. Protection. Maternal instinct. And you've had a feeling like there's something there when it's not."

Unconsciously, Electra rubbed the back of her head. "Why did they give me away?"

"They were attacked shortly before you were born," Marcus explained. "You were born early, delivered after Josie was declared dead. RC died a few hours later."

Samuel explained. "Selene told us that your mate was in that pack. He loved you, wanted you. But his father poisoned his mind."

"You were to become the Luna and your son the next Alpha," Davis smiled. "As always, the moon goddess has a backup plan. A second chance."

"But I'm not a Luna or even an Alpha," Electra objected.

"No, you're Elder," Marcus said as he stood up and walked to her. "Look at my eyes, child."

Electra looked up and saw eyes just like hers. Curious, she looked at the other two elders. Davis had similar eyes with a thin bright blue around the edge and Samuel had silver.

"It's the mark of the Elders," Marcus explained. "Few ever look at our eyes, so they never see it."

"Electra," Emmeline said gently. "The choice is now yours. You can accept your position as Gelert, and the merge can happen. You can continue as you are with a hibernating wolf. Or you can reject your wolf."

"Take some time and think about it. Talk about it with your family and mate. But before you make a final decision, pray to the moon goddess."

"How would my life change?' Electra asked.

"You can become a full member of the council," Marcus answered. "You can decline the position or settle somewhere in between."

"My successor has a seat on the council while Samuel's only attends a few functions a year," Davis added.

"And your successor?" She asked the man in front of her.

"That's up to you."

Chapter 53

LOST
Crystal River Pack

Hadrian walked into the master bedroom and heard the water turn off in the attached bathroom. He knocked on the door and waited for Electra to tell him to enter. Carrying his beer and a glass of wine, he entered and closed the door behind him.

"Goddess, I missed seeing you in the tub," he handed her the glass and gave her a kiss before sitting down on the closed toilet. "How are you feeling?"

"Confused. Overwhelmed. Happy. Sad. All of it," she said and took a drink. "I'm just... lost, you know? It's like everything that I knew about me is wrong. I don't even know who I am."

"You, my lovely mate, are the most wonderful thing to ever happen to me," he said leaning towards her. "You are Momma E. You are a whizz with a sewing machine. You are absolutely the best at making blueberry pancakes. Emily is an expert on blueberry pancakes; she would never lie about that."

She snickered at his statement that was said with absolute sincerity and seriousness.

"You are a daughter who is loved and adored. A sister who would sacrifice herself; *has* sacrificed herself. An aunt who is looked up to. Partially, because they're shorter than you."

Electra giggled and splashed some water at Hadrian, "You're horrible."

"I probably am," he agreed as he pulled his shirt off. Tossing his shirt aside, he reached around the shower curtain and pulled the drain.

"What are you doing?" she laughed as her bubble level began to lower.

"Either you're getting out," he told her as he stood up and took off his jeans and boxers, "or I'm getting in."

His hardness bounced slightly as it was freed. Hadrian offered her a hand, and she eagerly accepted it. She stood and he wrapped an arm around her waist, lifting her out of the tub.

Electra wrapped her arms and legs around him as their lips crashed together. He turned and pressed her back against the wall. With one hand, he held her wrists together above her head. His mouth moved to her breast where he lightly bit her nipple before sucking it into his mouth.

"Hadrian…" She moaned as she arched her back. He grunted a response as his fingers began to tease between her legs.

Fighting against his hold, Electra broke free and grabbed his head. She pulled him up and attacked his lips. "I need you."

"I need to see you," he told her and then lifted his head to look down at her. "Do you trust me?"

"Yes, I will always trust my mate."

He shifted and carried her out into the bedroom. Hooking his foot on the leg of the bench at the foot of the bed, he pulled it towards the closet. He opened the closet door and then sat her on her feet. Once he had the mirror on the inside of the door and the bench where he wanted them, he sat down and held out his hand.

"Come here," he softly ordered, and she started to straddle his legs. "Turn around, babe."

She faced the mirror and found it oddly erotic to watch him sit her on his lap with her legs wide open. He caressed her breasts and pinched her nipples. When he slid a hand down her belly, she thought it odd not to see a scar.

But soon, his fingers were disappearing inside her. All thought left her as she laid back against his chest. Watching him made her orgasm build harder and faster. Hadrian guided her hand to her breast and they both caressed and teased her.

"Are you going to come for me?" he whispered against her neck, never taking his eyes off the mirror.

"Oh, goddess, yes," Electra cried as she crested over the edge. Her walls clamped down around his fingers and her juices flowed out onto his hand. "Hadrian!"

"Goddess, you're beautiful," he turned her face towards him, and he kissed her. "I love you, Electra."

"I love you, too, Hadrian."

He pulled his fingers out of her and lifted them to his mouth. She grabbed his wrist and pulled his hand to her own mouth. Growling with desire, he watched her suck her juices off his fingers. With his other arm around her waist, he lifted her up and positioned her over his cock. Then he turned them both to face the mirror.

She sank down, impaling her softness with his hardness. A sigh escaped her around his remaining finger. Hadrian dipped his head and lightly bit her on her marking. Teasing the sensitive spot with his teeth, tongue and lips, he began to guide her movements.

"Oh, goddess."

"Mmmmm...." He nipped at her mark one last time. "Put your arms around my neck."

Electra reached up and clasped her hands together behind his neck. This caused her to arch, and he hit new spots inside her. Her eyes widened in wonder before they half closed in pleasure.

"That's it, baby," Hadrian encouraged as he gripped her hips. "Does that feel good?"

She tried to answer but could only moan. He chuckled and increased the speed and rhythm. Her moans and cries got louder as she neared her release. Her body trembled just before it tensed, and she cried out loudly.

Aftershocks racked her body as she tried to hold onto Hadrian's neck. It was now slick with sweat, and she could not get a grip.

"It's okay, I got you baby," he said, placing one arm around her waist and the other across her chest and grabbing her shoulder. He then stood up and stepped backwards over the bench. "Knees on the bench, spread apart."

Electra did as he said and again found herself drawn to the mirror. She watched as he began to pump in and out of her. His hands moved back to her hips, and he pumped harder and faster.

She leaned forward slightly, and Hadrian moved his hands to her shoulders. They both watched each other in the mirror. His eyes focused on her hand that slid between her legs to tease her clit.

"Electra, my beloved mate, come for me," Hadrian commanded as he neared his own release. He bared his fangs and bit her, marking her for a second time.

Pain and pleasure coursed through her as she found her release and pulled him with her. He shot ropes of cum inside her. In her mind, the image of her heavy with a pup appeared.

Chapter 54

SUCCESSORS

Crystal River Pack

N yla had been woken up with her fellow Elder Successor forcing her way into the mind link.

The Elders think that it might help if we talk with her. Road trip?

Arguing was pointless, so Nyla met Dawn in New York, where they rented a car. They took turns driving while the other navigated. Both were laughing at the others' lack of skills at either objective. They only got lost once but were quickly back on the road. The other detours were side quests for tourist traps.

The guard at the security gate at the edge of town looked at the credentials declaring that they worked for the council and waved them through. It was late. He was tired. And the two she-wolves appeared to pose no threat to him or the pack.

It was nearly two in the morning when they finally arrived at the packhouse for Crystal River, unsurprisingly very few people had been up. The guard on duty went to wake the Alpha when Elder Alpha Davis informed the warrior that the two women were guests of the Elders.

The morning came a few hours after they arrived. The two young women sat at a table by themselves in the packhouse dining hall enjoying black coffee and omelets. They laughed and chatted amongst themselves.

"Hello, I'm-."

"Alpha Celeste," Dawn smiled up at the tattooed woman. "Elder Dawn and she is Elder Nyla."

Celeste stared at the dark woman with black eyes except for the thin line of bright blue. Her hair was in box braids that were braided into a large braid down to her mid back. She wore khaki slacks and a bright teal halter top. Gold and silver chains hung around her neck and at least two dozen bangles graced each arm. Gold and silver hoops hung in her ears along with industrial bars at the top. She had a silver lip ring and a decorative septum ring.

"Is that silver or platinum?"

"Silver. It's an advantage of being an Elder," Dawn said motioning for the woman to sit. "You should sit in your condition."

"Not because you're pregnant, but because your donuts are being brought over," Nyla clarified with a smile.

Nyla wore a black skirt and hot pink blouse. The Asian woman was much more conservatively dressed, but her dark purple hair with pink tips showed that she was very much like her friend. She wore a gold wedding band and simple gold studs in her ears. Her black eyes were ringed with silver.

Celeste sat down as one of the omega women sat a plate of donuts and a cup of decaf coffee on the table, "Thank you, Lexie."

"That's the Naples family?" Nyla asked of the large family entering the dining hall.

"Yes," Celeste answered as Electra and Hadrian entered from the other door.

Electra froze as if she were being pulled towards the other two. A wave of power flowed through the room as the three Elder Successors were together for the first time. The air crackled as an unseen breeze shuffled napkins and papers around, knocking them to the floor.

"She's powerful," Dawn murmured as both her and Nyla's eyes flashed bright.

"She hasn't fully merged yet," Nyla said as Electra approached their table.

"Luna," Electra said, baring her neck.

"Sister, you are an Elder. You submit to no one except the moon goddess herself," Dawn said gently. "They..." she tilted her head towards Celeste, "will submit to you."

"I'm not that kind of person," Electra said softly as she sat down.

"I get that," Nyla said. "I was born and raised Omega. When the Elders came for my merge, my Alpha had to submit to me. It was strange."

"My old Alpha had me fixed because he thought I was wolf-less," Electra whispered.

"I would make them submit for sure," Dawn said. "My Alpha didn't even know that I existed. And I lived in his household," she shrugged. "He argued with the elders that a woman couldn't be an elder."

"What happened?" Electra asked.

"The moon goddess took his pack," Dawn said and then looked at Celeste. "Alpha, do you mind?"

She had not been so easily dismissed in a long time, and it took her by surprise. She did have other things to take care of, but she would rather eavesdrop on these three. Standing up, she bared her neck to the Elder Successors and called for Teuf to go with her. He whined under the table.

"Take this for him," Nyla said, handing Celeste the plate of her half-eaten omelet. "Go, hound."

Teuf followed his mistress, never taking his eyes off the plate.

"Would you like something to eat? Or drink?" Dawn asked.

"No, I'm... fine. I'm fine."

"You're nervous and anxious and worried that if you eat anything, it will make a return appearance," Dawn smiled at her. "We've been there. So has your wolf."

"Has anyone told you about the merge process?" Nyla asked.

"No," Electra shook her head.

"Have you had really vivid dreams that felt like you were there?" Nyla asked and Electra nodded. "Known things that you probably shouldn't? Know about places you've never been?"

"All the time."

"That's your wolf. Elder wolves retain memories and knowledge from all their lives. Before you merge, their past lives will leak into your life," she explained. "When you merge, all of those lives flood into you. Every experience. Every memory. Every emotion. Every piece of knowledge. Every *stupid* thing that they ever did."

Dawn started laughing and Nyla glared at her.

"Shut. Up."

"I'm sorry..." Dawn said, laughing even harder. "But you... you jumped... from a... hot... air... balloon..."

Nyla rolled her eyes before looking at Electra, "I am terrified of heights. And in one of my lives, I was an aeronaut." Smirking, she looked at the other woman, "At least I wasn't a prostitute."

"Temple concubine," Dawn said, trying to sound important but ended up laughing more.

Nyla rolled her eyes again but started laughing also.

"At least I won't have that many lives. Gelert didn't live that long ago," Electra said.

They both looked at her.

"Electra, the first Gelert, was the daughter of Remus," Dawn said quietly. "She is the first elder."

She sat in stunned silence for a moment. "I don't think that I can do this."

"Electra, it has been over a hundred years since the goddess chose three female elders. And nearly three hundred since she called on the Gelert," Nyla said, taking the other woman's hand in hers. "She wants to make changes. Ones that only women can make."

Chapter 55

FAMILY MEETING

Crystal River Pack

After her impromptu meeting with the other two successors, she and Hadrian met with the elders. And then the triplets. By early afternoon, she thought that she had possibly made her final decision.

She knew that her decision would affect so many more than just herself.

They met again with Marcus, this time as her grandfather and not as an elder. As they were leaving, Marcus pulled Hadrian off to the side and gave him the only piece of advice that he could.

"Whatever she decides, she is going to need your full support."

Currently, they were sitting in a room at the orphanage where some of the youth groups met at. The room was filled with assorted furniture that had been donated or rediscovered in pack storage. Nothing in the large room matched and it just added to the charm.

All of her and Hadrian's family were present. All the kids were there this time. The Elders and Alphas were not present in the room but had let it be known that they were on the property.

"If I do this, I will be required to go to the council meetings every quarter. It's about a week every February, May, August and November," Electra explained as she hugged a wiggly Emily who sat in her lap.

"Does that mean that you're going to leave us?" Emily asked quietly. "I don't want you to leave us mommy."

"Oh, no, baby," she kissed the top of Emily's head and held her arm out for Marie. The older girl rushed into the open embrace. "I'm not leaving you. In fact, most of these, you'll get to go to."

"There's one in November that we have to go to," Hadrian said as he sat down on the couch and placed his daughter in his lap. "Your mother has petitioned for custody."

"Mommy?" Marie asked.

"No, honey, your birth mother," Electra said. "But when we spoke to the priestess earlier, we scheduled a mating ceremony and for you two to be bound to me."

"Are we going to have to go with her? Our first mother?" Emily asked with tears in her eyes and voice.

"No," Hadrian said harshly. Electra touched his arm, and he relaxed. "I've spoken with the Alpha's lawyer, and she said that Mitzi has no claim to either of you. She signed away her rights and broke her bond."

"If you become an elder," Aiden asked, "would it help?"

Electra and Hadrian smiled at each other. He nodded and she took a deep breath.

"Yes. I would have a seat on the council."

"Seriously?" Troy asked. "So, you could punish Dark Sky for what they did to you?"

"Yes," Electra blushed and looked down. Hadrian placed an arm around her shoulders and pulled her to him. He kissed her hair and murmured something that made her smile.

Her eyes flashed gold as she looked back up. "I have been told that Gelert can be very vindictive and cruel. When Mitzi tried to get to Marie, I felt Gelert, she wasn't fully awake, but I wanted to kill Mitzi. I wanted her blood. I felt like I needed it."

She pulled both girls close to her. "But I overruled her. Once we merge, it will be a mix of her and me and all the previous lives. Only the really strong can overcome her. That's why my birth parents were killed. People feared her."

"Do you fear her?" Mike asked his daughter.

"No. I feel her. I feel her pain. I feel her sadness. I feel her need to protect, to mother. But I also feel me, and I survived AJ and everything that he and his father did to me. I believe that I am strong enough to control her."

"What if you're not?" her mother asked, worried about her.

"I am," she answered softly, looking up at her mate. "I am strong enough to survive Dark Sky. I survived being raped. And beaten. I survived being mutilated. I survived being rejected. I survived healing. And I am strong enough to control the Gelert."

"Yes, you are," Hadrian kissed her as Marie made a face of disgust and Emily squealed happily. "Are you telling them?"

"Not yet. I want to talk to the moon goddess first. If you don't mind," she answered softly, a little uncertain.

"Whatever makes you comfortable," he smiled at her as he leaned in and kissed her hair, inhaling her scent that was now an addiction he did not want to break.

"When do you see the moon goddess?" Helena asked.

"Saturday night," Electra smiled. "I go before her after our mating ceremony, and I am bound to the girls."

"Saturday?" Allison and Jenny said at the same time.

"That's not enough time!" Allison objected.

"You can't get anything planned that quickly!" Jenny pointed out at the same time.

"Moms!" Claire yelled before they really got going. "How are you two planning on getting a mating ceremony planned in less than a week?"

The room fell silent as they all looked at the couple that were grinning like Cheshire cats.

"I have two other Elder Successors, three Elder Alphas, two Alphas and a werecat helping," Electra said with a little laugh. "They are taking care of the actual ceremony, and I am doing the dresses."

"Jill or Sles will be getting in touch with you about what needs to be done," Hadrian said, shaking his head. "I still can't believe that I'm calling the Luna Sles."

"I can't believe that my Alpha and Luna are planning a mating ceremony for me," Electra laughed.

Chapter 56

DRESSES

Crystal River Pack

Electra took the girls to school on Monday and walked them both to their classrooms. The teachers had all heard the rumors that Hadrian had left his new mate. They were surprised when Electra brought them to class and said that they were having a mating ceremony on Saturday.

Neither smelled a wolf on the woman and simply just smiled when Emily said that Electra was going to be on the council. It quickly went around the school and Marie confirmed it.

By the end of the day, they were both being picked on. It never bothered Emily. Marie just smiled and ignored them. She knew she was right.

After all, Sunday night, they had dinner with the Alpha family and had watched the two Alphas, and his parents submit to Electra. She had been quick to tell them not to do that. It was strange for her.

Now that the school day was over, the kids were gathering in the foyer of the school for dismissal when the door opened and the teachers and staff quickly fell to their knees. The students were quickly told to do the same as Elder Alpha Marcus walked into the building.

"Marie, Emily," he called out. "Are you ready?"

"Where's mommy?" Emily asked as both girls popped up and grabbed their backpacks.

"She had to go to the temple and be fitted for her robes," Marcus said as they each took one of his hands. There was a murmur that ran through the area as they turned to walk out. "We're meeting her at the fabric store."

"Are her robes black like yours?" Marie asked as they approached the exit.

"Hers will be gray until she takes my place," he answered as his assistant opened the door. "Thank you, James."

Marcus asked them about their days as they went to the sedan. A booster seat was already installed for Emily, and she fastened herself in as she talked about Missy Thompson laughing so hard that milk came out of her nose.

"What was she laughing at?" Marcus asked from the front seat as James drove away from the school.

"Jack Goldsmith said that he had wolf ears and no one believed him and he pulled out his sister's headband from last year when she was the mascot in Crystal Springs and he was like, see I told you and then Jordan Quesada, she's a girl, said that he was nothing but a liar and Steven Underwood said that she was a boring stick in the mud and Jordan told him that he would know about mud because he was dirty and then her brother, Chad, asked if he was dirty, why did she have a crush on him and Missy started laughing and chocolate milk came out of her nose."

"Breathe, child, breathe," Marcus laughed.

James was laughing also as they drove towards the material store in Crystal Springs. Marie told them about her much less exciting day. As they pulled into the parking lot, the younger man took pity on his boss.

"Sir, it's not going to matter if you remember the names, or who did what," James said softly. "It's going to matter that you were there and that you listened. That's what is going to matter."

"Thank you," Marcus said. "It's been a while since I was around young girls. That did not sound right."

"Since I have six girls, I will give you all the advice you need."

"Still trying for a boy?"

"Nope. My own softball team."

Emily was going through another story with full names and direct quotes as they entered the fabric store. Jenny, Electra's mother, waved at the girls as they ran for the fancy material. Emily loved the silks, satin, velvet, brocade and chiffon. Lace, she told anyone who would listen, was a necessity.

Ne-ces-si-ty.

Oxygen was almost as important.

Marie on the other hand, preferred simple things. She was enthralled by her Aunt Bridget and her goth look. Allison advised her new daughter to prepare herself for a skull phase.

Before anyone could stop her, Emily had already picked out three silks, two velvets and a gold brocade. All in various shades of pink. Electra was certain that she could get a bottle of Pepto-Bismol and Emily would love it.

"Honey, you only need one dress," Jenny told her.

"Princess Kate had three," the little fashionista stated.

"And when you marry the Prince of Wales, you can have just as many," Electra said looking at the selection.

After laying the silk and then the velvet against the brocade, she picked one of each and pushed the others aside. Then she grabbed her sketchpad and drew out a dress. A bodice made from the brocade. A full silk skirt and long sleeves. And because Emily kept begging for one, a cloak, just like a real princess.

Emily gushed at the drawing. "It's perfect, mommy."

The clerk looked at the drawing. "That is beautiful. I don't know if we have a pattern like that."

"I make my own patterns," Electra said gently as she figured out how much material she would need.

"Mommy?" Marie said, holding a deep purple velvet and light purple silk.

"Oh, that's beautiful. Do you want a cloak also?" When she saw her little face light up, Electra smiled at her. "Is there a dark gray velvet? I think that would be perfect for you."

Marie sat the two bolts of material down and then dashed back over to the velvet. Electra turned the page and then sketched out a simple dress with a square neck, long sleeves and floor length skirt. She added in a waistline and made hash marks across the top indicating the velvet.

She then added a cloak, complete with hood and pockets. Deciding that since both her girls had cloaks, she would too. Flipping back to the drawing of her halter dress with a high-low skirt. She lowered the hemline and made it into an A-line before adding a cloak to it.

"You do know that part of your office robes includes a cloak, right?" Marcus asked with a grin.

"Seriously?" Electra asked looking up.

"Seriously," he answered. "And if you do that in cream or ivory it would look really good with the gray cloak."

"Have personal experience?"

"My mate, when we were married, she wore a cloak to match my robes."

"That's a nice idea," Hadrian said as he, Parker and Darius approached them.

"No," she answered, snuggling into his arms. "I like your fancy uniform with the little funny hat."

Smiling, he leaned in and kissed her. "I'll even wear the funny hat for you."

"What are you doing here?" Marie asked, putting the velvet on the counter.

"We had a mutual aid call, and he saw your mom's car. Had to stop so he could get kisses," Parker rolled her eyes. "That's pretty. Your mom is going to make you a dress with that?"

"A cloak to go with my dress for the ceremonies," Marie said with a little blush.

"Are you excited?" Parker asked.

"More importantly, are they always that gross?" Darius asked, motioning towards the couple still embracing.

"Always," both girls answered. One gushed and the other sighed.

"Be nice," Hadrian warned lightly, "or I'll steal kisses from you two next time I take you to school."

"Dad, you wouldn't!" Marie said horrified.

"He would, and you know he would," Parker laughed. "We need to get back to the station. It's Rodriguez and Hamilton's turn to cook dinner. I want front row seats for that shit show."

"Hey, what's a tisp?" Darius said in an imitation of Rodriguez.

"Tisp?" Jenny asked curiously.

"Teaspoon," the three firefighters answered.

"Let me know if I need to bring you anything," Electra said and kissed her mate just before he stepped away.

"We have pizza delivery on speed dial," Hadrian assured her.

"I like that chicken pasta thing," Darius smiled.

"Don't you have a wife?" Parker teased.

"Yes. And if I want to live, I do the cooking," Darius shuddered.

"I think Rodriguez knows more than your wife does," Hadrian said as they made their way out of the building.

Chapter 57

CEREMONIES

Crystal River Pack

Hadrian and Electra would have preferred a simple ceremony. They kept telling the Blessed Three this. Each time that they said it, she simply told them something along the lines of 'Sure thing,' or 'You betcha' before going back to planning a large ceremony.

Emmeline smirked at them, "You do, you do, they do, we sing, we dance... are we having a wedding or a Broadway musical?"

The couple relaxed after her comment and truly handed it over to them and Celeste and her best friend Jill. The large werecat looked at Electra and her colorful hair before suggesting that they do the wedding to match the colors of her hair.

"Emily can have her pink, Marie her purple and you get to shine like the star that you are."

Their families, his girls and a few friends. They had even chosen to have their mating ceremony and the bonding in the open-air temple to reduce the number of guests.

It did not work as they had planned.

The fire department showed up. Even the crews on shift brought the rigs.

Teachers, staff, students and parents from the elementary school were there.

The Alpha's and their families. But of course, that was a given.

The Elders, their successors and all their families. That was also a given since Electra would join them.

Then there were the friends. Friends of friends.

And their neighbors' second cousin's college roommates' best friend from elementary school second grade teacher's pet goldfish former owner's ex-husbands current girlfriend.

This time, Hadrian thought, they probably even brought the goldfish.

The outer courtyard had been decorated for the party afterwards. A dance floor had been set up. Along with a couple dozen tables. A buffet table with finger foods and a second table for the cakes.

All of this was cleared away and chairs brought in for the dignitaries. It was standing room only as Mike walked his adopted daughter down the makeshift aisle.

The white twinkle lights remained in the trees and tiki torches were set up around the perimeter. As they were nearing the time for the ceremony to start, the clouds dissipated, and the crescent moon shone brightly above them.

Marie and Emily stood with Hadrian next to the high priestess where an altar had been erected. They each wore the dresses and cloaks that Electra had made. The cold wind that blew around them made her glad that she had made the cloaks.

Hadrian wore his dress uniform with his awards and ribbons proudly displayed. When she had seen them, Electra imagined that they were for saving someone or a heroic rescue inside a fire.

"I assure you; it's nothing that exciting," Hadrian gave a small laugh and then pointed to each one explaining what it was for. Years of service, various training and certifications, even local, state and national competitions that he had won. He barely paused on the one for Valor and she did not press for more.

Electra wore a cream-colored halter tea length dress with a dark gray cloak. Since she had not merged with her wolf, or assumed her position, there were no markings on it. Her freshly recolored mermaid hair was in an elegant French twist.

Emily and Marie had picked out her shoes when they saw the platform heels with a mermaid air brushed on each of their blue heels. Around her neck were the pearls from Jenny's maternal family.

When they reached the altar, Mike hugged Electra and kissed her hair, "I love you. You have been a blessing to our family. Don't ever doubt that, little girl."

"I don't, daddy," she whispered back through her tears. "I love you too."

Mike gave her one more tight squeeze and then handed her over to Hadrian. He smiled broadly as Electra stepped over to him and his daughters.

The high priestess positioned them so that they were facing each other and holding each other's right forearm. Using a gold rope, she wrapped it around both of their hands and tied a knot above their hands.

"You've already marked each other and exchanged vows, right?" the high priestess asked.

They both confirmed it, and she nodded, stepping back for Marcus. He picked up the silver rope and smiled at Hadrian. "This is going to sting a bit."

Hadrian hissed as the silver touched his skin. It turned red and his skin started to welt. "A bit?" he said between just teeth.

The high priestess smiled at him. "It will get better in just a moment," she placed a hand on both of their arms, carefully avoiding the silver.

"Blessed mother above, in the light of your moon, I ask you to bless this union of your daughter and her mate."

Moonlight shined down on them and the pain disappeared. The redness and welts faded. There was a feeling of power that surged through Electra's body and passed into Hadrian's.

As they watched, both ropes dissolved into their skin leaving faint outlines of where they had been.

"Cool, huh?" the priestess asked quietly as both girls gave a soft "wow."

"Okay, girls, your turn," the high priestess motioned for the Elders who picked up the girls and had them place their hands over Hadrian and Electra's arms.

Marcus held his hand above theirs and the silver and gold ropes slid up over the girls' arms.

"That tickles," Emily giggled.

"Blessed mother, bind this family together. Unite their lives, hearts and souls," the high priestess said.

The ropes faded leaving lines on all four arms. A warm feeling engulfed them and then settled inside them all.

"That's it?" Marie whispered.

The priestess chuckled, "The moon goddess may do more when Electra meets with her. That is all that we need to do."

The Elders sat the two girls down and all three returned to their seats. Hadrian leaned over and kissed Electra before they turned and faced the audience.

"Ladies and gentlemen, Hadrian O'Reilly and family," the high priestess announced.

Chapter 58

RECEPTION

Crystal River Pack

The chairs were moved to create a seating area around the edges of the meadow. A temporary dance floor was laid out in the center and a table set up opposite the altar held the bridal and groom's cakes. A small gathering of children, and the Luna, stood waiting in anticipation of cake.

Wyatt rolled his eyes and loudly declared, "My wife has eaten all the sweets that she brought. She's by the cakes with the children. I see gestational diabetes in her future."

With an amused smile, Electra cut the cake with Hadrian and let both of the girls feed her a piece. They insisted on feeding some to their dad also. And then he gave them each some also. He even smeared a little icing on each of their noses.

Teuf stood by ready to help clean the little faces. His mistress stood by ready for cake. Or any sweets.

Hadrian led Electra over to where the dance floor had been moved outside. Music began to play from hidden speakers. Laying her head against his shoulder, and wrapping their arms around each other, they began to sway to a Nat King Cole song. Hadrian sang along to *Unforgettable*, one of her favorite songs.

At the end, Mike took his place as father and daughter slowly danced to *Dream a Little Dream*. She had always been drawn to jazz music. When she learned who her parents were, she discovered that her dad had played the saxophone, and her mother had been a music teacher. They always had music playing in the house, much like Electra did now.

"I'm so happy for you, little girl."

"Me too, daddy. I never thought that I would have something like this. A mate. Pups. A calling from the moon goddess."

"I always thought that you were destined for more than Dark Sky. I never set my sights on the moon."

"You always told me that there were already footprints on the moon. Aim to leave mine somewhere no one has been before."

"Your little one has really taken that to heart," he smiled down at her. "Your. Little. One."

She smiled back. "My. Little. One. They're both mine. I have the bond to prove it."

"The bond. Their love and adoration. Him," he tilted his head towards his new son-in-law. "His love and adoration. You've got a great little family there, little girl."

"Thanks, daddy," Electra smiled as she laid her head on his chest, and he rested his chin on top of her head. "I love you, daddy."

"I love you, too, Electra O'Reilly," Mike said, squeezing her close. "Looks like our song is nearly over and someone else is wanting a dance."

"I did promise a dance to a few others."

"Hope you don't mind, I'm going to go dance with my granddaughters," he said, and she looked up with tears in her eyes that he wiped away with his thumb. "None of that, little girl."

Mike kissed her forehead and then led her over to Aiden. "Sir, it is my honor to present my daughter as your daughter. Treat her well, love her and treasure her."

Aiden smiled at the blushing bride. "I could do no less, sir," he lifted her hand to his lips. "I give my son to you as the thief of your daughter. Treat him as well as you can, love him when you can and remind him of the treasure that he has received as often as possible."

There had been a collective awe when Mike presented Electra. When Aiden presented Hadrian, the sweet awe was replaced with laughter. But then it changed back to a soft sigh as he continued.

"I also share my granddaughters with you. Help me to guide them, teach them and protect them. And remind both our children that it is our duty and responsibility to spoil our grandchildren."

"Ours too!" Jenny called out.

"Hell yeah!" Allison agreed.

"We're in trouble," Hadrian laughed.

"Ha!" Nyla scoffed. "You boys have nothing on Elders."

"I have no idea what she's talking about," Samuel said nonchalantly.

"Not a clue," Davis agreed as their successors glared at them.

"Rome," Dawn counted off on her fingers. "Cairo. Hong Kong. London. Geneva. Rio. And they are not going to remember anything from their trips because my oldest is seven."

"Good point," Marcus said. "We should go again."

Both women growled at him. The high priestess counted something out on her fingers before smiling.

"You should bring Electra to my temple in Rome," The high priestess suggested. "I recommend early June. Maybe late May."

"Before you go anywhere, I'm getting a dance," Aiden said as he took Electra by the hand and led her to the empty dance floor. "I had to call to find out the name of the song about Mona Lisa."

Nat King Cole's *Mona Lisa Song* started to play. She smiled at him.

"I want you to know how happy Hadrian and the girls are with you," Aiden said as they did a slow waltz. "Except for when he was being an idiot. I'm glad he got his head out of his ass."

"Me too. They make me happy, too," she admitted. "Thank you for making my family feel welcome."

"That's the Alpha and Luna. They want the whole pack to feel like a big family."

"Jill is the crazy aunt no one talks about?"

Aiden threw his head back and laughed. "He and the Luna take turns with that title."

"Elders," The triplets called in unison. "It's time."

Chapter 59

THE MOON GODDESS

Crystal River Pack/Dream Realm

Hadrian walked over and gave his bride a light kiss. Smiling, he assured her, "I'll be here with our girls, go do what you need to do."

She gave him a nervous smile and quick kiss before she was guided into the temple. Nyla and Dawn helped Electra change out of her dress and into ceremonial gray robes. The ones that she currently wore had no embellishments or designations.

The ones that she would wear after her ascension, had small colorful squares lining the inside to remind her that she did not represent a single pack, but all packs. Her sleeves had embellishments on them indicating her wolf's lineage and position. There were other markings to remind her that all decisions had consequences.

Beads were stitched to create the spider Anasazi with intricate stitching creating a spiderweb. When she asked Marcus, he explained that they all had the storytelling spider and his web to remind them that their choices were connected like a web. And that just like walking into a spiderweb, decisions can cause chaos.

The Blessed Three led the way into the sacred clearing. The Elders followed with their successors on their arms. Teuf trailed them and shifted into his hell hound form just before he entered the clearing.

Marcus walked Electra to the center of the clearing. He had her kneel on a soft patch of grass and squatted down in front of her.

"After you speak with Selene, you will merge with the Gelert. It's going to hurt. You'll be here at the temple for the next few days. Are you ready for this?"

"Yes," Electra said confidently.

"Okay, the hound will be with you the whole time," Marcus stood up as Teuf huffed air over her head, letting her know he was there.

The high priestess took her place as the Blessed Three formed a loose circle around them. The Elders formed a larger circle around them.

"Do you still have your necklace?" the priestess asked, and Electra pulled it out of her robes and let it hang from her neck. "Concentrate on the crystal if the pain gets to be too much."

When she was in her position in the outer circle, the triplets began to hum. Soon the meadow was filled with the humming sound and a thick blue fog. Bare feet appeared in front of her and when Electra looked up, she found herself looking at the moon goddess.

"Hello, Electra," she said in a very familiar ethereal voice.

"H-hello."

Selene held her hand out and helped Electra to her feet, "Walk with me."

They walked into the fog and when they left it, Electra found that they were in a lush garden filled with moon flowers, evening primrose, chocolate daisies and other night blooming flowers. Nightingale birds sang in the branches of the trees as owls hooted cheerfully.

"You have questions for me," it was a statement and not a question because the moon goddess already knew that she had questions.

"Why me?"

"Ask what you really want to know."

"Why was I treated so badly?"

"I knew that when people found out that I was calling on the Gelert, they would be upset," Selene touched a plant, and a queen of the night bloomed. "I did not think that they would try to kill an innocent infant. But they did."

They reached the heart of the garden, and the goddess sat on the edge of the creek. She waved her hand over the water, and a small baby appeared.

"Your birth parents died protecting you. I took you to Mike because he knows the legends. He knows the history. I knew that he would teach you the ancient stories and he did. And Jenny loves you as her own."

"I delivered you myself. Placed you in Jenny's arms and told her the only thing I could."

"Gelert," Electra said, watching the scene play out in the water.

"You were to face trials as all Elder wolves must do. But they were taken away by the pack. You were to become the Luna. Your son was to become Alpha and father my next Blessed Three."

A scene of Electra, AJ and their son played on the water's surface. In this watery portal, AJ was a loving husband and doting father. This was a scene that had been planned but never came to fruition.

"That road has not yet been traveled," The goddess said, waving her hand over the water erasing the ideal scene.

"I cannot have pups," Electra said sitting next to her.

"And yet, a son grows in your belly."

She placed a hand over her stomach and looked at the goddess. "How?"

"The Gelert is old. She is the oldest of my children. She is also one of the strongest."

Selene looked at Electra and sighed, "It is the human side of you that says that I control everything. That all the deities sit around controlling all of your lives. We don't. We set you on a path. But once you are on earth, we have no control over you or your choices."

With another flick of her wrist, the water began to boil, every bubble that rose to the surface carried a prayer within it. The prayer was released when the bubble reached the surface and popped. "I don't care who wins the football game. Or if you steal the pack of gum. I could care less if your crush notices you. Or if you're straight, gay or somewhere in between. None of us do."

Larger bubbles began to surface with scenes that ex-
ploded across the water only to sink and rise again,
"We have children starving and when we provide the
knowledge or tools to help, they are cast aside as evil.
You have people fighting over whether a pup should be
born and once it's born, they turn their backs. We do not
control when you conceive. There is a lot that is left up to
biology."

Electra reached out and touched the goddess' hand. "I
don't blame you. Somehow, she has always been there
in my mind, quietly guiding me through everything. She
always told me that there would be something great at
the end of my trials. I had just assumed that she was a
figment of my imagination. Something that I created to
lean on when it all got too much to handle."

"No, child," Selene said with a calm voice. "That is the
Gelert. She has lived many times and will live many more
times. She has a good idea of how things will turn out,
if she can reach out to you before you merge, and you
don't give into her bloodlust, you are strong enough for
her."

"I almost did," Electra admitted as she pulled her hand
back. She glanced at the water and saw the scene where
she shifted to protect Marie. "My pup was in danger."

"Gelert was always a very protective mother. What did
you do to reign her in?"

"I told her no one should suffer like I did."

"That's it?" the goddess asked. "And she submitted?"

"She did," Electra touched the water, but did not feel it.
"There was this incredible sense of pain and sadness. It

was like she felt all her past pain and then I was in control but in wolf form. I've never experienced anything like that before."

"You are definitely strong enough, but do you want the responsibility?"

"I have thought about this a lot. I keep coming back to the same question," Electra admitted. "Can I help others to not suffer as I have? To prevent other omegas and wolf-less people from being abused?"

"And do you have an answer?"

Chapter 60

THE MERGE

Crystal River Pack/Dream Realm/Past

When Electra opened her eyes, she was right back where she had been. Kneeling in the center of the sacred clearing, the triplets and elders surrounded her.

"Concentrate on the crystal if the pain gets to be too much," The high priestess said before taking her position.

It was an odd sense of déjà vu as the triplets began to hum, and the clearing filled with a fog. This time, it was white and large wolf paws appeared in front of her. She looked up and found herself looking into her own eyes. Except it was a wolf that looked back at her. Reaching up, she touched the wolf's cheek.

"Gelert?" Electra whispered and the wolf's head inclined slightly. Electra leaned forward and pressed her forehead to the fur covered one.

Deep in Electra's mind, Selene softly whispered, "There is no way for me to lessen this pain, it must be endured."

The instant that their foreheads touched, there was a flash of light. She was standing in a white hallway with paintings on the wall. Voices were coming from down the hall that she walked towards.

She was a little girl and wore a simple white shift dress. A regal purple rope was tied at her waist, and she had no shoes on her feet. The tiles on her feet were cold as she neared the end of the hall.

Stopping just outside the doorway she listened to the two people arguing. Gelert told her that they were her parents.

"Remus are you telling me that she may be like that?" the woman yelled.

"Diana, I'm telling you that she is like me," the man replied calmly.

"No! I did not give birth to a freak!"

"Do not call her that!"

"And what would you call her?" the woman screamed.

"Call her Gelert. That is her name."

"I will not raise a ... a ... a dog!"

"Wolf," he corrected.

"That does not make it any better!"

"Then I will find her a mother that will love her."

"Where will you find a mother for that creature?"

"The gods will provide."

"And you will just set me aside?"

"You did that yourself."

Gelert was starting to take them away from there when Electra demanded more answers.

Wait! What about your new mother?

It was almost as though they changed directions. They sank down into a field and Electra could tell that they were a few years older.

"Gelert!" a woman called with a laugh.

She turned and saw a beautiful woman in her early twenties. Black hair was half contained in a loose braid down to her waist. A simple empire waist dress covered her very pregnant belly. Her olive skin glistened in the sunlight with perspiration. Her smile reached her eyes that sparkled.

"What mommy?"

"Come feel the baby kick!"

She ran over and the woman placed her little hand on the rounded belly. Electra felt the baby kick and her child eyes widened in wonder.

"Did I feel like that too?"

"I'm sure you did," The woman smiled. "And someday, you'll feel a baby move inside you. And you'll love that baby as much as I love you."

The light engulfed her, and they were whisked away to another memory, another life, another rejection. Again, Electra demanded to see something else. An acceptance, love, being cherished. With each life, Gelert showed her the horrible memories. With each life, Electra forced her to remember the good moments.

With each death that Gelert remembered, Electra wanted to see the life after. The good memories that Gelert had pushed away were brought to the front.

Then, there was a night in a castle. She sat in her human form, nursing her little boy. The door creaked open with a wolf in it.

I remember this...

Electra murmured as she watched the memory unfold and the Gelert gave a warning.

Wait until we get to your memories. It will be hard to keep yourself separated from your body.

They watched the memory as Gelert's head popped up in the back of the woman's mind as she smelled *him*. Carefully, she stood up and approached the bassinet.

"Who sent you?" the woman, Gelert, asked as she placed the child in his bed. The wolf growled but she understood what he said. He was sent by Actis, a jealous god who despised the special treatment that the werewolves received. "You will not get him," she warned him as she shifted.

They fought and Gelert won, ripping out his throat as she flung him against the wall. The tapestry fell and covered his body. Her injuries were healing as she limped over to check on the baby. In this form, she could not turn the bassinet upright and was about to shift when she heard her husband coming up the stairs.

He did not know that she was a Were. She had hidden it well. Her wolf form had been presented to him as a wedding gift. She could not shift yet, but once he was gone, she would shift back. She watched as he entered the room and saw the mess. Seeing it through his eyes, she regretted not shifting.

Llewelyn drew his sword and quickly cut off her head.

Sadness permeated both Electra and her wolf. The light started to come but Electra refused to move. She watched as Llewelyn heard the baby and found him carefully tucked away in the upturned bassinet. After picking up his son, he turned to see his beheaded wife on the floor. Taking a step towards her, his foot hit something solid under the fallen tapestry.

The king knelt and moved the tapestry. A wild wolf that had fought with Gelert lay dead with a gaping hole in his neck.

"What have I done?" the king cried out as he slumped over his wife.

Guards entered the room and were shocked to see such a mess.

"Sire?" one said.

"I thought that she had killed the baby. But she had defended him."

"Her clothes, sire?"

"The wolf must have ripped them off and she continued to fight him," he stood up and handed the crying baby to a maid that had joined them. "Take my son. I am going to bury my wife myself."

"Sire..."

He held up a hand and stopped the guard. "It was my hands that she died by. It will be by my hands that she finds rest and comfort."

You did not know?

Electra asked Gelert who shook her large wolf head no.

He loved you.

This time when the light came, they both willingly went into it. They continued through the lives that Gelert had lived. Electra continued to search for the good while Gelert focused on the bad. They continued for quite some time as the wolf controlled the narrative. But then, Electra wondered if she could also determine what they saw. Concentrating hard, she found what she was looking for.

Three women sat on the dais at the head of the council chambers. It was gray stone with high windows and large fireplaces on three walls. The women wore dresses around the seventeenth century; corsets, petticoats and more layers than any woman should wear. The men wore dress coats and high pants from the period.

The women on the dais wore black robes similar to the ones Electra had been fitted for. To their right sat a set of blessed three. To their left sat their male successors.

The crowd was quite upset with the declaration that the elders had just made. Some were objecting, others cheering it on. They were arguing, yelling and throwing accusations amongst themselves.

"Hound," The Senior Elder called, and a large Irish wolf hound stood and stretched before walking to sit in front of the dais. "Calm yourselves, or I will let her feast."

With a shake of her body, the dog shifted into a hell hound. It's red eyes glowing eerily in the smoke from her breath.

The crowd settled down and found their seats. Once it was quiet again, the hound shook her body again and returned to her regular form. With a nod from the Elders, she lay down at their feet.

"We will have no more slaves," the silver eyed Elder declared. "You have until the winter solstice to free your slaves."

"What will we do with them?"

"Are they not part of your pack?" all three elders demanded. "Are you not their Alpha? Do you not take care of your pack now?"

The blue eyed Elder stood up and Electra recognized her as the Gelert. "Your slaves will be set free, and they will receive the same rights as any other were. They will have the ability to leave and join a new pack. If families have been separated, they will need to be reunited if possible."

You did this?

Electra asked her wolf as she pulled the light herself. Gelert answered, turning the memories back to earlier in that life.

I did.

She was about nine years old and was being forced into a room with other slave children. They had all been stripped of their clothes and shackled together. A young woman came through with a rag and bucket of water. Cold soapy water was moved over their bodies before a man doused them with a bucket of cold water.

They were all shivering when the buyers were shown in. They were all Omega born slaves and knew better than to look up. Even when their faces were lifted so the men could look at their teeth.

In the end, the man that bought her and two other girls along with one of the older men. He gave them each a crimson-colored sheath dress and long cream-colored apron. They were then loaded into a small carriage and taken away.

Did you ever see your family again?

Electra asked quietly as they both called the light. Softly Gelert answered with sadness in her voice.

No. My mother was bred by a warrior to produce a strong slave. I was taken away from her when I was three so she could be bred again.

Now that they were working together, they were quickly bouncing between lives. They went back and forth in time. For every question that popped into Electra's mind, Gelert took them to a memory.

This doesn't hurt as bad as I thought it would.

Electra said and Gelert laughed.

You're not feeling your body right now. Do you know how long we've been going through my memories?

A few hours. I hate this one.

Electra said as the light dropped them in the memory of her rejection. The Gelert gave a small snicker at the time and then offered a few words that gave her human self small amount of comfort.

A few hours. We're nearly done.

It was the yule ball and Electra was working at the drink station tucked away at the back corner in the dark. It was her birthday, but she was wolf-less, no one cared. No one outside of her family.

Suddenly there was a commotion as AJ made his way across the floor. His father was right on his heels. He stopped, grabbing the counter.

"You!" AJ screamed as he realized who he had been tracking. "I will not be mated to someone like you! I, Anthony Thomas Diamante Junior, reject your worthless ass, Electra Diane Naples, as my mate and future mother of my pups."

As pain ripped through Electra, AJ turned and walked away. The Alpha scoffed at her and her pain.

"Get her out of here. I don't want that filth near my guests."

Two security guards grabbed her by her arms and drug her out of the ballroom. One pushed open the door and they roughly tossed her out into the alley. Electra tried to catch herself against the wall but heard the pop of her wrist. As she fell to the ground, her ankle twisted.

Wolf-less.

Rejected.

Injured.

She did not think that the night could get any worse. Looking back, she now knew it could.

Do we have to go through this?

Electra asked, suddenly feeling all the pain from the merge.

Yes, we must. Trust us. And remember, you survived.

The younger Electra tried to stand. Placing her weight on her ankle made her cry out in pain as she fell back to the ground. Tears streamed down her face as she sat on the ground, leaning against the brick wall. She was uncertain of how long she sat there, but the stars were bright on the moonless night.

Hold fast, little one. I have great plans for you.

Electra remembered the ethereal voice telling her that just before *it* happened. The angry voice had been quiet and the presence that she had always felt was not there. It was as if part of her was missing. Dormant.

Figures appeared at the end of the alley. She was helpless when the males surrounded her. Injured, she could not run away as they grabbed her. She could not fight them as they ripped her clothes off her. She could not cry out for help as they bound and gagged her.

"You're supposed to be my mate," AJ snarled in his Alpha voice as he forced her legs apart. "As long as I am Alpha, you are not allowed to speak to me or against me. And you will always submit to me and my demands."

He thrust into her, ripping her virginity from her. He pounded into her until he found his release. When he was done, he tossed her towards the other men.

"Go ahead. Enjoy her. I'll have her fixed in the morning so we can have a plaything."

The sun was coming up when Electra was finally left alone. She was battered and bruised. Her uniform was torn to shreds and used to hold her in place over a box. Her arms were stretched out and tied to the dumpster while her legs were tied to the box, holding them apart.

Here the pack priest found her just as he had been told he would. His servants untied her and wrapped her in a rough blue blanket. No more tears came as they flung her over one of their shoulders. All her tears had already been exhausted. She barely even felt anything as the men at the temple took their turn with her.

Even when the priest mounted her, she could shed no tears. Feel no emotion. When they were done, they gave her some medicine.

It was later that day that she finally felt something. She woke up to find her father sitting beside her hospital bed. Tears filled his eyes as he smiled at her with love.

"I'm sorry, little girl. We had no choice. Either we let them take your womb, or they would kill us. The younger ones would become slaves. He said that he would take Athena as a concubine."

She reached out and touched his hand. He did not recoil. Instead, he clutched her hand in both of his and kissed it.

"I'll be okay," Electra whispered. There was no way that she would allow her eight-year-old sister to become a concubine. "Tell me a story. My favorite story."

Mike smiled at her and started telling her the story about King Llewellyn and Gelert.

Chapter 61

PAIN

Crystal River Pack

The temple omegas had moved Electra's body into a small room in the temple. If Hadrian had to leave, then Marcus, the high priestess or one of the blessed three were to always be with her. Once she had been made comfortable, an omega had brought Hadrian in.

He found her in an empty room with only a small window high in the outside wall allowing sunlight to filter in, the bare walls were painted a plain white with no trim or molding. Even the floor was plain with large white tiles and matching grout.

Electra lay on a large thick palette on the floor with a white sheet lightly draped over her. Her eyes twitched and moved as if she were watching a million things at once. On occasion a hand or foot would twitch.

"She's fine," the high priestess whispered to Hadrian. "Sit with her, let her know that you're here."

"Will she hear me?"

"Yes, and no," Marcus said softly from behind him. "She will hear you and draw strength from you. But it will not really penetrate her mind right now. Towards the end, she will reach out for you, she will need you."

Hadrian sat down next to her and took her hand in his. Then he leaned over and kissed her forehead. "I love you. I'm here."

As the sun came up, Allison and Jenny came in and sat with Electra. Hadrian grabbed a shower at the temple and then sat down in a small dining room to eat with his girls. They asked a lot of questions that he did not know how to answer.

Imogen had entered during one of the more difficult questions. She smiled understandingly at him and suggested that they hang out with her that day. With that solved, he went back to his mate.

Mike came by to check on her. He told Hadrian stories about Electra's childhood. She was outgoing and caring, always wanting to help with the pups. Didn't even mind the dirty diapers.

Mike took the girls home for dinner and Marcus brought a meal for them to share. Marcus helped sit Electra up and Hadrian put a glass of juice to her lips. Rubbing her neck, he encouraged her to swallow.

"You're a good healer," Marcus told him as Hadrian tipped the glass again.

"I'm not a healer," Hadrian replied, wiping his mate's mouth. "I've just trained as a paramedic."

"And what is a paramedic if not a type of healer?" the older man asked as they lay her back down. "Healers have been called many things through the years. Doctors. Nurses. Witches. Paramedic. Corpsman. Isn't that what your Alpha was in the military?"

"Yes. In the navy," he was stroking her colorful hair away from her forehead. "What is she going through?"

"The past lives of her wolf," Marcus smiled. "The reason we are called elder is because our wolves are some of the oldest. Her wolf was the first born of Remus. Before his brother killed him. She has a younger brother, Ithacaus. He, currently, is merged with Davis."

Marcus sat back with his tea. "Samuel is host to Xiao Wei. At one point, Xiao Wei served with Genghis Khan. Dawn is the host of Maleio. Don't ever ask her about being a Wayfinder. Think Moana with a thousand years of stories to tell. Nyla is host to Abagunda. Shaka Zulu wishes he had the army that Abagunda commanded."

They sat in silence for a few minutes; both lost in their own thoughts. One worried about his mate. The other hopeful for the impending changes.

Marcus smirked, before whispering, "The goddess is getting ready to make some big changes."

"How do you know?"

"The next Elders are all women warriors hosted by nurturers mated to healers. They were all omega raised, all abused, and all remained sweet and kind."

His own wolf spoke to him, and he nodded in agreement.

"The last time she did it like this, they abolished slavery," Marcus looked at the young woman as she twitched under the sheet. "Can't wait to see what they do."

Hadrian placed a hand on her cheek, and she calmed down. "Who do you host?"

"Thorson," the Elder said and Teuf lifted his head from where he lay at the foot of the palette. "Yes, Garm, I am speaking of our old days."

Teuf shifted and laid his body along Electra's legs.

"We have lived many lifetimes together. He is not bonded to her, but the moon goddess told him to protect her during this, and he will," he stroked the shepherd's fur.

Electra spoke softly in a strange language. Hadrian lifted her hand to his lips.

"I'm here," he whispered softly.

"She still has quite a way to go. Get some rest with her," Marcus said as he gathered the remnants of their meal.

Hadrian lay down next to her and inhaled her scent. It calmed him and excited him at the same time. Her scent was slowly changing as she merged with her wolf, just as she changed.

She was stronger. Her muscles are firmer. More determined. More confident. Her uncertainty was fading to the back.

When he woke up the next morning, the high priestess was tending to Electra. The woman was careful about checking on her while keeping her hands just off Electra's body. Hadrian sat up, worried.

"She's doing really well," the high priestess smiled at him. "I don't think that we have actually met. I'm Hari, Harriet, but I prefer Hari."

"Hadrian," he replied and offered a hand before pulling it back. "Sorry, I forgot."

"It's a lot to remember. Only you and Marcus are allowed to touch her. You cannot touch anyone else. Restrictions on your diet and clothing. It's why we have mates stay with the Elders at the temple," she sat back on her heels and looked at him. "How are you handling all of this?"

"Better than I thought I would. A bit of a headache," he touched his temple.

"Already?" her smile brightened. "She is doing very well. She is elevating to Alpha and taking you with her. She should start the final phase tonight. We'll need to bring the pups back to the temple."

"Will they also become Alpha?"

She looked at him confused, "Do you not know what your daughters are?"

"I was told that Emily could commune and would need to train with the oracle."

"Yes. She will very likely be the next oracle for the pack. Has no one said anything about Marie?"

"No. She's my little bookworm and tomboy."

"We'll talk more after all of this. There is a reason why your ex suddenly wants her daughters."

Seeing his eyes darken with anger, she made a motion with her hands causing him to relax.

"It's nothing bad, I promise you that. In fact, it is very good. And the girls are now bonded to an Elder. The council will not sever that bond."

"Both my girls are safe?"

"Very much so," with that, Hari stood up and left the room.

A few hours later, Imogen brought in more juice and a meal for Hadrian. Marcus came to help him give Electra some more of the drink. When he asked the older man about the girls, his eyes sparkled, and he simply said it was not the time.

After Marcus left, Hadrian gave Electra a sponge bath with the warm water and herbs that the omega brought in. Once she was clean and dry, he used the lotion provided to cover her skin. When he was done, Teuf returned to his post at her feet.

Around dinner time, Emmeline and Hari brought the girls in. They sat on the floor next to the wall as the two priestesses checked on Electra. When they agreed that she was in control, they motioned for the girls to join them.

"Will it be like this for us?" Marie asked quietly.

"No, dear," Hari said with a smile. "Elders are different. With most werewolves, it is like sharing your body with a wolf. They can have completely different personalities. But Elders merge with their wolves. They share memories and knowledge. Their decisions are made from extensive personal experience and collective knowledge. That's how they guide us."

The older woman was patient with all their questions. And being young girls, they had a lot of questions.

"How do you know if you are an Elder?" Marie asked.

"There are marks," Hari lifted her shirt on her left side and showed them her crowned moon birth mark on her abdomen. "The crown indicates that I am the high priestess. The blessed three have their marks in the same place. The Elder mark is the thin line around the iris."

"Hadrian..." Electra murmured.

"I'm here," he told her as she cried out for him. "What do I do?"

"Hold the crystal in her hand with yours," Hari said, ushering the two girls onto the blanket. "Let her know that you're here. Girls, hold her hand over here, and no matter what, do not break contact with her."

Chapter 62

MORNING

Crystal River Pack

E lectra slowly opened her eyes and looked around the room. It took a moment to remember that she was still at the temple. Her eyes were drawn to movement as Teuf stood up and stretched. He met her eyes, and she heard him in her head telling her that he would be back.

The dog sauntered out of the half-opened door in search of something to eat.

Electra moved her head slowly to look at her mate. He was still asleep and looked peaceful. Slowly looking at her pups on the other side of her, she could not help but smile.

They are perfect.

They are.

"You're awake," Hadrian whispered as he sat up. "How do you feel? Marcus said it was like you got hit by a truck."

"More like a convoy," she admitted quietly with a grin.

He leaned down and kissed her lips lightly, "I love you, mate."

"Mmm," she smiled up at him. "I like the sound of that. I love you, too, mate."

"I like the sound of that," he kissed her again and they heard little giggles.

"Come here, girls," Electra said softly.

Hadrian stood up as Marie moved to lay her head on Electra's shoulder. He picked up Emily and sat her on the other side and she mirrored her sister.

"I'll be right back," he said softly before leaving the room.

"Do you have a wolf now?" Emily asked, looking at her new mom.

"I do," she smiled at the cherub face looking at her.

"Is she nice?" Marie asked and Electra worried over why she would ask that.

"Not exactly," Electra answered and Gelert scoffed in their mind. "But she's already in love with both of you."

I'm nice.

You ripped a man's throat out. Not exactly nice.

"Will she hurt us?" Marie whispered.

I can compel her to talk.

Not now.

Smiling at the two girls, Electra silenced the wolf. "No, sweetheart. We will never hurt you. Either of you."

Emily relaxed as she laid her head back on Electra's shoulder, "I love you, mommy."

"I love you, too," she kissed both of their heads as Hadrian and the high priestess came back in.

"I would ask how you feel, but I won't," Hari smiled. "The good news is, you're nearly done."

"There's more?" Electra asked in shock.

"You just need to shift," Emmeline smiled as she and her sisters entered. "You'll feel better afterwards."

"But..." Electra started as Gelert chuckled in her head.

We're Elder. We can shift during the first part of our pregnancy.

"Oh," she blushed as the other two women looked at her funny. "It's okay. I guess I answered my own question."

"All right, girls, why don't you go help in the kitchen," Hari suggested. "Your grandparents will be there shortly."

Imogen stepped out into the hall and walked with the two girls down to the temple kitchen. Marcus stood in the doorway with Nyla and Dawn behind him.

"Are we ready?" Marcus asked with a smile.

"No," Electra said softly.

"We're here, sister," Nyla said. squeezing around the Elder.

"I'm right here," Hadrian said as he sat down next to her.

I want to run!

Gelert screamed inside her head.

"Okay," Electra said as she tried to sit up. "Oh, shit."

"Let us help," Dawn said as she and Nyla helped her to sit up before moving to her hands and knees. "The good news is that you will feel so much better soon."

"What's the bad news?" Electra gritted out.

"It's going to suck really fucking bad until then," Nyla warned.

She's not wrong.

"Focus on me," Hadrian said, moving in front of her.

Nodding she focused on his soft brown eyes and then let out a deep breath. Listening to what Gelert was telling her, she relaxed and felt a surge of heat flow through her body. Her muscles and joints relaxed and then they snapped and popped as her body shifted.

Her head felt like it was being cracked open like an egg as it changed shape. Her fingers became claws as her feet also shifted. Her back arched up and her spine extended into a tail. Shaking her body a beautiful mocha colored coat of fur rippled with golden caramel highlights.

She took a deep breath through her nose and was assaulted with scents. Shaking her head to clear it, she took a hesitant step backwards.

Then Gelert was in control, and she yipped happily at Hadrian. Smiling, he looked over at Harl who nodded at him. Quickly stripping out of his clothes, he shifted, and they bolted out of the door and down the hall. Once they made it outside, they disappeared into the trees.

Hadrian chased his mate through the woods until she reached the river. They splashed into the water, frolicking like young pups. He rubbed his cheek against hers and licked her nose before they returned to the temple.

Chapter 63

LUNCH AT THE FIREHOUSE

Crystal River Pack

The house fire had been brutal and the whole crew was exhausted. As the rigs pulled into the bay, no one noticed the Durango in the parking lot. Silently, they put their SCBA gear away and dropped their bunker coats and pants into the laundry room as they made their way into the station house.

The house had been a total loss with damage to three surrounding houses. Four families out of their homes. At least two would have to be completely rebuilt. All because someone, literally, let their kid play with matches.

The nine-year-old, his four-year-old sister and the seven-year-old neighbor were all in the hospital with smoke inhalation and minor burns. The mom had some bad burns, but she would heal in a few hours. The dad was passed out drunk in the backyard, quite a feat for a werewolf.

When he had come to, seeing the flames shooting out of his house, he had slapped his wife. The cops had to get involved. Then the Alpha and Luna were called. Once the patients had been transferred to the hospital, the ambulance crew returned to the fire scene.

By the time that they had returned, the other two Crystal Pass stations and two additional trucks from Crystal Springs were on the scene. The neighbors all wanted a piece of the dad, and no one really blamed them. The Alpha sent him to sleep it off in the drunk tank and would only intervene if needed.

That was why Wyatt was such a well loved and respected Alpha. He knew what was going on. He always showed up at major scenes. He took a personal interest in his pack members.

But he trusted the members of his pack to do their jobs. The police and patrol units kept crime down and the streets secure. Hadrian and his fellow fire fighters kept the pack safe. The court system kept everyone in line. The hospital and healers kept everyone healthy.

The Crystal River pack was lucky. And Hadrian knew it. He had heard the stories about Dark Sky and similar packs. Had even seen the way other packs treated their omegas when he had gone to hunts. The pack was lucky. He was lucky. And Electra was damned lucky.

He was thinking about how lucky it had been that the Luna had found her as he went through the door. She was in his thoughts so much that he was certain that he could smell her.

"Elder?" Johnson said from the day room.

"Electra is fine," Electra corrected, and Hadrian could hear her smile. He turned towards the day room with the rest of the crew and saw her in the kitchen. "It will be a few minutes until lunch is ready, if you want to get showers."

"What did the doctor say?" Hadrian asked as he walked over to her.

Electra leaned over and kissed him quickly on the lips. "Go get a shower, and I'll tell you over lunch," she said as she turned back to the stew on the stove.

Grumbling, he followed the others down to the shower room. About fifteen minutes later they started reappearing and found the stew, cornbread and biscuits.

"Elder, this smells wonderful," Parker said as she sat down.

"Please, it's just Electra," she smiled as she sat more bowls on the table. "Stevens, you're vegetarian, right?"

"Yes, Elder," he said as he sat down.

"Please, do not make me compel you to not call me Elder," Electra pleaded. "With my luck, you'll end up clucking like a chicken."

"Yes, Eld-ectra," Captain McMurray said catching himself.

"I'll take it," she laughed as Hadrian pulled her into his lap.

"Where are our girls?" he asked, nuzzling her neck.

"On their way over," she smiled as the door opened, and her parents and siblings walked in. Marcus walked in behind them and went straight to her. "Yes."

Marcus kissed her temple and took a deep breath of her scent.

"So, what's going on?" Mike asked as Marcus helped himself to a bowl of stew.

"Just waiting on my parents," Hadrian told them. "I'm assuming that's who they're with?"

"No, they're with the Alphas," she said as the oven beeped. "Those should be the cookies."

"Cookies?" Celeste asked as she entered the room carrying her son with Wyatt following with Hadrian's girls in his arms. Electra laughed as she pulled two racks of cookies out of both ovens. "Are those your cherry cookies?"

"Chocolate pumpkin spice," Electra said, sitting back down in Hadrian's lap as his brother and his family arrived. "Just your parents now."

"Aren't they both working today?" Gerard asked. "And why aren't the girls in school?"

Electra blushed. "It seems that when you call and say that you're an Elder, you can get whatever you want. I promise, I'm not going to abuse-."

"Abuse it," Marcus interrupted. "Abuse your authority any time you need to make an announcement. Or you want to cook for me."

"She is a very good cook," Aiden said, taking the happy baby from Celeste. "What's up little man?"

"Okay, what the hell is going on? And thank you for getting me out of that training meeting," Allison said after coming through the door.

Electra looked at her mate who grinned like an excited schoolboy.

"I'm pregnant," she finally said.

There were several congratulations offered, and Aiden and Alison whooped in excitement. Electra's family looked confused.

"But...," Mike asked. "The surgery? Didn't they...?"

"The Dark Sky pack took my uterus," she confirmed. "My wolf..."

"Her wolf repaired the damage done," Marcus explained. "When she was around her second chance mate, the healing process sped up. But once they claimed each other, it was amplified. Do you know how far you are?"

"The high priestess and Adeline say about a month," she smiled. "I had my first doctor appointment this morning."

"You don't have the scent of pregnancy," Helena pointed out.

"Only for my mate and other Elders," Electra said, feeling Hadrian's hand move protectively over her belly.

"Elder wolves are very protective of themselves and their lineage," Marcus said. "Which is why they don't have a wolf scent until they are accepted by their mate. But there's another reason for the impromptu meeting?"

"I'm going to step back and just be a volunteer," Hadrian said. "The council is providing us with housing and a monthly stipend. And as an Elders' mate, I will accompany her wherever she goes. So will the pups."

"What about school?" Gerard pressed.

"They will continue school as usual, but they will also have tutors," Hadrian took a deep breath and slowly let it out. "It has been confirmed that Emily will be an oracle. She will start her training after her next birthday because she is already exhibiting skills."

Marcus placed his hands on Hadrian and Electra's shoulders, pushing calmness into them. "Marie will need to go to the high temple before she shifts. Aiden, your mother and grandmother were healers?" Aiden nodded at his question and wondered if his granddaughter would also be a healer.

"Am I a healer?" Marie asked quietly, voicing the question all the adults were wondering.

"Yes. And the high priestess believes that you may be a divine healer," Marcus replied.

"What's that?" Marie asked.

"It's like the high priestess," Wyatt explained, "but for healers."

Chapter 64

HALLOWEEN

Crystal River Pack

H adrian rubbed his forehead in utter frustration. In fifteen minutes, they were supposed to be at the park for trunks and treats. Marie sat on the couch in her elaborate witch costume. She, Dee and Taylor were the Sanders sisters from *Hocus Pocus*. Electra and Hadrian were going as Hercules and Meg.

Emily was going as Anna. Or Moana. Or Lilo. Or Cinderella. Or Marida. Or Sleeping Beauty. Or Jasmine. Or Snow White. Or Rapunzel. Or Ariel. Or Belle. Or Tiana. Or Nala. Or Elsa. Or Mulan. Or Esmerelda. Or Pocahontas.

Just how many Disney princesses were there? And how did his wife sew that many dresses in such a short period of time?

Finally, Meg and Tiana, with a stuffed frog on her wrist, came down the stairs. They loaded up into the Durango and headed to the park where Marie ran off with Dee and Taylor and Emily took her bag to collect as much candy as she could.

"What do we do now?" Electra asked as Hadrian opened the back of the car.

He turned on the battery-operated twinkle lights and emptied several bags of candy into a large bowl. "Leave the candy and go visit."

"Visit with who?" she asked as he took her hand and began to lead her across the parking lot.

"Whoever. You, my lovely Greek goddess, are an Elder Successor and everyone will want to visit."

Just as he finished speaking, a woman approached them. "Elder," she bowed her head and offered Electra a carved turnip.

"Thank you," Electra said, accepting the gift. The woman bowed slightly and then scurried away.

"Turnip carving predates the pumpkin. The pumpkin is more of an American thing."

"I did not know that. I just thought we did turnips because we were werewolves," he admitted as a woman gave them each a soul cake. "Just another part of our pagan heritage."

"Wiccan," Electra said softly. "Halloween is based on the Wiccan holiday Samhain. Our lineage predates that branch of religion."

A man wished them a happy Halloween and gave them each a large goodie bag. Thanking him, Electra placed her turnip in the bag before opening the soul cake.

"These are some of the better ones I've had," Hadrian said of the quartered cookie style flaky cake.

"Tastes like she used a pie crust recipe," Electra said, accepting another gift with a warm smile and thanks. "This is the origin of trick or treating. You would give a soul cake, and the recipient would pray for your dead relatives."

"What was the earliest memory you have of Gelert?"

"Rome. My father chose me over his wife because she could not accept what we were."

That's what you got out of our memory?

Gelert asked in Electra's mind and she gave her wolf a small chuckle.

"Do you remember the last time you lived?"

"I was born a slave," she smiled up at him. "We ended the practice. All three of us that were Elders at that time were all born slaves."

"Do you know why the goddess has called on you this time?"

"No. She doesn't tell us. It's not like oh, hey, it's Tuesday, let's end slavery."

Hadrian chuckled. "But Tuesday is a good day to end slavery."

"If I remember, it was actually on a Thursday."

"Still a good day," he leaned down and kissed her lightly.

"None of that," Allison teased as she approached the couple, "there's kids here."

"So, no dancing naked under the moonlight?" Hadrian asked his mom.

"Only in the privacy of your own backyard," she hugged him and then Electra. "You two look great. I saw the Sanders sisters, who also looked amazing. What princess did Emily finally settle on?"

"Tiana," Electra laughed. "She wanted to bring all of her dresses and change throughout the night."

Allison laughed. "Like her wardrobe changes during her party?"

Hadrian shook his head in dismay. "I'm dreading the teen years."

"Did you bring the jeep or just the Durango?" Aiden asked as he joined them, placing an arm around his wife.

"Just the Durango," Hadrian confirmed.

"I'll take you and the girls home," he said as the group came around the corner and they saw the Durango completely surrounded by offerings.

"Is this normal?" Electra asked.

"Yes," Imogen said as she walked across the lot from her car. "Just wait until it's the winter solstice. Especially with it being your birthday."

"I'm never going to get used to this," Electra said as tears filled her eyes. "Even in the past, Gelert was never really welcomed."

"Times change," Imogen smiled. "And the new generation is much more open to change. They are making their own changes."

"The Hunt," Hadrian said.

"Yes," Imogen agreed. "We have our suspicions about what the goddess is wanting to do. But she always looks at the long game. We mortals never look past our own lives."

Chapter 65

CRESCENT CITY

Crescent City Pack

Electra and her family arrived in New Orleans a few days before the fall Council Meeting and did the typical tourist things. Jackson Square, Bourbon Street, Riverboat cruise, Aquarium, Charles Street Trolley. And just for Marie, a cemetery tour with a stop by the grave of Marie Leveau.

Despite what she was now telling everyone, no, she was not named for Marie Leveau. No matter how much she wanted it to be true.

The last werewolf touristy thing they did was to go tour the packhouse. The pack's territory included the majority of southern Louisiana from the Mississippi River down to Grand Isle and just east of Baton Rouge.

Crescent City had their packhouse just outside of Slidell on an old plantation. The house was grand with large columns and a wraparound porch and balcony. The large ballroom was set up for the Alpha dinner the following night.

After a tour of the house, Elder Marcus walked them over to the council chambers which were housed in a round building that was sunk into the ground with stadium seating leading down to the floor. On the floor sat a raised dais with three ornate throne style chairs with a smaller one to the right of each. They had elaborate carvings indicating the position of each Elder.

Gelert looked at the center throne and memories of the last time that she sat in it flooded through her and Electra's shared mind. Memories of that life also filled them. The hunger, loneliness and desperation. When the Elders came to collect her, she remembered thinking that she had been sold, yet again. The memories were so realistic that Electra's body became heavy with the silver and Wolf's Bane that the slaves were given each day.

"That is not this life," Electra whispered softly, and the weight dissipated.

It was not much different.

Gelert pointed out and Electra turned their body around, placing the throne behind her.

Across from the Elder's dais was a lower one with smaller, but equally ornate, thrones. The Alpha and Luna were the largest. Beta and gamma sat to the right and the priestess, oracle and healer to the left. The higher-ranking Alphas and their assistants would sit closer to the bottom. The higher the seat, the lower the ranking. The upper landing was open for spectators.

"Do they all look like this?" Emily asked quietly where she and her sister sat on the cushioned bench of the front row. Her young voice echoed beautifully through the room.

"No," Marcus smiled. "This is an older chamber. At least by American standards. There are some in Europe and Asia that date back millennia."

"I've been here," Electra whispered as more of Gelert's memories continued to flood through her. "It had just been finished. We took up the question of slaves here."

"You did. It was one of the first issues that you three considered," Marcus confirmed. "Tomorrow, you will not come out with us. You will be presented to the council along with your family, when Davis calls for you. Let me show you the room that you will wait in."

Following him down the lower hallway, Electra asked, "Why am I not being presented at the beginning?"

"Because I want Dark Sky to bury themselves before being confronted with the Elder that they abused and enslaved. The same Elder that outlawed slavery," Davis said, meeting them in the hallway. "I've been told that I have a mean streak in me."

He opened the door and motioned for them to enter a room that was lavishly decorated with several custom couches and a fully stocked bar along one wall. The woodwork was detailed with 3D ivy vines made from mahogany climbing the casings. Flat screen TVs hung on three walls and currently played a slideshow of the Crescent City Pack.

"You'll be able to watch all the events live. In the next room is where the girls can stay with their tutor," Marcus explained.

"We haven't gotten one yet," Electra admitted.

"They have their class work and we've been keeping up with it that way," Hadrian added. "We were planning on interviewing over winter break."

Both Elders nodded. "It's new territory," Marcus smiled, and Davis added; "You've never had to deal with this before. Talk with your sister Elders, they struggled also."

Hadrian and Electra nodded, admitting they were out of their depth. That night, they met Dawn and Nyla and their families at a restaurant on the river. The other two successors commiserated with Electra.

"As if being a mother isn't hard enough," Nyla laughed. "Here, have some additional responsibilities."

"And, oh, by the way, the entire werewolf world will scrutinize everything you do," Dawn added.

Chapter 66

TRIAL
Crescent City Pack

The council chambers were full as Alphas and their entourages mingled. The wives were mainly in the spectators' seats. But several Alphas were now including them in their staff. The wife of the Beta to a neighboring pack to Crystal River handed a bag to Celeste.

"Beignets from Café du Monde. I hear you have a sweet tooth."

Greedily Celeste accepted the bag, "You are my new best friend."

"Until her actual best friend gets here, or someone else gives her sweets," Wyatt teased as he brushed powdered sugar off his wife's face and growing belly. "Or she runs out."

"You did this to me," Celeste said around a mouthful of pastry.

"And I'm sure we both enjoyed it," he shot back, and the Beta laughed as she went to find her seat.

The hierarchy of the Crescent City Pack entered the room and mounted the smaller dais. They stood in front of their chairs and the Alpha stepped up to the microphone. The crowd found their way to their assigned seats and the large room, filled with approximately two thousand werewolves, fell silent.

"Alphas. Lunas. Betas, and distinguished guests. I am Alexander du Monte, and this is my lovely Luna, Cherry. My Beta, Joseph Betancourt, and his mate, Lucille. My Gamma, Tabitha Ming and her mate, Daniel. I am also joined by my healer, Diamond, oracle, Cheyenne and priestess, Ophelia. Welcome to the Crescent City Pack."

There was a thunderous applause punctuated by howls and yips. Alexander raised his hands to silence the crowd.

"I remember watching my dad do this when I was just a pup and thought that if I ever got to do this, there was something that I had to do," he took a deep breath and winked at his mate who was hiding behind her hands and shaking her head. "LET'S GET READY TO RUMBLE!"

There was another round of applause and laughter. In the crowd were several Alphas and Betas who grinned at each other. Some even admitted that they too had thought about doing the same thing.

"I'm not going to lie. That was awesome," he admitted into the microphone. "So awesome that I will willingly sleep on the couch for the next two weeks while my mate plots my demise."

"You think I don't already have a plan?" Cherry demanded and Alexander blew her a kiss.

"Ladies and gentlemen," he said in a much more professional tone, "please stand for the Elder Alphas."

The three elders walked out onto the dais. Samuel and Davis each had their successors on their arms. Like the others in the room, the three men wore suits with the Council Crest on the breast and ties indicating their host packs. Similarly, the two women wore tailored skirt suits with the same triple wolf crest on the jacket.

After they settled in their own seats, Davis nodded at the Alpha across from him. With a nod of acknowledgement, Alexander moved to stand before his own chair, "I now declare the session open."

Davis switched on his microphone attached to his collar. "Please be seated," there was a hushed silence as the entire room took their seats. "I fear that we are doomed to repeat history. In 1653, during the first council meeting held in this chamber, the Elders took up the issue of slavery. For two years they heard from packs around the world. Today, we are confronted with accusations of a pack violating our laws and keeping slaves."

There were murmurs as the crowd whispered amongst themselves.

"Dark Sky pack," the five elders called out in unison, "we call you to the floor."

Alpha Anthony, Beta Salvador and AJ made their way to the floor. All three wore black suits with the Dark Sky crest on the breast pocket.

'Don't worry, I control her,' AJ told his father and Beta through the mind link.

'You better,' His father replied.

They took their places on the floor, looking at the dress shoes of the Elders.

"Do you have slaves in your pack?" Dawn asked.

The three men stood silent.

"She is an Elder Wolf. You will answer her," Davis warned. "Either willingly, or under compulsion."

"We have servants, sir, but we do not have slaves," the Alpha replied.

"It was not I that asked the question. Disrespect the Successors again and you will suffer the consequences," Davis bared his teeth, and his claws tapped out a rhythm on the arm of the chair.

"These servants, as you insist that they are, they receive the same treatment and benefits as any other pack member?" Nyla asked.

"They do."

"And they may leave the pack? Attend council functions? Attend Solstice Hunts in order to meet their mates?" Dawn pressed.

"They may. But many choose not to."

"Do they choose not to?" Dawn leaned forward, extending her own fangs. "Or are they unaware that they have this option?"

"Choose your words wisely," Nyla warned. "We have a very convincing witness that will speak the truth."

"If you're talking about that wolf-less bitch," AJ said, "that whore would spread her legs for anyone."

"No. I have not spoken with a wolf-less bitch. Sister?" Nyla looked at the other Successor.

"Nor I," Dawn grinned. "Do tell us about this whore. Where is she? Will you bring her to defend yourself?"

"She left our pack," the Alpha replied.

"Are there others?" Dawn asked. "Surely this one woman was not your only slave."

"No, she's not," AJ sneered.

"She's not the only slave?" Dawn clarified with a hungry smile.

"What my son means is that she's not a slave," Anthony gave his son a warning look. *'Watch yourself,'* he warned through the mind link.

"Not anymore, you mean?" Nyla asked with a grin. "If your omegas are free to come and go as other pack members, why have there been none attending the hunts?"

"They choose to remain in the pack and seek a mate at home," Anthony answered.

"Danielle," Dawn called out to Anthony's oldest daughter. "Join your father and brother," There were quiet murmurs as she walked down the steps to the floor from the spectators' seats. As she passed by a Japanese delegation, the youngest son of the Dragon Moon Alpha gently squeezed her hand. She smiled down at her fated mate without stopping.

"Do you agree with what they are saying?" Nyla asked before issuing a warning. "Lying to the council or an Elder wolf can result in your death."

"No, Elder, I do not. There are slaves in the pack. Omegas do not go because they are told who they will be mated to," Danielle answered. "If a match is deemed unsuitable, it is denied, as mine was. The woman that they speak of was sterilized to ensure the purity of the pack."

"Her family consented," AJ shouted at his sister.

"After you threatened to make her sister your concubine," Danielle spat back at him.

"Concubines are not illegal, girl," their father reminded her.

"They are when the child is eight!"

There was a collective gasp at her declaration. Without thinking, Anthony slapped her so hard across the face that she stumbled.

"Yuto," Davis ordered as all five on the dais stood, fangs and claws extended, "see to your mate." Before the sentence was even finished, the Japanese man was moving towards the woman. "Have the Alpha and his son bound."

Guards moved quickly to bind the two men. They were forced onto their knees, and silver collars fastened around their necks. Heavy chains were anchored from the floor to the collars and handcuffs.

"Beta, you may join your leaders, or stand on your own," Samuel offered. "They are already looking at the death penalty."

"Elder, my granddaughter is an omega, and I fear for her safety," he answered honestly. Lowering his head to bare his neck in submission, he held his hands out to the sides showing his empty palms to prove he was no threat, "Ask of me what you will."

The five Elders sat back in their chairs and Davis motioned for the Successors to continue their interrogation.

"How many slaves are in your pack?" Nyla asked.

"About a hundred."

"I'll kill you," Anthony warned.

"Silence!" all five of the Elders commanded.

"I believe it is time for Marcus to make an announcement," Davis said, motioning for the Beta and the couple to return to their seats. "Danielle, please take your father's place. Yuto, accompany your mate."

Marcus stood and the door under the seats leading into the hall opened. "Recently, my Successor was found and merged with her wolf. She is the oldest of the next generation of Elders and she will become the Senior Elder. Her wolf," Marcus smiled at the two bound men as they caught sight of Electra, "is the Gelert. Ladies and gentlemen, Elder Successor Electra."

Chapter 67

ELDER ELECTRA
Crescent City Pack

The screens showed the Elders, the host pack and the floor. When AJ and his father stepped out onto the floor, Gelert became agitated. Electra began to pace the floor as his voice flowed from the speakers. Gelert growled loud enough for their mate to hear it, and Blaze whimpered.

Hadrian stood up from the wooden couch with dark purple cushions and approached his mate. He wore a fitted suit that matched her dress. Where the Crystal River crest used to be was now an emblem designating his mate's position. As was the custom, he wore the tie for their host pack with the Crystal River pale blue and tiny crimson red diamonds.

Stopping Electra in the middle of her pacing he linked their fingers together. Lifting her hands to his lips, he kissed each of her knuckles. His gentle touch soothed the beast inside her. The loving gesture calmed the woman.

"This is not my Electra," Hadrian whispered. "My Electra would not be worried about some two-bit asshole. She faced down rogues when she thought she was wolf-less."

Smiling, she looked up at him, "Thank you."

"You're welcome," he kissed her lightly. "There is nothing that they can do to you. You hold their lives in your hands," he kissed her palms. "These hands. These hands that hold me close. These hands that make our daughters way more dresses than they need."

"With pockets," Electra laughed.

"Yes. With pockets and skirts for twirling. You, Electra, are stronger than they are. Even without the Gelert, you are stronger," he smiled at her as her eyes flashed in warning. "But with the Gelert, you hold the power and authority to destroy them."

"Part of me wants to rip them limb from limb until there is nothing left," she admitted. "But another part of me wants to never think about them ever again."

"I advise somewhere in between."

"So, maybe just rip off their balls?"

"That's my girl," Hadrian pulled her into a comforting embrace. "Don't let them see anything but the strength of the Gelert and the compassion of the survivor."

Electra slipped her arms around his neck, "And the love of the mate and mother."

He kissed her, ignoring the Omega at the door, "Exactly. I think that they are ready for us."

"Let's go rip some balls off."

Hadrian chuckled before kissing her, "Maybe we should wait for the girls to be out of the room first."

"Probably," she replied and heard Lizzie snicker. "I'm still not used to having a servant."

"If it makes you feel any better," the teen in black slacks, gray Oxford shirt and black tennis shoes said from the doorway, "I'm not used to serving someone who cooks and sews for me."

"Well, I'm a bit different," Electra admitted as she turned and linked her arm with her mate. "Let's go show these assholes who they fucked with."

Smiling, Lizzie went and opened the door to the room where the girls sat doing schoolwork. Marie was working through her math as quickly as possible so she could get her latest Rick Riordan book. Emily was taking her time coloring the bubble letter page. Again. She had already discovered that she could trace the picture onto a blank page and have more pages to color.

After the last few days, it was confirmed that they needed a tutor, if for no other reason than to keep them focused. And doing all the work, not just the favorites.

"Come on, ladies," Lizzie said brightly, and both girls dropped what they were doing.

"Is Teuf out there?" Emily excitedly shook out her gray dress. Crayon wrappers fell to the floor.

"I'm sure he's with the Alpha," Lizzie confirmed as she went to pick up the colorful scraps of paper.

"Lizzie," Hadrian said firmly, "she can clean up her mess when she returns."

"Yes, sir," the Omega said obediently.

The sisters each grabbed one of Lizzie's hands; she might be Electra's assistant, but the two young girls saw her as a big sister. Smiling at them, they followed the couple through the doors into the council chambers.

The adults were just as overwhelmed as the two girls. Yesterday when they were here, it was large and imposing. Today, it was more imposing and intimidating with all the people standing watching the new Elder Successor enter.

The men all wore suits or traditional garb for their pack in pack colors. Crests were on the left breast of both the men and women. The women mainly wore dresses in pack colors with long sleeves or jackets. There were a few short-sleeved dresses and one sleeveless dress showing off multiple tattoos.

Electra met Celeste's eyes in the third row and gave a small smile. The Alpha was known for throwing tradition out the window. Today was no different. Celeste inclined her head slightly and smiled at the Elder and her friend.

Hadrian looked forward, afraid that if he looked anywhere else, nerves would make him puke. Inside his head, he did the only thing he could think of to keep himself calm. Thankfully, Blaze joined in on the Jetsons theme song.

His oldest daughter was wondering if this inspired the court room in Harry Potter. His youngest quietly called out to Teuf as they crossed the floor. His head popped up as his paws landed on the back of chairs on the lower row. With little encouragement from the girl, he went to join the family.

"You fucking bitch!" AJ yelled. "What is the meaning of this?"

"SILENCE!" Davis ordered as Electra and Hadrian mounted the steps with their daughters behind them. Teuf silently followed them and ignoring his mistress commanding him to return to her.

The whole room was on their feet with their heads bowed in submission. At the Senior Elders command even AJ fell silent but he continued to glare at Electra.

Marcus kissed her cheek and motioned for her to stand in front of her chair. She stood next to her grandfather and faced the two men on the floor before her.

What do I do now?

You let me handle them. I promise, no blood in front of the pups.

Gelert pushed to the front of their mind and her eyes glowed gold. Fangs extended and when she looked at AJ and his father, she saw their fear.

"You dare to show such insolence and disrespect!" Electra's voice rang out in the chamber. "Cast your eyes downward and do not challenge me again!" Immediately both men looked at the ground unable to do anything else.

Gelert receded to the back and gave control back to Electra.

I'm here when you need me.

Thank you.

"It is my honor to introduce Elder Electra and her mate, Hadrian," Marcus declared. "And their daughters, Marie and Emily."

"And Lizzie!" Emily said as she tried to tug the young woman up on the dais. She shook her head no but then Teuf nudged her up.

"And Lizzie," Marcus said, offering a hand to the now embarrassed teen.

"Sorry," Lizzie muttered quietly as Electra squeezed her hand.

Chapter 68

REVENGE
Crescent City Pack

The council took a thirty-minute break, allowing Electra and Hadrian time to settle the girls in the room. Cherry sent a pack nanny over to keep the girls entertained. Lizzie took her position at the table below the dais with her laptop and cell phone.

She was picking up her duties quickly and receiving assistance from the other aids. Marcus had his aid, Thomas, help her and he handed her a bottle of water as they settled back in before the Elders returned.

"The girls seem to like you," Thomas said, taking his seat.

Similar to Lizzie, the assistants were all dressed in slacks and oxford shirts with pins on their collars, indicating which successor they assisted. While Dawn and Nyla' assistants wore gray shirts with golden pins, the other three assistants wore white shirts with similar pins and the Council Crest on their breast pockets.

"I was so embarrassed," Lizzie admitted quietly with a little blush.

"Don't be," Luisa, Dawn's aid, laughed. "Reggie recently told someone I was his mom's wife. Needless to say, his dad was a bit surprised. I, on the other hand, was mortified."

"Dawn probably laughed her ass off," James, the aid for Davis, grinned.

"You know she did," Luisa confirmed.

"They are on their way in," James said, nodding towards the host Alpha who stood, and the room grew silent.

"Ladies and gentlemen, please stand for the Elder Alphas," Alpha Alexander said before bowing his own head.

They entered in the silence with the Successors on the arms of the respective Alpha. Once on the dais, Electra looked towards where her mate sat with the other mates. He lifted his head slightly and met her gaze with a smile.

We'll do this together. My bloodlust. Your compassion. Their pain.

Gelert assured Electra as the Elders walked back into the Council Chambers.

"Please be seated," Davis commanded once the Elders and Successors were seated. He waited until everyone was settled before continuing.

As one, the six commanded, "Bring in the prisoners."

The disgraced Alpha and AJ were led back in and chained to the floor again. AJ mouthed something to Electra and Gelert grinned back at him.

"Anthony, I will give you one more chance to recant anything that you have previously said," Davis offered. "Is there anything that you or your son has said that you would like to be stricken from the record?"

"No, Elder," AJ answered believing that he could still control Electra.

"Very well. Elder Electra will continue with the questioning," Davis nodded at her and then sat back to watch the entertainment.

"Anthony, both junior and senior, you will answer any questions that the Elder Successor poses to you. Or you will suffer her wrath," Marcus warned them.

AJ pushed into Electra's mind.

You will drop all charges and recant any statement already made. You will have us set free and you will return to Dark Sky as the good little bitch that I've made you. Do it now, and maybe I'll be nice and only let the Betas have you.

AJ grinned at her as she nodded her head in understanding. What he did not know was that Gelert was repeating everything that he said in a whining voice. She mocked him before letting her human host hear the bloodlust in her voice.

Oh, no, he's going to let his Betas have us. Beta, it's what's for dinner.

Electra threw her head back and laughed. She laughed so hard a tear slipped out of her eye. When she stopped, she looked at the man who rejected her and abused her for his amusement. His own wolf whimpered in his mind as he watched in horror, recognizing the powerful wolf that now stalked them.

"Allow me to remind you that under the laws that govern our society, your title of Alpha has temporarily been stripped. You are no longer my Alpha. In fact, you are nobody's Alpha. All your privileges and protections are gone. You no longer have the ability to compel me to do a damned thing."

Electra's amused grin became sinister, "But I can. Now, why don't you tell everyone what you just tried to compel me to do. I would personally enjoy it if you refused."

"You're nothing but a wolf-less bitch-."

AJ fell silent as Electra's eyes began to glow gold and fangs extended in her grin.

Gelert's voice echoed around the chamber, "I compel you to repeat what you just told me in the link, out loud for everyone to hear."

"You will drop all charges and recant any statement already made. You will have us set free and you will return to Dark Sky as the good little bitch that I've made you. Do it now, and maybe I'll be nice and only let the Betas have you," he recited.

"Mmmmm…. Betas," Gelert growled out loud. "A tasty meal before we feast on you for dessert."

Electra pushed to the front but left her eyes glowing. "Trust me, she would love to tear you to shreds. And I am tempted to let her. Tell the council if you have met your mate."

"You know I have," he sneered.

"And what happened?"

"I rejected your worthless ass."

"My worthless ass?" She laughed and her eyes flashed. "That's priceless coming from a ... chicken."

Instantly, his hands went to his armpits and he began to scratch at the floor with his foot. He pecked at the ground and began to move like a chicken as much as the chains would allow. A look of surprise crossed his face as he clucked and cleaned feathers that only he could see.

"And after?" With a wave if her hand, he quit acting like a chicken but remained under her control. "What happened after you rejected me?"

He fought against her control, after losing the silent battle of wills, he said, "My friends and I shared you."

Electra stood up and stepped off the dais walking towards him. Her fangs remained extended, and her claws were out. The golden eyes shimmered as she and Gelert shared control.

"You raped me," both voices echoed around the chamber.

There was a collective gasp from the council at the accusation. Electra gave a small hand gesture to Lizzie, who sent the slide show to the screens. Pictures of a younger Electra filled the TV screens around the spectator seating and the tablets for the council members. She was battered and bruised.

More pictures came up. More bruises. Black eyes. Cuts and abrasions. Matted hair from blood. As she aged in the pictures, the beatings had obviously intensified.

Then there were pictures of her in a hospital bed. Pictures of her seven-inch scar across her abdomen after her surgery. The brands that were burned into her skin.

"What does that mark mean?" Electra asked with a single claw under Anthony's chin forcing his head upward to see the large screen TV.

"Dark Sky slave," Anthony answered to the shock of the council.

"And that one?"

"Sterilized," AJ answered and there was an angry response from the audience.

"As I told you, we have a very persuasive witness," Davis said standing up and the collective grew silent. "You."

"This is not fair," AJ complained.

"Fair!" Electra demanded grasping his face with her claws digging into his cheeks. She forced him to his feet as much as the chains would allow.

"You mutilated me! You raped me! You encouraged others to rape and beat me. You threatened my family. You threatened to take my eight-year-old sister as a concubine. And I'm not the only one. I'm just the one you treated the worst because I was supposed to be your mate."

She reached out and tore away the chains with no effort.

"Let me tell you something before you are executed," she told him quietly. "My wolf is strong. Her lineage is powerful. With the blessing of the moon goddess, I have what you took from me. A child grows inside me. And your line ends here."

Electra tossed him to the ground where he was quickly chained again. She sat in her chair and nodded at Davis.

"Is there anyone who will speak in defense of Dark Sky?" Davis called and there was a silence in the room as no one moved.

Everyone turned as Danielle stood up from her chair, "Elders, if I may."

"Please," Davis motioned for her to continue.

"There are many issues and flaws within my pack. But we also have good people. We have strong warriors. We have supportive females. I believe that we can be more. With the right leadership and guidance, we can become a great asset to the werewolf community. Please, Elders, punish the guilty. But not the victims."

The six Elders spoke in the mind link before the other five turned to look at Electra.

"Your pleas have not fallen on deaf ears. The former Alpha will face execution. Titles and positions will be stripped from the executive leadership. Danielle, you and your mate will assume the roles of Alpha. Is there an Alpha who will volunteer to guide them."

"If it pleases the elders," Amato said, standing up, "the Dragon Moon pack will offer support and guidance."

"As will Harbor Moon," the female Alpha declared.

"Silver Moon," Sirius declared after a motion from his sister.

"Crystal River," Wyatt offered.

"Big Sky," Another Alpha stood up.

"Glacial Coast."

"Pueblo Crest."

"Buffalo Bayou."

Davis held his hand up silencing the other Alphas who were standing. "Alpha Danielle and Alpha Yuto, do you accept this position?"

"Yes, Elder," they both answered, and she wiped tears from her eyes.

"Thank you, Elders. I promise to be the best Luna-."

"Alpha," Electra cut her off.

Danielle swallowed hard. "I promise to do the best for my pack and my people. What about my brother?"

"He will return to the Marines. There, he will learn what being a leader really means," Davis smiled kindly at the young woman. "He is stripped of his title, position and protections. When the Marines Pack releases him, he will go to Crystal River as an omega. If the moon goddess deems him worthy of a second chance mate, I hope he sees her wisdom."

He looked at his own mates and smiled before turning his attention to the man in question.

"Too often as leaders we forget that we have partners to support us. As such, we often forget what treasures we have. Mine, like to remind me that without the two of them, I would be dead. Or at least, a lot grumpier."

There was a light ripple of laughter.

Chapter 69

TIRED

Crystal River Pack

Tuesday afternoon they headed to the airport to fly back to Crystal Pass. Dawn hugged Electra and gave her a little hope, before snatching it away.

"We have three months to recover and then we have the February meeting in Sydney."

Allison met them at the airport with Electra's Durango. She promised to have them over to the house for dinner that weekend. After they all had time to rest and recover. With that assurance, she climbed into the passenger seat of the patrol car and let the officer drive her back to the police station.

By the time Electra and Hadrian walked into their house, they were exhausted, and the girls were asleep. They laid the girls on the couch, and he settled into the recliner with her in his lap. Lizzie had gone back to the orphanage where she was still staying. The luggage in the Durango was not going to walk away and could stay there a little longer.

"Pizza?" Hadrian offered as he put the feet up and laid them back.

"Yes," Electra agreed, settling in and closing her eyes.

"Mommy," Emily said, shaking them. "Daddy."

They opened their eyes and discovered that the sun had set.

"We're hungry," Marie said. "And someone's at the door."

As Hadrian started to put the feet down, there was a tap-tap-tap on the door. He stood up and sat Electra on her feet before moving to the door. To be honest, he was a little surprised that they had not yanked open the door themselves.

Opening it, he was confronted with a large black werecat and the delicious aroma of chili. The scent hit him like a punch to the gut, and he suddenly realized just how hungry he was. Eying the slow cooker in Jill's hands, he hoped the chili tasted as good as it smelled.

"Lizzie was tired as hell, I guessed that you guys are also," Jill said as Hadrian opened the door more for him to enter.

"Jill, that smells fabulous," Electra said, going into the kitchen.

"Chili in the slow cooker is always a go to for cold weather," Jill said, setting the slow cooker on the counter and plugging it in. "I have corn bread in the car."

"I'll get it!" Marie yelled as she ran for the door.

"OK, I admit that I'm here on a mission of mercy also," Jill admitted as Electra handed him a ladle. "Other than drooling over your man. Please tell me, he looks awesome naked."

"Gross," Emily said.

"I think I look adorable in the nude," Hadrian wrapped his arms around his mate and rested a protective hand over her stomach.

"Yes, you do," Jill said appreciatively.

Electra laughed as Marie came back into the house. "He does."

Jill started purring when both the girls hugged him. Laughing, he held them to his chest, "All my babies like it when I purr."

"It's comforting," Marie said.

"What is your ulterior motive?" Hadrian asked.

"Huh? Oh! My mission of mercy," Jill leaned against the counter with an arm around each girl. "The bestie is having to get a nanny, something she did not want to do. But, as I'm sure you two now know, something that is needed."

"Yes," Hadrian sighed.

"Here's an idea. She doesn't want a full-time nanny. You don't want a full-time nanny. Since we are the area representative for the council, you'll be going to a lot of the same events."

"Crescent City is one of the few host packs that don't set up events for the kids. Probably because he is an only child and never went to the events until he was of age. She came from an island pack and never went to an event until she did her hunt."

He chuckled at the couple that looked at him with mild amusement and confusion. He shrugged, "What can I say, when you have a colicky baby, you have plenty of time to read."

"I remember those nights," Hadrian winked at his daughters.

"So, my idea is that you two share a nanny."

"That's actually a really good idea," Electra agreed.

"The other part of my mission...." Jill took a deep breath. "Jodi wants to work for you. She's really good at sewing, but just the basics-."

"Tomorrow, as soon as she's out of school," Electra cut him off. "Weekends will be a must because of the Yule ball."

"She'll be here by three thirty. And she'll be excited."

"So am I. Between my new duties, the dress shop and my pregnancy, I feel like I'm missing my girls."

Chapter 70

NEW HOUSE

Crystal River Pack

The first weekend in December, a handful of omegas and some volunteers from the fire and police departments showed up at the house to move the family. They were moving to a larger house closer to the Alpha. Troy and his family were moving into the old house. The Dressing Room, as Electra had named her shop, was staying in the basement.

It was a compromise because Electra was not ready to give up her little shop. Hadrian had made it for her, and it held special memories.

Along with Jodi after school, Electra's mother and sister-in-law were also helping her. Lizzie was doing double duty as the Elder aid and teaching Hadrian how to run the business end of the dress shop. The decision had already been made to locate a larger shop and expanding her staff for a second location. Including someone to create her patterns in a computer program and use the new large printer that Marcus had gifted her.

With all the help they had that weekend, it did not take long for them to be moved into the new house. Wyatt had given Electra and the girls free reign through the warehouse of furniture that the pack had. Even Lizzie found furniture that she liked for her detached apartment.

Hadrian discovered that he enjoyed being a stay-at-home dad. Now that he was a volunteer with the department, a lot of pressure was off him, but he still got to do what he loved. Twice a week, he joined Jill at a cooking class in Crystal Springs. During the first class the teacher assumed that they were a couple, and they rolled with it.

Suddenly, Hadrian and Electra were moving in circles that neither thought they would ever be in. She had been a wolf-less slave and he was a mid-level Beta. And now, they were moving into what used to be the gamma house.

When Wyatt took on the mantle of Alpha, as expected by tradition and transition, his father's Beta and gamma resigned. Stephen filled the role of Beta almost immediately. It had always been the two of them that a third seemed like overkill. The duties of the gamma were distributed among the other cabinet members and the position never filled. Many packs were now moving away from having the position.

Although, if he had to take a third to a meeting, it was usually Jack or Gunny. He respected them both, they were always straight with him, and they considered the pack their family. Plus, they were good leaders and close friends with Celeste.

As an added bonus, it was fun to watch other packs wrap their heads around a human being a gamma.

Wyatt took Jill once.

Only once.

Wyatt spent more time trying to get the werecat to focus on something other than the males than getting anything accomplished. When he got home from the trip, his lovely mate took one look at him, doubled over laughing, holding her then large belly with their first pup and laughed until she cried with hiccups.

"I warned you."

Never again did he not heed her warning about one of her friends. Doc had moved into the packhouse last month and she had already advised against him having a cabinet position. Instead, he would be attending the fire academy at the local college and working with the fire department.

It was while they were moving that Hadrian had met the man. Jill had insisted that he accompany them to the next class.

"If the teacher says anything," Jill said as he wrapped an arm around Hadrian's waist, "you're my secret lover, but my adoring husband," he placed a loud kiss on Hadrian's cheek, "thinks we're still just friends."

"What the hell?" Hadrian demanded. "Why do you get a secret lover, and I don't?"

"Because you got your side piece pregnant," Jill countered as Electra followed Parker and her husband into the room.

"You're just his side piece, now?" Doc asked Electra with a grin.

"Only during cooking class," she laughed as her husband and his friend argued about plot lines.

"I see they're still writing the next soap opera," Parker said, shaking her head.

"I'd watch it," her husband teased, placing a kiss on her head before going back for another box from the rented moving truck.

"I probably would too," Parker admitted. "I miss his antics at the station."

"I'll send him your way a little more often," Electra said as the microwave dinged in the background.

A moment later, Doc placed an arm around each woman's shoulders. He had a large bag of popcorn in one hand and three bottled Sprites in the other. They sat on the couch watching the two men.

"I like snacks with my romcoms," Doc said, and the two women laughed.

The bag of popcorn was nearly gone by the time the two men realized that they had an audience. Jill, being Jill, dipped Hadrian declaring his undying love until Celeste walked through and said she had cookies. Hadrian found himself abandoned on the floor as his audience laughed.

"Chocolate chip cookies always take precedence over a fake boyfriend," Jill declared.

Chapter 71

YULE BALL
Crystal River Pack

Electra walked into the ballroom, completely in awe of the beautiful room. The large pentagon-shaped building across the street from the packhouse was surrounded by tall Corinthian columns providing shade and protection on the oversized landings and balconies.

The white marble floors reflected the light from the thousands of candles in tall golden candelabras and chandeliers. The walls were painted a pale blue with cream colored trim, picture rail and crown molding. Portraits of past Alphas and Lunas hung on the walls of the upper walkway. Crimson red rugs lined the stairs and walkways.

Round tables with cream-colored tablecloths and golden and cream chairs filled the room. A matching long rectangular table sat along one wall flanked by a staircase on either side.

Electra stood in the middle of the dance floor taking it all in. She wore a light gray halter dress with the same shoes she wore at her mating ceremony. Hadrian held her cloak with her position markings on it over his arm, and another that she had made earlier in the day. Hers was a darker gray and the black stitching was set off by the occasional bead and crystal.

He stood watching her in amusement, forgetting the discomfort of his black tuxedo. The Elder's crest was on his breast where previously the pack crest would have been. He was proud of his mate, not just because of her position, but because of who she was.

When the Elders asked what she wanted to do with the Dark Sky pack, she could have had the entire pack executed. Instead, she only had the Alpha executed and the cabinet demoted. The son was stripped of everything and exiled from pack lands.

The pack was given a second chance to rebuild under the daughter and her previously forbidden mate. The first thing that they did was to give equal rights to all pack members. Protections were given to abused spouses and children. Gunny, the Viking triplets and a few others were there setting up a new police department and security protocols.

Given the opportunity, many of the women in the pack wanted to learn something outside the house. Many of the younger males agreed while some of the older males fought against the changes. Many had been cast out as rogues when they refused to pledge allegiance to the new Alphas.

The priest had been sent to Rome for the high priestess to deal with. His trial would be in January. Electra would have to travel to Rome to testify. But for tonight, she was going to enjoy her first Yule ball. And celebrate her birthday for the first time in years.

"Electra?" Anna said approaching them. "The Alphas are waiting upstairs for you. If you'll follow me, I'll take you up."

They followed the woman in a jade green dress that had been made in Electra's basement. The satin material hugged her body and flowed down to the floor in a full skirt. As with all of her dresses, it had pockets big enough for a phone and other necessities.

At the top of the stairs, they turned left, and Anna led them into a lounge where the pack council sat. Celeste sat in a chair with her feet in the Alphas lap as he massaged them. Her dress was in her signature sapphire blue and silver white silk with no sleeves, an open back and high slit. The Alpha adored his wife and her many tattoos.

He wore a fitted tuxedo shirt with the vest and jacket tossed carelessly on a table. The tie was hanging loose around his neck with the top buttons of the shirt undone. He smiled at his wife who was in paradise with his attention.

Stephen sat in a nearby chair with his own tuxedo in the same state of disarray. His wife sat on his lap with her head on his shoulder. Her shoes were also discarded and her much more conservative dress was unzipped in the back.

"Ellie, is something wrong with the dress?" Electra asked, concerned.

"Oh, no. It was perfect," she shifted and showed the dampness of where her breast milk had leaked.

"I thought about that," Electra said, and Hadrian handed her the short cape he was holding. It was a black velveteen with jade green satin roses hiding the clasps.

"That's beautiful," Imogen said as she sat between her two mates. Her knee-length dress was a deep violet with thin gold chains making shoulder straps. They were braided in the front and separated to form an intricate pattern on the back.

Both of her mates wore tuxedo pants and shirts. The dark-skinned one smiled at Electra. "We love this dress. Can you do one in something sheer?"

"And much shorter?" the blonde added.

"Boys!" Imogen laughed.

"Someone has to make up for me not getting my mates pregnant," Emmeline said from the bar where she sat with her two mates. The three women chuckled at the long running joke.

"Adeline," Rosa said rubbing her belly, "you can have the next one."

Adeline and Henry link hands over her belly. Rosa kissed her before laying her head on his chest. Smiling at one mate, he kissed the top of the other's head.

"If that's an option," Sammi declared, "I'm in!"

"Are there Were seahorses?" Gunny asked.

"I don't think so," Jill laughed. "Girl, sit your pregnant ass down and you, you lovely hunk of man meat, get comfortable."

"In other words, he wants to see your muscles," Jack rolled his eyes.

"Is that not what I just said?"

"It's what I heard," Doc answered, pulling his phone out and aiming the camera at Hadrian. "Whenever you're ready."

Laughing at the men and her own mate's strip tease, Electra sat down and kicked her shoes off. As he tossed his jacket towards Jill, Aiden and Allison walked into the room.

"He learned those moves from me," Aiden boasted as he tossed his jacket on the back of a chair.

"I have a video of you dancing on the fireman's pole. So, I can confirm, his moves are better," Allison countered as she sat down next to the police chief.

An hour later, Anna came back and informed them that they had opened the doors. Thirty minutes after that, the men started to put their jackets on and tie their ties. The women straightened their dresses and put their shoes on.

Electra and Hadrian were the last to go down the stairs since she was the highest-ranking Alpha. She had never been to a Yule ball other than the one on her birthday when AJ rejected her. Seeing so many people lowering their heads to her was overwhelming.

Halfway down the stairs she stopped. "Ladies, at least half of you are wearing dresses from my shop. Gentlemen, I probably have seen your wife or daughter. Please don't start treating me like a princess in a tower. I'm still Electra. I just have a split personality now."

Wyatt and Celeste were the first to laugh. Soon it rippled through the large hall. The mood lightened and Electra relaxed.

"I love you," Hadrian told her as they reached the bottom of the stairs. "You make my life complete."

"I love you, too. And you mispronounced complicated."

Chapter 72

ROME
Crystal River Pack

In January, Electra and Hadrian flew to Rome with the girls for the trial. At the insistence of Davis, they stayed at his villa just outside of the city. After the trial, he promised to take the family to Venice and Cecily. The divine oracle, Neema, confirmed that Emily was an oracle herself.

Neema admitted that it was surprising that Emily could already communicate with the animals. Even more surprising was that she had sensed and spoken with Gelert while she was still hibernating. When Neema asked the high priestess about this, the woman simply smiled and gave a simple piece of advice.

"Hold fast, little one, for I have great plans for you."

At hearing these words, in the ethereal voice that Electra had heard her entire life, fear flooded through her. A calming hand was placed on her shoulder and when she turned, she watched the Moon Goddess dissipate into mist. She experienced a similar feeling later when they visited the divine healer, Zsa Zsa.

When she took Marie into the inner sanctum of her own temple, she confirmed that Marie's wolf would make its appearance in the next few years. When that happened, she would begin training with Adeline. Her spot was already reserved at the healer's academy.

The following morning, Davis's mates and Zoe, the shared nanny for Electra's girls and Celeste's son, kept them entertained while their parents went to the trial. Just like at the Crescent City pack, they had been taken to the council chambers so that they would be prepared and knew what to expect the following day.

Just like so many other buildings that were utilized by the Were community, they were hidden in plain sight. The ancient ruins that had once been a great structure and were now a tourist trap, sat on top of the oldest council chambers that were still used. A velvet rope blocked off the entrance to the underground city. Guards with large K9 dogs stood on either side of the open staircase ensuring that no one went down the stone staircase.

Unless, of course, you were supposed to.

The guards nodded to Electra and her entourage as they let them through. Even the hell hounds lowered their heads in respect. Teuf was a large dog, even larger in his hell hound form, but next to these hellhounds, he looked like a young pup.

As they went down the well-worn stone stairs, Celeste linked her arm with her husband and leaned into him. "The last time that I was here was for Aria's trial."

Wyatt placed an arm around her shoulder and tucked her in next to him before kissing the top of her head. He could have told her that he loved her, but instead he opted to tell her the one word that had carried her and her friends through multiple deployments and other events. With his lips still on her hair, he murmured, "Hydrate."

Reaching the bottom of the stairs, she snuggled into his chest and wrapped her arms around his waist. Looking up at him, she grinned, "Hydrate."

Electra and Hadrian stopped next to them, and they could all feel the excited energy that radiated out from her as Gelert paced in her mind. Hadrian placed a comforting hand on his wife's back and Blaze went to his mate to calm her. Teuf moved from next to Celeste to lean into Electra's legs.

Stroking the dog's head, Electra grinned, her eyes glowing brightly in the dimly lit reception area and waited for security to check them in. The room slowly fell silent as people turned to face the two Lycan dominant Alphas towering over the Elder Successor. Two large members of the security detail approached the group.

"Elder, if you'll come with us," the blonde man motioned for them to go ahead of him.

The darker skinned man motioned for the crowd to move out of their way as he guided the four towards the door at the far end of the room. He bypassed the security checks and guided them into the hall.

When the hallway split, he directed Wyatt and Celeste to go one direction, "The ushers at the door will help you to your seats. Elder, sir, if you will follow me this way."

Entering the Elder's room, Electra looked up at the carved stone ceiling and searched for the carving that had intrigued Gelert as a child. The moon goddess walked through a garden and called forth her children to live two lives shared in one body. Memories of her past lives washed over her as she stood in the original council chambers.

This was much smaller than the other chambers that the council typically used. Originally built to hold the leaders of the original 35 tribes of Rome and representatives of the other tribes. This was before they had organized into packs and were still grouped as tribes. When they finally connected with their beasts, they also connected with the other gifts that the moon goddess had given them.

Rapid healing.

Heightened senses.

Mind link between family and pack members.

Strength.

The beasts had their own personalities and had to learn to work with the humans that they shared a body and mind with.

Gelert pushed to the surface, and all her memories were forced to the back of her and Electra's shared mind.

Let me handle this, you've endured enough in this lifetime. I can handle this little flea.

Electra easily agreed and let her beast have control. She was only vaguely aware of when the ushers took the mates away and then when Marcus took her arm to guide her out to the trial. The Elders and their Successors entered the underground amphitheater that was now only used for trials. Vent shafts allowed air flow, and the occasional torch and small fires lit the cavern.

The high priestess read out the charges against the former priest and his followers. The first witnesses were called to the witness box; they all spoke about what they had seen or endured themselves. Electra was called to give her testimony.

Instead of moving to the witness box, Gelert pushed Electra's memories out through the mind links and the members of the executive council experienced her memories firsthand.

"Enough!" Davis commanded and the single word echoed around the cavern.

Gelert pulled back the memories and the amphitheater was eerily silent as the soft sobs began to echo around the room. The high priestess stepped back up to the podium and called for an hour recess.

"If you don't mind," Davis interrupted, "I think everyone would prefer to vote and to put this whole debacle behind us."

"Very well," she said with a nod. "Everyone who finds the accused guilty, please stand up."

Every single body of the hundred plus members of the Executive Council rose to their feet.

Chapter 73

MARTIN AND LLEWELYN

Crystal River Pack

Gelert woke up early on a March morning and stretched in Electra's mind. There was a new life in the pack, her pack. A life that she needed to protect.

Being an elder, in fact, the oldest elder, she could see the moon goddess's plans. But she also knew that just because the moon goddess laid out a plan, that did not mean that the wolf would follow it. They all had choice and free will.

Electra moved in the bed, waking Hadrian up, "Is it the baby?"

She chuckled, "Yes, but not ours."

Moving closer to his wife and mate, he placed a hand on her rounded belly. He pressed a kiss to her temple, "Who's baby?"

"I think Celeste had their second son."

"We'll go by after the sun is up," he assured her. "Let them have some time to themselves and you sleep a little more."

Rolling to her side, she pulled him with her, and he spooned her with a light kiss to the back of her head. In the warm embrace of the man she loved, Electra slipped back into sleep and the Gelert paced restlessly as she looked into the future.

The visions of the Gelert moved through the woman's mind like dreams of years past. Now she knew that the visions of battles and attacks were memories. The visions of her holding her own baby, surrounded by a loving family were more than just wishful dreams. They were predictions, glimpses of the future.

And now as she watched her unborn pup grow up with the newborn that would become his best friend, she knew that the packs that she loved so much would be the ones to lead the Were Community into the next chapter.

Once the sun came up, the girls went to eat breakfast with Lizzie while Electra and Hadrian went to the packhouse to meet the newest member of the Crystal River Pack.

Anna took them up to the family's floor in the packhouse. After a quick knock, Wyatt called for her to "Show the Elder in." This confirmed for both Electra and Hadrian that the Omega had spoken to them through the pack link.

Celeste sat in her large bed with her newborn son asleep in her arms. Her mate sat on one side of her and their oldest son lay asleep on the other. Pulling her into him, Wyatt kissed her temple before releasing her shoulders and standing up to greet their visitors.

"Please, Elder, sit," Wyatt motioned for Electra to take his place.

She sat down and the baby stirred in her womb as the baby in Celeste's arms also stirred. The newborn stretched his legs as he fussed. When his foot touched Electra's belly, his cries stopped, and he grew still.

"These three," Electra said with the Gelert's voice of their sons, "will do great things. And these two will lead their packs with grace and valor."

Celeste looked at her sleeping toddler, "Not Aiden?"

Shaking her head, Electra smiled as her eyes glowed, "He has a different path to follow. It will be a daughter who leads both Crystal River and Silver Lake."

"I'm not telling him that he's going to be a girl dad," Celeste said softly as she looked down at her son. "He was hoping that they were wrong and that Martin would be a little girl."

"Who is Martin named after?"

Looking at her mate who was speaking with Hadrian near the door to the nursery, Celeste smiled, "One of the men that Wyatt served with. I'm still planning on naming my daughter after you."

"I'm named after a Greek goddess, make sure all your daughters are named after goddesses."

Celeste nodded, "I can do that."

Three months later, the roles were reversed as Electra sat in her bed holding her newborn son. Hadrian sat at the foot of their bed with Emily and Marie on either side of Electra and their newborn brother. Adeline escorted the two Alphas into the bedroom and then quietly excused herself.

Where Hadrian had always done the varying shades of gray for simplicity, Electra loved the colors. All the colors. He would have been content with gray or white walls. But she loved the bright blue-green color that covered the walls. Floating shelves, painted to match the walls, flanked both sides of the brass bed. Each had a matching brass sconce above it.

His simple black furniture had been replaced with customized built-ins for both walk-in closets and the dressing area. A rocking chair sat next to the large windows that looked out over the lush backyard. A table with a book on top sat on the other side of the rocking chair. Across from the bed was a flatscreen TV that hung above a low bookshelf that was full of books and nick knacks.

The bed itself was covered in what could only be described as a boho chic blanket and multiple contrasting pillows of varying sizes and shapes, all in bright jewel tones. The whole house was now filled with color, just as their lives had been too.

"Hi," Celeste said as she handed over a baby blue blanket to the new father. "I'm supposed to take credit for this, but we all know that I had nothing to do with this other than bringing it."

He chuckled, "It's okay, I have the ones that Luna Elizabeth made the girls. I'm assuming that she made this one for Llewelyn too?"

Wyatt kissed the top of his wife's head. "Actually, Sammy made it."

"How does that woman have time?" Electra asked.

Celeste shook her head. "I have no idea. Maybe while Gunny is-"

Wyatt placed his hand over her mouth, "The girls do not need to know what Gunny does to Sammy."

She pulled her husband's hand away from her mouth and told him, "I was going to say while he puts the kids to bed. After dinner, anyone under the age of eighteen, and not still breastfeeding, is the responsibility of their father."

"Sammi is a brilliant woman," Electra mused.

Chapter 74

NEW PACK HOUSE

Dark Sky Pack

Just after Llewellyn's first birthday, Danielle and Yuto welcomed their first pup. She was a precocious little girl named Pearl. Electra and Hadrian went back to the Dark Sky Pack to celebrate the newest member of their family and see how the pack was faring. Electra's old pack was rebuilding and remaking itself exactly as the pack members wanted.

The large imposing federalist style building that had been the packhouse had been converted into a school. Half a mile down the road, a new packhouse was being built. Under the guidance of the volunteer packs, they had already reestablished their pack and services. Roads had been repaired. Sewage and water services had been improved.

Everywhere that Electra went, things looked completely different. The old pack library had been torn down and a new one was built. It was open to all pack members, no matter what their station or rank was. Popham Park in the center of town was now open to the public. While the wrought iron fence had been left in place, the gates had been permanently anchored open.

Currently Electra and Hadrian stood in the large common area of the new packhouse with Danielle and Yuto. The metal frame was daunting, and it would be a large building when completed. A total of seven stories with four wings coming out of a central ring. There was a wing that faced each of the cardinal directions.

"We have no orphanage," Danielle was explaining, "it was something that we never had. Orphans were simply enslaved and forced to work at the farms or in upper-level households."

She looked at Electra apologetically. The Elder merely smiled. Electra had never received any maltreatment from Danielle and did not hold her responsible for the actions of her father and brother.

Yuto pointed towards the east wing, the only one close to being completed. "This wing will become the children's wing. My sister is staying here to get it up and running from the ground up. We decided that we wanted a true packhouse," he looked down at his mate lovingly.

She leaned against his chest wrapping her arms around his waist as he wrapped his around her shoulders.

"The next wing to be completed will be the north wing. That will hold council chambers and leadership offices. Our intention is to make a compass. The east, where the sun rises, is our future, our children. The north will guide us. The west will become a place for our older wolves that no longer have family here," Danielle explained.

"The south will be our anchor," Yuto added. "It will have our apartment, guest quarters and communal dining hall. Our apartment will be one of the last built."

"We burned the Omega Ward," Danielle gave a little laugh. "The whole district was condemned and when we asked them what they wanted to do with it, the consensus was to watch it burn. So, every family had time to get their stuff out, and then they got to set it on fire."

"We built apartments for them while we rebuilt the Wards. Except we're renaming everything. New neighborhoods are being built and they're being integrated. Homes are being assigned by family size and need; not status."

"How are people reacting to all the changes?" Hadrian asked.

"We laid out a few changes that we insisted on. The rest of them, the pack is making the decisions. We have the pack cabinet, and we also have the city council," Danielle smiled. "We just finished the new municipal building, if you want to see it."

"Would love to," Electra smiled as they began to move out of the construction zone.

In the few hours that they had been at Dark Sky, the atmosphere seemed completely different from when Electra had lived there. Women wore jeans and shorts. Children ran and played. Men moved out of the way instead of forcing their way through.

"The more people interacted with other packs and the outside world, the more they wanted to change," Yuto waved at an older woman who waved back. "More and more families were sending their daughters to human colleges to give them a better chance."

"We'll cut through the park," Danielle said as she pressed a button on the crosswalk.

"This will be a first," Electra admitted softly.

Danielle smiled at the other woman as the light changed, and the walk signal appeared. "There's been a few changes."

Crossing the streets, the first thing that Electra noticed was that the large statue of the Alpha wolf was gone. On the plinth was a man and woman with a young child standing between them. Their features were generic and did not resemble the former Alpha or his long lineage of tyrants.

Electra looked at the front of the plinth and expected to see the Dark Sky Pack crest. The circular shield, with a background of deep, velvety black. At the top of the crest, a silver crescent moon emerges from behind a cloud, casting a dim glow over a powerful and sleek werewolf with fur that was a mix of deep black and dark gray, blending with the night. On either side of the werewolf, towering pine trees stand with their branches reaching upward, creating a frame around the shield.

A banner unfolds below the werewolf, bearing the pack's motto in bold, silver letters: "Umbrae Noctis, Virtus Luporum" – translating to "Shadows of the Night, Strength of Wolves" from Latin. A border encircles the entire crest, adorned with swirling patterns resembling storm clouds.

Electra knew the crest well. It had been everywhere when she had been growing up. The dark werewolf seemed to always be watching, judging, condemning. She had always hated the crest. It surprised her when she did not see the crest.

In its place there was a new crest. A clear moonless night with the stars shining above the tree line. The North Star being the biggest and brightest. When she knelt to look at it a little closer, she discovered that there were pin prick holes in the stars and an LED bulb poked through the North Star. A silver banner with bold letters declaring A DARK SKY WITH A GUIDING LIGHT.

"We held a contest to create a new crest," Danielle said with a soft catch in her voice. "This one won by a huge majority."

Chapter 75

RACE VS HUNT

Pearl of the Atlantic Pack

It was the quarterly Council meeting before the annual Hunt. This would be the fifth Hunt since Wyatt broke with tradition and had what he had dubbed a non-Hunt. Several of the older Alphas were getting quite upset over the fact that the Elder Alphas were not forcing the host pack to have a traditional hunt.

Alphas and Betas railed at each other. They stood and were yelling all around the large council chambers. There were two factions within the werewolf community. The traditional members that thought the Hunt needed to resume as they had always known it. And the progressives who liked it as it was and wanted it to continue.

Elder Alpha Davis stood on the raised dais and lifted his hands high in the air. "SILENCE!" he commanded over the loud voices.

Instantly, the large, cavernous room in the Pearl of the Atlantic pack council building in Dubrovnik, Croatia, fell silent. Lowering his hands to his side, he cast a cold and frustrated look at the men and women around the room. His two fellow Elders joined him at the edge of the dais; their successors stood in front of their smaller thrones.

All six of their eyes glowed, showing that the ancient wolves that they shared a mind and body with were in control.

"Find your seats," came a much quieter order.

Unable to disobey the Senior Elder and his commands, everyone that had left their chairs found their way back to them. The large chamber remained eerily silent with so many people in the large stone room.

The three Elder Alphas stood looking out at their audience, their eyes glowing the color of the rings around their pupils. All six remained in their position until the entire room lowered their heads and exposed their necks in submission, then the two Elders moved back to stand before their thrones. The three successors also sank back into their seats.

"We will settle this, here and now!" Elder Alpha Davis commanded. "Each host pack can choose how they wish to hold the annual Hunt. They may choose what is said at the beginning, may choose the location of the race and who all may participate. The changes that have been implemented on the recent Hunts have all been done with our blessings."

With his glowing eyes, indicating that his wolf was in charge and demanding submission, he looked around the room.

"Thankfully, we are blessed to have a wolf that was there during some of the first Summer Solstice activities," he turned and walked to stand before Electra. Currently, he held the position of Senior Elder, but even he knew that his wolf was below this woman's wolf. Other than Remus and Romulus, hers was the oldest wolf.

"Elder Alpha Gelert," the Senior Elder said as he offered his neck in submission, "would you please enlighten us with your knowledge of the original Hunt?"

Her own eyes glowed gold and a deep guttural growl came from her as she snarled at the man. When she stood up, Senior Elder Alpha Davis moved back to his own large throne.

Stepping to the front of the dais, a louder growl issued from deep in her throat and she felt the battle in her mind between herself and the strong and angry wolf.

"I AM THE GELERT!" she declared loudly. Legends and horror stories of the Gelert and her atrocities were well known. Through every life that the Moon Goddess had given the wolf, she was blood thirsty and angry, with no remorse for any life that she took.

The scent of fear filled the cavernous room, and Electra could feel the excitement that the scent caused in the beast inside her. A small tremor ran through her body as her claws extended, and her fangs elongated slightly. She let the beast inside have control but kept a tight rein on her.

"It was during my first life, when I was born unto the first, Remus. I was seven when my father and his brother fought, and Romulus was victorious. My brother was not yet born. After Remus died, we were taken into my uncle's house and claimed by him."

"The summer of my tenth year, on the longest day of the year, Romulus held the first race."

A light ripple of confusion coursed through the audience.

"It did not start as a hunt; it was not until man corrupted it that it became a *hunt*," the sneer and derision that she said hunt with told everyone what her opinion of the modern hunt was. It was not a very high opinion.

"Originally, the race was held to find the strongest women to mate with the wolf-men. If they were not strong enough, the pregnancy would kill the mother. Very few were making it to full term. Even fewer were ending with a living child. And even those had a low survival rate."

"This Hunt, the version that you know, has been done for less than a thousand years. Only two of my previous lives experienced this abomination."

As the oldest child of Romulus, Gelert was the first of the Elder Alphas. She held the oldest memories of all their previous lives. She was the one that the Moon Goddess relied on to make changes. Usually drastic changes. Frequently with a blood trail.

"The 35 tribes of Rome would gather on the longest day of the year and hold the Greek games," Electra declared as she looked out over the crowd that held their heads down. "The Olympiads! The males would show off their prowess and strength. The women would show their endurance and try to catch the eye of a male. But at the end, it was the female that had the final say."

Nervous shuffling filled the room.

"Do you wish to dispute this?" Electra demanded loudly and the room was still almost instantly.

She stepped off the dais and approached one of the older Alphas who was objecting to the changes. The Gelert forced her way into his mind and the smaller wolf whimpered and cowered in fear. The man cast his eyes down and offered his neck in submission.

Pulling back, she walked towards a wolf that was refusing to look away from her. She bared her teeth and issued a low warning growl. When the wolf still refused to back down, Electra released her hold on the beast slightly and she easily slashed the man's throat open.

"Who else would like to challenge me?" The Gelert demanded, her rough voice echoing across the room and through the mind links.

The Alpha lay at her feet, his body twitching as the blood drained out around her. Eyes were cast down and even the fellow Elders submitted. A lone figure moved through the chamber and stopped in front of the bloodied woman.

Much as he had done a few years before at the trial of the murder of an Alpha, Hadrian cupped the face of his mate and smiled at her. The change was slow, but it was visible. Her shoulders relaxed and her claws and fangs retracted. Her eyes were the last thing to change as the glow faded, and they became their typical light brown.

"Hello, mate," he said softly, and Electra smiled at him,

Chapter 76

MIDNIGHT CALL

Crystal River Pack

The phone call came unexpectedly, and Taylor had said very little. But both Electra and Gelert were wide awake with the soft spoken "Momma E?" Gelert growled protectively inside Electra's mind as she asked where the frightened little girl was.

"What's wrong?" Hadrian asked as his wife got out of bed.

"Taylor just asked me to come get her and her brother from the hospital," came the answer as she got dressed inside the open closet. "Go back to sleep, I'll let you know when I'm headed home."

He looked up at her as she walked to his side of the bed, "I guess I finally get to know what it's like when I get a call."

Chuckling, she kissed him before leaving. Watching her retreating figure, he enjoyed the view of her rounded bottom in the jeans. His eyes tracked up to the snug gray t-shirt that she wore.

Years ago, when he first met her, he would never have imagined that wearing an outfit like that would be such a big deal. Then he got to know her and the hell she came from. Saw the Dark Sky pack as it had been, watched the former Alpha's son attack her.

But he also got to see her bloom into the kind woman that she was. Even before they discovered that she was not only an Elder Alpha, but the oldest and strongest of the Elders. And the deadliest. Yet, she was also forgiving.

AJ had been injured and would be discharged from the Marines in a few months. When Alpha Wyatt approached them about him coming to the pack, she readily agreed. Even went to the veteran's hospital to see him.

"Yeah, this kinda sucks," he said, giving up on trying to settle back down and go back to sleep.

His mind was working now and focusing on the man who had once abused his wife. There was no way he was getting back to sleep. Giving up, he got started on breakfast. Soon the house was filled with the scent of blueberry muffins.

Several hours later, Electra returned with a bruised Taylor and her little brother William. Marie and Emily were excited that their friends were staying with them. But at the same time, they were upset about Taylor being injured.

Alpha Wyatt made the decision to leave the kids with the O'Reilly family. At least until after the trial. Or their mother, Victoria, had healed from her own wounds.

When Stephen Chambers tried to lie on the witness stand during the trial, Gelert bared her teeth, and the truth spilled out. He had beaten his wife their whole relationship, but the first time he beat his daughter, she called for help.

Celeste had seen events like this too many times before. She insisted that an example be made of him.

Victoria was sent back to her home pack to heal away from the prying eyes of the Chambers extended family. She was advised to break the mate bond before her husband was executed. She did not and died shortly after he did.

The Chambers family did not try to get custody of the pups afterwards. After filing a petition to the council, the Elders granted Electra and Hadrian custody. At the next council meeting, Taylor and William were also bonded to the family.

Arriving home from the council meeting in Taiwan, they were greeted with the announcement that AJ was now here. Electra took a few days to come to terms with this fact. Then on Sunday, they would go to the pack picnic that was held every week after the Veterans Support Group Meeting.

The light dusting of snow that was falling would not stop them from having the picnic. But with there being so many young pups, they were having it inside the civic center. Tables were set up and everyone attending filled them with food that they brought.

Electra still was not used to everyone standing and submitting to her when she entered the room. After so many years, she should be used to it by now. She was not. And was not certain that she would ever get used to it.

Looking at the veteran in the wheelchair, she saw a very changed man. He had been humbled. It was a hard lesson to learn, and he had learned it in the worst way. He was still learning it.

Big Jake, an army veteran who had lost his leg and now used a prosthetic, stood with his arms crossed his chest as he glared at AJ. The large muscular man could still intimidate people with only one leg and a wolf that rarely came out anymore. One of his mates placed a hand on his shoulder and he visibly relaxed as Electra approached them.

The room was full of veterans and their families, but the small area that AJ was sitting in suddenly became empty. Even Jake's partner walked away with the small signal that he received from the guard with the large hellhound that accompanied Electra everywhere now.

This was something else that she was having to get used to. It still was unusual to have a guard assigned to her. Especially one that even made Teuf seem small in his hellhound form. But Mörker was now a common sight with the Elder and her family.

"Jake," Electra smiled at him, indicating that he should stay. "Would you do me the honor of helping our newest pack member adjust to life here."

His scowl softened and he gave the Elder with multicolored hair a small smile. "If that is your wish."

Smiling, she nodded, "It is, my friend. And if he gives you any problems, let the Gelert know." Letting her beast take the lead, her eyes glowed and fangs extended. The voice that came from the gentle woman was that of the angry wolf, "I still want to taste your blood."

Pushing her way into the man's mind, the Gelert found the injured wolf curled up and whimpering at her approach. She bared her teeth and growled in warning. He tried to scoot away from her, whining with every movement.

Get up.

I can't. I'm injured.

She nudged him with her snout, and he yelped in fear and pain. Squinting at him, she snapped at his remaining legs until he stood. He whimpered as he slowly moved away from her.

What is your name, wolf?

Frykt.

The older wolf smirked at the quiet answer.

That is Norwegian for fear. You used to induce it. Now, you experience it. The goddess has plans for you. Otherwise, I would put you out of your misery now.

With that declaration she pulled out of his mind. The man looked up at her with fear in his eyes and she simply smiled at him. Electra gave him a knowing smile, as she caught a small glimpse of the woman in a moonbeam dress with stars at her waist and a dark shawl made of the night sky surrounding her.

There had been a glimpse of his future. And how he was important for another life. She would not question the goddess. For Selene was older than herself, and ultimately, it would be his choice.

Chapter 77

CHOICES

Rome/Crystal River Pack

The divine healer watched her students with knowing green eyes. There was one that excelled as she had expected. It all came natural to her. She enjoyed it. She enjoyed helping others.

But her heart was not in it as it should be.

After the class was done and the healer had dismissed the others, the older woman pulled Marie into her private office. The light sand-colored walls had camel colored trim and shelves that were filled with books ranging from old tomes to modern paperbacks. She had a small desk that was covered with papers and notebooks.

She removed her official robes and hung them on the peg before sitting in the armchair in the seating area. The seating area was made up of two dark red wingback chairs and a small dark wood table that matched her desk. A brass lamp with a red glass lampshade sat on the table, offering a light glow that warmed the area.

"Join me," she motioned to the other chair and Marie sat down. "Any who show the skills of a healer are trained. Not to become a healer, but so they know how to control their powers."

Marie nodded, "I'm trying my best."

"You are doing well, child. But this is not the path that you wish to follow. Is it?"

"No, mistress," Marie admitted, looking at her hands in her lap. She toyed with the trim of her apprentice robes. As apprentices they were required to wear white robes while at the academy. They reminded her of a pale version of the Harry Potter robes. Her description for her family had been Harry Potter meets 1950's nursing uniforms.

"The position of healer is a choice. As is that of a divine healer. Your mark will have appeared at birth and faded by the first moon," Zsa Zsa explained. "If you choose to accept the position, the mark will return. The goddess herself will touch you to mark you."

The divine healer sat forward and took the teens hands in her own. "But you must choose. Do not choose because you have been told that this is your fate. Choose because this is what you want to do."

"I wanted..." she paused considering her words. "Did mom have a choice? To be an Elder?"

"Yes. Maybe you need to go home and talk to her."

Marie nodded and then left the office to return to her dorm. She hung up her robe and grabbed her shower kit and a sundress before heading down the hall to the communal bathroom. As she washed her body and hair, she thought about what Zsa Zsa had said in her office.

After drying off, she pulled on her sundress and gathered up her clothes and shower kit. Back in the small room with a desk, small chair and bed, she toweled her hair dry as she looked at the pictures on her walls. These were the important people in her life – her family, the Crystal Pass Fire Department and her friends here. Ignoring the time difference, she clicked on her mother's picture and waited for Electra to answer.

"Hello, baby girl."

Halfway across the world, the warmth and love of the woman at the other end of the line surrounded her and she instantly felt better. At the same time, she felt so alone.

"Momma, can I come home?" Marie asked on the verge of tears.

"Always. Nyla is in Spain, I'll see if she can send the plane over."

A few hours later, Marie was on the private plane for the Elders on her way home. Usually, she slept on the long flight across the Atlantic. Today, she couldn't seem to sit still. An Omega kept checking on her; offering food, drink, pillow, blanket, everything shy of her own soul.

Eventually the plane landed, and Hadrian was waiting at the private airport. Marie hugged him as the Omega put her bag in the back of the SUV.

"Is momma busy?" she asked, fighting back her tears.

"Making your favorite cookies," he said softly. "I wanted some time alone with you."

"Oh?"

"You want to see the new firehouse?" he led her over to the passenger door and opened it for her.

"Yes!" she said enthusiastically as she hopped inside.

Smiling, he closed the door. That was his little girl. The next generation at the fire department.

As he drove, he told her about the improvements that had been made in the year she had been away. The new station has a full training facility. He explained how the Alpha had arranged with the local college to offer classes, and the cost of the facility was split between the city and the college.

Hadrian took a turn after the station and pulled into a small campus. "This is the university annex," he explained, pulling into a parking spot. Pointing at the different buildings, he listed what they were for. "Dorms. Classes. Student center and food court. Library."

"This is really cool, dad."

"Thanks. Your training as a healer will help as a paramedic."

"You know?" she asked quietly, looking at her hands in her lap.

"Since the moment we were told that you were a healer," he admitted with a smile. "Being a divine healer..." he shook his head. "That's not you. This, the department, is what pulls you."

"You're not disappointed?"

"Only if you do something you don't want to do," he reached over and tugged on her hair lightly. "It's your choice."

"Did momma have a hard time deciding?"

"She did. It's not an easy choice. She worried about all the time she would be away from you kids. She worried about controlling the Gelert. She was afraid that you would think that her duties were more important than her family."

"But she's done so well."

"She has," he smiled at her. "We have. It was a lot of work that I don't think you were aware of. We had a lot of fights." Hadrian nodded when his daughter looked at him in surprise. "Oh, yeah. I know you saw us arguing sometimes, but some of those arguments went for days."

"We never knew that."

"I know. We did our best to keep the big fights from you. Like the fact that the Elders refused to hear from your birth mother. Electra wanted her to have a chance to say why she left."

"Did she ever tell you?"

"She wanted more. She grew up dirt poor in a poor pack. Summer Moon is one that has survived off the charity of the Council for years. They were content in their lives. Saw no reason to change."

"What happened to them?"

"The Alpha became accustomed to receiving money from the Council. His son saw no reason to change. His son sold out to Keebler. When Keebler was executed, Summer Moon fell to the nearest district leader which was Harbor Moon. Under the Alpha's sister as their Alpha, they are turning it around."

"And what about her? Mitzi?"

"She was sent back to her home pack. The new Alpha, Alpha Madison, gave her a position in her secondary cabinet as an overseer of a pack farm. She's doing well. Mitzi never got a second chance mate. But she does have two sons with her new husband, and one also shows the signs of a healer."

"Can I go see her?"

"We can probably make that happen."

"I love you, daddy."

They leaned across the center console and hugged each other. He kissed her temple. "I love you, too."

Chapter 78

GRADUATION

Crystal River Pack

It was the first graduating class of the new fire academy. To no one's surprise, Marie O'Reilly was the valedictorian. She had finished her training as a healer and returned just in time to start the first class. Now she sat on the stage in the fire academy auditorium, preparing to give her speech.

After a round of applause, the provost of the academy turned to smile at her. Nervously she stood and approached the podium. Running her damp palms along the legs of her uniform pants, she looked out at the audience.

Sitting in the center of the front row were her parents, Hadrian, Electra and Mitzi. On either side of the three were her siblings; full, half and adopted. Turning to look behind her on the opposite side of the stage from the graduates, she smiled at the Alpha family. At the nod from the two Alphas, she turned her attention back to the audience.

"First, I would like to thank Alpha Wyatt for giving us the opportunity to attend a fire academy here at home," there was a round of applause. "And, of course, Alpha

Celeste for overseeing the project." There was another round of applause. "And most of all, Terry, Anna and all the other omegas who did all the actual work."

To the surprise of most of the omegas, the two Alphas led the audience in a standing ovation. It lasted for a few minutes before the two leaders sat back down. Alpha Wyatt's voice popped into her head, and it gave her the confidence to continue.

I always knew that you would be the next generation of O'Reilly for the fire department.

Taking a deep breath, she smiled at the people seated in front of her. A red-headed man that she met at a council meeting in Rio smiled back at her. He was a few years older but was willing to move to her pack to allow her to pursue her dream. A young she-wolf could ask for nothing better than a mate that supported her. He winked at her and blew her a kiss, and she felt her cheeks turn pink.

"I spent most of my high school years in Rome training as a healer. The divine healer drilled it into us that omegas were the backbone of our society. At first, I honestly did not get this. Then I had the chance to reconnect with my birth mother at her home pack. She was born an omega and strived for something better. It was not until she returned to her home pack at the order of the Elders that she found her place."

She looked at her parents and all three smiled at her encouragingly. "It was her strength, my mother's guidance and my father's faith in me that brought me home.

Here, to find my place," she turned and smiled at her fellow classmates. "To find our place."

Marie turned back to the audience.

"Let me give you a few facts about our charter graduating class. Of the twenty-five of us, seventeen are omegas, two were rogue born, five of us are Betas. If you were keeping count, that left one. One Alpha. I was not Alpha born. I was born a Beta and elevated when my dad married Elder Electra. There is so much that happened that year. And several of my fellow graduates were with me through it."

"When I came home and entered the academy, we had a few rough days. No one was certain how to address me. After all, I was now an adult Alpha. The daughter of an Elder," she made a face and there was a small ripple of laughter.

"But then Chief Buchanan walked in and said I don't give a damn who your daddy is, what your rank is or where you're from. Your asses are now the dirt under my boots."

"After that, we figured out real quick, we were not going to make it unless we banded together. Chief ran the hell out of us. We stuck together and here we are. With the support of our families, the fear of Chief and a collective determination, all of us who entered two years ago are leaving together."

"Ladies and gentlemen, I am proud to say that we are the charter class of the Crystal Pass Fire Academy."

There was another standing ovation for the class as she motioned for her fellow graduates to stand. It was several minutes before the captain could award their diplomas. As all twenty-five names were called the audience erupted in applause. At the end, Chief Buchanan stepped up to the microphone.

"I want everyone here to know that I am very proud of this inaugural class. And I want to thank our Alphas for this opportunity. And to let all four packs that have graduates know, you are getting some of the best that we have. When Alpha Wyatt called me and asked me to head up the school, I was afraid that I would be stepping on toes. Chief Hayes and Commissioner O'Reilly have been here for a long time. And just in case you did not catch it, there was one of each in this class."

"The Alpha wanted to make sure that there was no special treatment. And there was not. Nor is there with the next class. Especially since that one has four Alpha born cadets. But as Firefighter O'Reilly put it, they are dirt under my boots for twelve more months."

"Congratulations, graduates. It has been my pleasure to be your instructor. Go, make me proud."

"Actually, Chief," Charles Hayes said, approaching him with a box. "We have a present for you."

The gruff drill instructor turned firefighter turned instructor looked surprised. He accepted the gift and opened the box. Inside, encased in clear resin, was his missing whistle. He had used it every morning to wake them up. And as they progressed, he would randomly blow the whistle and time their response.

On top of the block was a small brass plate. Underneath was another plate with all twenty-five names. He wiped away some tears before he read the top plate out loud.

"To Chief Buchanan, from your first class to respond to ALARM! ALARM! ALARM! MOVE YOUR ASSES! Thanks for everything."

"Chief?" Jason Stewart of the second class handed him a smaller box. He took the box and inside was a new whistle. "We're going to need this back in about twelve months."

Thirty years later, when Marie took over the academy, the cubes had become a tradition. The first one that she received was just as important as the first one she gave. The second cube she received had her son's name listed.

Chapter 79

ORACLE

Crystal River Pack/Denali Pack

Emily sat on the floor of the main room of the Oracle's temple of the Crystal River Temple complex with the large hellhound asleep next to her. The walls were painted a soft blue, and one couch was a bright red while the other was a soft cream that matched the two armchairs. Light wood tables were scattered throughout the room.

Imogen was always tickled with Emily and her scenarios. As she got older, they got more detailed and dramatic. Gone were the days of the simple childish questions.

"What if mom gets pregnant? I can't say anything?"

Now, at nineteen, the scenarios were outlandish. Such as today's scenario. And to be honest, Imogen had quit listening after the zombie apocalypse. But now, she realized her pupil had quit speaking.

Sighing, Imogen told her, "Even if robot-controlled zombies are at the border, you cannot say anything."

"I knew you weren't listening," Emily grinned.

"Please don't go through it again," Emmeline pleaded as she rubbed her forehead. "Is this normal?"

"There is nothing about me that's normal," Emily replied, playing with her hell hound, Hades.

"True story," Imogen agreed. "Now, are you excited about the hunt?"

"Yes," Emily squealed. "Is it normal?"

"To be excited?" Emmeline asked.

"To talk to your mate before you meet."

"What do you mean?" Adeline asked as all three sisters sat up and started paying attention.

"I've been dreaming that I'm talking to him," she admitted, and the three sisters looked at each other.

"It may simply be that you and your wolf are creating a mate in your mind," Imogen said. With this suggestion, the triplet sisters relaxed.

"He tries to get me to look in the mirror or glass so that he can see me."

Even more alarmed, the triplets sat up again and spoke to one another through the mind link.

"Do you?" her mentor asks. "Do you ever look at your reflection in your dreams?"

"No," Emily shook her head. "During training we were told to never look at a reflection in our dreams."

"Yes. It is dangerous. Does he ever tell you his name?" Imogen agreed.

"No. He says that he wants it to be a surprise."

"Have you ever had these dreams before?" Emmeline asked.

"No. Not like this. When Taylor would cry at night, I would go to her, and we would play in a meadow. Sometimes, I would imagine what Gelert was like in a past life."

"When you say that you would go to her," Emmeline asked, "do you mean that you would go into her dreams?"

"Yeah," Emily realized that the three sisters were watching her closely. "Can't all seers do this?"

"No, Emily," Adeline explained. "It's a very rare talent."

"When you get back, you will need to learn to control your dreams," Imogen smiled. "Go. Your mother will be looking for you soon."

Two days later, under the midnight sun of the Denali pack, Emily finally laid eyes on her mate. Staring at the man in front of her, she had a hard time formulating words. Light brown hair that was slightly disheveled with a stylish scruff covering his cheeks. He had dark olive skin and bright green eyes.

"Emily?" Joseph Graham said as he stood in complete shock.

He had graduated two years before Marie. He had been the varsity quarterback and captain. Emily had dated his younger brother in high school. Marie had a secret crush on him. Dee and Taylor had both tried to date him.

With this thought in mind, she busted out laughing. "My sisters had the biggest crushes on you."

"And you?" he asked, keeping his distance as her escort eyed him.

"No," she shook her head. "You were Gaston."

"And you wanted the beast?"

"I wanted a prince to sweep me off my feet," she admitted.

He held his hand out to her; he could not touch her until she allowed it. Curious about what he would do, she placed her hand in his. He pulled her into his arms and began to waltz as he sang a mash-up of Disney songs.

Laughing, she let herself be spun around their imaginary dance floor in the middle of an Alaskan meadow.

"I love me a good romance," she admitted, laying her head on his shoulder.

"Anything you want, princess," he whispered looking at her. "Anything at all."

"What pack are you in?"

"I'm still a River. But I've been off getting my MD. I just graduated and will start my residency when we get back."

After the Summer Solstice hunt, they returned to Crystal River. Joseph moved into an apartment and Emily stayed with her parents as they got to know each other. While her regular studies continued, she learned how to control her dream walking. It was not a common trait for werewolves, not even for their oracles. But it is something that a voodoo priestess in the pack could do.

Just as with her other studies, she was a quick learner and mastered the skill. Before summer was over, they were sharing an apartment as she continued her training with Imogen and her sisters. On New Year's Eve, Emily and Joseph were mated in the clearing of the Temple Complex.

With the dress that Electra made her, and the decorations, it truly was a fairy tale wedding. Perfect for someone who had been obsessed with princesses her whole life. The skirt was full enough for her mate to twirl her around the dance floor.

And inside a hidden pocket was a note embroidered on a silk handkerchief from her parents telling her how proud they were of her.

Chapter 80

DARK SKY ALPHA

Crystal River Pack

Llewellyn came home after going to the Dark Sky pack for his mom. Although he did this for her from time to time, there was something about this trip that felt different. Electra did not question the goddess; she said that he needed to go by himself.

When she questioned the Blessed Three, Imogen had advised, "Never doubt the goddess. She gives us choices. But certain things are destined."

When Llewellyn walked into the house Electra knew that there was something that had happened. There was a change in his scent. A change in him. He entered the kitchen, and she smiled.

"You met your mate," she said, not turning from the stove.

"How did you know? Was it Emily that said I needed to go?"

Electra turned the burner off as she laughed at her youngest child. "She did but did not say why. However much it may kill her, she cannot say anything, and she cannot influence."

"And it kills her," he chuckled.

"I can smell her on you," Electra admitted. "Is it Pearl?"

He didn't have to say anything. The look on his face said it all. She opened her arms, and he moved into the embrace. He was no longer her little boy, and she rested her cheek against his chest as he had done as a child.

He was a spitting image of his father at that age. The only difference was that he had a little scruff on his jaw. Hadrian never had it because of fire department regulations.

They were still in the same position when Hadrian came into the house. He wrapped his arms around them both and squeezed them tightly.

"You just let me know when you're ready to have a mating ceremony." Hadrian told his son. "And why the hell you're back here without your mate."

Llewellyn laughed. "Because I still have duties to perform."

"Don't worry," Electra said. "William will be home soon. He can assume your duties."

"What about his mate?" her son asked. "I thought she didn't want to come here."

"When her Alpha found out that she mated with an American he kicked her out," Hadrian explained with a grin. "Celeste and your mom flew to Russia and gave him an earful. Although he changed his mind after dealing with the Gelert and an angry female Alpha."

Llewellyn laughed, "That I have no problem believing."

Electra shrugged, "We're still working on her temper."

That night, Llewellyn walked out onto the patio looking for his mom. She sat on a bench swing with a glass of wine in her hand. He sat on a chair and propped a foot on the edge of the swing, gently pushing it.

Electra turned and put both legs up on the swing and faced her son. "What's on your mind?"

"I don't know if I'm ready to be an Alpha," he admitted.

"Why not? You trained with Aiden and Martin. You already have contacts with other Alphas around the world," she pointed out.

"Did you know?" he asked quietly.

"I had my suspicions," she replied over her wine glass.

"Mom."

"When I assumed the position of Elder, I took oaths. Anything that the gods tell us, remains between us."

"So, the moon goddess told you."

She smiled at him in the dark. He knew that she would not confirm anything.

Chapter 81

OMEGA
Highland Loch Pack

It was the first council meeting that the three women had on their own. Over the last several years, their mentors had them handle more issues and requests on their own. But this time, they sat on the dais in the large thrones by themselves. The first day was complete and they sat out on a balcony at the Highland Loch pack-house.

Somewhere below them, guards with hellhounds patrolled the grounds. They each had a hellhound that lay close to them and the handlers stood guard in the hall-way to their suites. All three of the Elders were strong wolves, old and wise beyond their human years. And all three were warriors with no qualms about taking a life.

The three Elders were drinking wine and looking out over Loch Lomond with stars sparkling above them and reflecting below them. Occasionally there was a cool breeze and somewhere an owl hooted. In the rooms behind them, their mates slept, oblivious to their wives being outside.

All three wore sweatpants, hoodies and thick socks. They had aged slowly, as Elders usually did, so none looked as though they were nearing their fifth decade. Electra still had her mermaid hair, Nyla sported long blue box braids and Dawn currently had short hair dyed light pink with turquoise tips.

"Did you ever think that you would grow up and be sitting here?" Nyla asked.

"Honestly, no," Electra admitted. "Hell, there were days that I didn't think I would live to see the next day."

"Yeah," Dawn agreed. "Some days I wondered if I was going to eat."

"It's really not fair, is it," Nyla mused. "Alphas and Betas live like kings. Omegas scrape by."

"Not all," Electra thought of the Omegas at Crystal River and then the ones at Dark Sky. "Dark Sky was horrible about classes."

"What was it like? Going from Dark Sky to Crystal River?" Nyla asked.

"If someone had told me that I had landed on Mars, I would have believed it," she laughed and the other two joined her. "I mean, I went from no rights, no options, no life and the only time that pack leadership noticed me was to beat me or rape me. And then I end up with an Alpha who takes her husband to strip clubs, and yes, they still go."

"Here's to keeping the fire burning!" Nyla raised her glass and the other two joined her in the salute.

"My first week at River, I had lunch with the Luna, the Alpha arranged for me to have a makeover, and I was told that I could do whatever I wanted to do. In less than six months, I went from slave to Elder."

"Did it feel good killing the Alpha?" Dawn asked.

"Gelert enjoyed it," she gave a small half shrug. "Then again, she probably would have gone swimming in his blood."

Just bathe in it. Not enough blood in one man to go swimming.

Electra rolled her eyes at her wolf and joined the other two in laughter.

"What about his son?" Nyla asked. "He's at River, now, isn't he?"

Electra nodded, "For several years now. He had a hard time adjusting, after he lost his leg. But he met his second chance mate and..." she trailed off with a little smile. "That's a story for another time. What about you two? What was it like going from Omega to Elder?"

Through the years, they have discussed their lives in both phases. What they had deemed before and after they were elevated to Elder. But not once in all their years of knowing each other had they ever talked about how they reacted to the change.

"The Alpha of the Welsh Dragon pack is a prude," Dawn said of her host Alpha. "I doubt that he even has sex unless it's to get the Luna pregnant. He sure as hell ain't ever been in a damned strip club."

They all busted out laughing.

"Not mine!" Nyla laughed. "That fucker has a dozen wives and concubines! All living in one house!"

"Oh goddess!" Dawn laughed. "All those women PMS-ing at one time!"

"Where the hell do you think you're going?" Electra acted like an upset wife with PMS.

"The fuck away from here, bitch!" Dawn answered and they all laughed some more.

"OK, seriously, now," Nyla said as they settled down. "Don't you think that the treatment of Omegas is a bit harsh? Sometimes downright cruel?"

"I have," Dawn admitted soberly. "We all came from harsh backgrounds."

"We can't get rid of the classes," Electra pointed out.

"No. No. Not what I was thinking," Nyla said. "Don't you have Omegas in your security teams?"

"I do," Electra nodded. "And a half blood."

"Yeah. Me too," Dawn said as she topped off their glasses.

"They make up the majority of our society," Electra gave a small laugh. "Celeste once told me that not everyone could be an Alpha. I never thought much about it at the time. I just thought that she was telling me that it was OK that I was wolf-less."

"But now?" Nyla asked, wrapping her blanket a little tighter around her shoulders as the cold wind picked up.

"If everyone was an Alpha, not a damned thing would get done," Dawn said as she too pulled her blanket a little tighter.

"Wyatt and Celeste have no problem getting their hands dirty. Even now, Selene is getting ready to take her place as Alpha and she insisted on living with the Omegas out on one of the farms. She worked with them for six months," Electra took a sip of her wine. "She moved into an apartment and spent the past year working various jobs."

"I think more Alphas should do that," Nyla said.

"What brought this on?" Dawn asked quietly.

There was a strained silence among the three friends. When a soft sob escaped Nyla, the other two women rushed to comfort her.

"I found my Successor. He had nearly starved as a child. The omegas only got the leftovers."

Neither knew what to say. They simply held her and offered comfort. Slowly, in the late hours of the night and early hours of the morning, an idea came to life.

The following morning, the Elders took their seats on the dais. The cold stone room had been the same one that Gelert had helped to abolish slavery in a previous life. After a long night of discussion and deliberation, they reached a consensus.

Electra sat in the middle as the Senior Elder. She motioned to Lizzie who stood and walked to a small door. A lowly Omega with dirt-stained hands and near threadbare clothes stepped inside. He quickly pulled his soft cap off his gray hair. Keeping his eyes down he followed the younger woman to the center of the floor.

"Sir," Electra said gently. "Please tell the council your name, rank and job."

"Aye, Elder. Me name is James McPherson and I'm an Omega for the Highland Loch pack. I'm just a tenant farmer and tend to the sheep and crops."

"Not just," Electra smiled. "If it were not for you and others like you, we would have nothing to eat or wear."

In unison the three Alphas moved off the dais and stood in front of him. Nyla and Dawn each placed a hand on his shoulders as Electra took his hands in hers.

"We want to thank you for taking time away from your important duties to speak with us," Nyla said, and he nodded.

"We want to encourage you to speak your mind without fear of consequences," Dawn added.

"You will be your pack's representative during this investigation. Please, speak the truth and let the goddess guide you," Electra finished before kissing his forehead in a blessing.

"Thank you, mistress," he murmured as a single tear slipped out of his eye.

The three elders returned to the dais but did not sit.

"The treatment of the omegas has been brought to our attention," Dawn declared. "Most packs treat them well. But many fail to protect their most vital pack members. We are instituting a new position for leadership."

"When we asked several people here to point us to a trusted and respected Omega for the Highland Loch pack," Nyla smiled at the omega, "Mr. McPherson was the one they all pointed to."

"Ladies and gentlemen, I present to you, the first Omega liaison," Electra said. "If you accept the position, you will join the high council staff and assist the investigation. With your findings and recommendations, we will make changes in our laws."

"Me?"

"Yes, sir. And we recommend that all packs also create a position for an Omega liaison," Electra confirmed with a smile.

The old man lifted his gaze and was surprised to find that the council was lowering their eyes in respect to a member of the high council. He gave a soft affirmative answer. Nyla advised her sisters through their link to look at the high window across from them.

The woman with the long blue-black shawl over her white dress nodded approvingly at her daughters before disappearing.

Chapter 82

SNEAK PEAK – VOODOO

In Book Three of the Crystal River series, we meet a single mom of three who is raising the children that her sister abandoned. After a series of events that she has no control over, Skylar finds herself in a position where she must start over. After moving to Crystal Pass, she discovers that werewolves are real.

And that she's been surrounded by them her whole life.

On a lonely night, in a new house, in a new town, she calls upon the Mother Goddess who lives behind the moon, the Goddess that her mother had always told her about. With a soft-spoken prayer under a full moon, she pleads for a partner that can meet the needs of each of her children.

The Mother Goddess who lives behind the moon answers her prayer. But not in the way that she is expecting.

Chapter 83

SNEAK PEAK – NEESHA

Ridgefield/Little Ridge Pack

"Oh my God, Sky!" Tanisha squealed. "We were about to leave! Where are the kids?"

My kids – Skylar corrected in her mind. She gritted her teeth and knew that the whirlwind of her sister would not stay long.

"They are with friends." She said unlocking the door and walking in. Tanisha and the biker that was with her followed her inside. Skylar sat the groceries on the kitchen counter and then put away the milk and sugar-free ice cream. Without saying a word, she walked back out to get the remaining bags.

Walking back in, she found the man sitting on her couch. Her sister was on his lap. Their faces were currently glued to each other. Skylar hoped that they could quit that before too long.

Rolling her eyes, she put away the groceries. Then she washed the vegetables for the lunches for the next week. She cut up cucumbers, celery and carrots, placing them in four sets of five divided containers.

Skylar had red, Asher had blue, Tiffany had pink and Fiona had purple. All the lunches, except sandwiches, were made over the weekend. It made the mornings go by so much easier. Next, she portioned out chips and boxed cookies into similar containers. Sliced apples and grapes went into another container.

Anything leftover went into storage bags for evening snacks. All the fruits and veggies went into the refrigerator and the chips and cookies into the pantry. Cleaning off the counter and washing the knife and cutting board were the last steps.

Walking out of her little galley kitchen, her anger rose. The couple were still stuck to each other. Tanisha was now straddling the man and one hand of his was under her shirt. Hopefully, if there was a God out there, they would be gone before her kids got home.

Skylar had three people coming over tomorrow for their hair to be done. She gathered up her work towels and put them in the washer behind the slatted folding doors next to the kitchen. The washer started and seemed to pull Tanisha and her latest fling out of their own world.

"Oh! Are you done?" Tanisha asked, turning around in his lap.

His hand remained under the shirt but did at least move down to her stomach. Skylar really hoped that her sister wasn't pregnant again.

"Yeah."

"Sit down, we want to talk to you." Tanisha was excited.

Skylar had a bad feeling as she sat down in the recliner. Her home wasn't much. The brown leather living
room set with coordinating tables and lamps had been
paid for by weekly payments. The dining room table
and chairs came from a garage sale when they were
kids. The windows were covered only by the mini blinds
that the complex provided. The walls were covered by
school and sports team pictures. And Tiffany in her
Brownies uniform. Fiona would start in fall and couldn't
wait.

"I'm getting married!" Tanisha squealed and the man
smiled.

"Congratulations." Skylar smiled. "To who?"

"To Frankie!" She laughed.

"Are you Frankie?" Skylar asked the man.

He gave a deep laugh. "Yes, ma'am. John Franklin,
everyone calls me Frankie."

He was a handsome man with bright blue eyes and
dark brown hair down to his shoulders and a three-inch
goatee. His lips were full, and his nose was broad.

They both wore jeans and Harley Davidson T-shirts.
Black motorcycle boots covered their feet. He wore a
leather vest, and Skylar saw a patch with a wolf on the
back. The tattoos on his arm indicated that he had been
a mechanic in the army.

"We want your kids to be in the wedding." Frankie
said. "Neesha keeps telling me about your kids. I was
hoping to meet them."

"Asher had a game this morning." Skylar said. "They
went with some friends for the afternoon."

There was a knock on the door, and she got up to answer it. As she opened the door, Babs walked in with a magazine opened to a haircut that she liked.

"Can you make me look like this?" She asked without preamble.

Looking at the bob with block coloring Skylar nodded. "What color do you want?"

"Do you have blue?" Babs asked excitedly.

"I have the Marge Simpson blue that I use for Amelia." Skylar said, thinking of what was in her personal supplies here. "And I can always lighten it, or I can add a little plum to it to darken it."

"That. Let's do that."

"Okay, I have three appointments tomorrow-."

"Tonight?" She asked and Skylar motioned to the couple on the couch. "Oh. Ummm..."

"Go ahead, Sky." Tanisha encouraged.

"Give me thirty?"

Chapter 84

SNEAK PEAK – NEW UNCLE

Ridgefield/Little Ridge Pack

Sunday morning, Frankie and Tanisha came back and took the kids out for a few hours. It let Skylar get her appointments done and the kids got to spend time with their 'aunt Neesha' and new uncle.

Asher did not want to go.

He had been old enough to remember his mother walking away from him. And then when she came back, pregnant with Tiffany, only to leave again. Tiffany was not even a year old when Tanisha came back, pregnant again.

Before she left the third time, Tanisha had signed adoption papers. Since then, Tanisha had called and sent an occasional holiday card. But she had not been back.

Asher had finally agreed to go because he didn't want his sisters with her alone. Especially Fiona. Not only did he remember her leaving, but he also remembered her rejecting 'that deformed thing' when Fiona was born.

When they got back, the girls insisted on showing Auntie Neesha their room. Skylar was cleaning up the dining room from where she had done her hair appointments.

"I've got this." Asher said getting the broom out of the hall closet.

"Thanks." Skylar smiled at him as she carried the towels to the washer.

"Can I talk to you?" Frankie asked, making a motion with his head towards the door.

"Sure. Asher?"

"I'm good, mom." He replied not looking up from what he was doing.

Skylar smiled sadly at him and then followed her future brother-in-law outside.

"Your son doesn't like his aunt much." Frankie said without waiting for the door to close behind them.

"No. He doesn't."

"I don't know what you've told him, but Neesha has done nothing but brag on you and your kids. I really want this wedding to be perfect for her. She really wants you there."

"What I've told him?" Skylar asked slowly. "And just what do you think I've told him?"

"I don't know." He admitted. "But she's been going on and on about you. When I found out that you were only a few hours away and suggested that we should come see you, Neesha was afraid that you wouldn't want to see her. That you would have told your kids horrible stories about her."

"No, I haven't." Skylar said sitting down on the little bench in her small patch of grass. "I tell them that they have an aunt. When she calls, I let them talk to her if they want. Asher doesn't want to. He has his reasons and I'm not going to force him."

"You're his mother-."

"Exactly." She said coldly.

They stared at each other for a moment. Neither budging.

"Can we come to his next game?" Frankie finally asked.

Skylar nodded. "Bring your own chairs and refreshments. Don't know if the concession stand will be open."

"He seems like a good kid. They all do." He gave a small smile. "I wouldn't mind having one or two of our own. Actually, I think she may be pregnant. Or it was just nerves that had her throwing up the last two mornings."

Great. Skylar thought. At least this guy seemed like he would stick around. The real question was, would Tanisha?

"You need to talk with her." Skylar said with a sigh. "I think that there are things that you two need to discuss before you get married."

The front door opened, and Tanisha walked out, smiling from ear to ear. She wrapped her arms around his waist, and he draped an arm around her shoulders. He kissed the top of her head lovingly.

"Sky, your kids are wonderful!" Tanisha beamed. "I hope someday I can have kids just as great."

There was a soft gasp and when they turned to look, Asher stood in the doorway. His face looked like he had just been punched in the gut. Then the pain and hurt passed and was replaced with angry rage.

He gave Tanisha a withering look just before he slammed the door. Skylar looked like she was going to cry. Tanisha had no reaction. Frankie was just confused over their reactions.

"I think it's time for you to go." Skylar said softly before she stood up and walked into the apartment. There was the distinct sound of the lock clicking into place.

As the couple outside slowly walked away to Frankie's crew cab pickup, Skylar walked down the hall to the bedrooms.

"Momma?" Tiffany asked from their room and Skylar gave a small hmmm. "Is Asher okay?"

"Yeah, baby, he's just having a bad day." Skylar said with a forced smile. "Why don't you girls go and start a movie?"

One of the older women at the salon got Disney movies every month. She always got the ones with the digital code and after she uploaded the code or whatever she did, she would bring the movie to Skylar. The basic cable TV and the large movie collection kept them entertained.

As the girls went down the hall, they debated which Iron Man movie would make their brother happy. Skylar opened the door and saw her son completely under his Iron Man blanket. She slid under the blanket and pulled him close. Her head was on his pillow, and she kissed the top of his head through the blanket.

"What did I ever do wrong?" he asked from his hiding place. She could hear the tears in his voice, and it broke her heart.

"Nothing, baby. You did nothing wrong." She squeezed him close to her.

"Why doesn't she want us? Why doesn't she want me?"

"I don't know. But I know that I got the best son. And I got two great daughters. I wouldn't trade my life for anything."

"Maybe for a date?" he smirked as he peeked out of the blanket.

"You do realize that if I went out on a date, I would have to shave my legs? And wear actual clothes? And shoes! Ugh!"

"A skirt and heels." Asher corrected and his mom groaned as he laughed.

"I'm pretty sure that the girls have picked an Iron Man movie to make you feel better. And there's ice cream in the freezer."

"Cookies and cream?" he asked hopefully.

"Yup. And maybe we'll have pizza for dinner."

"I love you, momma." He said turning around and hugging her. "I got the best mom in the world."

"I love you too, kid." Skylar hugged him back and wished that they would never have that conversation again. But she knew that they would.

Chapter 85

SNEAK PEAK – SUNDAY MEETING

Crystal River Pack

S hane was making coffee for the veterans' group that met every Sunday at the community center. There was a second pot for decaf because two of the female veterans were pregnant. Pressing the start button, he looked up as Frankie and his brother Jake came in.

Shane and Frankie had been friends since school. Jake had always been a bit aloof. Now he was just an asshole. Jake gave a slight nod to Shane as he went and spoke to Gunny.

"How did last weekend go?" Shane asked Frankie as he leaned against the coffee bar.

"I thought that it went okay." Frankie said running his hand through his hair. "We were supposed to go to the boys' soccer game yesterday. Sky called Neesha Thursday and said that she didn't want us there."

"Neesha did say she was a bit of a bitch." Shane pointed out.

"I know. Her son, Cash, smells like he's getting ready to shift. I don't know if she even knows." Frankie shrugged.

"What are you going to do?" Shane asked as the Alpha and Luna walked in.

"I have no idea." Frankie admitted. "Neesha is a mess. She's not even sure if Sky will come to the wedding."

Other veterans started arriving and soon the meeting started. For two hours the group talked about good days, bad days, friends and future plans. When it was over, Frankie found himself telling several people about the visit to her future sister-in-law.

Everyone loved Neesha and could not imagine her sister being so cold to her. When they moved outside to where the families were gathered for the weekly picnic, Neesha was surrounded by women that were comforting her.

"Babe, what's wrong?" Frankie asked as he sat down on the bench and pulled her into his lap.

"That may be our fault." Heather said with a weak smile. "We were wanting to know about her sister."

"I just can't believe that your sister would be so mean because of her decisions." Darla said to her son's fiancé. "You're not the one that had a kid in high school."

"And then had two more with two different men." Clara added.

Tanisha buried her face in Frankie's chest. Maybe she should have told them the truth. But now that they all loved her, she couldn't. No, they loved Neesha. Now everyone believes that Sky is a selfish bitch and when she didn't show up to the wedding, Tanisha would not have to admit that she never invited her.

As a pick me up, some of the women made plans for a girl's day. Mani/pedi, hair, shopping, the works. All of it would be a treat for Tanisha.

"I'll call Mal." Jake said shocking everyone around him. But before anything else could be said, he walked away, reaching out to his friends' wife.

Tanisha knew that she couldn't go back now. Even Jake was starting to like her. Making up her mind, she decided to just cut her sister out of her life. It wouldn't be hard to do that. Again.

Wiping tears off her face, she turned and faced the group. "I couldn't ask for a better group of friends than all of you."

"You're part of the pack now." Frankie said pressing a kiss to her temple.

A few feet away, the alpha and Gunny were texting back and forth. It didn't matter that they were standing next to each other. This was what they did when they did not want anyone to know what they were discussing. Gunny was human and did not have the mind link, and texting had pictures, emojis and gif.

They both felt as though something was off about this woman. Neither of them could quite put their fingers on it. Gunny did a deep dive on her and came up empty. Nothing came up for a twenty-four-year-old Neesha Johnson born July first. There were always those that wanted to get away from their past, but there was usually something.

> I'm still only pulling up a Skylar Marie Johnson.

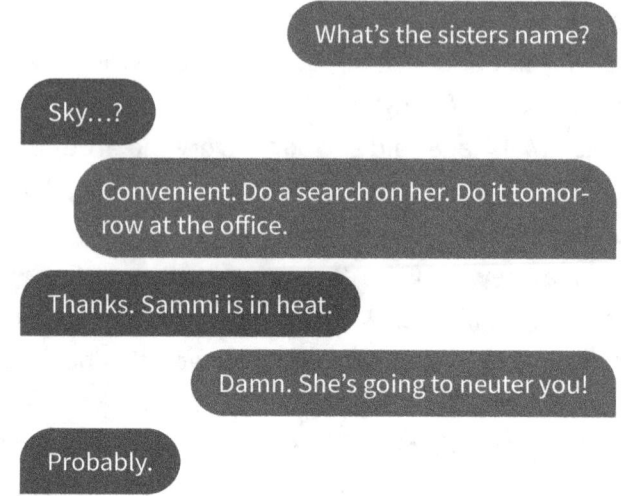

The two friends grinned at each other before going to their own mates. Gunny's kids were running around and playing with the other kids. Wyatt's oldest was running around with them while his second child was being spoiled by whoever was currently holding him.

"So, Darla was telling me that everything was set for Frankie's wedding. She has her final dress fitting week after next." Sammi was telling Celeste as the men approached.

"I'm glad he found someone that makes him happy." Celeste smiled as Wyatt wrapped his arms around her waist and sniffed her neck. "Get me pregnant and I will kill you."

"Noted. Might want to tell your friend that also." He winked at Sammi.

She glared at Gunny who just grinned at his mate.